SHAKESPEARE Vs
CTHULHU

An anthologie of fine stories inspir'd by
the Bard of Stratford and the Lovecraftian
Mythos

Edited by Mr Jonathan Green

Proudly published by Snowbooks

Copyright © 2016 Jonathan Green, Jonathan Oliver, Michael Carroll, Adrian Tchiachovsky, C L Werner, Josh Reynolds, Nimue Brown, Andrew Lane, Ian Edginton, Adrian Chamberlin, Guy Haley, Danie Ware, James Lovegrove, Ed Fortune, Pat Kelleher, John Reppion, Graham McNeill, Jan Siegel

Snowbooks Ltd

email: info@snowbooks.com | www.snowbooks.com.

British Library Cataloguing in Publication Data.
A catalogue record for this book is available
from the British Library.

Paperback / softback

ISBN 9781909679863

First published August 2016

Printed in Denmark by Nørhaven

SHAKESPEARE Vs
CTHULHU

Edited by Mr JONATHAN GREEN

Featuring divers tales of terror by
Mr JONATHAN OLIVER

Mr MICHAEL CARROLL

Mr ADRIAN TCHAIKOVSKY

Mr C L WERNER

Mr JOSH REYNOLDS

Mistress NIMUE BROWN

Mr ANDREW LANE

Mr IAN EDGINTON

Mr ADRIAN CHAMBERLIN

Mr GUY HALEY

Mistress DANIE WARE

Mr JAMES LOVEGROVE

Mr ED FORTUNE

Mr PAT KELLEHER

Mr JOHN REPPION

Mr GRAHAM MCNEILL

Mistress JAN SIEGEL

Illustrated by
Mr MALCOLM BARTER, Mr KEV CROSSLEY,
Mr TONY HOUGH, Mr RUSS NICHOLSON,
Mr NEIL ROBERTS & Mr TIERNEN TREVALLION

SHAKESPEARE Vs
CTHULHU

Interlude

Act Three

Epilogue

Curtain

Dramatis Personae

THAT WAY MADNESS LIES

JONATHAN GREEN

"To die, to sleep.
To sleep, perchance to dream - ay, there's the rub.
For in that sleep of death what dreams may come..."

Hamlet, Act III, Scene I.

"In his house at R'lyeh, dead Cthulhu waits dreaming."

The Call of Cthulhu.

Imagine if it had been William Shakespeare, England's greatest playwright, who had discovered the truth about the Great Old Ones and the cosmic entity we know as Cthulhu, rather than the American horror writer H P Lovecraft. Imagine if Stratford's favourite son had been the one to learn of the dangers of seeking after forbidden knowledge and of the war waged between the Elder Gods in the Outer Darkness, and had passed on that message, to those with eyes to see it, through his plays and poetry... Welcome to the world of Shakespearean Cthulhu!

The 400th anniversary of the death of William Shakespeare, on 23rd April 2016, seemed like the perfect time to bring together the fantastical worlds of the Bard's plays and Lovecraft's most terrifying creations, and so I set about gathering together a group of like-minded individuals: a cult, if you like, of authors who I knew could do justice to both the legacy of the Cthulhu Mythos and the greatest writer ever in the history of the English language.

After all, Cthulhu and Shakespeare are the perfect match. There is a trail of madness and horror that runs through much of Shakespeare's work – from Lear's ranting at the heavens on the blasted moor and the macabre cooking suggestions of *Titus Andronicus*, to *Macbeth's* weird sisters and Ophelia's downward spiral into insanity and ultimately death.

I

Just as in many of Lovecraft's stories the only sane response, when faced with the truth of the uncaring nature of the universe and man's insignificant place within it, is to lose one's sanity, so madness is a recurring theme in Shakespeare's plays – from Othello's green-ey'd monster, to Lady Macbeth's suicide-inducing insomnia. Of course during the Bard's lifetime medical practitioners still held on to the belief that mental illness was more often than not the result of the malignant attentions of dark powers; how appropriate.

But Shakespeare's life is just as fascinating as any of his plays, as much because of what we don't know about the Bard of Stratford, as what we do. Considering he is the world's most famous and most popular playwright, despite commemorating the occasion of his birth (and his death) on 23rd April, we don't actually know when he was born. We don't know the date of his marriage to Anne Hathaway. We don't know for certain the identity of the Dark Lady, to whom he wrote some of his most famous sonnets, and neither are we absolutely sure who the Fair Youth was to whom many of the remainder are dedicated. We're not even sure what he looked like.

It is precisely because of this lack of information that some have argued that William Shakespeare did not write his plays at all, although that is not an argument you will find upheld here. The man was a certifiable genius, rather than just certifiable (as are so many of the victims of the stories contained within this anthology).

Of particular interest to scholars of Shakespeare's life are the infamous "lost years", a seven-year period between 1585, following the birth of his twins, Hamnet and Judith, and 1592, the year Robert Greene published his pamphlet in which he referred to Shakespeare as an "upstart crow". During this time Shakespeare left no historical traces, other than being party to a lawsuit to recover part of his mother's estate, which had been mortgaged and lost by default. Many have surmised what he was up to during that time – was he a sailor, a soldier, a clerk of law, a teacher, or even a spy? – but is the truth that he was really out there in the world, fighting monsters and thwarting the schemes of the cultists of Cthulhu?

That's what three particular stories bound up within the anthology deal with. This trilogy begins with Josh Reynolds' *A Tiger's Heart, A Player's Hide*, set during the summer of 1592, when an outbreak of plague resulted in the closure of all of the theatres in London. Next comes Guy Haley's *A Reckoning*, which takes as its inspiration the circumstances surrounding the murder of Shakespeare's friend, and fellow playwright, Christopher "Kit" Marlowe in a tavern brawl in Deptford, in 1593. The last of these stories, John Reppion's *Exeunt*, takes place towards the end of Shakespeare's life, in 1616, and to say any more would spoil the surprise.

The rest of the stories take some of Shakespeare's most famous works and give them an appropriately dark, Lovecraftian twist. Indeed, Shakespeare's plays are such an inspiration to so many that more than one play has produced more than one story for the anthology.

Take *Romeo and Juliet*, for example. Jonathan Oliver's *Star-Crossed* forms the Prologue to our performance, set as it is in the present day, while Michael Carroll's *A Madness Most Discreet* throws us back through time, into the Machiavellian world of Renaissance Italy. Likewise, *The Tempest* is responsible for two entries in this book. First there is Ian Edginton's *The Undiscovered Country*, which considers what befell the sorcerer and wronged Duke of Milan Prospero before he and his baby daughter Miranda made landfall on Sycorax's magical island, while the anthology concludes with Jan Siegel's very different *#Tempest*, a teasing tale for the Twitter generation.

Another contemporary retelling is Graham McNeill's *Something Wicked This Way Comes*, which relocates Shakespeare's infamous Scottish Play to the present day and considers the dangers of the modern cult of celebrity.

Of course Shakespeare wasn't only a playwright, he was a poet as well, most famous for his 154 sonnets. Nimue Brown's *What Dreams May Come* and Danie Ware's *The Green-Ey'd Monster* form a fitting tribute to the Bard of Stratford whilst also honouring Lovecraft's literary legacy.

No play is free from the taint of the Great Old Ones and the Outer Gods in this anthology, whether tragedy, history or comedy. Shakespeare's most widely performed tragedy, that of *Hamlet*, is the inspiration behind Adrian Tchaikovsky's *Something Rotten*, and has the doomed Prince of Denmark having to deal with more than just his obsession with death, while Pat Kelleher's *The Terrors of the Earth* puts a new spin on an old story, that of the mythical monarch of Britain,

King Lear. And then there's Andrew Lane's *The "Iä"s of March*, which revisits the Rome of Julius Caesar, and puts the plotting and scheming of Brutus and his fellow conspirators into a new and terrifying context.

Henry V, that Shakespearean celebration of English might, is revisited in C L Werner's *Once More Unto the Breach*, while Adrian Chamberlin takes *Richard III* as his subject in *The Suns of York*, turning the hunchbacked Duke of Gloucester into even more of a monster.

There's little to laugh at in the tales of Lovecraft, and the same is true of Ed Fortune's *The King in Yellow Stockings*, which takes one of the Bard's most famous comedies, *Twelfth Night*, and turns it into an abject tragedy.

Even stage directions are not safe from the warped imaginings of our Cthulhu-inspired authors, and Shakespeare's most famous stage direction – *"Exit, pursued by a bear"* – from *The Winter's Tale* forms the basis of an entire story in James Lovegrove's *Exit, pursued by...?*

But before you turn the page and dive into the plethora of disturbing delights that await you within, I must first pass on a word of warning from the Bard himself:

"That way madness lies."

King Lear, Act III, Scene IV.

JONATHAN GREEN
JULY 2016, LONDON

4

Prologue

"I defy you, stars."

Romeo and Juliet, Act V, Scene I.

STAR-CROSSED

JONATHAN OLIVER

A BIRD FLYING over Ardenton would not notice anything remarkable about this small Midlands town, yet it is here that we set our scene.

Two will meet, the offspring of two magical families, two lives that will be governed by cosmic forces they can neither understand nor fully control.

Above – far, far above our fictional bird – stars are moving, constellations coming into alignment like courtiers waiting to take their places in an ancient and arcane dance. Beneath the earth, tectonic plates shift infinitesimally, too little to register on any charts – but it is enough.

The conditions will be met. The gates will open, and the actions of our lovers will seek to unleash upon the world forces that could consume it entire.

"I SEE A stranger."

"Tall, dark and handsome no doubt. Really, is that the best you can do?"

"This card suggests a new start: a meeting that will lead to new opportunities. And this..." Jasmine's mother turned over another card. "Is..."

"Is that supposed to be The Hanged Man?"

Penelope turned the card to face her. "Well, obviously... It's, erm... Hand me those instructions again will you?"

"And you've got how many boxes of these, Mum?"

"Around fifteen. I think."

"You think?"

"Okay. I have thirty."

"Great. And how are you going to shift thirty boxes of tarot cards when no one can tell what the pictures on them are supposed to be?"

"Special offer? Buy one get one free?"

"Bloody hell, Mum. Please tell me that you got these on sale or return."

"No... No, I didn't."

Jasmine sighed and looked around the poky little shop. Her mother had once been a highly-valued member of the magical community – a reliable psychic, gifted clairvoyant, and a white witch of considerable power and reach. Now she was reduced to this: selling trinkets and junk to the impressionable and desperate.

"Look, let's put half a box's worth out on display for now and see how it goes," Penelope said, attempting to sound hopeful. "In the meantime the rest of them are in the kitchen, if you don't mind taking them downstairs."

Jasmine did mind. The basement was at the bottom of three turns of a stone spiral staircase – like something from a medieval dungeon – and it took her a good half hour to lug all the boxes down. The basement had a low ceiling and smelled of mould. On days when it rained heavily there was the disconcerting sound of what seemed like a river's worth of water flowing just beyond the walls.

Jasmine opened the basement door, revealing barely half a metre of free floor space before the towers of boxes and miscellaneous junk that filled the rest of the room.

"Thanks a lot, Mum!" she shouted up the stairs.

A lot of the boxes were either half- or two-thirds full, and Jasmine spent almost an hour redistributing stock, and making room. A stack of cartons towards the rear of the basement budged barely an inch when she tried to move them, the topmost box swaying threateningly towards her.

"Gods! What is in these?" she said, looking for a product description. "*Obsidian skull essential oil vaporisers*. Fantastic!"

Jasmine sighed and wrapped her arms around the stack again. It leaned ominously, looking like it was about to topple, and, reacting on instinct, she thrust out her hands, pushing the boxes away.

The tower fell with the sound of heavy things breaking.

It wasn't just the ornamental skulls within that had broken, however. One of the boxes had fallen against a damp section of basement wall, shattering the plaster and revealing a space within.

The smell of mould intensified, but there was something else; something more animal.

Jasmine knelt and cautiously peered into the hole she had inadvertently created.

Inside, resting on an inch of dust was a book wrapped in cloth.

She briefly thought of calling out to her mother to come and see what she had discovered, but then something told her that this was just for her.

Jasmine reached for the book and withdrew her hand the moment she touched the wrapping. It hadn't felt like cotton or hessian, but something unpleasantly organic.

Stealing herself against disgust, Jasmine snatched up the book, quickly throwing off its noisome shroud.

It looked ancient. Evidently hand-written, the tome was illustrated throughout; some of the pictures made her flesh crawl. Screw the magical knickknacks and mass-produced enchantments her mother pedalled, she thought, this was the real thing. The book was likely worth a fortune, and it might well be just what Jasmine needed to turn things around.

"THE BOOK HAS been found."

Uncle's voice jolted him out of his contemplations, so suddenly had it been dropped into the silence. In the study, the only light came from a guttering candle on the mantelpiece. They did not require light for their studies. Any strong illumination would only dampen the potency of their manipulations and transgressions.

Arodias stood. "Is it nearby?" he said.

"Yes."

"Then you were right to bring us here. Rest now, Uncle. Your work is done."

The sigh of the old man's final exhalation filled the room as the smell of decay bloomed from his body. Come the morning there would be little of him left; perhaps just a smear of grease where he had sat.

Arodias crossed to the mantel and lit another candle. In the spotted and tarnished mirror his gaunt face looked back at him. He looked old.

And he was old, his life extended well beyond his naturally allotted span of years. But that was alright, Arodias could change.

BY THE TIME term had started at the new college, Jasmine had begun to translate the book. At first she thought it was written in Latin, but after a few failed attempts at trying to make sense of the text with the aid of Babelfish, she realised that what she was looking at was archaic English. It was written in such a crabbed hand and expressed in such an esoteric style that it took her a whole afternoon of staring at one page before the words began to give up their meaning.

It wasn't like any book on magic Jasmine had ever read, and her mother had an impressive library, even if she herself now made little use of it. Jasmine was well-acquainted with nature magic, magical thinking and the various branches of sympathetic sorcery, but the arcane text in the ancient book referred to none of these things.

The passages that she had so far been able to decipher described all manner of beings – or were they gods? – but it focused on one in particular.

This creature was a manifestation of nothing, though it wielded great power. It had once been a pharaoh, but had since returned to the darkness 'betwixt the stars'. The author of the book – this title-less tome that was as much a diary as it was a treatise on the supernatural – had been attempting to make contact with this entity, though for what purpose wasn't entirely clear.

"What are you reading?"

The boy sitting opposite her on one of the ratty armchairs that filled the student lounge had fine mousy hair cut in an unfashionable style, and was dressed in a way that said not so much hipster as failed 1950s' beat poet.

"Sorry?" Jasmine said.

"What are you reading?" He leaned forward, his gaze on the book rather than her.

"Oh, this? Just a history book. It's a bit boring actually."

"May I?" He thrust out his hand abruptly, making Jasmine flinch.

"I'm sorry. You are...?"

"Oh." The hand was withdrawn, a confused expression on the boy's face as though he had forgotten himself. "I'm Richard. May I?"

The hand was back again.

"Look. The thing is that it's really quite fragile. And it isn't mine, so I really shouldn't. I'm Jasmine, by the way."

"I see," Richard said, got to his feet and left the lounge.

Jasmine blinked and looked back down at the book. She realised it would take time to make friends at the new college, but she hadn't expected to immediately attract the resident weirdo.

NATHANIEL CREED WAS the author of the book, and he had once owned the building in which her mother's shop resided. He had been a famous 17th century magician, or so he claimed, though much of the book seemed to detail his failures, rather than his successes.

"Then maybe you had better find a way!"

Jasmine was snapped out of her studies by her mother's cry of frustration as she slammed down the phone. The silence that followed was worse, and she crept down to the kitchen to find Penelope with her head on the table, quietly crying.

"Mum?"

Penelope looked up and Jasmine's stomach clenched when she saw the despair on her mother's face.

"Oh, sweetie, I tried, but we're going to lose the shop."

"What? How?"

"The rent's too high, the footfall too low. I tried. Really, I did."

Jasmine put her arms around her mother. "I know you did, Mum. I'm not blaming you. You did your best."

"Thing is, we may lose the house too. All my finances were tied up in the shop, and with that gone..."

Jasmine could have sworn, could have smashed something, but instead she let her mother cry into her shoulder, wishing that Penelope could again be the mother who had been the provider of such comfort, who had been her faith in a world that had more in it than most could reckon. Some sort of radical change was what her mother needed, and once Penelope would have been able to use magical means to enact such change herself. She had long ago lost her self-confidence, and Jasmine didn't know whether her mother even had it in her anymore to perform the most basic of cantrips.

However, there were still those who believed in Peneope; colleagues and friends who could be called upon to bring their own talents to bear.

"JASMINE."

"Jasmine?"

"Jasmine Cooper. I'm Penelope Cooper's daughter?"

"Oh, Penelope, bless her. How is she doing these days?"

"Not good, I'm afraid. She's losing her business and it looks like we're going to lose the house."

"Oh, goddess! I'm so sorry. That's terrible. Is there anything that I can do?"

"Actually, that's what I was calling about. You and Mum were once pretty close in the magical community, and I was wondering whether you could use your power – perhaps call on some others, too – to help turn things around for us... Hello?"

"Yes, I'm still here. I'm sorry, Jasmine, I don't quite know what you expect of me."

"A spell or two, perhaps? I don't know... don't you have some kind of magic to help a witch in need?"

"That's really not the way it works, my dear."

"But Mum told me you used to get up to all sorts. She told me about things you'd seen, the stories of the magic you'd worked –"

"Jasmine, slow down. Your mother was always one for stories, I'm afraid, and that's what they mostly were."

"But... she said the spells really worked."

"And did you ever witness any that ever did? Magic just isn't like that, Jasmine. It never was. Look, I think that Penelope was trying to impress you, entertain you maybe. I'm sure she meant no harm."

"But there's really nothing you can do? That any of you can do?"

"I'm so sorry, Jasmine. Naturally, I'll be thinking of you both, praying for you. And do tell Penelope, if she ever wants to give me a call –"

"Fine. Bye."

ARODIAS LOOKED AT the boy in the mirror. It had been a long time since he had worn such a youthful face; decades since he had spoken to anyone outside the circle of his own family, let alone a woman.

There had been women once, before his studies had intervened, before his discoveries had reshaped his world and himself. Once he had been married. Once he had loved and, if he cast his mind back, Arodias thought that he could just about remember how that had been.

"Hi, I'm Richard," he said to his reflection. "I'm sorry about all that... strangeness before. May we talk?"

JASMINE HAD READ somewhere that one of the best ways of coping with grief – or mental trauma of any kind – is to throw oneself into work, or study.

For all of the disorientation and anxiety she had experienced in her first few weeks of college, she soon found herself settling in. Her Modern English Literature course was well-taught and engaging, and there was a wide variety of societies and clubs on offer.

One afternoon, she was handed a leaflet advertising open auditions for a forthcoming production of *Romeo and Juliet*, and though it had been a while since she had last trod the boards in Drama Club at school, she decided to give it a go.

At first, she had thought of going in for one of the significant, though smaller, female roles – Nurse, or Lady Montague or Capulet perhaps – but deciding to throw caution to the wind, Jasmine put herself down for Juliet.

"Okay, people. I need a Romeo and a Juliet, and we're going to go with the balcony scene. Who do we have?"

Jasmine raised her hand and saw only a handful of prospective Romeos do the same. Her heart sank when she saw that one of them was the weirdo who had quizzed her about the book.

"Right, Romeo, we'll start with... you. Yes, you. Chap in the black T-shirt. Richard? And" – the director cast her eye over the clutch of Juliets. Jasmine was just about to lower her hand when she was singled out. "Yes, you my lovely. You are...?"

"Jasmine."

"Jasmine and Richard, splendid. Let's go from, 'But soft, what light...'"

She wasn't expecting there to be any chemistry between them, but Richard spoke his lines as though he meant them; he was a generous actor, bringing her more fully into the role, helping Jasmine give a performance that at least felt halfway real.

She left the auditions feeling quietly confident and was going over her lines again in the cafeteria when Richard sat down opposite her. It may have been the light or the fact that she wasn't as tense as she had been at their first meeting, but he looked younger somehow.

"Hi," he said.

"Hi."

"I thought you did really well today."

"Yeah, you too."

"Look, I just wanted to apologise about all that... *strangeness* before, with the book."

"Oh, don't worry about it. I'd forgotten all about that to be honest."

"It's just that old books are a bit of a hobby of mine."

"What kind of things are you into?"

"Areas of esoteric study and research mainly. What some may call magic."

"Hah! You should talk to my mother. She used to be into all that stuff. She owns the shop on the High Street – *Destiny*. Well, she did. It's going to close down."

"I'm sorry to hear that."

"Nothing to be done about it now, I suppose."

"And what was the book you were reading?"

"Just some old diary. I thought" – *that it could help, that there was magic there that I could use* – "it looked interesting, but it's a bit boring to be honest."

"Even so, I'd like to see it, if I may." Richard leaned in a little too close and Jasmine drew back. For a moment there had been a strange, musty smell and an expression crossed his face that made him look old. She blinked and he was leaning back in his chair. "It might be that I could help you understand what is in the book. Some of the more esoteric texts need a little translating. That is, if you would like?"

She thought back to when she had found the book, and the feeling she'd had that it was somehow meant to be hers.

"That sounds great," Jasmine said, "I'd like that."

"Splendid. Well then, if we two are to be Romeo and Juliet, as I very much hope, then why not bring it along to one of the rehearsals, and we'll see what we can do."

He held out his hand and Jasmine saw that he had the most beautiful, slender fingers

"Thanks, Romeo... God! I mean, Richard. Richard is what I meant, of course. I'm so sorry." Jasmine was sure that her embarrassment had lit her up like a beacon, but Richard smiled.

"No need to be. Soon then, my Juliet."

ARODIAS WAS CONFIDENT the roles would be theirs. After all, on the morning of the auditions, he had taken the precaution of burning certain powders while describing complex geometries over the smoke.

He had always suspected that the book had remained in the home of Nathaniel Creed. No doubt Creed had set up wards to keep it from his sight. In any case, Nathaniel was hundreds of years dead and the book was back in the world.

And the girl may be useful, beyond being his route to the book. When he had first seen her, she had been reading Nathaniel's words not just with a glimmer of understanding, but a hunger for more.

Yes, she had something, this Jasmine. He may yet have need of her.

"OH GOD, YOU utter *utter* idiot. 'Thanks, Romeo.' *Romeo!* Oh yeah, well played Jasmine. Top of the class."

She blushed as she remembered the conversation. She'd never spoken like that to a boy before. And he'd hardly been the master of subtlety himself. *My Juliet.* Any other time, she'd have been running for the hills, but there was something about Richard – a certain intensity, an alluring intelligence. She didn't know quite what it was, but she did know that she wanted to see him again.

"'Thanks, Romeo'. Oh God oh God oh God!"

There was a soft knocking on her bedroom door. "Are you okay in there, my love?"

"Fine, Mum. Just struggling with some homework."

"Is there anything that I can do?"

"No, I'm fine really."

"Okay then. Well... I love you, you know?"

"Yeah, I know, Mum."

Jasmine waited until she heard her mother's footsteps recede before she took Nathaniel Creed's diary from under her bed.

She needed something to focus her mind, to take her away from thoughts of Richard for a while. Perhaps he had been right to be so interested in the book. Word by word, it was starting to speak to her.

"WELL, MY LOVELIES, we have our Romeo and Juliet. Round of applause please." Richard looked at Jasmine and winked. She smiled, a little abashed, and gave him a thumbs-up.

Just as she'd promised, she had brought the book with her, and it was this that was on her mind that afternoon, rather than the words of the play.

"That was terrific, Jasmine. Very stirring," the director said, after they had read through Juliet's first scene.

"Really?" Jasmine said. "I think I tripped over a couple of the lines."

"No, no, that was perfect, really."

She looked from the glassy sheen in the director's eyes to the disgruntled expressions on some of the other actors' faces, and felt that the cast were not in agreement.

But then they were onto Mercutio and Romeo's verbal sparring, and Jasmine's thoughts returned to what she had learned the previous evening.

Nathaniel Creed's philosophy was unlike anything she had encountered in the world of magic, either through her mother or her own studies. Creed's approach was unusually anti-human, and concerned itself not so much with discovering the spiritual side of oneself, as denying the individual's place in the universe. Indeed, he referred to the human race as an 'accident'; a by-product of a vast process humanity didn't have the capacity to understand. He wrote about the importance of erasing one's own identity, becoming a nothingness — a gateway through which something could enter.

Jasmine looked up as Richard sat down beside her. On the stage Friar Lawrence was going through his morning ablutions.

"Penny for your thoughts," Richard said.

"Oh I was just wondering who this Al-Hazred is that the author mentions. Any ideas?"

Richard looked briefly taken aback.

"Are you okay?" Jasmine said.

"Yes, fine. Fine. Just a bit tired. But, yes, that name does ring a bell. Listen, I was thinking that we could take a look at the book together, tomorrow evening, over dinner at my house."

"Your house?"

"Of course. I'll have a meal prepared for us and... Oh, I see. No, nothing like that of course. It's just that we'd have access to my library and —"

"Look, why don't you come over to mine instead? We have a pretty impressive collection of books ourselves, and I'm sure that you and Mum would get on like a house on fire, being into magic and all that."

"'And all that?'"

"Oh, you know what I mean. I also cook a pretty mean curry. And we can learn more about this."

Jasmine gestured with the book and Richard's hand shot out, as though he meant to grab it.

"Sorry," he said. "May I... may I just take a quick look?"

"Romeo and Juliet," the director called, "you're up. Party scene run through, yeah?"

"Of course," Richard replied, and, managing a weak smile, he turned back to Jasmine. "Later then."

"Since when did you start cooking?"

"Since you stopped bothering, Mum."

"Heh. Fair point. Are we having guests?"

"Just a boy from college. Richard."

"A boy from college, eh?"

"Don't start. It's not like that." At least, she didn't think it was. Richard was simply coming over to help her understand Creed's book, and Creed's book would help her with their shitty life. She was sure of it. "Anyway, I think you'll like him. He's into all that weird stuff."

"How flattering, Jasmine. Thank you so much."

Richard was alarmingly punctual. Jasmine had been intending to change before they sat down to eat, but instead she had to answer the door in tracksuit bottoms and an ancient T-shirt. Richard himself was dressed so formerly that it looked like he was on his way to a funeral. As he stepped over the threshold, he brought with him a faint odour of mothballs. He hadn't brought any flowers or wine, but then Jasmine didn't think that it would have occurred to him to do so.

"Dinner's almost ready," she said. "Oh, and this is Mum."

"Mrs Cooper. A pleasure to meet you."

Richard held out his hand and Penelope didn't take it.

Well isn't this getting off to a flying start? Jasmine thought. "Right, well. As I said, dinner is pretty much ready, so why don't we go and sit down?"

Penelope kept up the silent treatment all through the meal, and glared at Richard as though daring him to make a wrong move. Jasmine had no idea what had got into her. She had never been this off with any of her other boyfriends; not that Richard was boyfriend material, she reminded herself.

Richard bolted down the meal as though desperate to get it over with.

"Okay, then," Jasmine said as she cleared the plates. "Shall we make a start on those lines then Richard?"

"Lines?" Penelope said.

"Oh, I haven't told you have I? Richard and I have been cast in the college production of *Romeo and Juliet*, as the leads."

Penelope couldn't have looked less delighted if Jasmine had told her she was pregnant.

"So, we're just going to go over our lines. Okay?"

Her mother didn't respond, but she did hold Richard with a baleful glare as they left the room.

"I'm so sorry about Mum," Jasmine said, once the bedroom door was closed behind them. "She's been going through a lot, you know?"

Richard didn't answer. He was standing at the dresser with his back to her, staring down at the book.

"So, here it is," he said, reverence in his voice. "Nathaniel Creed's book. I'd heard so much. Had no idea it was so close." Richard turned around with the book in his hands. "Where did you find it?"

"It was under a pile of junk in the basement of Mum's shop." Jasmine wasn't sure why she felt the need for the white lie, perhaps it was the intensity in Richard's eyes as he opened the book. "Where did you hear about the book in the first place?"

"Creed and I..." Richard cleared his throat and started again. "Nathaniel Creed's work is very well known within certain circles."

"Famous wizard. Got it."

"Wizard is far too... *trite* a word for what Creed was. Creed was..." Richard gestured with the book, as he sought for the right words. "*This* is not magic."

"It's not?"

"No, the knowledge within this book concerns itself with something far greater. Magic is often mere wish fulfilment; ludicrous ritual, offering, at best, a temporary salve to suffering." Jasmine thought of all the junk in her mother's shop and nodded. "But Creed *knew*. To involve oneself with true knowledge, one must entirely forget oneself. Humanity is nothing; less than nothing – a cosmic joke. There are beings... out there that have terrible, infinite power. True sorcery, real magic, lies in attracting their attention."

"But Creed never managed it, did he?" Jasmine said.

"What do you mean?"

"Well I've been reading the book, and from what I can work out, it's mostly about his failures. He never seemed to do any actual magic. And the book... well, it ends halfway through a sentence. What do you think happened to him?"

Richard ignored the question and said, "Creed knew more than he would let himself realise. His philosophy was mostly sound, but his ritual technique was all –"

"– wrong. Yes, that's what I thought." Jasmine said, interrupting him. "There's a bit where he really seems to be onto something."

Richard looked at her as though he were only now truly seeing her; Jasmine thought that if she wasn't careful she could lose herself in those eyes.

"Show me?" Richard said, holding out the book.

He sat beside her on the bed as she carefully turned the brittle pages.

"Here we are. It's like the words of the ritual are mostly right, but the cadence, the rhythm is all wrong."

"Yes," Richard said, leaning in closer. "I must admit that had never occurred to me."

"It's about patterns. See this diagram? He's got the basic idea right, but he's not followed it through."

Jasmine pointed to a picture drawn in dark brown ink. Richard nodded emphatically and put his hand over hers where it rested on the page. She looked up; his face was inches from her own.

"'And palm to palm is holy palmer's kiss'," he said, entwining his fingers with hers.

"Richard?"

"Yes, Jasmine."

"I believe that's my line."

She leaned in and kissed him. For a moment his lips didn't seem to know what to do, but then they found their place. Jasmine moved away and smiled.

"'You kiss by the book'," she said and Richard laughed. "Anyway, shall we carry on?"

"Yes, Jasmine."

*   *   *

22

As SHE CLOSED the front door behind Richard, Penelope said, "Jasmine? A word."

"Christ! You made me jump. And don't talk to me like that. I'm not five. Anyway, I have things I need to be getting on with."

"Stand right there and bloody well listen."

Jasmine had never seen her mother so angry, but there was also an edge of fear in her voice.

"Jasmine, I love you. You know that. But I will not have that boy in our house again."

"What? He was polite as could be during dinner. I only wish I could say the same for you. Honestly, Mum, I have no idea what's got into you."

"You really don't see it do you?" Penelope took her daughter by the shoulders, and though she tried to pull away, held her firm. "Listen to me. This is important. Richard is... *polluted*. It's been a long time since I've encountered someone with an aura so awry, but trust me when I say he's bad news. Rare as it is, I know genuine evil when I see it."

Jasmine knocked her mother's hands away. "Oh, please! Don't spin me any more of your Harry Potter bullshit."

"I just want you to be safe."

"No, you're just afraid of what will happen when I take control of my life."

Jasmine did something then that she hadn't done since her early teens: she stormed upstairs and slammed her bedroom door.

She could still smell Richard in the room — incense and mothballs — and Nathaniel Creed's book lay open on the bed where they had sat.

Jasmine looked at the diagram in the book before picking up a notepad and a pen, and correcting Creed's mistakes. The ritual he had been attempting to realise was all about the sounds and rhythms of words spoken aloud, except that Nathaniel had been no poet, had no feeling for verse and his attempt to formulate a chant had fallen at every hurdle. He understood the concept; he just hadn't had the wherewithal to put it into practice.

"The problem, Creed," Jasmine said, "is that you lack poetry."

She looked at her version of the diagram, studying its overlapping lines and symbols. "Poetry..."

Jasmine took up the script, flicking through the text, trying to get a feel for Shakespeare's words. She read aloud from *Romeo and Juliet*, while she traced the intricacies of the diagram with her right hand.

"Look to behold this night,
The all-seeing sun
Ne'er saw her match since first the world begun."

She shaped the text to her will and as she spoke, she became aware of another will, beginning to impose itself upon the world. It was coming from an almost impossibly far distance, and it was approaching fast.

"Our solemn hymn to sullen dirges change."

Her body was filled with a pleasant languor, a seductive dream state.

"Tears distilled by moans."

Jasmine closed her eyes, noting, as she did so, the closeness of the darkness beyond her bedroom window. Her right hand spasmed and twitched as it continued to trace the complex geometries of the diagram.

"Thou sober-suited matron all in black
All the world will be in love with night."

Boundless space surrounded her – a formless chaos imbued with life by each word.

"Thus I enforce thy rotten jaws to open."

A wind rose from nowhere; Jasmine faltered and she grasped for her next line before the power could elude her.

A voice spoke into the void.

"In fair Verona, where we lay our scene."

Jasmine opened her eyes, to find herself sitting in a plaza in the environs of an extraordinary city.

Every building, every tower, minaret and spire, had been constructed from the same obsidian stone. Above her, a depthless sky was strewn with the jewels of a million unfamiliar constellations. Across from where she sat, a fountain sang with dark wine – its heady perfume undercut with the scent of bitter herbs. Such a vast city should be home to a vast population, yet she appeared to be alone, even though voices and the sound of footsteps surrounded her; she felt the touch of silk and heard feminine laughter as something brushed past. From a church across the way, strange music sounded, as of many pipes playing, not always to the same purpose.

Jasmine looked down at her hands to find that she still held Nathaniel Creed's book, though of *Romeo and Juliet* there was no sign.

She rose to her feet and, across the way, a section of wall seemed to detach and come towards her. It took Jasmine a moment to realise that it was the figure of a man, cast from the same stone as the city. His clothes had been spun from a midnight thread – or was she seeing the absence of clothes on the absence of a man? – and neither colour nor lightness relieved his darkness.

"Jasmine," he said, and described a courtly bow, his right foot forward, his right arm swept low. He was dressed like a Renaissance prince or nobleman, and his features were youthful, though Jasmine suspected she would never be able to determine his true age. As he rose, she gasped, for the depths she had first seen in Richard's eyes were here limitless.

He saw the book in her hands, and laughed. "You used Nathaniel Creed's words to summon me?"

"I used the ideas behind the words. The words themselves were from a different source, as I'm sure you're aware," she said, gesturing to the city that surrounded them.

The discordant music coming from the church ceased. Above them the stars began to fall. Sickly yellow light bled from the church's windows and the doors opened; within, she could hear the sound of something massive shuffling across a stone floor – it put her in mind of the elephant house at the zoo. She wasn't sure that she wanted to enter the church, or see what would emerge, but the obsidian man held out his hand and there was nothing that she could do but take it.

"My lady?" he said, gesturing to the church, and together they stepped forward.

ARODIAS FELT INVIGORATED, full of a boundless energy and a breathless anticipation such as he hadn't experienced in many a year. There had been a period in the late 18th century when he had lived, for a time, in the catacombs of a deconsecrated and abandoned monastery where

– after much meditation and the ingestion of a number of highly toxic fungi – he had encountered a being that had instilled in him a similar feeling. But that had been an inter-planar entity, and Jasmine was a mortal human woman; one who understood the truth, and in whom Arodias sensed a desire to set it free.

When he opened the front door, he felt like announcing to the entire household that he was in love, but no one would answer, not with Uncle gone and the rest of them lost in their own esoteric venturings.

Still, he had to tell someone.

He found Cousin in the dining room. He had clearly been sitting at the large dark wood table for some time; a mantle of dust rested on his shoulders and a spider had made its home between his left ear and the back of the chair on which he sat.

Cousin was a long way away, but Arodias brought him back.

"Arodias," he said, "is it time to attempt to open the gates again so soon?"

"Not quite, Cousin, but not long now." Arodias leaned forward and then recoiled when he got a whiff of his relative's fetid odour. "I have met someone. A girl."

Cousin's dry laugh rattled loose two of his teeth. "A girl? Arodias, are you not a bit beyond that, your present form excepted?"

"But, this is no schoolboy crush. She was the one who discovered Nathanial Creed's book, and she *understands it*, Cousin. The dark truths and arcane secrets speak to her."

"You know better than to let love interfere with your esoteric commitments."

"But that's just it, Cousin. None of us – not one member of this family, over however many centuries it's been – has been able to open the gates and call *him* into this world. But with Jasmine it feels not just possible, but probable. The stars are right. You feel it, don't you Cousin?"

"Be careful, Arodias."

"You know that he is near. Don't tell me that you don't."

Cousin expelled a breath and leaned forwards, shedding dust and destroying his spider companion's home. His right hand came up with the crackle of dry tendons stretching. There was the sound of ancient bone fracturing, but he showed no pain as his hand made the sign of the Crawling Chaos.

"Yes, Arodias," Cousin said. "He is near."

JASMINE WAS IN love. She had not slept, yet she was wide awake. Penelope noticed her buoyant mood at breakfast and had scowled at her daughter when she had been asked to pass the butter.

"Mum, lighten up. Let's forget about last night and start over, okay? Richard means nothing to me. He *is* nothing."

"I'm glad to hear it," Penelope said, but there was wariness in her words, as though she were a little afraid of her daughter.

The world revealed itself anew as Jasmine walked to college that morning; no more real than scenery painted on cloth and poorly hung, and now that she saw this, she felt confident that she could recast it to her own desires. All she needed was her obsidian man. If she gave him access to their universe, he had promised that there would be a corner of reality that was eternally hers. It didn't matter that everything else would be gone; what mattered was that Jasmine would be able to rectify the mistakes of the past: the divorce that had changed everything, the misfortune that had dogged her and her mother at every turn. And whether any of it were true or not, well, what did that matter? The obsidian man had told her the truth, or at least hinted at it, and though a part of Jasmine had shrunk away in the face of it, wanted to erase the knowledge that been revealed to her, she realised that unless she embraced the chaos, it would destroy her.

And she was in love. The entity that had eluded Nathaniel Creed had noticed her, and taken her by the hand. Unlike Creed, she understood the true power of words, how the sounds and rhythms they made were as important as their meaning. Jasmine wished that she could share this knowledge with her fellow English Literature students, but her new lover had forbidden it.

Richard greeted her effusively at the lunchtime rehearsal, even going so far as to lean in for a kiss, which she didn't reciprocate, much to the amused glances and raised eyebrows of the rest of the cast.

Once she was in character, none of that mattered. The college disappeared and they were in Verona.

Jasmine felt every line, every word of the fated tragedy. This would be her ritual. When she kissed Romeo she could taste the grave and that which waited beyond.

"Okay, and let's leave it there," called the director, shattering the illusion, leaving Jasmine blinking in a shaft of sunlight that streamed in through one of the windows.

"Jasmine? That was excellent, but I'm wondering if we're over-playing it a little. I think you can rein in some of that intensity without lessening the performance."

What did she know? Jasmine merely smiled and tilted her head in something approximating a nod.

"That was amazing," Richard said, leaning in again for a kiss, which this time was returned. "Did you bring the book?"

"I think that you love Creed's book more than me."

"I can assure you that's not the case." And she was amused to see that he was genuinely mortified she would think such a thing. "I just really enjoyed our time together last night, that's all."

"No, I didn't bring the book. But we can return to it soon."

"Listen, I was thinking that after the play, maybe we could go out for dinner some time? Without the book; just the two of us. We don't even have to talk about the occult."

After the play. Jasmine smiled. "After the play, Richard, all manner of things will be possible."

For the first time in several hundred years, Arodias was having doubts.

Jasmine could help him complete the ritual – that he was sure of – but he could not guarantee her safety once the gates were opened. His god didn't give a fig for human relationships, let alone love. He might grant Arodias mastery over chaos, but he could also take away the first person he had genuinely cared about in a very long time.

Usually, he would change out of his college clothes at the end of the day – and sometimes he even changed form – but that evening his troubled mind insisted that he seek counsel.

He couldn't find Cousin anywhere, and both Brothers had shut themselves in the scullery, from which blasphemous sounds and peculiar smells emanated. Arodias found Sister in the attic, studying the patterns of spiders as they spun their webs between the roof beams.

"Arodias," she said, without turning around, "you appear to be flustered."

"Where is Cousin?"

"I believe that he has taken himself to Leng."

Then he wouldn't see Cousin for some time, if at all.

"You should be in a much more jubilant mood, Arodias. The stars are right, yet I detect in you a certain melancholy."

"Do you ever have doubts, Sister?"

"Doubts, Arodias?"

"About whether what we're doing is right."

"Come now, you know not to apply morality to these matters."

"The situation has changed. Sister, I'm in love."

Sister did turn then, and she laughed, the malice in her mirth distorting her already terrible visage.

"Oh, but that is priceless. Just because you have become a teenage boy, Arodias, it doesn't mean that you have to act like one. Does anybody else in the family know?"

"Just Cousin."

"Yes, well that would explain his sudden departure. Arodias, do I have to remind you what happened the last time you permitted yourself to fall in love?"

Katherine had been a publican's daughter, and normally Arodias wouldn't have given her a second glance, but there was a wickedness in her that appealed to him. At first they had shared only a bed, but over time, and despite himself, Arodias had revealed certain arcane secrets to her, hinting at the dark realities that lay just beneath their own. One evening, after a long and uncomfortable carriage ride back from Bristol, he had found her paging through a tome from his private library – access to which he had strictly forbidden. Arodias hadn't castigated her, or cast her out, but had instead taken the book from her hands and helped Katherine to understand what was written there. He wished he hadn't.

One stiflingly warm night, not long after, as Arodias had tossed and turned in fitful sleep, while beside him Katherine slept as one dead, something had descended from the moon on membranous wings and plucked his lover from their bed. The shadows thrown by the single guttering candle meant that Arodias only caught a hint of this horror's true from, but it had been enough to send him to a sanatorium for a prolonged period.

The thing that had stolen his lover might as well have taken his heart.

"Really, Arodias," Sister said, "you should have left your humanity behind with the rest of us a long time ago. Were we wrong to make you our avatar?"

In Jasme, he had found something of his humanity again. Much to his surprise he found that he cared what happened to her. The hunger in her eyes for forbidden knowledge – the underlying desperation to impose her will upon the world – reminded him all too keenly of Katherine. This time, however, he could make sure that such a terrible fate did not befall his beloved. For her sake he must put aside his diabolical mission. True, it would mean regaining his mortality – oblivion would come for him in the end – but better that than the eternal alien cruelty he saw in Sister's eyes as she waited for his answer.

"No, Sister," Arodias lied, "you were not wrong." He raised his right hand in the sign of the Crawling Chaos. "Thank you for your council. Praise Nyarlathotep."

JASMINE LOST HERSELF in Juliet. She had come to know the play intimately, had memorised not just her own lines, but the words of every character in every scene. She could recite Shakespeare's play backwards if needs be, though she didn't think that it would ultimately add anything to the ritual. Instead, she focused on the words that held weight; the verses that would best give themselves to her purpose.

No, not mine, Jasmine reminded herself. *His.*

Often, after rehearsals, some of the cast would get together for a drink, and although Jasmine was usually invited, she would never join them. She didn't want to think of any of the other cast members outside of their characters; it would diminish their role in the ritual. Richard, she did keep onside, allowing him to join her for the occasional coffee, or lunch get-together in the canteen. Though he was keen for them to be closer, she had allowed little more than hand-holding and the odd chaste kiss.

"Jasmine?" There was a knock on her bedroom door – Penelope. "Jasmine, my love?"

"I'm studying, Mum. Go away."

The door opened and Jasmine quickly closed Nathaniel Creed's book, shoving it under a stack of papers.

"I just thought that you could use a cup of tea. You've been at it ever since you got home, and you hardly touched your dinner."

"Really, it's fine. I've got a lot to get through."

But to her frustration, Penelope sat on the bed beside her and put her hand on her shoulder.

"Look, I'm glad that you're not seeing Richard outside of college, but that doesn't mean you shouldn't have a social life. You're young, Jasmine, you should be enjoying yourself."

Jasmine brushed her mother's hand away, and without looking up said, "I have a lot to do. I do not need a cup of tea, and I do not need you constantly disturbing me."

Penelope didn't back away but leaned in closer.

"Something's gone wrong. Something isn't... *normal* here." She stood and started to pace the room. "I could burn some sage, a cleansing ritual would perhaps –"

Jasmine snorted a contemptuous laugh and turned to glare at her mother. She didn't say anything, just held her with her eyes until she backed out of the room and quietly closed the door.

Jasmine shook her head. If only her mother realised that she was doing this for them.

She turned back to the desk and closed her eyes. As she'd expected, the obsidian man was just on the other side of the darkness.

He was leaning against the fountain in the middle of the night-black plaza, an amused expression on his face, as though he had been witness to the mother/daughter stand-off. The stars above him were closer than ever; blazing ethereal torches that Jasmine felt she could reach up and pluck from the heavens, if she so wished.

"I must say," said the obsidian man, filling a wine glass from the black stream pouring from the fountain, "that using the words of the Bard, the energy of performance, to enact the ritual is a stroke of genius. You are far more gifted than Nathaniel Creed was, or Arodias Thorne could ever hope to be.

"Who is Arodias Thorne?" Jasmine said, taking the cup offered to her.

But the obsidian man only replied with a cruel smile.

As THE FIRST night of the play drew near, so the tension in Jasmine rose. Any fluffed line, any misreading of a stage direction from any of the cast was met with a rolling of her eyes and a sigh of exasperation. During one of the final dress rehearsals she had cut Mercutio short with a cry of, "No, you idiot! The emphasis should be on *Queen*, not *Mab*."

The director had had to pull her aside. "Jasmine, you need to remember who is directing this play, okay? And you need to relax. Take the rest of the evening off. You certainly know your lines well enough, so perhaps it's time to give the others room to deliver theirs, okay?"

Seeing the colour rise in Jasmine's cheeks, and her glare change from one of annoyance to baleful intent, Richard intervened. "Come on, Jasmine, this is supposed to be fun. Why don't we step out and grab a coffee?"

She turned on Richard as though she intended to launch herself at him, but the warmth in his eyes and his smile cut through her rage, bringing her back to herself. He really did look every bit the youthful, brash, daring and reckless Romeo.

"I... I'm sorry," she said, letting him take her hand. "Yes, let's get a coffee."

In the café, she tried to talk to Richard about Creed's book, but he showed little interest and instead, asked, "How have things been, really? How's your Mum, Jasmine?"

But she shook her head and said, "I don't know."

On the opening night, Penelope was as excited as her daughter was agitated.

"I'm proud of you, you know?" she said, as she drove them to the college. "And your dad, he —"

"I know, Mum. I know. Please don't cry. You'll only set me off."

Night had fallen in Ardenton. Across the fields, on the edge of town, a low mist had begun to roll in. No moon shone, but the sky was clear and the stars bright and cold. The air seemed to shimmer as Jasmine stepped from the car and just for a moment, she saw those other, alien stars. Her right hand trembled as she remembered the diagrams and strange geometries Creed has described in his book.

"First night nerves?" Penelope said. "Don't worry, I'm sure you'll be fantastic. Now, away, I shall see you inside. Break a leg."

The discordant music Jasmine heard as she prepared herself backstage was only the college orchestra warming up. As she applied her make-up in the dressing room mirror there was a shadow standing in the corner that she knew no amount of light would dispel.

She forgot all about the night as the house lights came down, and it was summer in Verona.

The spell was almost broken in the first act when the young man playing Tybalt tripped over a line and then forgot the next. He must have seen the look of pure murder that Jasmine shot him from the wings because he quickly recovered. Thankfully that was the worst of the missteps and Jasmine began to sense the reality of the play imposing itself upon the fabric of the universe. The audience must have felt it too, because the gasp of horror when Tybalt was run through by Romeo sounded genuine. Even Richard looked shaken, as though he truly had blood on his hands.

The director glanced at Jasmine and smiled nervously as she prepared for her next cue. Whatever happened on the stage it was out of the director's control; this was no longer her play.

Jasmine allowed herself a thought of what might have been as she shared a kiss with Romeo in Friar Lawrence's cell. Richard held her lips for just a moment too long, as if afraid to let the fated tragedy take its course.

By the beginning of the last act, the chill of the tomb filled the stage. There was a fetid odour too, and Jasmine heard the skitter of claws on stone, putting her in mind of rats within the walls. The stars were so close that their song put all thoughts of death from her mind. Soon she would be in control of her world, and if it was just a dream, she would make sure it was the sweetest dream ever dreamt.

The tomb on which she lay felt like cold stone, though she knew it to be wood. She whispered along to the lines of the actors, feeling how each word was another key turned, another gate opened.

She opened her eyes a crack and risked a glance at her mother, and was surprised to see tears streaming down Penelope's face. She wanted to sit up and tell her that everything was going to be okay, but she would know that soon enough.

Romeo leaned in for a final kiss, believing her as one dead, but she opened her eyes and he stumbled over his next line.

"A... a dateless bargain to engrossing death."

"Richard, do you love me?" Jasmine whispered.

He glanced at the audience nervously before whispering back, "With all my heart."

Before he could pick up the thread of his soliloquy, Jasmine withdrew the knife she had concealed in her robes and buried it up to the hilt in Richard's chest.

ARODIAS CHOKED OUT a gasp and looked down at the knife handle protruding from his chest. Blood was pouring from the wound, but before it could reach the boards the flow was reversed, as the thing that had invaded his body began to use him up. Once he would have rejoiced at this touch of true chaos, but now he could only glance over at his lover with a wounded look as the darkness consumed him.

*　　*　　*

JASMINE WATCHED IN fascinated horror as Richard dropped to his knees. The mortal wound she had struck was now bloodless, but there was no life left in him – at least, no human life.

Blackness clouded Richard's eyes, like ink dropped in water. His mouth stretched in a silent scream, his jaw gaping wide enough to tear his lips into a ragged smile. Richard's head dropped and a stygian torrent poured from his mouth, falling not into a pool, but the form of her obsidian man.

People were running for the exits now but whip-thin tendrils erupted from the torso of the obsidian man and dropped them to their knees. The night that he had brought with him began to fill the theatre, and when Jasmine felt its touch, she looked to Penelope.

Her mother was on her feet, though black tendrils held her in place; she was straining against them as she fought to get to her daughter.

Jasmine knew then that she had made a dreadful mistake. The obsidian man could not give them a world her mother would want to live in. She remembered what Penelope had said about Richard, that he was *polluted*, and now so was she. She looked over at the husk that had contained her lover, and there was no longer anything recognisably human there.

The walls were beginning to dissolve as the tide of infinite chaos washed up against them. Those of the audience who were not dead were either catatonic with fear or gripped by hysteria – crying, laughing, singing. One man in the second row was repeatedly pounding his forehead into the seat back before him, chanting. "Iä, Iä, Iä, Iä, Iä, Iä."

"Mum," Jasmine said. "Mum, I'm so sorry."

But Penelope could not respond and, in any case, it was too late.

The obsidian man strode to the front of the stage and, looking down on the huddle of broken humanity that made up his audience, smiled.

He opened his arms wide as the tide of chaos poured from him, and said, "Never was a story of more woe."

Act One

"Though this be madness, yet there is method in't."

Hamlet, Act II, Scene II.

A MADNESS MOST DISCREET

MICHAEL CARROLL

MY TALE CONCERNS three households, all alike in dignity, in Verona.

Not *"fair* Verona" as other scribes might have it, for like all cities Verona is clad in a blithe veneer that hides a midden of corruption and woe. A cadaver may be draped in exquisite finery, garlanded with spring blossoms and laced with sweet perfume, but – for all that – it remains a corpse.

I was a page to Count Paris, a man three years my senior, but in social standing countless leagues my superior. Some have painted him cruel to his servants, citing his aloof bearing and his often brusque manner when dealing with those beneath his station, but I knew him to be strong-willed and driven. That he was at times quick to rage and would demonstrate such through application of the whip or his ironclad fists was to be expected: a man who has been borne aloft for all his days will accept that as the norm, and does not dwell on the disposition of those bearing him.

Men – of high birth or low – rarely allow their gaze to drift below their own horizon. We do not truly see what lies beneath us. We no more consider the plight of the lives of those who serve us than we do the well-being of the dirt underfoot. This is true for all. As a page in a great house, I was regarded with deference by the common villagers and farmers. To them, my lowly position was as unattainable as the count's was to me. While on an errand for the count I carried myself as would a king, eyes aloft and manner stately, then shed that mask upon the instant of my return, approaching my master with small steps and bowed head.

That is the nature of man: we look up with envy or ambition, and down with scorn or pity, and any man who claims contrary is a liar, a fool, or a conniving peddler.

It is true for all, even the most high, and though I have always known this to be a fact, I did not – and *could* not – understand it in full until the time of my master's encounter with the houses of Montague and Capulet.

* * *

SOME BELIEVE THAT it begins with Montague, with his concern for the well-being of his son, Romeo, who was a youth of an outward melancholic and wistful nature. Montague himself was genial and well-regarded by all, but his gentle, understanding ways gave young Romeo leave to wallow in unwarranted sorrow.

I once happened upon Romeo and his good friend Mercutio as they led their horses through the city – allowing their steeds some respite after a prolonged hunt, I recall. Both were deep in discourse of a heady nature and still young enough to be unmindful of their surroundings: a true gentleman might not openly acknowledge the serfs around him, but with age he learns to choose his words with care.

Romeo and Mercutio passed me by without a glance in my direction, so all-consuming was their conversation.

"I would swim against the *tide* for her," Romeo said. "At night, too, in the face of a hurricane, and... and..."

"With one arm tied?" Mercutio suggested, a smile upon those thin lips.

"Yes! With an arm tied and stones filling my pockets!" Romeo laughed. "She is the *sun*, and I am a mighty oak, nurtured by her warm light."

"A mighty oak? I think not. A sapling, perhaps. Or maybe a weed."

Romeo cast a playful strike at Mercutio with his crop. "She is magnificent in her beauty and a delight in her manner. She is sweeter than sugar'd honey and as refreshing as the underside of the pillow on a sweltering night. Just the *sight* of her lifts my spirits – and other things besides."

"And yet, if you asked her, fair Rosaline would not deign to inform you whether 'twas dusk or dawn."

Romeo nodded. "This much is true. But the heart forges connections that the mind cannot fathom. She is mine, and I am hers, and it is only time that separates us."

"My father said that time is a mountain we all must climb," Mercutio said. "At its foothills, looking up, it seems an impossible task. But years and miles later, looking back the way we have come, it seems to have been little struggle at all, and we can more easily see the other paths we might have taken."

At that, Romeo and Mercutio passed from earshot and I carried on about my errands, but I have always remembered Mercutio's words, and there have been times when they were my sole comfort.

I CAME INTO the employ of my Lord Paris through the officers of his uncle, Prince Escalus, who had found me orphaned in the Lagarina Valley. I have no memories of this, for I was no more than two years old when it occurred, so all I had ever known was the life of a servant. It suited me well, I think. I believe I was as well-regarded for my discretion as I was for my abilities to carry out my duties, whatever they may be.

Once, in my presence, Prince Escalus asked a particularly unsavoury task of Count Paris. I cannot and will not divulge the exact nature of that task, but I will say that it was at the time deemed necessary, though unbecoming of a man of high-born stature. The prince spied me and curtailed his words, replacing them with, "Can that boy be trusted?"

My lord glanced at me and said, "He can, Uncle. I trust him above all."

They then resumed the discussion of their plans, but I scarce absorbed them, I was in such shock. For the count to so acknowledge me was without precedent. I fancied, for a time, that in another life perhaps Count Paris and I might have been friends.

My master never again made mention of the compliment, and nor did I, but it lifted me, and that was more than sufficient to ensure my loyalty.

And loyal I was. When the count asked me to procure for him a particular object from a certain apothecary, despite the wretched nature of the object, I agreed to acquire it without question, though I was moved to request a greatly increased stipend.

"Why so?" asked Count Paris, for once looking up from the ancient volumes that covered his writing desk.

"My lord, the apothecary wears a veil of decency. His reputation among the gentry is unimpeached, and he knows that I am your man.

He will not admit to one such as I that he trades in objects of a... base nature. I will need to employ a proxy to acquire that which you need. And even that might not be sufficient. He will part with the item, but only to the right person and only for a sizeable sum."

Count Paris leaned back in his chair and regarded the ceiling for a moment. "The sum is scant consideration, but... perhaps the wisest move would be to apply a degree of stealth in place of coin. For if the item is purchased, then the fellow will know that someone has it, and might make use of it. Best if it is taken without his knowledge." He tapped the end of his quill against his lips for a moment, then smiled. "Yes. I will request that he calls upon me for a consultation, and while he is here, you will find entry to his stores and retrieve the item." He stood, and fixed me with his gaze. "Can this be done?"

That was the manner of Count Paris. His words were, "Can this be done?" but their intent was somewhat different: "You *will* find a way to do this."

That very night saw me, shrouded in black and with muffling cloths wrapped around my feet, watching from the shadows as the apothecary hastened toward the palace, his pack laden with potions and salves. Once gone, I pried open the door to the shop and began to search through the shelves.

The fates were on my side that night, for I located the item within moments – or perhaps it was not the fates, but something darker that guided my willing hand – and was back on my horse and on the road with such alacrity that I actually passed the apothecary before he reached the home of Count Paris.

Thus it was that when he was presented to the count, I was at my master's side, as always, with none any the wiser that I had ever left – and little chance of suspicion being cast upon me should the apothecary later discover that his stores had been plundered.

The count, playing his part, informed the apothecary that his request for a consultation had been a ruse. "In truth," he told him, "I would know of the health of the Capulet girl."

The apothecary at first declined to provide any information, for he was intent on maintaining the illusion of propriety he had so carefully crafted. "It would not be right to speak of such matters, my lord," he told the count.

Count Paris's coin-purse became a little easier to bear, but still the apothecary was reluctant to pierce another's privacy. The coin-purse then strangely disappeared entirely from the count's possession, and the apothecary found himself moved by such loss to placate my master with tales of positive news from around the city.

"I have heard," said he, "that the daughter of Lord and Lady Capulet is said to be in excellent health. And still a maiden, though that is neither here nor there and should not be the concern of anyone outside the Capulet household."

"Indeed," Count Paris said. "It is my understanding that Lady Juliet's welfare is the primary role of her nurse. A good woman, she? Trustworthy and vigilant?"

"I believe so, my lord. Unimpeachable. As one would expect."

"And Lord Capulet himself... Is he well? I ask because upon our last encounter it seemed to me that he was of sallow complexion and had shed a number of pounds."

The apothecary simply nodded at this, but remained silent, and so the count turned to me. "More wine for my guest. Bring the finest."

Much as the application of lamp-oil will free a rusted hinge and allow an intruder unhindered passage, a good wine – in sufficient quantities – will enable words to more easily pass through hitherto locked lips. The apothecary stayed long into the night, and he and Count Paris relaxed into the conversation to the point where simile and metaphor were almost entirely set aside in favour of directness.

"Capulet has the *plague*," the apothecary said. "There are some who – for reasons known only to God – will suffer the blackness but not dispense it to others, and for that we must thank the Lord, else we would all be stricken. Capulet is shuffling toward the grave as we speak. He is a vile man who deserves no less, but his coin flows like water and so I would not be quick to see his end. I have been administering potions to keep the sickness at bay and sustain his life, but the plague fights like a cornered dog and soon the cost of potions will outstrip Capulet's wealth."

"I would have his daughter," Count Paris said. "But he loves her more than life itself."

"A beautiful sentiment, my lord. Would that it were so. In truth, I suspect that Capulet would gladly exchange his daughter *and* his wife for one more year of life."

"But a businessman such as yourself would prefer coin as payment, not women."

"That is so, my lord. Coin will fill a purse, where women would empty one."

AND SO IT was that some days later I accompanied my master to House Capulet.

With the knowledge that Capulet was skirting the edge of poverty, I looked upon his home with different eyes. The servants seemed downcast, the tapestries faded, the food and drink almost vapid. Were it not for his departing hair, sunken eyes and loose, wrinkled jowls, Capulet himself would have seemed a boy wearing his father's clothes, so thin had he become.

Lady Capulet, as ever, presented herself as though she were wrapped in the finest corsets from ankle to throat. Always a striking woman, though demure and content to observe rather than participate, it seemed to me that she was now stepping out from her husband's shrinking shadow. She greeted Count Paris in proper terms, with all accordant courtesy and curtsies, but it was plain to those who were aware that her rich perfume was inadequate to mask a certain anxiety for the future: if her husband passed before Juliet were wed, control of the Capulet estate would likely move to her nephew, Tybalt.

Lady Juliet was presented in due course, and my lord Count Paris excelled himself in his restraint as he greeted her. "My lady... A pleasure. As always, you are a balm for the eyes and a tonic for the soul."

"You are too kind, my lord," Juliet said, and it seemed to me that she was taken by him. In truth, my master was considered handsome and kind, and his presence brought a certain fluster to many women, young or old, wed or unwed.

With the greetings done, the women were dismissed and Capulet took Paris into the smallest of the reception rooms. Much later, I discovered that this was because the other reception rooms had been stripped of their fittings: for now, Lord Capulet was maintaining his illusion of comfort.

I stood by the door as Capulet's servant Potpan served bread and wine, then he was dismissed and I was, apparently, forgotten.

"Count Paris, please do me the favour of thanking your uncle for his decision regarding the altercation between my servants and those of House Montague."

My master seemed bemused at this. "I was of the understanding that the Prince threatened that further occurrences would be met with execution?"

"And so he did, wisely. Fear of death has put an end to their squabbling." Capulet reached for his cup and sipped at his wine. "It is always a pleasure, Paris, to accommodate you, but I am curious as to the purpose of your welcome but unexpected visit this day."

"I will have your daughter, on the provision that her maidenhead remains inviolate."

Such directness sparked the expected feint of indignant surprise from Lord Capulet, but the count immediately dismissed it. "Set your theatrics aside, Capulet. You are dying, scarcely able to pay your apothecary's bills. The fates conspire that you are damned to lose either your life or your wealth – you may no longer have both. Which is it to be?"

If eyes could spit fire, Count Paris would have roasted. "What *truly* brings you to my door, Paris? If it is to gloat, then by God's bread I will see you –"

"There will be an accord between us. I will have Juliet but I seek no dowry – which I know you can ill afford. In fact, I will give you enough coin to pay your debts a score over."

Capulet's bluster was washed away, replaced by a trembling gratitude, but he said, "Count Paris, Juliet is but thirteen. While I appreciate your offer, I must insist that you wait for her hand. Two years, at least."

Paris considered that, and countered with, "Two years at *most*."

"Is that so long to wait?"

"It is more time than you have at your disposal, Lord Capulet." Paris looked around the small room. "I should commit the paintings and ornaments to memory, for I am sure they will be gone long before I set foot in this house anon."

"Two years, Paris," Lord Capulet said, his resolve briefly turning to steel. "Anything less would not be proper. And, yes, by that time I will likely have departed this mortal coil. Unless..."

"Unless I help you to settle your debts in the meanwhile."

Capulet nodded at that, and, after a moment's silence, the two men shook hands and struck a monstrous deal that sealed both their fates.

In celebration of his new wealth – and to assuage any suspicions among his peers regarding his finances – Capulet decided that a ball should be held, and everyone of import would be invited. The sole notable exception was the Montagues, for their rivalry with House Capulet had deep and strong roots that would not easily be snapped.

As a page to such an important man as Count Paris, I was known to the servants of all the great Houses and as such well-placed to learn from Potpan and Gregory that when Lord Capulet told his wife of Paris's intent to take Juliet as his bride, Lady Capulet had been almost overwhelmed with joy and relief, and she'd set about the planning of the ball with great enthusiasm.

At the ball, my master again encountered Lady Juliet. He took her aside, and told her, "You will be mine. It has been agreed."

"*I* have not agreed, Count Paris!" she spat back at him. "You will *not* have me, not while I have breath left in my body!"

This vexed him considerably, for on their last meeting the young lady had seemed enamoured of him. Every woman is in possession of her own mind – and its accompanying thoughts and emotions – but Count Paris had never known any woman to so clearly reject him. I have come to suspect, in the years hence, that Lady Juliet must have been eavesdropping on my master's conversation with her father.

They parted on poor terms, both returning to the ball where they masked their feelings and made play that all was well.

It was that same ball that young Romeo attended in the hope of meeting his beloved Rosaline. Being of House Montague and thus an enemy of the Capulets, Romeo had not received an invitation to the ball, but a young man of considerable cunning and burning loins will always find a path to the object of his desire.

All thoughts of Rosaline vanished forever when Romeo chanced upon Juliet. That meeting was the pebble that triggered the avalanche, for Juliet's cousin Tybalt discovered the interloping Romeo, and set about him with a fury.

It was Lord Capulet himself who stopped Tybalt from killing Romeo, for it is considered an omen of great ill-fortune for a guest – invited or otherwise – to be killed at a celebration, and Capulet was already embroiled in his own battle with the fates.

But the spark between Juliet and Romeo had ignited a flame that could not be extinguished, not by any number of years of animosity between their families. They met in secret, and their love blossomed instantly and ferociously.

With the aid of Juliet's nurse they approached Friar Laurence – a man who had long bemoaned the Montague and Capulet rivalry and wished for it to be over – and begged for him to wed them. The deluded Friar agreed. Had he not, had he dismissed them as mere infatuated children and sent them on their way, perhaps all would have been different.

My lord Paris knew none of this. Nor did I, at the time. The count was slowly but steadily parting with portions of his land, and other possessions, in order to raise enough coin to honour his deal with Lord Capulet.

His obsession with Juliet grew, as did his fears that her blood might be tainted before she could be his.

I took this to mean that she must remain intact and that Paris wished to be the first to breach her womanly defences, but later I learned that I was mistaken. An understandable error, I think, for I did not then know the extent of my master's plan.

I did, however, know that certain of Count Paris's skills lay beyond those of mortal training. It was said that he could charm the stars from the sky, the fish from the sea, and persuade any man to do his bidding, but those who said such things did so in jest, in casual banter that only served to highlight their admiration for him.

They did not comprehend what he could truly do. On an excursion to Castagnaro I witnessed my master persuade a young peasant boy to cut off his own thumb, all because that boy had not bowed as we passed.

I once saw him whisper to two comely young mothers, who then abandoned their infants and followed the count into the woods. He emerged hours later, unkempt and eager to move on. I have learned that the women were never seen again.

The truly strong of will can resist his urges – as he experienced with Juliet – but if a man has the slightest leaning in a particular direction, Count Paris is a master of the words that will encourage him to take that path.

It was this skill that my master employed when he encountered Tybalt of House Capulet shortly after that fateful ball. The count had already learned of Juliet's liaisons with Romeo, though he did not yet know they had been secretly wed. Rather, my master feared that their passion was such that Juliet might soon surrender her maidenhead to the Montague boy.

He spoke to Tybalt, and did so with that calm, measured tone that I knew to mean he was employing his skills. "Romeo has insulted House Capulet. *Your* house, Tybalt. He has captured Juliet's eye, and, more, her heart... But Juliet is promised to me, and when we wed, I shall ensure your rightful place in the family. Can the same be said of Romeo, your enemy, should he be the one to take Juliet as his bride? I think not. He has stolen your beloved cousin and with her your future. What is to become of you now?"

Tybalt said, "You jest, Count Paris. I know Juliet's mind – she would not be swayed by a Montague."

"If your certainty on that matter is as a rock against the tide, then I shall say no more and bid you farewell, Lord Tybalt. But... if there is doubt? That Juliet is possessed of a strong will is without dispute, but she is young, and the young are fickle with their affections."

Tybalt began to respond, but my master was not yet done.

"Juliet has been *wronged*, Tybalt. You know this to be true. Montague has bedazzled her with his youth and charm, and in so doing he has destroyed House Capulet, forever." My master rested one hand on Tybalt's shoulder. "You will soon be cast out, and that saddens me. Stripped of your social standing, you will be forced to leave Verona, for who would take in a stray from a dishonoured family? This is likely the last time we will speak as equals, friend Tybalt. Once Romeo is accepted into your family, the gap between us will be insurmountable."

"I understand, Count Paris," Tybalt said, "and by all accounts my uncle should have let me end Romeo at the ball. But it was not to be."

My master handed Tybalt his sword, a jewel-handled blade of exquisite workmanship. "A parting gift, then. Perhaps you will wish to sell it, or exchange it for food and lodgings. Or put it to its intended use." He leaned closer to Tybalt, fixed his gaze on the young man's eyes. "Romeo is but a boy. A boy who has wronged you greatly. And you have unfinished business with him. A man who does not defend his honour and title against a sworn enemy is hardly a man at all."

Tybalt began to swing the blade, slashing at the grasses at their feet. "I am a man."

"It is not I that you need to persuade," Count Paris said. "Go now. Do what you will. Honour your family, and cast aside any fear of consequence. Lord and Lady Capulet do not wish for their daughter to be wed to a Montague. And..." here, the count's voice dropped to a whisper, "should there be witnesses, you must remember that my uncle is the prince, and I have his ear."

It was – like so many of my master's plans – almost without the possibility of failure, regardless of the outcome.

Tybalt confronted Romeo, and challenged him. But Romeo – beset with honour and likely with unfounded hope for the future of their Houses – refused to duel.

I am told that Tybalt, his ire fuelled by Count Paris's words, would not relent and he assaulted Romeo and House Montague with a barrage of insults. Still, Romeo refused to fight, but his friend Mercutio could take no more of Tybalt's discourtesy, and rushed to action.

It was a duel that ended badly, but then so few end well. Mercutio died, and – enraged beyond all measure of control – Romeo struck out at Tybalt, killing him.

I was with Count Paris and Prince Escalus when Montague came to plead for mercy on his son's behalf. "Tybalt was slain, but not murdered, by Romeo, your highness," Montague said. "It was not his choice to fight, and he had seen his closest friend struck down by Lord Tybalt. He reacted as would any honourable man."

My master leaned close to Prince Escalus, and whispered, "Uncle... You have already decreed that fighting between Capulets and Montagues would be punishable by death. I do not wish for that, but a leader must be seen to be consistent. Would that it were otherwise, but it seems you have no choice but to put the boy to the sword."

The Prince turned to him, "Mercutio was my cousin. My *blood*."

"As he was mine, your highness. Were it *my* hands scribing the laws, I would pardon Romeo without hesitation. But the burden of law rests on shoulders greater than mine, and its roots are stronger than blood."

Count Paris stepped back, and allowed his words to echo through his uncle's mind.

The others spoke. Romeo's cousin Benvolio related the encounter in considerable detail and without, it seemed to me, any true bias. Lady Capulet spoke for her beloved nephew, and pleaded for the prince to take the sword to Romeo.

But my master's skills of persuasion were not quite strong enough to influence Prince Escalus to adhere to his earlier proclamation. Romeo would be spared... but exiled.

It was a small victory, but enough. With Tybalt dead and Romeo banished, Juliet's blood would more likely remain pure long enough for Capulet's two-year condition to pass... If her blood was not *already* tainted.

LATER, MY MASTER again called for the apothecary. This time, there was little need for lubricating wine to ensure the steady flow of conversation.

My master said, "It is likely that Montague and Juliet lay as husband and wife."

"Very likely, yes," the apothecary agreed, "it was such base urges that first drew them together. Does this cause upset to your plans?"

"Only if she is already with child."

The apothecary pursed his lips. "Hmm... Such a situation, if it is so, cannot be determined at this early stage. It will be months before her belly begins to swell."

"Is there no other method available to you? Be mindful that cost is not to be considered."

"Cost is irrelevant, your lordship. There is nothing that can detect the presence of new life so early... but there are methods that will *end* a new life should it already be flourishing."

"That is of no use to me, apothecary. If life is there, my plans are for naught. It seems my only path is to allow time – and, with it, girth – to be the messenger."

"Perhaps if I knew what your plans were, my lord, I would be able to help?"

That was not the right thing to say: my master could countenance such impudence up to a point, and the apothecary had now clearly taken a step beyond that point. By asking to become more involved, he had inspired the count to reconsider their already clandestine relationship.

Count Paris leaned closer to the apothecary, and said, "You and I are not friends. We have a business arrangement, that is all. You will supply me with what I need, as you would with any other customer, but our relationship goes no further."

"My apologies, lord, I merely wish to be of service."

"Go. I will visit you tomorrow with a list of items I require. Save that, our business is concluded."

AND SO IT was that, by chance, I was well-placed to witness the next step in our unfolding tale. The next day, after my master had paid a visit to House Capulet and spoken with the Lord and Lady, I was accompanying him to the apothecary's shop when I spied a young woman ahead of us.

Though she was cloaked and moved from shadow to shadow, I recognised her immediately as Juliet, as did Count Paris.

"She makes for the friary," my master said, and spurred his horse on to greater speed. We passed Lady Juliet without a glance, and reached the friary before her.

Inside, Friar Laurence tried to hide his displeasure upon seeing my master, and wore his mask of piety and respect with his usual grace.

"I will be married to Juliet of House Capulet on Thursday," Count Paris told him.

"On Thursday, sir? The time is very short."

The count explained that Lord Capulet had agreed to hasten the marriage for Juliet's sake, that she should have something to distract her from the grief of losing her beloved cousin Tybalt. In truth, Capulet feared for the future: with Tybalt in his tomb, the House no longer had a male heir.

When Juliet entered the friary, she well masked her surprise at seeing the count, though she addressed her intended husband with a measured tone and scant enthusiasm.

Inwardly enraged, Count Paris took his leave, and I followed. But as the door closed behind me he silently bade me to wait. He mounted his steed and departed noisily, taking my own mare by the reins.

I approached the closed door and – having cast a glance around me for witnesses, and finding none – I pressed my ear against it.

I heard Lady Juliet bemoan her lot to the friar, and from her very lips I learned that she and Romeo had been secretly wed. I quenched the urge to race after my master and inform him thus, for there was more to come.

Friar Laurence expressed sympathy toward the girl's plight, though he was shocked when she threatened to end her own life rather than marry Count Paris.

And then, to my own shock, that wretched friar offered her a vial containing a potion that, when consumed, would place her in a death-like state. He would send Friar John with a letter to Romeo, informing him of the truth, then when Juliet had been laid to rest, Romeo would come for her and they could be together.

I hastened after my master, and spied our horses outside the shop of the apothecary.

Though he was occupied with business inside, and a good servant never interrupts his master, I plucked at the count's sleeve until he gave me his attention, then I motioned that this was a matter of the utmost urgency, and he followed me back outside, where he glared at me in a fashion that – in other circumstances – would have had me fearing for my life.

Out of earshot of the apothecary, I dispensed with the expected apology and quickly explained to my master what I had learned.

"So I am betrayed by Juliet herself," Count Paris said. "She is already a bride. Besides, she would choose exile with Romeo over marriage to me."

His scowl slowly became a thin-lipped smile, and he looked past me and said, "All is not yet lost. Now comes Friar John."

The young friar was hastening from the friary, and did not even see Count Paris until his way was blocked.

"Good day to you, priest," my master said.

"Good day, my lord," said Friar John. His gaze flickered to the road ahead. "If you will forgive me, I have an urgent matter that –"

"I will take that letter, Friar John."

"I... I know of no letter, Count Paris."

"Come now. You are a man of God, so surely you know that dissemblance is a sin. You carry a letter intended for the exile Romeo, of House Montague. That letter will not reach its destination."

"I have been entrusted with a vital duty by Friar Laurence, and..." Already, the man was faltering. "I must carry out that duty."

Count Paris stepped closer to the man. "Must you? Perhaps you should not. The road is long and its dangers many. Perhaps you are waylaid somehow, and the letter never falls into Romeo's hands."

"Sir, I... I..."

The count leaned closer still, and whispered into the friar's ear certain words in a tongue with which I was unfamiliar. In the course of my duties I had encountered many visitors from foreign lands, but I had never heard a language so coarse, so brutal, so laden with foul intent.

Friar John's eyes grew wide, and his breath became shallow. His body stiffened, and slowly he nodded, once, to my master, then turned and continued on his way with notably less haste than before.

"Come," Paris said to me. "Word must be sent to Romeo by other means."

I did not understand, but my station forbade me to seek elucidation.

Upon return to the palace, my master waited in his study throughout the night, dismissing all visitors – and there were many, for it was believed that he would shortly be wed to Juliet and they came to wish him well – and instead lingered over his many ancient books.

Even the appearance in his study of Prince Escalus – bearing good wishes and hearty, well-intended advice – did little to fracture my master's composure, for he was now so mired in those archaic, unfathomable texts that I had to almost force him to eat a little bread and cheese, lest he collapse from hunger.

The morning came, and with it the news of Juliet's apparent passing.

Grief surged through Verona like the evening tide through Venice, for Juliet was much loved by all.

She was laid to rest in the Capulet crypt, and while Count Paris attended the ceremonies, I did not, for he had instructed me to make contact with the Montagues' servant Balthasar, whom I knew to be close to Romeo.

I found the man in the kitchens of the Montague home, along with his fellows. Though none present would have shed a single tear at the death of Capulet himself, nor any man in his household, the loss of the fair Juliet had shaken them, especially coming so soon after the exile of their beloved Romeo.

I took Balthasar aside, and said to him, "You know of the connection between Juliet and your master. Do not deny it. Not now that she has passed."

"I will not deny that, but... what brings you here? Your own master was promised to Lady Juliet, was he not?"

"He was. His loss is immeasurable, his heart is as a block of ice cast from atop the highest steeple onto stony ground. And surely he would despatch me to the wolves were he to discover that I had come to you. But... though I have not yet *known* true love, I have learned to recognise the shadow it casts. Fair Juliet and noble, headstrong Romeo had a lifetime's love in a handful of days."

Balthasar nodded, and tears swelled in his eyes.

"The Capulet tomb will be sealed on the morrow," I informed him, "and my lord will be expected to sit in vigil until dawn, long after all other mourners away to their homes. But my lord Paris is *not* a man given to extended mourning. Do you understand, friend? Does my meaning alight on fertile soil?"

Again, he nodded, but now the slightest smile crossed his face. "Count Paris will depart before dawn. And Juliet's tomb will be empty, save for her."

"A wise man might seize such a chance to bid a last farewell to his love."

I left him then, knowing that within minutes he would be on his way to Romeo.

And so the stage was set.

I MIGHT MAKE the argument that I was merely carrying out the instructions of my master, that I could not be held accountable for what followed, but that is a craven stance, and I am no coward.

I returned to the churchyard, where Count Paris knelt in prayer with the other mourners, and I looked upon Lady Juliet and – though I knew the truth – I myself was almost moved to weep.

The shadows grew long and the sky red, then black. As the night chill rose and shuddered through their bodies, Lord and Lady Capulet departed for home. They could give no more tears, for they had cried themselves dry. They turned to my master, the last remaining mourner, but their mouths, too, had run dry.

It was clear to me that Lady Capulet blamed Count Paris for her daughter's seeming death, but in truth the Lady herself should have borne a large portion of that blame, for it was she who had insisted that Juliet would marry Paris, against the girl's objections.

And then they were gone. The count asked of me, "Is all in place?"

"It is, my lord. Romeo's manservant has taken word to him, and I expect him to arrive before mid-night. But –" I stopped myself.

"You have a question?"

I almost did not answer. A page should not question his master, that is a simple and clear rule. But these were not simple or clear times, and so I spoke: "My lord, if you wished Romeo to come, wherefore did you stop Friar John from taking him the message that Lady Juliet truly lives?"

"Because a man encumbered with sorrow will not be as alert as a man buoyed by joy and hope, and I do not wish Romeo to become aware of my presence too soon." He patted my arm, the first time he had ever done so. "And that is something for which you, my loyal page, should be thankful."

I did not grasp his meaning at that moment, but it was to be clear enough before the night was out.

We hid ourselves in the shadows of the Capulet tomb, I crouched and unmoving for so long that I thought my joints would lock forever, and my master nearby, quietly muttering prayers in that strange tongue as he carefully anointed his arms, face and chest with balms and potions, many of which I recognised as items acquired from the apothecary.

With my cloak pulled tight around me, I succumbed to a cosy drowsiness and settled into that state for an interminable time, until it was shattered by approaching footsteps. Within the minute, Romeo of House Montague was at the tomb's entrance, his head low, his hands trembling.

My master burst forth from the shadows, his sword in hand, and – somehow – I saw then another piece of Count Paris's plan: should Romeo escape alive, or someone else happen upon the scene, my lord would claim that he mistook Romeo for a grave-robber, or a vandal.

But he had emerged too soon, giving Romeo time to leap back and draw his weapon. Sword clashed against sword with such ferocity I feared the noise would prematurely rouse Juliet from her slumber.

I had hoped to remain in shadow, but Romeo saw me, and – through instinct – I shouted that I would call the Watch, and made to leave.

I did *not* leave, because to inform the Watch would surely invoke the wrath of my lord, and such a thing could be fatal. I considered this as I watched him clash with Romeo, and that consideration led me to a new understanding, though I cannot speak to its exact source. The notion merely arrived, unbidden, in my head...

My master wanted Romeo in the tomb because a human sacrifice was required to appease his *own* dark master.

Had Romeo not returned to Verona that night, my lord would have had to choose another victim for the sacrifice. And I was the only other person present.

My realisation of this almost spurred me to join in the fight against Romeo, but unarmed I would be no match for the young Montague's flashing blade.

Nor was Count Paris. Though skilled, Romeo was still but a boy, and it was clear that my lord was his superior... But Romeo's anger and grief were fuels to his strength, and Count Paris had been sitting, unmoving, for hours.

Romeo struck one final time, his blade passing beneath my master's mis-timed swing, and cut him deep from loin to sternum.

A fatal blow, I knew. No medic alive possessed the skill to stitch such a wound. Count Paris fell to his knees, staring down at the splash of his own blood on the dusty ground. He moved to clutch at the wound, but was too late: a length of bloodied intestine slipped out, and my master screamed in equal pain and anger.

Through scarlet-flecked lips he said, "I am slain... I am finished."

Romeo cast his sword aside, and moved to Paris as one would rush to an injured friend. "My Lord Paris..." he began, but his words failed him.

"If you have an ounce of mercy, Montague, lay me beside her," Paris said. "So that we might be together in death, at least."

Paris collapsed once more, and Romeo honoured his last wish, lifting him onto death's stone serving-platter, next to Juliet.

I watched in shock from the shelter of a headstone, unsure as to the move I should next make. My lord Paris, dying... His killer only yards away, now with his back to me as he looked down at Juliet's inert form.

I am not a coward, as I have explained, but then I am not a fool. Besides, before I could act, Romeo removed something from within the folds of his clothing, and began to speak.

"You are gone," Romeo said, looking down at the inert body of his love. "Snatched from this world by grief that we could not be together, and by anger that your future was given against your will to this man dying at your side."

And now Romeo turned to my master. "Oh noble Paris. Perhaps you mistook me for a vandal, your own sorrow blinding you, for you could not have known that Juliet and I were *already* wed, and thus she could never be your bride."

From my hidden vantage point, I could see that the Count still lived, his limbs trembling.

"Rest now, my lord," Romeo said. "Allow the final slumber to take you, as it has taken this lady whom we both adored."

Romeo bit the stopper from the small glass vial in his hand, briefly turned to spit it aside, and I saw the grief on his face. In that moment the whole of my part in this wretched affair became clear to me.

Paris was a monster, and I, his willing hand, no less guilty of his crimes. For my actions, I will spend eternity in dismal hell, and even that punishment would not be sufficient.

Two lives already needlessly lost – Mercutio and Tybalt – and a third, my lord, moments away from joining them.

Romeo raised the vial to his lips and I broke cover, screaming "No!" as I ran toward him. I could not allow a fourth life to be extinguished.

I do not know – and will never know, I fear – whether the young Montague heard me or not. He quaffed the contents of the vial and instantly collapsed to his knees.

For a brief moment, he remained there, swaying gently to and fro, then pulled himself toward Juliet's static form. "Oh true apothecary... Thy drugs *are* quick."

He leaned close enough for his lips to give Juliet's the slightest touch. "Thus with a kiss, I die." Romeo of House Montague fell backward to the ground, forever still.

Perhaps it was the noise of his collapse, though a more fanciful storyteller would have you believe that it was true love's final kiss, but at that moment sweet Juliet awoke.

She looked about her, confused at first and then in shock. "What now? What is this? The friar's potion did as he promised, but... Oh lord, 'tis Count Paris, dead at my side! And... no! No! Oh sweet Romeo, your eyes fixed in death! This cannot be!"

I stepped closer. "My Lady Capulet..."

She spun to face me. "Who...? Oh, I know you. Count Paris's page. What wickedness transpired, page? Romeo returned as my letter begged, yet he is dead, and not from a wound as Paris."

"Poison, my lady. Acquired from the apothecary. Believing you gone, he extinguished himself."

"Then... then I would be *truly* gone! I will join my love in the next life! Hand me your dagger, page, or a sword!"

"My lady, I cannot. This mad cycle of death must end, I beg you! It began with my master's desire for you, let it not end with you dying by his side!"

Juliet turned from me, and reached for Paris's belt, seeking a weapon. And she found one.

It was the item that he had me steal from the apothecary's shop. A tiny fragile bone knife, scarcely the length of a man's finger, its blade curved. For all the world it reminded me of a length of orange-rind, though bleached white. It was *not* orange-rind. I knew what it was.

"This, though small, will suffice!" Juliet said. "Away with you, page. I would not have you witness my suicide."

I was not fast enough to stop her. She stabbed the small curved knife into her breast, at an angle I knew had pierced her heart. She fell back, eyes wide with pain and fear and grief. In seconds, she was gone.

It is done, I thought. *All done*. The young lovers, star-crossed to the end.

I turned to leave, but was halted by a rasping breath behind me. It was my master, still not passed over into death's realm.

With great effort he beckoned me forward. "One final task, page. You are sworn to follow my orders while I still live... Lift me. Place me atop fair Juliet, that her sacred blood will mingle with mine."

"Lord... She has *passed*. Such an act would be a foul desecration!"

"You are already damned far beyond blasphemy, boy. Do it!"

I remained where I stood. I did not know the vile purpose of this, my master's final act, but I would play no further role in it.

With a last, Herculean surge of strength, Count Paris rolled Juliet's body onto his, face down. It looked almost like a lovers' embrace, but it was far from thus. Her blood spilled from her chest, and seeped into his mortal wound.

The small bone knife fell from Juliet's hand, and I moved forward to step on it, crushing it. A despicable thing, and although it had already done its business, I could not allow its existence to continue.

I knew what it was. Oh, yes, I had known from the beginning, and it is to my shame that I blindly – no, *willingly* – followed my lord's plans.

Carved from the skull of an infant that had been poisoned by its mother, and inscribed with the markings of a language older than humanity itself, the knife – when lubricated by the blood of a woman untainted by motherhood – was sharp enough to slice a path from this realm to another. A darker realm.

My master's body shuddered one final time, and Juliet's corpse slipped from him, falling to the ground to lie next to her beloved Romeo.

Had I the presence of mind, I would have snatched up my master's sword and hacked at his throat until his head fell clear of his body.

But I did not act, and perhaps it would have made no difference.

Juliet's clean blood had mixed with Paris's, and though now dead, his body was not still. Something moved within his chest.

A sound, next. A wretched, hacking laugh, that came not from my master's throat, but from somewhere deep within him, somewhere beyond life and death.

I backed away, knowing that I could not stay to witness what came next.

Romeo's horse was nearby, and I ran for it, jumped into its saddle and began to ride and did not stop.

The horse collapsed from exhaustion a day later, and then I ran, and kept running. And though half a century has now passed, I am running still.

All of Europe lies in permanent, putrid darkness with Verona at its wretched heart. The houses of Capulet, Montague and Paris are gone, all but forgotten, and the rest of the world struggles, with noble futility, against the slithering forms that come to feed on us each night.

And always the darkness grows, each plundered soul adding to its strength. The creature that was once a man I called "Master" is its guide and its gateway to this Earthly realm. Paris had long sought power, but true power had sought – and found – him.

He was a freezing man who invited a tiger into his hut for the warmth it might provide, but a tiger's needs and strength are greater than a man's and cannot be harnessed.

The few who have escaped the darkness bring with them tales of wings – giant, black and leather-like – blocking out the stars, of odours so rank that they inflict an instant nausea, of scaled creatures bearing fangs longer than a man's arm, of flickering tongues that drip a burning venom, of boneless, sinewy limbs that reach from the shadows to coldly – almost lovingly – caress soft human flesh... and then take hold.

I fear that one day I shall see my master again, in the foul form he now takes, and I pray to whatever gods remain that when he gazes upon me with his many eyes he will recall my good work and regard me with mercy.

But I no longer fear damnation, for Hell has come to Earth, and I played no small part in that.

It is no consolation to suggest that this was all inevitable, that Paris would have found a path to Juliet's blood regardless of Romeo's interference, but there is a modicum of comfort in knowing that the two young lovers were spared the true horrors that followed their deaths.

For never was a story of more woe than this, of Juliet and her Romeo.

SOMETHING ROTTEN

ADRIAN TCHAIKOVSKY

THIS IS NOT what I told Fortinbras, Prince of Norway, when he arrived with his little band of followers; the desperate adventurer who had heard the Danish royal family was failing and had come to stake his claim.

Well, he has it all now: Norway, Denmark, all of it. And perhaps he sleeps easy, believing what I told him. But he never entered Elsinore. He never saw what I saw, what nobody should have to see. It's better that way. Let him sleep easy right up until the restless history of that castle returns from that undiscovered country.

You've heard the story, of course, the one I told to Fortinbras. I made it lurid and bloody enough that nobody would think to go behind it and find the far more lurid and bloody truth.

But let me introduce myself: I am Horatio. I had the privilege of being the Prince of Denmark's only confidant. And even now I cannot tell you what was true, what he did not confide in me, whether or not he was mad. I would far rather Hamlet had been mad.

And yet I fear — and it keeps me awake at nights — that there was method in it.

I KNEW HAMLET at Wittenberg. We were students together. He had an insatiable thirst for learning; he said that, back where he came from, they did not care for the new sciences. He was a child of his mother, though, and she had sent him away from Elsinore at a young age to be educated. He very seldom returned home. Often, when he threatened it, she came to see him instead. His father he described as "distant, almost faceless." But then, Old Hamlet was the King. Small wonder he had no time to be a loving parent as well.

And then news came to Wittenberg that Old Hamlet the King was dead. Word came to summon young Hamlet to court for the funeral. He was slow to respond. He told me his mother had warned him that one day he would revisit Elsinore, and never leave. I had always assumed this meant duties of state.

I travelled with him to that dark and shrouded castle by the sea, God help me. He needed me. He knew there was something terrible in wait in his ancestral home, in his past, in himself.

Even before we got there, the rumours were rife. Hamlet's uncle Claudius was publicly over-familiar with the widowed Queen. Not hard to see why the common tongues were wagging about infidelity. Not so great a step from that to murder. Had Claudius done away with his brother so he could make room in Gertrude's bed? Ask any tosspot in any tavern in Denmark and they'd tell you so. Hamlet must have heard the accusations as we travelled to Elsinore.

And yes, that is the story I put about, when Fortinbras came calling. Why would I so shame the family of my dead friend? Believe me, I was protecting their reputation. I was protecting everyone.

We arrived to find Old Hamlet had been interred with suspicious haste, and Claudius enthroned and wed to Gertrude, further feeding all that tavern speculation. The wake had become the wedding breakfast, though both were sparsely attended. The Danish court seemed like an atrophied stump of earlier days. I met them all, that cast of wonders. It should have been the social opportunity of a lifetime for a poor scholar like me but I was already wishing I'd stayed in Wittenberg.

There were the twins, a pair of simpletons who spent their time obsessively tossing coins and would talk in garbled tones of a deterministic universe where free will counted for nothing and we were all the pawns of vast and cosmic powers. There was a handful of ageing retainers and guards. There was Ophelia, her brother and her father.

The brother, Laertes, I had seen occasionally at Wittenberg. He was a rake and a brawler, given to sudden passions and angers, quick to act and quick to regret. I had not known he had a sister, much less one so striking as Ophelia.

I say "striking" advisedly. She was beautiful, but there was something about her that disconcerted. I was put in mind of those poor working girls that all students know, whose beauty is a brief bloom of a handful of years before hard life, pox and childbirth bring their long winter.

Ophelia's beauty burned like a fever that must kill or pass. And what she would become, in her season, I could not have said.

Yes, she drowned, of course. Or that is how I told it. I saw her in the water, that much is certain.

And there was her father, Polonius, advisor to the crown since time immemorial. An old, old man, now – too old surely to have such young children, and no word of who their mother was. And disfigured, they said – so gnarled by time or disease that he must hide his face behind a veil that fluttered and undulated when his whispering voice issued from behind it.

So Hamlet, who had come home for a funeral, found himself the guest at a wedding. They did not let him look upon his father's body. It had been a closed casket from the start. I wish we'd just gone, then. I wish I'd never tried to help.

But Hamlet was suspicious, itching to find some evidence against his uncle. And I was his friend, and in truth Claudius did not delight my eye. He was a big man, the fine clothes straining about the bulges of his body, and there was something unwholesome about his makeup, the wide eyes, the broad mouth, the boneless way he slumped upon the throne.

So I went to speak to the retainers, and with proper applications of flattery and familiarity and rum I began to hear strange stories. Hamlet's father had been seen after the funeral, dancing atop the waves at midnight, far out to sea.

And I was a fool and told my friend, who began to worry that his father's restless spirit was seeking someone to avenge its murder. Was it because he had barely known Old Hamlet that Young Hamlet felt his filial duty so keenly? Was it because he had been kept from Elsinore so long that he now made the unravelling of that knot his grand purpose? Or was some other voice speaking to him, soft and low where no-one else could hear?

That was when his mind began to slip. And from here on there is much I cannot know, because the truth of it existed solely in Hamlet's brain. He took to the battlements, staring out over the endless waves as though he could see into the great sunken depths they hid. He said he saw his father there, just as the retainers whispered they had.

The sight of the ghost reproached him, he said. It bobbed and turned over in the water like a drowned thing.

I did not see it. I could not look out at those waters for long without turning away. I cannot vouch for ghosts, but the seas off Elsinore were murky and troubled, and there were motions in the water that wind and wave cannot account for. I averted my gaze because I did not want to see what might surface like the kraken, if I watched another moment. And so Hamlet would stand and look out into the maelstrom while I, the coward, sat with my back to the crenulations and shivered in the spray.

So there was the business of the proof. Hamlet was an educated man. He was not going to mount a coup because of a remarriage and a revenant. He was even then starting to distrust his own judgment. And so he found some players and concocted... I know not what. I have heard people say my version of events is tenuous, with the poison in the ear and whatnot, and I cannot deny it. I was making it all up as I went along; Fortinbras's arrival had not given me much time to prepare.

That was not the play Hamlet ordered them to put on. No *Murder of Gonzago*, but another piece. You may have heard of it. It was a play about a king. There was a city by a lake. There was a creature in it, half fish, half man. There was a great deluge and a drowning. And I cannot say what it was that caused Claudius to rise like a man who has seen his own death, but the new king stumbled blindly from the chamber and that was Hamlet's proof. Despite my pleas he was on his uncle's trail in moments, with murder on his mind.

I found him later, pale and shaking and stabbing his bodkin at the castle walls until I thought the blade would break.

"I couldn't do it," he told me, and then, "I found him at his prayers."

And I, naive that I was, agreed that it was a hard thing, to kill a man at prayer, and waxed scholarly about the state of men's souls, until Hamlet cut me off angrily and told me it was not piety that had stayed his hand. "It was the sight of what he prayed to," he said, and then would say no more.

IN MY STORY to Fortinbras I left plenty of room for my friend's mental state to be just a clever ruse, to throw off the suspicions of Claudius and the shambling, masked figure of Polonius. The truth is somewhat different. I cannot say if Hamlet was mad, by the end, or if his actions were those of a sane man confronted with a mad world.

He went to his mother. Aside from me – and what help could I be? – she was his only ally. Unless he tried to speak of it to Ophelia – I saw them talking closely several times – but she was a part of the old Denmark, the world of his father and uncle, that his mother had married into twice.

This is where my account must begin to break down. I papered over the holes for Fortinbras, but then he was a simple man and ready to believe the penny-ballad lies I told him.

Hamlet went to his mother, that much is true. I think he went to accuse her of complicity in his father's murder, or to reproach her for her remarriage. Or perhaps it was to ask questions best not asked, of what dire secrets had so irrevocably bound her to the Danish royal line. All I know is that they were not alone. I can only imagine the horror when, in some fraught pause between himself and Gertrude, Hamlet heard the eavesdropper's laboured, liquid breathing.

He killed Polonius. That much he told me. He stabbed the old man through the tapestry because he thought it was his uncle there. Then, when he drew back the hanging and saw what was revealed, behind the disordered robes and fallen veil, he stabbed and stabbed again. He did not need to hide the body, he told me. It was deliquescing even as he finished his work, and the ichor stung his hands though he scrubbed at it with soap. The details of what he had seen, the deformities of old Polonius, he would not say with clarity, only references to goatish features, to tendrils that pulsed and darkened in time with the old man's failing breath…

Events began to move swiftly after that. Hamlet was a changed man, from what he had seen and what he learned from his mother. The light of an unhallowed knowledge was in his eyes.

I told Fortinbras he was banished to England. England, that island nation, is such a useful shorthand. It is easy to say that Denmark has a long maritime tradition of maintaining diplomatic ties to *England*. People will understand, when you state that the Danish royal line has many blood ties to the *English*, and that the faces of Hamlet's ancestors often manifested that *English* look in so many of their features.

It is true, there was a sea voyage that Hamlet undertook in the company of the witless twins. I overcame my fears that once, and watched his boat through a telescope, as he rowed it far out across the midnight sea. I saw him stand up in it, as though daring it to capsize. He cast his weighty burden into the waters and I saw the waves go still as glass around him. I heard his voice echo out as he cried out the name of his father, and something vast and fungous moved beneath the boat as though coming in answer to his call. Or perhaps my hands shook, and I did not see these things. Perhaps I cannot, in the end, tell a hawk from a handsaw after all.

But I know that I saw Ophelia in the water, later. I saw her pass in the river, lithe as an undine. I know what I told Fortinbras, but in truth she was waving, not drowning.

We went to the tomb after that. I had given my sanity and my life over to Hamlet's cause by then; I would dare anything with him. And he was fired with madness or purpose, and the two are so often indistinguishable. He found the gravedigger and he threatened the old man until the family sepulchre was opened, the lid of the tomb raised. So it was we looked upon the final resting place of Old Hamlet.

It was empty, a cenotaph where should have been a grave. And then Hamlet took the tools from the cowering gravedigger and set to his grandfather's memorial, and then his great-grandfather's, demolishing his line a king at a time. None showed the common signs of human mortality; not a corpse did we find, no dust, no bones, as though all those hoary generations of Danes had not succumbed to death after all, but had gone on, transformed, to some other life beyond the understanding of men. And I remember sitting amongst the broken tombs as dawn came up, as Hamlet raved and trembled at this fresh evidence that the world as we knew it was just a skin over some vaster mystery. I remember marking how, as the carven tombs grew older, so their decoration was more of the ocean: marble seawrack and fish, tentacled beasts and strangely manlike gilled things... and I thought of the old Danish tale, of the prince who takes as his bride the girl from the sea, who even now waits on her rock outside Copenhagen for her lover to return.

Then Hamlet chose one last tomb to desecrate — belonging to a mighty warrior ancestor from pagan times who was known to have fallen in battle against the sledded Pollack. Here was one who must surely be genuinely interred within the sepulchre.

And he was, that old ancestor. Bones only, we found in his stone sarcophagus, that was decorated with twining weed and eels and stranger things. It was the sight of those bones that drove Hamlet past the bounds of human sanity.

That warrior predecessor of his had been laid out in fine robes that had now mouldered, leaving only a skeletal framework of gold thread to show their contours. There was some golden jewellery too, marvellously yet curiously formed: a tiara or crown, a heavy torc and other pieces. None of it was worked in any familiar style and the crown in particular was shaped for a head of unusual proportions. We did not wonder at it, though, for we had before us the skull that crown was wrought for.

What can I say about that set of bones we were faced with? What will be believed? Shall I speak about the size and orientation of the eye sockets, the ranks of pointed teeth? The flatness and length of the skull? Or what about less certain matters — the quantity and proportions of the other bones, the length and slenderness of the fingers and toes, the delicate arches that flanked the neck. And these the remains of a man who was Hamlet's direct ancestor, some generations removed. Small wonder he lost his mind. I would have run away and set myself on fire, if I had seen within myself the echo of that terrible cadaver.

But Hamlet did not run. When he turned to me from those bones he was a changed man, his face forever altered by understandings no one should have to bear.

"What now?" I asked him.

"Now I go to the bosom of my family," he told me. And then, as if to himself, "I am the last son of the Danish crown."

We made for Elsinore, but we were intercepted on the road. A familiar face met us: Laertes, Polonius's son. He was raging, his bare steel drawn, demanding revenge for his father. I could only look into his pouchy, pop-eyed face and feel a horror. He had that *English* look to him as well, and I did not want to think about what Hamlet had seen in Laertes's father, when the old man's veil had dropped.

Polonius had been advisor to the crown for many generations, they said. None knew how old he truly was. Likewise, I cannot know how far his transformation had progressed.

Hamlet had a sword, and I thought he would be glad to meet a problem that could be solved with a blade. Instead, he put Laertes's point to his chest and told the angry youth that he would submit to the stroke, but first Laertes must hear him out.

He had me stand aside, then: I, Horatio, his closest friend. There were things he must reveal to Laertes it was not fit I know. It hurt at the time, when I thought he did not trust my resolve. Now I look back and believe that he sought to spare me. Perhaps that forbearance is the reason I am still alive, and only came to the very door of madness. Hamlet and Laertes passed that portal and ne'er looked back.

He was a long time talking to Laertes, and soon enough our attacker had lowered his sword and just listened, his face growing longer and longer. They returned to the tomb, then, and Hamlet showed the ranks of empty receptacles and the grotesque bones. That pagan warrior king had been Laertes's ancestor too.

And what else he told the man, I cannot know. All that I knew and more. There were things he must have read in his more esoteric researches in Wittenberg and there were the secrets vouchsafed him by his mother.

And perhaps there was other cryptic lore that came to him when he was out on the water. Perhaps that great spongy mass I thought I glimpsed had come to complete poor Hamlet's education, that the state of his family sepulchre only confirmed.

When he was done, Laertes's desire to kill him had faded, though, from his face, it had been replaced by even darker thoughts. Polonius's son set off at once for Elsinore and we followed at a distance.

"He will give out a challenge to me," Hamlet explained in tones almost carefree. "It will be announced as sport, but they will take it that he means to kill me. I do not think my uncle will shed tears, if he can still shed any."

"And then what will you do?" I asked. "You'll fight him?"

"He and I will fight," Hamlet said. "Horatio, you have nibbled at the edges of this business like a mouse. All you need to know is that it will be finished tonight. I am the last of my line, Laertes the last

"I would have run away and set myself on fire, if I had seen within myself the echo of that terrible cadaver."

Illustration by Russ Nicholson

of his, two noble Danish families whose roots go further back than genealogy can possibly record. What if I told you that, where Elsinore now stands, the people of these lands have come to the waters since time immemorial, and made terrible bargains with the sea? But we live in a modern, Christian age, now. Such things cannot be permitted to continue." And a shudder gripped him. "Though nothing any of us can do may touch what goes on beneath the waves and in the abyss of the deeps. We cannot stop them; perhaps we cannot even slow them. All we can do is show them that we are no longer their collaborators."

"I do not know what you mean," I protested, though it was not true. I had seen enough to guess at it.

"Do you know they marry the city of Venice to the sea?" Hamlet said wildly. "Aye, it's commonplace knowledge. Not so the sea-marriage we have perpetrated here in Denmark! But I shall furnish a divorce that even the Pope shall not condemn."

WHAT'S MORE TO say? Well, certainly there is the tale I spun Fortinbras, of duels and chalices and poison. And by the time he arrived with his men, I'd already set a torch to the bodies, just as Hamlet had instructed me. And well I did, given the irregular form of some of the corpses. But what actually transpired within Elsinore's halls that night, I cannot honestly vouch. I know that Claudius was slain, and Gertrude too, who knew more about the matter than any mortal should. Some others of the court I found dead, mostly by the blade. All were of the older Danish families – nobles and their ancestral retainers alike. The remainder, guards and servants come to the castle within the last generation, had fled its walls.

In the central hall, where Claudius stared glassily at the ceiling from bulging dead eyes, I found Laertes, run through. I do not know if it was by his own hand or by another, but there were footprints in the blood that could only have belonged to my friend.

I followed them, expecting at any moment to find his corpse laid out, for surely some of that blood was his. His halting steps led, however, to the battlements.

There, I was confronted only by the waves crashing against the rocks below, and the great roiling swell of the ocean beyond, and so in truth I cannot say what happened to Hamlet, my friend from Wittenberg. It is a strange thing, that the very best I can hope for is that he dashed himself to death against the rocks. Any other outcome would represent a victory for the forces and powers that he was fighting against. And yet they were within him. Who knows what they might have whispered to him, in those last moments? Who knows if, in the face of death, his resolve might not have crumbled?

But Fortinbras never knew, and did not count the bodies. He accepted what I told him, because it served his purposes and because he was a simple man.

And that was many years ago.

AND NOW I am an old man, and I tell you this before I travel to Elsinore one last time. The peasants there are restless. There are rumours, just as there were before, of something seen out to sea. The least credible of them swear it bears the face of the old royal line, that was so tragically cut short back in my youth. I think they are just superstitious peasants and fishermen who would take a seal or a dead fish for Our Lord Jesus Christ if they had drunk enough, but there are other possibilities that I strongly wish to be able to rule out.

And so I will be on my way, if you would pass me down that crossbow from the wall. Because, if something is still rotten in the state of Denmark, then I may be going to meet my oldest, dearest friend from university, and it is fitting that I bring an appropriate gift.

ONCE MORE UNTO THE
BREACH

C L WERNER

DARKNESS CLUNG CLOSE to the French countryside, the night as heavy and black as any the young King had ever witnessed. The dull glow of campfires seemed but the feeblest defiance of that darkness, the impertinence of mortal blood against powers and principalities old beyond reckoning. The voices that rose from the tents of the English were less than whispers, humbled and subdued by the weight that bore down upon them. By contrast, the sounds arising from the French encampment fell upon his ears like the rumble of an angry sea. Song and laughter, the clamour of armourers pounding rivets into plate, the equine cries of destriers with the smell of battle in their noses, sometimes the haunting tones of a murmured Latin prayer.

Henry could see the fires of the French camp, blazing away beyond the shrouding darkness. They were vast and monstrous, betokening a force almost beyond measure. Well did his adversary, Charles d'Albret, Constable of France, appreciate the disparity between their armies. There was no need to conceal the enormity of his host, for by displaying the overwhelming superiority of arms the French enjoyed, Charles d'Albret hoped to take the heart from the English even before battle was joined.

Certainly the display had shaken the English King's confidence. Only a short time ago Henry had led his troops through the broken walls of Harfleur, rallying them to stir themselves for a final effort to capture the town. Through the breach they'd won a grand victory against the French, but now Henry appreciated just how much that victory had cost him in the end. The siege of Harfleur had taken too long, worn away too much of the fighting season. To spare his army a winter spent in enemy territory, he'd intended to withdraw to Calais. Instead, he found himself caught in the jaws of a French trap. Charles d'Albret had guessed his route of march and intercepted the withdrawing English near the village of Agincourt.

Henry hugged the long cloak Sir Thomas Erpingham had thrown over his vestment as a guard against the October chill. His hand touched the glove he'd thrust beneath his belt. A rueful smile pulled at his mouth as he thought about how he'd come to possess that glove. Unrecognised in his cloak, he'd joined conversation with three of his soldiers. The loyalty they'd expressed, their faith in their King, had moved him greatly, but at the last he'd provoked the ire of one Michael Williams when stating that their liege wouldn't allow himself to be ransomed should he be captured. The disagreement had ended in a challenge of honour should the two of them survive the morrow's battle. Henry had exchanged gloves with Williams as token of their arrangement, putting the soldier's glove under his belt while the commoner stuffed the King's beneath his cap of boiled leather. So fierce had been Williams' manner when it was suggested that his King should die in battle that Henry wondered what the soldier would say if he knew it was the King himself he'd challenged.

Such brave, bold and honest men! Henry felt pride that he could inspire loyalty from such as these. Yet with that pride came a terrible sense of guilt, for he'd led them into a conflict that was hopeless. The Constable of France had assembled an army many times that of Henry's five thousand archers and seven hundred knights. The French horde was larger by orders of magnitude. Scouts from the English camp had reported their foe was five, ten, even twenty times their strength. Nor was it peasants and mercenaries who marched under the banner of Charles d'Albret, but thousands of French nobles arrayed in the finest armour and riding the most magnificent warhorses. There was no question in Henry's mind the tactics his enemy would employ. Despite several defeats at the hands of the English over the years, the French stubbornly insisted upon massed charges of lance-armed knights to carry the day for them. In better circumstances, such awareness of his foe's intentions would have emboldened the shrewd Henry. Now, all they did was provoke a sense of impending doom.

The French were too numerous to rout, too well armoured to stave off from a distance. The English forces were weary from their long march across northern France, and many were sick with contemptible afflictions. Though their hearts and spirits were staunch and defiant, they lacked the strength to seriously oppose the Constable of France.

Only a miracle, an act of almighty God, could carry the day for the English. Henry had begun his campaign against the French certain of his divine right to these lands that had been wrested from the English crown. Now he was plagued by uncertainty. Was his claim just? Who was he after all, but the son of an usurper? Was this sorry end God's judgement against those who'd stolen the crown from Richard II?

The rustle of something moving through the brush snapped Henry from his thoughts. His hand sped from the glove tucked into his belt to the dagger hanging from it. His eyes struggled to pierce the darkness. Faintly he could make out a figure moving among the trees. "Who is there?" he called out in French.

The reply was rendered in accent so barbarous that Henry had a hard time making sense of the words. "One that would offer service to a king," the figure answered. Beyond its brutish inflection, the voice had a repulsive quality about it, like the scraping of a snake's belly across a gravel path. Without realising it, the King found he'd drawn the dagger, clenching it tight in his fist.

"Are you Frenchman or Englishman?" Henry demanded. He knew the question was foolish, for such a loathsome voice never issued from either French or English tongue. "Come forward and show yourself."

The figure stepped out from the darkness. Henry was surprised to find himself looking upon a man wearing a leather hauberk and a helm of *cuir boulli*, his leggings tattered and stained, his boots worn and scratched. The features were rough and weathered, the face of a professional soldier. In aspect, the man was alike to the soldiers Henry had so recently spoken with. It was something less tangible that set the King uneasy, something that offended him at a level far more base and primal than reason and sense.

The soldier bowed before Henry. "I'm only a humble man, sire, but I offer service to you." Again, the words had that primitive intonation that made the King's ears feel unclean to hear them.

"Your bow will be called upon on the morrow," Henry told the man. "Or if you have no bow, then there will be work enough for your sword." He moved to turn away from this strangely repugnant soldier when the man caught at the hem of Erpingham's cloak.

"The service I offer is worth a thousand bows, a thousand swords." The man waved his hand towards the distant fires of the French camp.

"No arms can win against that." A crooked smile worked across his face as he looked up into Henry's eyes. "You need a miracle, sire."

Henry would have laughed at that, but his humour faded when he considered that only a moment before his own thoughts had taken a similar turn. "Are you selling miracles?" he wondered.

The strange soldier straightened. "If you will forsake scruple and honour, there is a way to ensure your victory. How much do you want to triumph over the foe?"

Henry stared at the man, an almost superstitious dread gnawing at him. Somehow he felt this soldier could do exactly what he promised. The prospect frightened him, conjuring images of the Devil and the awful price paid by those who entered into compacts with the Infernal. Yet, at the same time there rose into his mind the responsibility he bore. The fortunes of not only his army but also his kingdom depended upon the morrow.

"Follow me," the man said, seeming to sense the King's uncertainty. "It is not far. You will see, and then you can judge for yourself if you have the courage to lead your army through to victory."

Reason roared its warning through Henry's mind, urging him to be quit of this man, to shout for his soldiers to seize him. But a strange fascination held the King in its grip. He was transfixed, held like a bird staring into the serpent's eyes. When the man withdrew into the shadows of Tramcourt woods, Henry followed after him, slipping past his own sentries as he pressed on through the brush.

The threat that he might be walking into a trap shouted at him to return to the English camp as he moved deeper and deeper into the forest. Spies had informed Henry that the Count d'Alencon had sworn to kill the English king or forfeit his life in the attempt. The count was known as a man whose bravery was only eclipsed by his cunning. Was this some subterfuge of his design? Even if it were, Henry found he was unable to resist the uncanny lure that drew him onwards.

The strange soldier finally came to a stop, standing in a little clearing deep within the wood. Henry half expected to see d'Alencon and his knights erupt from the underbrush but even when he stepped out into the open, such an ambush failed to manifest. Instead the man he'd been following dropped to his knees and began pushing leaves and branches away from a spot just a few yards from the middle of the clearing. As the man moved away the dead foliage, Henry noted for the first time the weathered grey stones that lay half-buried in the grass and dirt. There was something about them that seemed too orderly to belong to any natural formation, yet at the same time he found himself unable to decide what part such curiously angled stones could have played in any construction.

That they belonged to a ruin was soon undeniable. The soldier's labour had exposed a rough stone slab in which an oaken trap-door had been set. Curling his grubby fingers around the metal ring fastened to it, the man drew back the door and revealed a series of steps. Henry could make out only blackness below.

"Only a little farther now," the man said. "Don't let your regal spirit falter now, my liege."

Henry directed an angry glower at the impudence of the man, his anger all the worse for the accuracy of the taunt. He had felt a tremor of fear pass through him, primal and terrible. A nameless sense of repulsion had seized him, something that reached down into his innermost being with loathsome violation. He wanted nothing more than to be quit of this feeling, to flee from whatever had provoked it. Kingly pride restrained him. Henry was of royal blood. Where lesser men quailed, he would stand defiant and resolute.

The strange man smiled and gestured to the steps. Preceding the King, he descended into the earth. Henry tarried only a moment, then followed after the soldier. The dagger was in his hand. If there was an ambush waiting for him, his betrayer at least wouldn't live to boast about it.

Darkness and the electric reek of a thunderstorm closed in around Henry as he descended the steps. His guide had become just a shadow ahead of him, more a suggestion of motion than anything of shape or form. The King felt an impression of hideous loneliness press down upon him. Almost he would have welcomed d'Alencon and his assassins; anything to dispel the terrible isolation that gripped him.

Suddenly there was light. A green flame flared into gibbous luminance. By its eerie light, the vault into which he'd walked was revealed to Henry. The chamber was hoary with age, the stone walls and floor betraying the same atmosphere of grisly antiquity that had clung to the rubble above. The room was neither square nor circular, but a disorienting jumble of sharp angles and convex curves, some trick of light or construction making their uneven contours seem endowed with multiple properties at once.

The King hurried to turn his gaze away from the walls to the accoutrements strewn about the crypt-like hall. A splintered table groaning under the weight of alembics and pestles, glass bottles and copper tubes. A grubby shelf trembling beneath vellum-bound tomes and mouldy scrolls. Tangles of dried herbs and shrivelled weeds hung from the ceiling while desiccated animal carcasses lay stacked in one corner, odd bits and pieces trimmed from their mummified remains. Across the floor, cabbalistic symbols had been drawn in chalk and blood, circles and pentagrams bound with strange letters and hieroglyphs.

Henry felt a chill run down his spine. Sorcery! The revelation didn't surprise him, but to have his suspicions confirmed was still an unnerving thing. When he looked back at his companion, his unease was only magnified. The green light was emanating from the man's outstretched hand, spilling from it in ghostly ropes of mist.

The wizard grinned at Henry's alarm. With a flick of his hand he sent the ghostly light spinning towards the ceiling, leaving it to cling there like some glowing growth. He turned from the King and moved deeper into the room. As he did so, the glamour that had concealed him evaporated. No more was he the strange soldier arrayed in the style of the English yeomanry. His frame became taller, more twisted, his skin lightening into such a pallor that Henry was reminded of a frog's belly. The hair became a mane of snowy cobwebs, falling about the wizard's shoulders in matted clumps. The face was lean, the nose long and hooked like a vulture's beak. The eyes were vicious red pits, recalling nothing so much as those of a starving rat.

Henry had never seen a man who evoked such disgust as this sorcerer. Despite his tall, gaunt frame, his proportions were squashed and malformed, like some monstrous dwarf swollen into the semblance of a giant. There was something diseased about that pallid flesh, something far more unclean than the taint of any leper. Every motion, every breath that stirred the wizard was *wrong*, a violation against nature itself. Strange undulations, hideous suggestions of motion that stirred beneath the mantle of uncured animal skins the wizard wore made Henry dread what further abominations lay hidden from his eyes.

"Yes, my liege, magic," the sorcerer said, his eyes gleaming in the dark. "Magic that will alter the doom that threatens your army. Magic that will bring you victory."

The King felt an icy fist close about his heart. He'd prayed for a miracle; instead he found himself confronted by sorcery. His mind raced through the wisdom and lore he'd learned from his tutors, recalling the perils of black magic and those who appealed to infernal powers. It was an affront against God and decency to consort with witchcraft.

The wizard grinned and shook his head. "No, my liege, I am not the Devil. Would it ease your doubts if I told you there is no such being? There is no infernal power seeking to corrupt and tempt the souls of men. Mankind is far too insignificant to be granted such an adversary."

As he had before, Henry's pride rose at the wizard's mockery, making him forget his fear. "Who are you?" he demanded.

Walking around the table and its alchemical implements, the wizard answered Henry's question. "It pleases me at present to wear the name Vashtar. I am a relic, a living echo of a people long-since faded from these lands. Last of that school of men who were the true druids of old. Before the time of French or Roman, before Gaul and Celt, we were here. We built cities of stone and probed the great mysteries, piercing the veils between the mundane experiences of men and the ancient forces that govern existence." Vashtar's face curled back in a bitter scowl. "All that was built, all that was learned was cast down, crushed underfoot by ignorant savages incapable of understanding and frightened by the unknown."

The druid pointed a gnarled finger at Henry. "You too are frightened. I can see it clouding that energy which you think of as your soul. Yet you refuse to submit to that fear."

Henry gestured at the macabre paraphernalia that littered the wizard's lair. "I came here because you offered my army the hope of victory. That promise is all that interests me, not mysteries and horrors best left to the past."

A ghoulish chuckle rattled across Vashtar's lips. "Yes, it is with the past that we shall treat," he laughed. "The self-imagined limitations man imposes upon himself that he may constrain his understanding to elements restrained enough to be embraced by his intelligence. Place and time are but illusions, my liege, doors that can be flung open if one but has the Key." He tilted his head to one side, studying the King. "No, you will not believe unless you are shown." He pointed to a chalked circle marked on the floor. "Stand within that sigil and don't stir from it. I anticipated the need for a demonstration, and have prepared for it accordingly."

Henry hesitated, a feeling of monstrous menace engulfing him. He watched as Vashtar stepped around to a stone pedestal and set upon its surface a large sackcloth bag. Something squirmed within the bag, some trapped creature that struggled to be free. From beneath his cloak, the druid drew a crude knife of obsidian. He looked back at the King.

"It is elaborate theatre simply to kill you," Vashtar declared. "Quell your doubts for only a moment and you will see. Then you will know I have spoken truly, that it is in my power to deliver an English victory on the morrow."

Thoughts of his army, of all those bold and loyal men who were otherwise certain to perish, moved Henry. If the French were victorious they would kill the yeomanry out of hand. Such was their hatred of the English longbow that no archer would be extended any measure of mercy. Surrender or defeat, the finish would be the same for thousands of brave soldiers. If there was even a chance of averting such a massacre, Henry felt compelled to take it.

The moment Henry stood within the circle, he felt a gnawing chill rake his body. The cold of desolate places, the void beyond experience, the cosmic nothingness that astrologers described as a celestial sea in which the stars swam. His breath was a freezing mist, the perspiration that dripped from his brow became little fingers of ice. He heard a hammering in his ears and recognized it to be the pounding of his heart.

Across from him, Vashtar was shouting a glottal cadence, a string of vocal atrocities that were more grunt and yowl than speech. One intonation, however, thrust itself upon the King's awareness, a slobbering intonation. *Yog-Sothoth! Yog-Sothoth!*

Incredibly, the atmosphere within the druid's lair became even more hostile. Henry closed his eyes against a bright flash of light wrought from no such colour as he had ever seen. When the stinging light was gone, he was aware of figures standing outside the chalked circle. Any demon called from Hell could have been no more horrifying for the King, for the men who'd been conjured by Vashtar's sorcery were known to him. They were men he'd ordered executed for treason before embarking with his army for France. He was gazing upon the visages of Cambridge, Lord Scroop and Sir Thomas Grey.

These were no ghosts, no spectres drawn out from their graves. The traitors were living flesh, their faces betraying shock and wonder at their strange surroundings. It was when Grey spotted the King that the traitor recovered from his surprise. Drawing his sword, the nobleman rushed towards Henry. Grey gave no thought to either the bizarre translocation that had come upon him or his unnatural escape from the executioner. All that concerned him was the presence of the King and the prospect of regicide.

Henry drew back as Grey rushed at him. The traitor's sword flashed towards him, but amazingly it rebounded from the edge of the chalk circle. Instead of slashing across the King's body, it merely grazed the side of his head, nicking his ear and scratching his scalp.

Vashtar's voice rose in a bestial bellow. Again the strange light flared through the vault. When Henry's vision cleared, the three traitors were gone, vanished as though they'd never been there at all. Only the blood trickling from his scalp gave proof that what he'd witnessed had been more than an illusion.

"It was unwise to leave the circle," Vashtar scolded the King. After the bellowed cry that had dispelled the traitors, the druid's voice had become a feeble croak. His entire body trembled, shaking as though gripped by an ague. "Had I not opened the Gate and cast your enemies back into their own position within the skein of time-space, their murderous design might have prevailed. Even though all of them were executed before you left England."

Henry reached to his head, feeling the blood under his fingers. "I don't understand. How is it that you can call dead men back from an hour when they yet lived? I cannot deny what I have seen, but the doing of it strains my reason."

83

Vashtar stepped back behind the pedestal. Henry watched the wizard's fingers close about the handle of the stone knife. At the height of his incantation, the druid had plunged the obsidian blade down into the bag. The creature within it no longer moved. Blood slowly dripped from the bag onto the stone floor.

"Don't seek to understand, my liege," Vashtar warned. "Even among the druids there were those brought to madness by such wisdom. It is enough for you to know that such power is possible. Through Yog-Sothoth the illusions of time and place can be wiped away, for he is both the Key and the Gate." He pulled the knife from the bloodied bag, wiping its dark blade clean on the furs he wore. "I offer this power to you, to harness to your cause. I can put onto the field a force of arms that will bring the Constable of France to ruin!"

"And what is the price of such aid?" Henry asked. He had no doubts Vashtar could do what he claimed, but it remained to be seen what the wizard wanted in return. Even before he spoke, Henry knew it would be something monstrous.

"It is enough for me to see the usurpers brought to destruction," Vashtar said. "Those who rule now where greater have once dwelt." He looked down at the pedestal, watching the blood trickling to the floor. "There are rules to what you consider sorcery, esoteric laws that are as strange as they are inviolate. To open the Gate and summon the Key it is needful to make an offering, an offering that must be supplied by one who has dominion over it." He nodded at the sackcloth bag. "Tonight there is a peasant in Abbeyville with three pieces of silver in his hand and an empty cradle in his hut."

The druid's eyes gleamed with reptilian coldness when he gazed at Henry. "I will need another offering to open the Gate and summon the Key tomorrow. The celestial harmonies which your Church has designated as St. Crispin's Day are laden with vast potentialities, allowing a far greater effort than what you've witnessed here. But I must still have an offering to render to Yog-Sothoth, an offering which you, as King, are empowered to provide."

Henry felt sickness boiling in his stomach. He knew what the wizard meant, and it was a proposal that offended him to the very core of his being. Yet if he refused, if he rejected the druid's sorcery, then the French would annihilate his army on the morrow. When balanced against the lives of his army, the sacrifice of a single martyr was incontestable. "Take what you need from among my baggage train," Henry told Vashtar. "Do not speak of this to me again." He turned and hastened back up the stairs, desperate to be back in the clean air and away from the foulness of the wizard's lair.

"As you command, my liege," Vashtar called after him. "I shall take what is needed from among your baggage train."

THE ENGLISH MARCHED out onto the grassy field. Under six thousand men strong, Henry's force was largely dismounted archers and men-at-arms. Such knights as were among his force had left their horses behind in the camp, for today would offer no provision for gallant forays against the enemy ranks. Even concentrated into a single group, Henry's knights would be as flies buzzing around a raging lion beside the enormity of the French host.

Charles d'Albret had amassed a force not less than six times that of Henry's weary army. Nor were these peasant levies, but rather the cream of French chivalry. Thousands of armoured knights on magnificent warhorses, their thick plate gleaming in the morning sun, stood arrayed in a series of three battles, ready to engage the English. The horses in the first battle had thick barding guarding their heads and backs, protection against descending arrows. Their riders, encased in steel plate, eschewed the use of shields to favour brutal picks and hammers. Of course it would be the lance that brought them thundering into the English line, smashing into Henry's soldiers with the fury of an avalanche. Disciplined as his yeomen were, they couldn't match the martial prowess of the French knights. Loyalty and courage could take a man far, but they didn't have the same resilience as training and experience. The nobility of France measured their status among their peers by their prowess on the battlefield and spent their whole lives honing their military skills.

Pennants and banners flying above the French ranks proclaimed the presence of many renowned nobles. The Constable of France had positioned himself with the first battle, such was his contempt for the outnumbered English. With him was Duke Charles of Orleans, Duke

John of Bourbon and the renowned Marshal Boucicault in command of the vanguard. Count Louis de Vendôme and Sir Clignet de Brebant led small cavalry companies on the wings of d'Albret's first battle, menacing the flanks of Henry's force. A second battle of dismounted soldiers followed behind the first, with the standards of Duke Edward III of Bar, Count Phillip II d'Nevers, and Count John d'Alençon. Beyond them, Henry could see a vast reserve of mounted knights and dismounted crossbowmen. The Constable of France had even brought a pair of menacing wide-mouthed cannon to the battlefield, though it seemed d'Albret preferred to destroy the English by force of arms rather than bombardment.

The terrain was against the French horde. The forests of Agincourt and Tramcourt bordered either side of the field, forcing the French into a narrow frontage where their superior numbers couldn't be brought to bear. To guard against the menace of enemy cavalry, Henry commanded his archers to set stakes in the ground when they took position, presenting an obstacle that would either repel the warhorses or see the beasts impaled upon them. Henry put blocks of armoured men-at-arms and dismounted knights between the companies of bowmen, Lord Camoys in command on the left and Edward, Duke of York commanding the right. At the centre, the King himself held the ground, supported by Sir Thomas Erpingham and his household guard.

As the French began their march forwards, Henry tried to quell the fear that swept through his men. He enjoined them to count themselves fortunate that they were present for such a heroic battle, that their deeds would live on in legend and be written into the legacies of England for ages to come. He prevailed upon them that their claim and their cause were just and that it was the will of God, not force of arms, that would in the end decide the course of the battle.

Even as he delivered his speech, describing the glory of St. Crispin's Day, Henry felt dread in his heart. After consorting with a creature like Vashtar, could he honestly claim his cause was noble, or that he enjoyed the favour of God? In his despair he'd turned to dark forces and now he felt ashamed to call upon the name of the Most High. For what had he broken faith with all things noble and decent? Where was the druid's magic now that it was needed?

The blaring of trumpets and the clamour of drums announced the approach of the French herald. Riding a richly caparisoned palfrey, dressed in bright doublet and plumed cap, Montjoy presented a foppish contrast to the grim warriors of d'Albret's army. Holding the standard of France high, the herald bowed his head to Henry and then asked if he would surrender. When the King rejected the demand for capitulation, Montjoy asked what ransom the French should ask once Henry was their prisoner. Pride flared within the King's breast and with a snarl he dismissed the herald, daring the French to wrest what ransom they could from his royal carcass. His show of defiance wrought a cheer from the English line.

Henry's insolence roused the French. No sooner had Montjoy withdrawn past the second battle, than the French began their advance. The cavalry on the flanks of the first battle came galloping forwards. As Henry had feared, the volley of arrows loosed from the English longbows failed to bring down more than a couple of the barded warhorses and utterly failed to pierce the plate worn by the knights. In a thunder of hooves, the wings of d'Albret's army closed in upon the English.

Before the French could come crashing down upon the English line, a voice like thunder boomed out across the battlefield. Henry felt his insides turn to ice as he recognized the glottal intonations of Vashtar's spell. An obscene stench spilled down upon the field, causing men to retch and horses to panic. The uncanny light flared once more, a luminance of no earthly hue. Instead of dissipating as it had in the wizard's lair, the light pulsated with mounting intensity. Henry blinked against the glamour, stunned by the enormity of the druid's conjuring. If the brief flicker he'd seen in the vault had summoned the Southampton plotters, then what might be called by this still mightier magic? The bowmen who'd routed the French at Crécy perhaps, or the triumphant soldiers who'd won at Poitiers?

As the intensity of the light faded, Henry felt his gaze drawn upward. Above the battlefield, a jagged blemish marked the sky, a tear through the air itself. Darkness undulated beyond that rent, glistening with a brooding menace. The French, their charge disrupted by the panic of their horses, looked skyward at the marvellous manifestation, shouts of disbelief and amazement ringing out from behind their visored helms.

Wonder turned to terror as a ropey coil dropped down through the tear in the sky. To Henry it seemed a thing built of bubbles, vine-like in its outlines and shining with a dazzling discord of colours. Yards long, thicker around than a man's leg, the growth whipped earthward, twining around one of the French knights and his steed. From man and beast alike there rose a shriek of agony. Henry could only stare in horror as the knight and his horse disintegrated into dust, flesh and bone and armour crumbling to powder as the pulsating coil of bubbles grasped them.

More of the vines now dropped down from the tear in the sky, some far more slender than the first, others of such monstrous dimensions that they were thicker around than a church steeple. Slim or fat, the bubbly tendrils struck at the French warriors, visiting upon them a ghastly riot of destruction. Some of the French disintegrated in the same fashion as the first knight had, others suffered a weird diminishment, shrivelling up inside their armour, wilting in horrible and unspeakable fashion. When Henry saw one of the massive warhorses reduced to the dimensions of a newborn foal, he realized the awful destruction the thing from the sky was bringing to d'Albret's army. It was adding and retracting years from those it struck, heaping such enormous age upon some so that they became dust, taking away from others until they collapsed into an abominable foetal sludge. Nor was its power constrained to visit but one manifestation upon its prey. Henry saw one French duke caught up in the bubbly coils with the left side of his body crumbling to dust while his right side withered into an infantile husk.

Beside him, Henry heard the awed gasp of the Duke of Gloucester. "It is the avenging angel of God!" Similar exclamations rang out from across the English lines. The King knew better. It was no manifestation of God they witnessed, but the hideous force evoked by a monstrous wizard. Henry could still hear Vashtar's cry rising above the terror and agony of the stricken French.

"Yog-Sothoth! Yog-Sothoth!"

The reeling French horsemen turned about, such of them as remained, and fled back into the vanguard of d'Albret's first battle.

"Wonder turned to terror as a ropey coil dropped down through the tear in the sky."

Illustration by Neil Roberts

The thing in the sky pursued them, more of its eldritch mass seeping down from the tear. Now it was the first battle that was struck by the bubbly tendrils, the knights and soldiers of d'Albret's vanguard who perished in such grotesque fashion. Valiantly the Constable of France urged his soldiers forwards to help his vanguard, but the effort to reinforce his men was for naught. Sword and axe seemed incapable of working any true harm against the devilish tendrils. A stout swing of a sword might burst a single bubble, bathing the attacker in a shimmering slime that corroded his armour and seared his flesh.

The second battle now advanced, employing pole-axes and spears to keep the hideous coils at bay. Behind them, the crossbowmen took to the field, seeking to shoot the undulating mass that continued to stream down from the rent in the sky. Their bolts fell far short of the target, clattering down upon the heads of their own embattled comrades. The boom of the French cannons was equally futile, the cannonballs sweeping past the infernal tendrils to plough into the trees of Agincourt woods.

Havoc and destruction had descended upon the French. The day was lost to them, Vashtar's sorcery had secured victory for Henry. The King, however, felt only a terrible foreboding. It was more than the horror and dishonour of winning the battle in such a ghoulish manner. There was something here that went beyond the conflict of kings and countries. The druid had called to something that should not be, drawn it out from whatever hellish realm it belonged to. As he watched the slaughter of French chivalry, Henry noted a hideous correlation between the tear in the sky and the decimation of d'Albret's men. He saw the Constable himself drawn up into the horror's grip, his black armour falling from his writhing body in decayed strips. At the same time, the hole widened, allowing a little more of the abomination to spill out into the sky.

"Once more unto the breach," Henry whispered.

The thing Vashtar had summoned, the monstrosity that was decimating the French, it was somehow using the essence of its victims to widen the tear and thrust more of itself into the human world. Whatever barriers had held this terror at bay, the druid's spell had created a breach and now the thing was spilling through the hole.

"My King! My King!" The despairing cry came from behind Henry's line. He turned around to find the Welsh soldier Pistol rushing towards him. The man's face was stained with tears, his skin pale. "The baggage train, sire! They have been massacred!"

The anguished report shook Henry to the core. He knew it was no French attack that had claimed the English baggage train. It was by his own doing they'd been struck down. In his plotting with Vashtar he'd failed to imagine the enormity of what the druid intended. The wizard had gulled him into believing it would need but a single martyr to fuel his ritual and defeat the French. Instead the fiend had claimed them all, slaughtered them to call the Gate and summon the Key in a manner far beyond the spell he'd worked in his lair. By agreeing to the sacrifice of one man, Henry had condemned them all.

No, he had done more than that. Henry realized that Vashtar had deceived him as to his intentions. The druid didn't care about the conflict between Englishman and Frenchman. It had been a ruse to secure what he needed to open the breach and allow his monstrous god to penetrate the barriers of reality. Now, with the foothold afforded it by the wizard, the abomination was securing for itself the lives it needed to widen the hole. What would happen when the thing emerged completely was a question Henry didn't want to see answered.

Henry turned, raising the Duke of Gloucester from his knees, disabusing him of the religious adoration falling from his lips. "That is no manifestation of God, but a sending from Hell itself!"

He looked about, calling to his men, demanding they attend his words. "The horror that assails the French in this moment will soon enough reach out for us, for such a monster will make no distinction between English and French blood. If we stand aside and let it devour our fellow man, though they be our mortal enemy, who can say how far it will rove to sate its hunger? Nay, I say this abomination, this spawn of Satan, must be brought to heel here and now, while it struggles to pull itself down from the sky!

"Yeomen! Nock your arrows and raise your bows high!" Henry pointed his sword towards the embattled knights and the soldiers striving to fend off the tendrils spilling down from the sky. "The crossbows of the French are unequal to the task demanded of them! Remind our foe the strength that is in English yew and English resolve!"

At their King's command, thousands of English and Welsh archers took aim. Though the fear was upon them, loyalty to Henry steadied their hands. With a cry of "Loose", volleys of arrows went flying upwards, sailing towards the ghastly rent in the sky. As the first volley drove home, hundreds of the shimmering spheres burst open, discharging their temporal venom back into the void. Several of the descending vines lashed about in agitation, reacting to the sudden injury inflicted upon the thing. For an instant, the monster's assault upon the French faltered.

"*Iä Yog-Sothoth! Iä!*" the frenzied shouts of Vashtar boomed across the field of Agincourt. At the druid's call, the ovoid ropes returned their vicious attentions upon the French knights, disintegrating and evaporating entire clutches of nobles with each lash of the undulating coils.

Whatever the horror in the sky was, Henry realized there was some sympathy between it and the wizard. The abhorrent monster had been drawn to the field of Agincourt by Vashtar's sorcery; now it seemed the obscenity was being guided by the druid. Perhaps not commanded by him, but at least focused by Vashtar's urgings. If the wizard were eliminated, if the connection between Vashtar and the thing seeping through the breach could be broken, maybe it would withdraw back into its own infernal realm. If nothing more, the wizard would make for a far more natural foe than the entity he'd summoned.

"With me, brave comrades!" Henry called to his bodyguard. He pointed his sword towards the border of Tramcourt woods where Vashtar's voice continued to shriek and rave. "Lend me your blades and let us settle the villain who calls the Devil onto this field of honour!" No cheers greeted the King's decree, only a grim and stony silence. Sir Erpingham, the Dukes of Gloucester and York, hundreds of men-at-arms of both noble and common breed, these formed ranks around Henry, denying the terror in their own hearts as they followed him towards the forest.

The field of Agincourt was becoming a mire of blood and death. Thousands of Frenchmen had been slaughtered by the spherical tendrils, their mortal debris splashed across the earth in loathsome puddles. Half-dissolved horses, men with their chests crumbling to dust, knights screaming from inside the molten ruin of their armour, these and hundreds of other gruesome sights met the English as they rushed across the field.

Henry noted with apprehension that the sky above them was darkening. Soon a second breach, smaller than the first, ripped the air. A pair of shimmering coils flopped down from the rift, striking at the advancing English. Henry didn't know if the coils came from a second monster or simply an extension of the first. All he was certain of was that the tendrils stood between him and Vashtar.

"Sire, the French!" Sir Erpingham cried out. The knight swung around, his sword at the ready.

Against all odds, a small cadre of French warriors had won their way through the havoc, rushing towards Henry's retinue.

Among the French, the black armour and beaked helm of Count d'Alencon stood prominent. The Count led his men, sword clenched tight in his fist. As he neared the King, however, d'Alencon reversed his grip upon the blade, holding it by the edge rather than the grip.

"A truce, King of England," d'Alencon cried out. "This day is unfit for quarrels between Christians, even when their cause is just. If you fight against this hellspawn demon, then I would set aside my vow to see you dead."

Henry motioned Sir Erpingham and his guards to step aside. "A truce it is," he declared. Pointing to Tramcourt woods, he indicated the barbarous figure of the druid. "There is the one who brought this monster out of the netherworld." He hesitated, deciding it would be imprudent to provide the details behind how Vashtar had worked his magic. "If we cannot hurt his monster, it may be that we can still visit justice upon the wizard."

D'Alencon nodded. "We are with you," he said. "The reckoning between us will await the finish of this fight, King of England."

Reinforced by these boldest of d'Albret's warriors, Henry led his followers through the morbid debris. The shrieks of Vashtar were more distinct now, his cries of *"Iä Yog-Sothoth!"* becoming more frequent and frenzied. The second breach began to widen, more of the coils spilling downwards. A dozen English soldiers perished as one tendril whipped about them. The Duke of Bar was reduced to steaming paste when one of the spheroid nodules growing from the lashing vines burst open upon the horned crest of his helm. The Count of Nevers and his brother, the Duke of Brabant, were both caught up in one of the coils, wrenched up into the sky, their bodies withering into dust even before they could be drawn into the unnatural rift.

Henry could see that Vashtar had turned and was now facing towards the King and his comrades. The druid was shouting entreaties to the horror in the sky, fixing its attention on the warriors making for Tramcourt woods.

One of the ropey vines whipped through Edward, Duke of York. The nobleman collapsed in a quivering heap, his body undulating with the abominable energies inflicted by the demon. It was mercy rather than malice that caused Count d'Alencon to drive his dagger into Edward's mangled body and bring the English lord's life to an end.

The Duke of Gloucester was the next to fall, his mind cracking as he watched the knight running beside him corroded by the temporal venom of the monster's tentacles. Casting aside his helm and sword, the Duke simply sat down on the gory field and began to weep. Henry rushed to his vassal's side, determined to fend away the lashing coils should they seek to finish the horror-stricken man.

Instead it was the King who was attacked, one of the tendrils striking at him from behind. A shout of warning from Pistol had Henry turning just as the writhing coil would have caught him. The ovoid vine passed close to him, so near that its noxious energies seared a section of his crown and left it dangling broken and twisted from the rim of his helm. Part of his red-and-blue surcoat withered into a mess of frayed threads, but no harm came to the King himself.

A second rope of shining spheres and translucent bubbles came slashing at the King. This time the attack was met by Count d'Alencon. With cold deliberation, the Frenchman warded off the assault with his sword, granting a respite to the man he'd vowed to kill. Henry was unable to repay his enemy's gallantry. Before the King could act, another coil came spearing down from above, stabbing through the top of d'Alencon's helm and piercing the nobleman within. Ghastly energies twisted and mutilated the corpse as the tendril started to pull d'Alencon into the sky, a meaty froth of mortal corruption dripping earthward as the tentacle retreated towards the breach.

"We shall never win our way through!" Erpingham cried out.

Henry's heart grew sick when he realized the knight spoke the truth. Vashtar's incantation was drawing more of the coils striking down at them with every heartbeat. It was only a matter of time before they all suffered the doom that had claimed the Duke of York and Count d'Alencon. In his distress, however, the King spotted one of his yeomen, his English longbow slung over his shoulder as he dashed alongside the knights and nobles.

"Yeoman!" Henry called to the man. When the soldier turned the King was surprised to find him to be none other than the archer who'd challenged him the previous night. Michael Williams was a man weathered by a rough life, his face severe and grim, his eyes dark and intense. The hauberk he wore was split and torn, his leggings stained with the muck of disease and war, but the yew bow he gripped was polished to a pristine sheen, the fletching of the arrows in his quiver as sleek and sombre as sable coat. Here, Henry knew, was a man who knew his duty. "A purse of silver if your aim is true!" Hurriedly he pointed to the howling druid standing at the edge of Tramcourt woods.

With a haste surpassing that of his King, Michael Williams put arrow to string and let fly. The renowned skill of the English bowmen was served justly when the bodkin pierced Vashtar's breast. The druid staggered for an instant, his cries faltering.

Perhaps a single arrow wouldn't have been enough to settle the wizard, but Williams's shot served to break the power of his spell. The focus that Vashtar had urged upon the horror in the sky was broken. Spitefully, the demon struck out at him with its tendrils, bubbles of temporal energy closing about him, at once advancing his malformed body to extreme decay and retarding it back to foetal slime. Screams rose from the sorcerer as the god he'd invoked wrought its ghastly due from his damned flesh.

As the druid's life faded, so too did the awful rents in the sky. The monstrosity withdrew back beyond the rift as the breaches closed. Long after it was lost to sight, however, the violating stench of its obscene presence lingered over the field of Agincourt.

Henry looked over the devastation, the litter of dead, dying and insane left behind by the devil's wrath. It was a sight to curdle even a King's blood.

HENRY NEGOTIATED WITH the French as to how this strange and horrible event should be reported to the French King and, indeed, to his own court in London. Marshal Boucicat, representing the French army after the death of d'Albret, agreed that no mention of the monster should be made. He shared Henry's fear that should news of this event spread then some other witch or wizard might seek to conjure the demon Vashtar had summoned. A more mundane account of the battle was devised, crediting the English with an astounding victory while maintaining the courage and valour of their French foes.

The losses to the French had been incredible. While the English had lost only a few hundred men to the monster, the French dead numbered in the thousands. No less than a hundred dukes had been destroyed by the monster, the very flower of French chivalry. Hundreds of knights had survived the battle only to emerge in a hopelessly crazed state. Montjoy advised it would be more merciful for their families should these insane men be extended the mercy of a swift death, a mercy that it fell upon the English to administer. Even then, there were some among the mad too prominent for even the English to countenance executing. Duke Charles of Orleans, Duke John of Bourbon and others of similar status would be taken back to England as prisoners and held in the Tower of London. Their condition would be kept secret and such ransom as their families might offer would be quietly refused.

Sir Ysmbert d'Azincourt, lord of the nearby village, led a band of knights into Tramcourt woods to find Vashtar's lair and put its contents to the torch. When they were finished, the only evidence of what had occurred on this bloody St. Crispin's Day would be locked inside the memories of those who had survived it.

For King Henry V of England, they were memories that would haunt him to an early grave. For his remaining years he would be feted and celebrated for a victory that wasn't his.

Never again could he look into the sky without watching for some sign of another rift, some trace of the monster's return.

Indeed, on dark nights servants would find their King gazing out from his window, quietly murmuring to himself.

"Once more unto the breach, dear friends, once more..."

A Tiger's Heart,
A Player's Hide

Josh Reynolds

THE BODY WAS a devil's mess, and the heat of the day had done little to help matters. It sprawled on the floor of The Red Wolf, limbs stiff, jaws wide, leaking copiously from the knife wound which had reduced it from man to meat. Despite the stink, Doctor John Dee leaned forward, his gloved hands carefully probing the strange lesions that dotted the cooling flesh. They were not the marks of plague. Or, at least not the plague one might expect.

"Curious," he said. "Most curious."

"And what do you make of it then, Master Dee? Dead, or only mostly so?"

Dee turned a gimlet eye up at his apprentice. "Were it the one, rather than the other, rest assured you would know, young William," he said.

"God's truth."

William Sly was well named. The eyes of an imp peered out from behind a cherub's face, and he smiled too readily, and too long. He poked the body with the tip of his sword.

"Still, conclusions are but the cliff of ignorance, or so I've heard tell."

"From whom, I wonder?"

Dee glanced around the common room of The Red Wolf. The alehouse was empty now, thanks to the poor offal currently befouling the floor. The man had wandered in off the street, gibbering, clawing at patrons and generally making a nuisance until someone had thrust a dirk into him. The patrons had then fled, either out of fear of the gallows or the plague – or both.

"I cannot recall," Sly said. He shrugged and tapped his fingers against the pommel of the Turkish dirk thrust through his belt. "Perhaps I made it up."

Shaking his head, Dee bent over the body to continue his examination. "You would do well to still your tongue and speed your eyes, young William. Else you shall learn nothing of my art, and be even more useless to me than you are currently." The marks were not the familiar rosettes of the pestilence currently sweeping through London, but instead curiously-shaped encrustations. It put Dee in mind of a dream he'd once had, in which he'd seen himself naked, with his skin patterned like velvet, and strange words lost in the folds.

Sly laughed. "Still of more use than this poor fellow." He made to poke the body again. Dee caught his wrist.

"Stop poking the corpus, William."

"Faith, Master Dee. I do but examine it."

"Examine it without poking it," Dee said, firmly. He squeezed Sly's wrist, and was rewarded by a wince from the younger man. Despite his advanced years, Dee was still strong and healthy, a fact belied by his appearance. Clad in dark robes and frayed ruff, with a worn skullcap on his round, white head, Dee looked the very image of a scholar gone ever so slightly to seed. There was some truth to the illusion, and more than Dee cared to admit.

"As you say, Master," Sly said, as Dee released him. In contrast to his aged master, William Sly was a rakehell in dress as well as demeanour. But for all his frippery, the hand that sheathed his sword was calloused and scarred, and his features, though round with youth, were nonetheless etched with the hard lines of experience. Sly had been a soldier of sorts, once. Now he fought a different kind of war, as Dee's aide-de-camp.

It was a war which had begun fifteen years before, in 1577, with the discovery of a doll in the shape of the Queen, a single pin of gold driven through its breast, in the fields of Lincoln's Inn. Dee had been a different man then, with different priorities. Then, his greatest worry had been his studies. Now his fears had grown to encompass a nation, as befitted the man some called the Queen's Conjurer. Dee much preferred the title his friend, Sir Francis Walsingham, had bestowed upon him — the Royal Occultist.

Dee turned back to his examination. "Look here, William. See these lesions.... What do they look like to you?"

"Plague," Sly said, holding a scented handkerchief up to his face. "Are you sure you should be touching it?"

"I daresay that this particular ailment is not contagious," Dee said. "At least not as we understand such things." He felt certain of that, at least. While the curious disorder some called the Chattering Plague was spreading with alarming rapidity, it did not appear to be catching. At least not in the normal way. No one could say how or why those afflicted had come to be so, only that it appeared to be confined to Shoreditch, for the time being.

"What do they look like to you then, Master?" Sly asked, humbly.

"Words. Phrases," Dee said, absently. "It is as if this sickness has made a book of him, and stamped its story on his flesh. You see?" He traced a lesion. "These curves here, the whorl there, the way they twist in upon themselves and back again. It is writing of some sort, if my eyes do not deceive me."

It was the first time he'd been able to get a close look at one of the Afflicted, and he gave a silent prayer of thanks to the unknown knifeman. Usually, they twisted and moaned so abominably that it was all one could do to get close. And then you had to deal with their teeth.

"I must confess, Master, I do not see it," Sly said.

"No. I expect you do not, at that," Dee said, curtly. "But it is the same for all of them."

Those who contracted the Chattering Plague wandered through the streets, spewing gibberish while those who heard them sometimes complained of feeling ill. Some suffered from nightmares. One poor woman had drowned herself in the Thames after a night spent attempting to care for her husband. And every day, more of them. The devil alone knew where they were all coming from. But Dee intended to find out.

"I knew a certain scribe in Angoulême, who tattooed himself with verses drawn from the Bible. Perhaps this is something similar..."

Sly made a sound. Dee looked over as his apprentice sank to his haunches opposite him. "What is it?" he asked, wondering what Sly had seen that he had not.

"I know this face."

Dee frowned. "One of Walsingham's?" he asked, softly. Sly had been one of Sir Francis's hounds for a time, and knew many of the others by sight.

Sly shook his head. "No. He was an actor — more a hanger-on, really. One of Lord Strange's Men, I think. Or he dearly wished to be so." He said the last hesitantly, and Dee peered at him, curious. It was the first time he'd ever heard Sly sound almost... wistful.

"And why would you know such a man?"

Sly shrugged. "A man like myself may know many men, and of all sorts, Master." He made a face. "For a time, I fancied I might strut the boards, before Sir Francis convinced me that my talents were put to better use in his service." He smiled. "I once..."

"Yes?" Dee said.

"Nothing, Master." Sly looked at him and then back down at the body. "I confess I cannot recall his name. Perhaps they will tell us – the lesions, I mean – if they are indeed words."

"They are. And if I but had my library, I feel I would have the answer," Dee said, scowling. He rose to his feet with a groan. Though he was still sound in body and mind, age had its claws in his joints. Things made noise that ought not to, when he moved. "But Mortlake is scattered to the winds, and the tools of my art with it."

Upon his return from Germany not three years before, he'd found his home – his sanctum sanctorum – ransacked. Stripped of all of its furniture and reading equipment, down to the upholstery. And what good was a magician without his tools?

"We shall just have to make do on our own strengths, Master. Perhaps we should visit another alehouse, eh? A spot of lubrication for the delicate cogs and whirligigs of your mind might not go amiss," Sly said, as he stood.

"There is no time for such foolishness. The Queen has charged us to find the cause of this ungodly plague, and so we shall. If he is a player, as you say, we must needs visit a playhouse." Dee drew his robes to him and left the body for the watch to deal with. They would burn it, most likely, or toss it into a plague pit, there to be forgotten. Sly followed him, still wheedling.

"It has been hours since we last filled our bellies or wet our lips, Master," he said, as they stepped past the two watchmen set to prevent anyone from interfering with their investigations. Dee signalled that their services were no longer required. The two men looked at one another in relief and began to board up the alehouse.

"And it will be hours yet, if you continue to complain. The body is but a cage for the spirit, William... would you strengthen the bars?"

"Feed the body, feed the soul," Sly shot back, almost desperately.

"And did you make that up as well?"

Sly shrugged. "If not, I'll gladly claim credit."

Dee shook his head, annoyed. Sly had proven himself useful, at times, but he lacked a proper appreciation for the unseen world. Dee's first apprentice, Edward Kelley, had been far more appreciative — too much so, in fact. Dee frowned, and thrust the thought aside. Kelley had made his choice, and on his own head be it. It was not for Dee to hinder a man set on self-destruction. He had worries of his own, and plenty besides.

Walsingham had understood. But Walsingham was dead, and Dee was alive and that was that. Dee glanced at Sly, striding along at his side, whistling tunelessly. Sly had been Sir Francis's last gift to him — a rough rogue, red-handed and silver-tongued. One of Walsingham's own, forged in the black fires of the most secret of conflicts. Sly could speak three languages as well as a native, and write in two more. He was a practised swordsman, a capable garrotter and a less than enthusiastic horseman. But was he capable of being anything more?

The thought of a successor had begun to weigh on Dee since his return to England. Despite the necessities of his art, Dee did not see himself as a conjurer. Rather, he was the castellan of Her Majesty's aetheric provinces. And a castellan must have an heir. He had responsibilities. When Walsingham had died at the eleventh hour, no one had been capable of taking the reins, though both Lord Burghley and the Earl of Essex even now sought to fill his position. Dee was determined that such a fate not befall the office of Royal Occultist.

That grim thought rattling about his skull, Dee said, "Where did you last see him?" Sly looked at him blankly, and Dee snapped his fingers in irritation. "The dead man, William. You do not know his name, but you have seen him of late? Yes? Then where?"

"The Theatre," Sly said.

"Which theatre?"

"*The* Theatre, Master. Here in Shoreditch, and nearby, not a half-mile past Bishopsgate. Owned by a friend of mine," Sly said, gracefully side-stepping a woman with a yoke of water-casks across her shoulders as she hurried past.

Dee frowned. Painful experience had taught him that when Sly said "friend", he meant any number of things. But it was a thread in need of tugging. "Let us go there at once. I like not the foul humours of this place, and would be shed of it as soon as possible."

"Shoreditch isn't so bad, Master. A bit lively," Sly said, hurrying after Dee. Shoreditch was just outside the jurisdiction of the city fathers, making it attractive to the unlawful and disorderly alike. It harboured the dissolute in all their varied guises and was notorious for its brothels and gaming houses.

"To die in Shoreditch would be to ensure a miserable afterlife, William," Dee said. He cast about darkly. There were people everywhere, all going about their business at once, and in a great hurry. Somewhere, a bear roared in pain, and an unseen crowd set up a hue and cry.

Dee flinched back as a drunken man collapsed in the street, emptying the contents of his stomach. Shoreditch and its environs were a sour brown patch on London's vibrant peel. Even at its most cheerful, it echoed with foul emanations — the worst of man, cast into the air and woven into every breath. For Dee, who had trained his mind and soul to see and feel beyond the harsh realm of the waking world, it was akin to striding hip-deep through a sewer.

It was even worse now, with the plague. Both of them. Boarded up windows glared blindly from either side of the narrow street, and watchmen stood guard. Dee could hear weeping and cursing from those sealed apertures, and he flinched away from the emanations of grief and madness. There were things growing in those places, dark seeds soon to flower. But they were not his problem, not yet. And perhaps not at all. He glanced at Sly, again wondering whether his apprentice would be able to shoulder the burden.

"Master – look out!" Sly barked. He caught hold of Dee's arm and jerked him close. Dee was about to berate his apprentice when he saw the woman staggering past, muttering to herself. Her lesions were no less pronounced than those of the dead man, and her murmurings, though nonsensical, had the air of repetition. She pawed at herself as she stumbled away, scattering people to either side of the street. Urchins threw gobbets of mud and dung at her, but lost in her madness as she was, she paid them no heed.

She was not alone. Other Afflicted crouched in doorways or alleys, rocking back and forth and mumbling. Dee hesitated, listening, trying to discern some meaning in the noise. There was something familiar about it, about the words which were not words, at least not in any language he recognized. And yet still, he had heard it before. He tugged on his earlobe. "So many of them," he said.

"Shoreditch has never suffered a lack of the witless and the mad, but this is something else again," Sly said. "It sounds almost like they're... singing." The voices of the Afflicted rose and fell arhythmically, and they weighed heavily and strange upon the air.

"No. Not singing. Chanting," Dee said. And not just a chant. It was as if it was layered over another sound altogether. Like a rumble of distant thunder. Or the growl of some unseen beast. He looked up at the sky, and considered the clouds. Afternoon was waning into early evening, and the sky was growing dark.

Sly's hand fell to his sword. "Chanting what?"

"I do not know. But it is all different... As if they are reciting from different pages," Dee said, shaking his head. He looked at Sly. "Hearing it now, all at once... There is a strange sort regularity to it. A commonality. Why are they all clustered here?"

"Perhaps the answer lies in there," Sly said. Dee turned. "The Theatre," Sly continued, with a gesture. "I fear it has seen better days."

The Theatre was a rough-shaped timber building, with a tile roof. It had been an inn once, Dee thought, as Sly led him into the seemingly deserted playhouse. It was midday, and he'd expected at least a few faces. But there were none to be seen.

"Should it be so empty?" Dee asked.

"No," Sly said. "I noticed a bill of closure on the postern as we came in."

"You are observant, William," Dee said, silently chiding himself for having missed it.

"As you have taught me to be, Master," Sly said. As they entered, Dee saw three galleries surrounded the open yard. From one side extended a thrust stage, and the yard was cobbled. Dee thought it resembled a layman's attempt to replicate one of the great Roman amphitheatres of old. "And there he is," Sly said. "The man himself."

Dee saw a short, stocky man sitting on the stage, a drinking jack in one hand and a pipe in the other. The man took a forlorn pull from the jack, and then an equally desolate puff on the pipe. He didn't seem to enjoy either.

"There's my old friend Burbage," Sly called, as he strode forward, arms wide. "Where are your players, Master Cuthbert? Has the Widow Brayne driven you out of business at last? Or has competition from The Curtain grown too great?"

"William Sly, as I live and breathe," Burbage said, barely stirring.

"And this is Master Dee — Dr. John Dee, late of Mortlake," Sly said. Burbage gave no sign that he recognized Dee's name. Something neither unusual nor entirely unwelcome, from Dee's perspective. Especially in these uncertain times. It was a short walk from court magician to heretical witch, and one he had no intention of taking.

"Why are you here, William? I have no need of a Porrex for the *Seven Deadly Sins* this season, or any other I fear," Burbage began. Sly gestured frantically. Dee restrained a smile. It seemed that his apprentice had not entirely given up on walking the boards, whatever his assertions to the contrary.

"Where are your patrons, Cuthbert? Where are the actors, the hired men?" Sly said.

"Gone, gone, and gone," Burbage said, taking another pull from his pipe. "Plague, William. Didn't you see them all, out there?"

"Who? The Afflicted?"

"My patrons," Burbage said, spreading his arms. Ale sloshed onto the boards. "The watch closed me down yester eve, citing unsanitary conditions, the bastards. Chased everyone who could walk away. And all because a few loons decided to gibber in the wrong ears." He peered at Dee in suspicion. "Sly called you doctor. Are you a physician, then? Come to board me up in this waste of money?"

"That would be of little help, in this instance," Dee said. The pestilence spread like wildfire in cramped conditions — tenements, the holds of ships and playhouses all made for fertile ground. But this was no normal epidemic. It struck suddenly and without warning. And until now, they'd had no inkling as to the cause. He looked at Burbage. "Then they were overcome during a performance?"

"Not really a performance, as such. A reading," Burbage said. "They've done a fair few readings, these past weeks. Not just here. At The Curtain too." He said the name as if it were a curse. "And at The Lion and Crow."

Dee looked at Sly, who said, "A reading is a way of testing out material before a full performance. And a way to wet the punters' appetites for the full meal. A penny buys a scene."

"What was this material?" Dee asked.

"A few pages from a play they'll be performing tonight I believe — though not here, more's the pity." Burbage gestured over his shoulder with his pipe. "They left a few of them behind, I think, if you'd like to look at them."

"Oh yes, I would indeed," Dee said. Burbage heaved himself to his feet and ambled offstage. Dee turned to Sly. "I believe I have the shape of it at last, William. Though not the reason."

"A play?"

"The written word has ever been both blessing and curse to mankind. It is a door by which man may unlock knowledge and passion both, or find his deepest secrets laid bare." Dee turned. One of the Afflicted had wandered into the yard. "There are certain forces which regard mortal flesh as nothing more than clay, or, in this case, parchment. They burn themselves into the mind and body as easily as you or I might make a note in a ledger," he continued, watching the afflicted man stumble around the edges of the yard. "But they must first be read or spoken aloud to kindle that all-consuming fire."

"But in a play?"

"Where better? A play is but a story, and a story is most combustible – it can inflame men, and consume them utterly, if they are not wary. This plague has its origin in the playhouses, I'm certain of it. Grab him, please."

Sly turned. "What?"

"Grab him." Dee was pointing at the wretch. "If I am to prove my theory, I will need a comparison."

Sly hesitated, but moved to obey. He snatched up a coil of curtain rope as he trotted towards his prey. Dee turned back to the stage, as Burbage reappeared, a sheaf of papers in hand.

The theatre-owner squinted. "What's William up to? And who's that he's scuffling with?"

"One of your patrons come to complain. Is that it?"

Burbage handed the papers over, still watching Sly. "They left in a hurry. Should you help him?" Dee heard a cry, but didn't turn around. Sly was many things, but milk-blooded he was not.

"No. And who were they?" Dee asked, as he scanned the cramped scrawl that filled the pages. It was indeed a play. *The True Tragedy of Richard Duke of York and the Death of Good King Henry the Sixth*. It was a good one, he suspected, though he was no judge of such things. Words and phrases had been crossed out and replaced with others. His flesh prickled as he read these revisions, and his stomach lurched. To anyone else they would seem nothing more than gibberish, but Dee recognized the pattern, if not the meaning.

"Lord Strange's Men."

Dee looked up. Sly had mentioned them earlier, but the meaning of the name had only just now penetrated. "By which you mean Ferdinando Stanley, Lord Strange?" Stanley was a well-known supporter of the arts.

"The very same. He's their patron. And a motley crew they are... Kempe, Pope, Bryan... even my own brother, Richard. And that debauch'd scribbler, Shakespeare," Burbage said. "This is his latest. He owes me coin, the bastard."

"Will owes everyone coin, though he never spends any," Sly said. He had the Afflicted tied hand and foot, and a swelling bruise decorated the unconscious fellow's face. He caught Dee's look and shrugged. "I had to play harshly with him."

"So long as you brought him, I care not," Dee said. He sank down beside the unconscious man. He looked back and forth between man and paper. "Ha! See. Look here, William. You see this — no! Do not read it. Merely look," Dee said.

"Words," Sly said, in a hushed voice. "Those strange words on the page. How is that possible?" He looked at the paper more closely. "This is Will's scrawl, or I'm a fool." He shook his head. "What have you done now, Will? What are those words? Not French or Latin. Moorish?"

"No. The words — these words, scattered about through these simple verses — are in no human tongue. At least not one still spoken. They are something old and foul, I fear, though I cannot be certain." Dee looked at him. "Who is this Will?"

"Shakespeare. A playwright, sometimes actor. But I cannot see him being involved in something like this. What do these words say?" Sly asked, gripping the hilt of his sword.

"I do not know. I only know what they represent, and that we must stop whatever performance they are a part of," Dee said. He turned to Burbage, who'd been listening in puzzlement. "Where did this company of yours go?" he demanded, hoping, praying that the answer was not somewhere out of London.

"The — The Rose, I think," Burbage said, shrinking back from Dee.

"I know the place. It's near The Clink, just over the bridge on the southern bank," Sly said. Dee's heart fell. Across the river. It might as well be across the Channel. He shook his head.

"We must get there. And swiftly," Dee said, crushing the pages in his fist. "Else I fear the Chattering Plague will be the least of our worries this eve."

"A coach, Burbage." Sly looked at his friend. "I know you had one off the Widow Brayne in your last counter-suit." Burbage hesitated, glancing nervously at the unconscious man on the ground. Sly's hand fell to the hilt of his knife. "It's royal business we're on, Master Cuthbert." Burbage swallowed audibly and nodded.

"In the back."

Long minutes later, the coach burst out of the yard and onto the darkening street, Sly standing behind the horses' tails, lash in hand. Dee crouched in the coach, holding on for dear life. Rattling, rowling, rumbling, the coach wheels raced along, its driver filling the air with curse-laden shouts of warning. Sly controlled the reins with the skill of a born hack, narrowly avoiding a man with a basket on his arm. Sheep bawled and scattered as the coach sped towards London Bridge, along ancient paths between unchanging, ever-changing buildings.

As they hit the bridge, Sly shouted something. Dee barely heard him, but he understood well enough. They were not alone in their journey. Swarms of the Afflicted stumbled, lurched and ran through the crowds, wailing and moaning. Dee sat back, fingers pressed to his temples. He could feel something in the air, as he had in Shoreditch. An eerie resonance, as of the beating of a thousand wings or the stamping of a thousand hooves, faint, but growing stronger. "William — do you hear it? Something is coming. We must go faster — faster!"

Sly urged the horses on to greater speed. The bridge had been built and rebuilt a dozen times over the centuries. Over two hundred buildings, some nearly seven stories high, clung to its edges, overhanging the Thames or the road. The latter formed dark tunnels through which they had to pass. Dee thanked whatever spirits were listening that the bridge wasn't as congested as it usually was. He hoped they would be in time.

The coach slewed slightly as they left the bridge. Imprecations flew from pedestrians as they scrambled out of the way of the rearing horses. Sly laughed wildly as the coach rattled on towards its destination. The sky had gone dark. Night was falling, fast and true.

When it at last came into sight, Dee realized that The Rose was well-named. It resembled nothing so much as a bulging tulip, lit by torches and lanterns. He counted at least fourteen sides to the structure, each one a petal of timber and plaster.

Sly brought the coach to an abrupt halt. "We walk from here, Master," he said, hopping down. Dee gathered his robes and clambered out of the coach, somewhat shakily. He could still feel the reverberations of the ride in his bones.

The crowd waiting to get in was larger than he'd expected. There were groups of working men, householder's wives and their servants, even beggars, all flowing as one towards the single entrance. And among them, isolated by bubbles of empty space, the Afflicted. They stood swaying amidst the human tide, or else were carried along with it, mouthing incomprehensible words. More of them arrived with every minute, in dribs and drabs, all but unnoticed by the crowd at large. He could not say how they were getting into the playhouse, but they were. No one stopped them, or even seemed to see them. A chill ran through him, and he looked to the sky again. Were the clouds thickening? Was something moving, just behind them, in the dark reaches of the sky, among the flickering stars?

Shivering, Dee tore his eyes from the heavens. He was tempted to find the nearest watchman and have the Afflicted rounded up, but he knew that at best, it would be a waste of time. At worst, it might cause a riot.

"We need to get inside, William. And now," Dee hissed.

Sly nodded and led him through the press of bodies, opening a path with discrete kicks and shoves, or indiscrete and indiscriminate cursing. They circled around the side of the theatre, heading for an area behind the stage. Horses grazed there, and actors sat, reading lines or sleeping.

No one challenged them, though a few shouted greetings to Sly. Sly waved half-heartedly in reply. "In all honestly, Master, I don't know who they're talking to," he said.

"Whoever it is, I should like to thank him," Dee said. "Without him, we would be stuck outside. We must find this playwright of yours."

The backstage area was crowded with crates of clothing, tables, stools and men hard at their work. The noise from the yard and the galleries swept over the stage and into the wings. Beneath the voice of the crowd, Dee could just make out the insect-drone of the Afflicted. The sound of it pulled him in — if only he could decipher it...

"Doctor? Master Dee? Is that you?"

A hand fell on Dee's shoulder, startling him. He turned so swiftly that the speaker stepped back, hands raised. "It's me, sir... Ferdinando Stanley. We met at Oxford." Lord Strange was dressed handsomely, in pearls and lace. He carried a cane in one hand. "Have you come to see the show?"

"Not as such, Lord Strange," Dee said. "We are here on the Queen's business."

Stanley's face hardened. There were few in Elizabeth's court who did not have some idea of what services Dee performed for the Queen. And fewer still who would refuse to help him, if he asked. "What do you require, Doctor?"

"Shakespeare," Dee said.

Stanley blinked. "You mean Will? Easy enough." He raised his cane. "Will? Will Shakespeare — attend me!" The crowd of actors and stagehands grew still.

"Yes?" a quiet voice answered, after a moment.

Dee gestured. "William." Sly shot forward. The crowd parted. Sly vaulted the casks and tackled the playwright as he was revealed. Both men careened through a silk screen and crashed into the crates of costumes. Shakespeare was shouting for help, as was Sly. Stanley waved the onlookers aside and led Dee towards them.

Shakespeare staggered to his feet, collar askew, eyes wild. Stanley extended his cane and caught him in the chest. Sly was up a moment later, lip bleeding. He dabbed at his face and grinned at Dee. "Fie, but he has a tiger's heart in his player's hide and no mistake."

"What is the meaning of this?" Shakespeare protested, looking at Sly. "I told you I would pay you back anon. I'm a man of my word!" He was younger than Dee had expected. Black hair, pale features. Fingers stained with ink — every inch the scrivener. But there was something about him... A snap, a spark. Edward Kelley had it, and Sly did as well. There was more to William Shakespeare than met the eye.

"I'm not one to tackle over pennies, Will," Sly said. "And you can address yourself to these gentles, rather than me." He caught hold of Shakespeare's arm and twisted it behind his back. "And I'll warn you to speak true, else you'll be scribbling with your other hand."

"Ow — fine! Speak," Shakespeare said. Dee shoved the papers Burbage had given him under the playwright's nose.

"You wrote this?"

Shakespeare craned his head. "Yes?"

"Where is the rest of it?"

"That work is under revision," Shakespeare said.

"You're performing it tonight," Stanley said.

"There's always time for revisions," Shakespeare said. "Sebastian asked me to add in a few lines. He thought it could do with some punching up."

"Sebastian?"

"Melmoth," Stanley said. "A member of the company. An actor." He looked around. "I don't see him."

Dee gestured for Sly to release Shakespeare. "Where is the rest of the play?"

With some prodding from Sly, Shakespeare led them towards a table and stool in the corner, out of the way of foot traffic. It was blanketed in loose pages, each covered in Shakespeare's scrawling hand. Dee noted the revisions, and felt a surge of disgust. He placed a hand over the papers, as if to hide them from sight. "Where did you get these words from? This Melmoth?"

"He — he gave me a book," Shakespeare said. He licked his lips. His eyes flickered towards the table. Dee's hand shot forward, scattering pages as he retrieved a slim, green volume. Its cover was of badly cracked Moroccan leather and it was amateurishly bound. But when he touched it, he felt a heat in his fingers, as if he'd drawn too close to a lit candle.

"Witchcraft," Stanley breathed. He looked at the playwright. "What have you done?"

"Not I! Melmoth. He paid my debts, asked only this in return. What was I to do?" Shakespeare said helplessly. "I saw no harm in it... It was only a little thing."

"And that is how it begins. One thing always leads to another," Dee said.

"What is it, Master? It looks like no grimoire I've ever seen," Sly said.

"It is not a book of spells. More a... Guide," Dee said, softly. The pages felt damp to the touch, though they crackled as if dry. Words, diagrams, images, all swam before his eyes. Not in one language, but many. "The Aklo letters..."

He snapped the book shut and glared at Shakespeare. Even as he did so, he felt a twinge of admiration. Other men had gone insane reading such things. Shakespeare not only appeared to have retained his sanity, but managed to make some of them rhyme. "Where is Melmoth?"

"I don't know," Shakespeare said.

"And did he read these revisions of yours at The Theatre, and The Curtain?"

"Melmoth has done me a good turn. I wished to give him something in return," Shakespeare said. Dee held up the book.

"And would you do the same for the Devil, if he paid your way? Fool." He looked at Stanley. "We must find this Melmoth and put him to the question. This fool of a scrivener has, all unknowing, set something in motion. And we must find out what."

"He'll be here somewhere. He's playing the Earl of Warwick," Stanley said.

Dee gestured to Sly. "Go with Lord Strange. Find our actor. And do so before the show begins."

"Should I not cancel the performance?" Stanley said.

Dee shook his head. "There is no time. Can't you feel it? It has already begun. We must know what he has done, and put it right if we can."

As Stanley and Sly left, he turned to Shakespeare. "Do you understand these words? Or do you merely copy them?"

"In truth, I thought they were Turkish," Shakespeare said. Drums began to thump. "That's the signal for the actors to take their places." He looked at Dee. "I meant no harm."

"Playwrights rarely do, in my experience."

Dee tensed. He felt something, like a trickle of cold water running suddenly down his back.

He turned. The area was empty of all save props and costumes and screens, and yet he could feel eyes upon him. The droning of the Afflicted was audible from the yard, rising in volume with the growing crowd.

"You hear them, then," Shakespeare said, his voice soft. Dee looked at him in surprise. "I hear them too, now. I do not understand... But they say my words. Like actors reciting a line."

"Not your words," Dee said.

"No. Mine."

Dee and Shakespeare turned. A gaunt figure sat atop the table, legs crossed, pages in hand. How long it had been there, Dee couldn't say. It unfolded, stood and hopped to the ground with boneless ease. "You've fallen in with bad company, Master Shakespeare. Whatever will I do with you?"

"Sebastian," Shakespeare said.

Sebastian Melmoth smiled genially. "Allow me to announce myself. I am Melmoth, and Melmoth is me. Sebastian Melmoth, late of Wessex and other sundry and diverse regions." White teeth flashed within a carefully clipped black beard as he bowed mockingly to Dee. "And you'd be the high cony in the garden, unless I'm much mistaken."

"I am Dr. John Dee," Dee said. "And by the authority vested in me by Elizabeth, Queen of England and Ireland, I charge you to cease your witchery."

"Cease? Why I've hardly begun, sir..."

Melmoth motioned. Dee heard the creak of boards, and realized at once that Melmoth was not alone. Strong hands gripped his arms and shoulders, and a foot caught the back of his knees, forcing him to kneel. Shakespeare sank down beside him, a scowl on his face. Two men, stagehands by their dress. Both were hollow-eyed and with the look of men gripping hell's edge by their fingers.

"What is this, Sebastian?" Shakespeare said. "What are you doing? He's here on the orders of the Queen. Would you see us all for the Tyburn jig?"

"All? No. You? Most certainly, good Will. I confess, I find you tedious. A good stretch will do wonders for your personality," Melmoth said, tapping his neck for emphasis. His hand fell to his sword. "Though your scribblings have helped me, I will admit. A quick death, then."

"You will not kill him," Dee said, quickly.

"No?" Melmoth looked at him curiously.

"No," Dee said. "I will not let you."

Melmoth stared at him for a moment before laughing uproariously. "Upon my word, sir, you do indeed put one in mind of an old hen, clucking away. I shall have to tell friend Edward he was right." His men laughed as well, but in strained fashion.

"Edward? Edward Kelley?" Dee said, momentarily at a loss. "How do you know him?" he demanded, wondering what part his old apprentice played in these matters. Melmoth slapped his knee, as if in jest.

"How else? Desperate men find company where they can." He peered at Dee and smirked. "Though it availed him little enough, in the end. The stars are right, old man. The beasts are at the gate, and the birds fall silent." He spread his hands. "Behold, I stand at the door and knock. Thomas, Sackerson, hold them." He reached again for his sword.

Trumpets sounded from the yard. Melmoth turned. "Well, fate plays its tune. The show begins, and you earn a brief reprieve. Enjoy your seats, gentles all. And do not be afraid to applaud, should the mood so strike you."

Dee struggled to rise, but his captor forced him down. "He has damned you," he said. The man grunted in reply. From the stage, Melmoth's voice rolled out across the yard, and stretched upwards to the galleries. The Afflicted spoke with him, though not his words. "Before I see thine countenance *iot-sot-ot* seated in that throne, which now the House of Man usurps, I vow by hell these eyes shall ne'er close. This is the palace of the fearful queen, and this... This the regal seat," he shouted, flinging out his hands. "Possess it, *iot-sot-ot*; for this is thine and not Adam's heirs'!"

"He's changed my lines," Shakespeare said. "I did not write it that way!"

Dee understood it fully now. Melmoth was opening a door. But for that, he needed help. Minds and voices joined to his own. The afflicted were his chorus and his tools, the weight of their madness weakening the substance of one reality and reinforcing another, more terrible one. The words he'd had Shakespeare add were part of the rite, and they had burned themselves into susceptible minds – minds opened by the rhyme and rhythm of Shakespeare's play. And now, as with disparate embers gathered together, a monstrous flame was being kindled. A signal-fire, to light the way... But for what?

He had his answer a moment later. The world shook. Birds rose screaming from the roof. In the courtyard, horses shrieked. Men and women screamed. Something stepped from the stars, descending, its every step a peal of thunder. He could see nothing past the edge of the stage. Melmoth was laughing now, all pretence forgotten. The crowd was surging back, panicked, leaving the Afflicted swaying in place, their faces turned to the crawling sky.

"What is it?" Shakespeare croaked.

"The Devil," Dee said, flatly. The weight on his shoulders suddenly vanished. His captor sank down with a groan. The one holding Shakespeare whirled about, but too late as a Turkish dirk caught him in the belly. The man folded with a whimper and fell. Sly helped Dee to his feet. "I found Melmoth," he said, wiping his knife on his sleeve.

"So did I," Dee said.

"Stanley is trying to get the punters to leave without trampling one another," Sly said. "What has Melmoth done?"

"Opened a door," Dee said.

"How do we stop it?"

Dee started forward. "We close it, William." He began to speak in Adamical, the Holy Language. The words were old, and the syllables liquid. It was the language used in the world's creation, and by Adam and all the angels. Or so Kelley had insisted. Dee knew only that it had some power. He hoped it would be enough to send what was coming back into the void. He could feel the terrible weight of the thing bearing down on his soul and mind. In the crowd, men and women were going mad, their brains split by the force of its approach.

He walked onto the stage, words spilling from his lips, softly at first and then more loudly, as he drew strength from them. The aether churned like a storm. Scraps of cloth and backdrop whirled about him. Melmoth turned, mid-line. "What?"

Dee flung out a hand. He spat words, and the world turned red and gold at the edges. The sky was on fire, and the boards trembled beneath his feet. He did not look up.

"I bite my thumb at thee, sir," Melmoth said, laughing. "Indeed, I bite all of my fingers, and toes for good measure. This is a holy moment, and you seek to clutter it with your mumbling. No sir, I shall not have it!" He bounded forward, blade hissing from its sheath. Dee stumbled back, still chanting.

And then Sly was there, sword in hand. Steel met steel with a screech, and Melmoth leapt back. "Fie sir, would you stand between the tiger and his prey?"

"You have eyes," Sly said. "Use them."

Melmoth gave a bark of laughter and slid forward, as Sly lunged to meet him. Dee gave little heed to their duel, hoping that Sly was as good with a blade as he claimed. Out of the corner of his eye, he could see the scrivener, Shakespeare, ushering panicked actors off the stage and into the wings. Lord Strange was in the crowd, shouting and waving his cane. Dee could hear little save the thunder of that abominable tread.

Dee lifted his hands and caught at the strangely malleable air. It was as if the world was but a stage, and reality a curtain, blocking them from the sight of an unforgiving, inhuman audience. Melmoth was seeking to jerk that curtain aside; to what end, Dee couldn't say. Nor did he care. His fingers blistered, and his breath frosted the air. He felt cold inside, as if he'd drunk a bellyful of freezing water, though his fingers were burning.

The air fought him, twisting in his grip. It was as if he held the latch of a door that something pawed at from the other side. A rank odour, foul and burning, filled his nose and mouth, choking him, causing his incantation to falter. By their smell could men sometimes know those from Outside were near, or so the Moors said. If that was the case, then this thing was surely too close for comfort. Still, he did not look up. Seeing it would do no good.

The world shook. His muscles screamed and his mouth felt dry where it was not bloody. He caught a glimpse of something behemoth-like and yet shapeless, crouched just behind it all, despite his best efforts. It was all shapes and none, clad in shadow and dust. *Iot-sot-ot*. That was what Melmoth had called it, when he'd offered it Elizabeth's throne. Dee knew it by another name, though he wished to Heaven that he did not.

Tawil At-U'mr. The Dweller on the Threshold. An iridescent empire of one, roiling through unknown gulfs, as described in the Book of Dead Names. He felt as if he were weeping, and as if a canker had burst in him, and its bile burned in his gut. His limbs trembled as he fought to hold the door of the world shut. He could hear Melmoth's voice. The creature was still reciting its corrupted lines.

"Sly," he croaked. "William! Melmoth is the key – he is the anchor... you must silence him."

"I'm trying, Master!" Sly called out. Dee risked a glance, and saw his worst fears realised. Melmoth was not human. Or else what was human in him had long since given over to something other. A shape within a shape, unnatural and indescribable.

Sly's words from earlier came back to him — *tiger's heart and player's hide,* Dee thought.

Seemingly ogre-wide and giant-tall, Melmoth rained down blows on Sly, who gave ground, if unwillingly. Dee prayed that his apprentice could hold for but a moment longer. An instant, a heartbeat. Long enough for him to complete his incantation of banishing.

A cosmic roar echoed through the timbers of The Rose, rattling Dee down to his bones. A wave of heat rolled over him. In the yard, the Afflicted began to spasm and topple, blood oozing from their pores.

Melmoth slashed out, and Sly dropped his sword and stumbled back with a cry. Dee felt his heart stutter as his apprentice fell. He couldn't help Sly, it was all he could do to hold the awful presence back.

Melmoth's incantation rose to become a howl. And from behind Dee, Shakespeare's voice rose to meet it. "I here proclaim myself thy mortal foe; with resolution wheresoe'er I meet thee, as I will meet thee, if thou stir abroad, to plague thee for thy foul misleading me..."

Melmoth's voice stuttered to a halt, as the playwright shouted. Shakespeare stepped past Dee, hurling his words into the teeth of the rising storm. "And so, proud Warwick, I defy thee... I defy thee!"

Melmoth started towards Shakespeare, blade raised, teeth bared. But before he took two steps, he cried out and toppled from the stage, Sly's knife in his side. As he screamed, so too did that which he had summoned. Its cry was not born of pain, however, but frustration. A frustration as old as the stars. Dee roared out the final words to his incantation.

The air tensed, tightened, and then dissipated. The hideous strength retreated, and Dee sank to his knees, exhausted. He touched his face and his fingers came away red. His heart thundered in his chest as he fought to catch his breath. "William," he croaked. "How do you fare, apprentice?"

"Tolerable, Master," Sly said. He was pale, and had one hand pressed to his arm. He flexed his hand. "Quite a throw, if I do say so myself."

"Yes, indeed," Dee said. He tried to rise, but could not. The world swum about him. Sly and Shakespeare were there a moment later, each holding an arm. He looked out over the yard and saw only bodies — the Afflicted. "So many..."

"Lord Strange got most of the punters out," Shakespeare said. "Not all, though."

"No. Not all," Dee said. Whatever Melmoth had done to the Afflicted, it had claimed them all. Perhaps it was for the best. Even so, the thought sickened him. He would gladly turn the author of such tragedy over to the Queen's justice. "Where is Melmoth?" Dee said.

"He exited stage left, as if pursued by a bear," Sly said. "Took my best knife with him, the poltroon." There was blood on his hand when he pulled it away from his arm. "Should we pursue, Master?"

"No. The play is done, and his power broken," Dee said, after a moment's consideration. He remembered what he'd glimpsed during Sly's duel and shuddered. They were in no shape to run such a beast to ground. "Let him run. We shall give his name to Essex, or Burghley, and let them hound him until he prays for touch of the furies." He felt every one of his sixty-odd years.

He gestured to Sly's arm. "You are wounded, sir."

"A bit of blood for the cause," Sly said, wrapping his handkerchief around his arm. "I've shed more and worse, never fear, Master," he added, grinning. Dee nodded. For a moment, he'd thought he'd lost another apprentice. But Sly was proving more than adept, Dee thought. Perhaps he need not fear for the future after all. Hesitantly, he clapped Sly on his unwounded arm.

"You... Did well," he said.

"And built up quite a thirst in the doing," Sly said. "Can we find an alehouse now, Master? I think we deserve it."

Dee snorted and turned away. Shakespeare stood nearby, staring out at the empty courtyard. He held the green book in his hands. "Will we be welcomed back, I wonder?" he said.

"I should think so. Your verse shows promise," Dee said. "But probably not for some time." He looked at the playwright. "It was a brave thing, Master Shakespeare. To match words with him."

"They were my words before they were his," Shakespeare said, not looking at him.

"Yes. But even so, I shall be recommending that all playhouses be closed for the time being, just in case," Dee said.

"And what of us, then?"

"What of you? Go, write, perform. There are worlds more than this, and stages too. Just be careful you find the right ones," Dee said. He held out his hand. "The book, please."

"What happened, truly?" Shakespeare's eyes were haunted, full of wonder and horror. Dee wondered which of the two would win out in the end.

"Nothing," Dee said, gently. "A tempest, now safely past. And one you will hopefully soon forget." He crooked his fingers. "The book, playwright. Such words are not for the ears of your audience."

Shakespeare handed Dee the green book. "For here, I hope, begins our lasting joy," he said. "The last line of the play. My play, not his."

Dee nodded. He looked down at the book, and traced its cracked bindings. Such a small thing, responsible for so much evil, but then, that was always the way.

He looked at Shakespeare. "That is my hope as well," he said.

What Dreams May Come

Nimue Brown

To sleep, perchance to dream, it is my fear,

Accursed things shall reach into my mind.

The gibbous moon sheds pallid light, too near,

Unnamed and creeping dread comes close behind.

Dare I to close my eyes, what may befall,

My lips might taste another's charnel breath,

Myself I see as chilled, upon a pall,

Laid low in fetid tomb, possessed by death.

But my eternal nightmare shall not fade,

Eldritch evil holds me in its power,

Though deep in madness, deeper I must wade,

With little hope of peace in future hour.

If any man yet lives with eyes to see,

My hope is fled, I've nought to offer thee.

ACT TWO

"Hell is empty and all the devils are here."

The Tempest, Act I, Scene II.

The 'Iä's of March

Andrew Lane

"Clock strikes
BRUTUS: Peace! count the clock.
CASSIUS: The clock hath stricken three."

Julius Caesar, Act II, Scene I

THE IMPOSING PILLARS of the nearby public buildings loomed above Publius Servilius Casca Longus like rows of marble trees arranged geometrically by some modern day Roman Euclid. The heavy marble roofs supported by the pillars were like a sharp-edged, impenetrable canopy of closely packed white leaves. Or maybe heavy white clouds floating close to the ground; he wasn't sure. Casca wasn't a poet – he left that to people like Gaius Helvius Cinna. He did, however, have a way with words that had served him well in his political career. The tricks of rhetoric came easily to him, and the metaphors his mind was applying to the pillars made him wish – and not for the first time – that he was in the middle of a real forest instead of the centre of the most important city in the world. Despite the risk of bears and wolves and snakes it would have been a great deal safer for him, and at least he wouldn't have to watch in silence the destruction of everything he held dear.

From where he stood, half-way up the steps of the Temple of Saturn, he could see out over the entire Forum. The marketplace was filled with a milling throng of people so dense that it must have been impossible to move down there, let alone breathe properly. Some were talking, some calling to friends and others hailing the man they had come there to see, and the susurration of their voices blended into a general background drone punctuated by the occasional sharp burst of noise. Despite the crush, the general mood down there was good; maybe even euphoric. People were obviously happy to be there – small children had been hoisted onto their parents' shoulders for a better view of proceedings and flasks of wine were being passed from hand to hand, along with loaves of bread and long strings of sausages from which people took bites before giving them up to the next person. A festival air hung over everything.

At least the soldiers were keeping the steps of the temples and official buildings clear, which meant that Casca – one of the ten Tribunes of the People, and thus a relatively important man in Rome – could stand in some comfort and watch the victory procession of the man he hated most in the world.

Gaius Julius Caesar was instantly recognisable in the centre of the Forum. He stood on a chariot pulled by two pure white stallions, which meant that he was significantly above the crowd, but his aquiline features and swept-back hair were easily recognisable. He had the kind of profile that looked good on a coin, Casca thought bitterly.

He found his gaze moving from Caesar the man to Caesar the monument – to the imposing facades of the Basilica Julia and the Curia Julia that Caesar had ordered built. They fitted in well with the general architecture of the Forum, but they were larger of course. Everything that Caesar did was deliberately larger than the accomplishments of anyone else. That was his defining characteristic.

Caesar's procession – the chariot, the horses, the accompanying soldiers, members of his family and general hangers-on – stopped in front of the Temple of Jupiter Capitolinus. The crowd made a space for them. Instead of stepping down from the chariot and showing deference to the several hundred senators who were lined up to welcome him, however, Caesar remained for a moment on the wheeled platform. He turned and raised his arms to the crowd, and the resulting roar of approval was like the thunder from an overhead storm. Caesar just nodded slightly. It was, he obviously thought, only what he was due.

A wave of bitterness washed over Casca, leaving him trembling. Only a year ago Caesar had been a simple proconsul and Rome's disobedient son, disregarding the orders of the Senate to stand down from his military command after his victories against the tribes of Gaul and instead advancing on Rome and precipitating a confrontation with his former ally Gnaeus Pompeius Magnus. That developed into a full-scale civil war. The same mob who had been calling for Caesar's head when he went up against the popular Pompey were now throwing garlands of laurels at it. How fickle they were. How easily swayed by success and confidence.

Pompey. Casca's friend – now dead, assassinated in Egypt following his catastrophic losses at the Battle of Pharsalus, just as he thought he was taking refuge there. Caesar had ordered the assassins put to death, but then he had probably given them the order in the first place. There was an unpleasant symmetry about the process.

Caesar was now dismounting from his chariot, but when he climbed the steps of the temple he made sure he ended up on the same step as the senators, not a lower one. A few of the senators deliberately went up a step to make a point, but Caesar did the same, leaving him on the same level as some of them and above the rest. And Casca knew that Caesar would have made a mental note of who had tried to get above him and who hadn't. Caesar could bear a grudge for a long time – another defining characteristic.

After a few moments of confusion, the Princeps Senatus, Marcus Tullius Cicero, stepped forward. He was carrying something, and it took a few moments for Casca to see what it was. When he finally recognised it he felt as if, for a few moments, he had become disconnected from reality, as though he was floating above himself, looking down.

It was a crown.

They were offering Caesar a crown. They were, for all intents and purposes, deliberately inviting him to take on the role of Emperor. He was already occupying the role of Extraordinary Magistrate, colloquially known as Dictator, but that was limited to a set period of time for a specific reason. To make a Roman into an Emperor – it had never been done!

Cicero held the crown out towards Caesar. The crowd bayed, sounding as they did during the gladiatorial games. Caesar held up a theatrical hand, refusing the honour.

Cicero again held the crown out. The crowd seemed to a person to be yelling, "Yes! Yes!"

Again Caesar refused, shaking his head and turning his whole body away.

The crowd were almost on the verge or rioting now. Casca – no stranger to the arts of the public speaker and the business negotiator

– saw how the man was manipulating the populace through a few simple, overly dramatic gestures. Taking the crown at first blush would have seemed needy. Taking it at second blush would have seemed as though he wanted it but was just being polite, like a guest refusing an extra plate of larks' tongues at dinner. Taking it at the third offering would make it look like he really had tried to refuse it, but was giving in under pressure. Very clever.

Cicero turned to look at the representative senators, seemingly taking their advice. None of them dared shake their heads, but the nods weren't particularly enthusiastic. After a moment he turned back and held the crown out for a third time.

This time Caesar reached for it. The noise of the crowd was so loud it should have reached Olympus to offend the ears of the Gods. Just as Caesar's hands were about to take the crown, however, he seemed to crumple. His hand went to the back of his neck, and he fell to his knees.

A collective gasp ran through the crowd. The forum went silent. Senators clustered around Caesar, trying to find out what was wrong, and his wife rushed up the stairs to his side. With the press of people it was difficult to see what was going on, and Casca decided it was time to leave. Caesar had been indisposed for long enough that he wasn't playacting for the crowd – there was a rhythm in these things, Casca knew – and so the chances were that this was fatigue brought on by the relentless military campaigns he'd been on recently and his hasty rush back to Rome. There probably wasn't going to be much to see for a while – certainly no coronation. That would have to be put off until a more auspicious occasion.

Trying to stay on the cleared temple steps for as long as he could, he made his way out of the forum and towards home. Fortunately there were a lot of temples lining the forum, so he made good time. The crowd thinned rapidly once he was a little distance away, and he was wrapped in his own dark thoughts when he noticed, across the otherwise empty street, a citizen staring off into the distance, roughly in the direction of the forum. The man was tall and thin. He looked just like any other Roman, albeit he was bald and his skin was pale, as if he spent no time in the sunshine. The thing that attracted Casca's attention, however, was his toga.

Instead of being the standard white colour of most Romans, or the dark of mourners, or bearing the purple stripe of magistrates and freeborn male children, it was dyed a startling yellow. Some of the more… extreme… Romans were known to wear embroidered or painted togas, but usually only in the privacy of their own homes or at exclusive parties. Seeing a man out in the street wearing a yellow toga was surprising, almost shocking. Casca was surprised that the man hadn't been set upon by members of the public and stripped. He was about to call out something critical and warning when the man turned to look at him, and Casca found the words catching in his throat.

The man's eyes were just holes in his face; ragged holes, as if his eyes and the flesh around them had been ripped away. There was nothing visible within the wounds apart from darkness, which was probably for the best. A war wound perhaps, or agricultural accident? Casca had seen worse, although such people tended to shun public places. Either way the sight was disturbing, but the man didn't seem to be affected by it. In fact, he was looking directing towards Casca with his head held up. Surely, if he couldn't see then he would favour his ears, listening for people walking past?

The man's attitude was so arrogant, so domineering, despite his bizarre yellow tunic, that Casca just shook his head and walked on. Let someone else help the man.

He was still obsessing about the chance meeting when he was hailed.

"Casca – what's all the noise in aid of?"

He turned, startled. On the other side of the wide street he saw Marcus Junius Brutus standing with his brother-in-law, Gaius Cassius Longinus. Brutus was a stocky, soldierly man with dark hair and a pensive face while Cassius was leaner and blond, and generally looked like he was watching the world and judging everything he saw negatively. Casca was surprised to see them together: the rumour was that Brutus's recent appointment as Praetor Urbanis had severely offended Cassius, who had been given the lesser title of Praetor Peregrinus. As far as Casca was concerned they should have considered themselves fortunate. Both men had allied themselves with Pompey against Caesar in the civil war, and both had been forgiven by the magnanimous and politically astute victor. Forgiven for a while, at least.

It was Brutus who had called. As Casca crossed the street to them he replied: "I was at the forum, watching our esteemed Dictator refuse the crown three times before apparently fainting."

"They offered him the *crown*?" Cassius said, astounded. "What were they *thinking*?"

"They were thinking that the populace has enthusiastically thrown itself behind Caesar, and so the Senate must do likewise lest they appear out of step," Casca explained. He glanced from one man to the other. They were both looking tired and frustrated.

"A soothsayer stopped Caesar on his way to the forum," Brutus said. "We saw it."

Cassius nodded. "The soothsayer warned Caesar against some event that will happen on the Ides of March. He was remarkably unforthcoming on what this event actually *was*, however, and Caesar was unperturbed."

"I'm not surprised," Casca said, with a trace more bitterness in his voice than was, perhaps, safe. "Everything seems to be going Caesar's way at the moment. What next, above Emperor? Being raised to Godhood?"

Cassius and Brutus swapped glances, then looked around to see if anyone else was close enough to overhear what was being said. Once, Casca would have laughed at the amateur nature of the dramatics, but the way that things were in Rome he felt like doing the same. Caesar had agents and friends everywhere.

"You realise that there's no stopping him?" Brutus said quietly. "Once he gets absolute power he'll implement such a purge as the world has never seen. Every office will be filled with someone he trusts, and every marketplace will be stacked up with the bodies of those he doesn't."

"And we know what he thinks of *us*," Cassius added. "We'll be amongst the first to go."

"Such talk is dangerous, you know?" Casca warned softly.

"Then let us talk in private." Brutus extended a hand. "Join us for dinner at my house. Let us speak openly there. Even the slaves will be sent away."

Casca only hesitated for a moment before reaching out and taking Brutus's wrist. Brutus's hand similarly squeezed Casca's wrist. "I will," he said, "and let us talk of simple things, like where in the Republic we can move to so as to live out our lives in peace and harmony."

"Or," Cassius said, "what steps have to be taken to ensure that we can stay *here* in peace and harmony, even though those steps themselves may be neither peaceful nor harmonious."

Casca left the two men there, and walked on. His mind was abuzz with speculation. He thought he had just been invited to join a conspiracy, but he wasn't entirely sure. Joining such an undertaking – if there was one – was risky, but he knew that he, too, was on Caesar's list of people who needed to be disposed of when he took complete power. Anyone who had supported Pompey was on that list, as were Pompey's entire family, any soldier who had ever served under him and anyone who had known him at school. Casca had to pick a side, lest one was picked for him.

Later, after he had rested and completed some business negotiations, and the sun had dropped behind Esquilline Hill he decided to walk to Brutus's residence. He could have got his servants to carry him in a litter, or perhaps order them to tie a mule to a *carruca* and pull him there, but he loved the city at night: the sounds of the iron-bound wheels of the carriages and carts clattering against the cobbles and the smells of the flowers drifting down from the seven hills, the incense burning in the smaller temples and the feasts being cooked in the various residences. How much longer he would be able to stand on a street corner in the darkness, close his eyes and just appreciate the city was another matter – perhaps one that would be sorted out that night.

The city was quiet, apart from the sound of occasional raised voices from some gathering of friends and the occasional hoot of an owl. It was for that reason that Casca found himself listening to a regular tapping sound, like a stick hitting the stones of the road. By the time he consciously registered it the sound had been audible for some time. He looked around, expecting to see someone walking along with the aid of a stick, a blind man or a cripple perhaps, but the street was empty. In fact, now he came to concentrate more on it, the sound wasn't really like the tapping of a stick on stone. It was more regular, like a hammer on iron, but surely no blacksmith ever hit an anvil so precisely or for so long?

The sound faded as he walked, and Casca put the puzzle on a mental shelf, along with other things to which he had no answer, such as with the man with the yellow toga, and how Caesar could be so arrogant as to dismantle the Republic for his own personal ambition.

It was while he was cutting through a lower-class area of mixed businesses, temples and residences that he saw a man walking ahead of him. He was alone, with a hood pulled up over his head, but the way he held himself, the way he carried his head and the set of his shoulders were immediately recognisable.

It was Julius Caesar. There was no doubt.

Casca looked around, not quite believing it. Surely the fact that he had been thinking about Caesar had caused his mind to spontaneously generate some phantom? How could Caesar be here? *Why* would Caesar be here? No soldiers to guard him, no slaves to clear the path ahead of him, no sycophants to tell him how noble and powerful he was; nobody. Caesar was alone. And with the hood over his head it was obvious that he didn't want to be recognised.

But it was definitely, unmistakably him.

Casca was intrigued. What in Jupiter's name could Caesar be doing out so late at night, and so alone?

The figure up ahead suddenly darted down a narrow alley. When he got to the corner, Casca gazed down its shadowed length. He looked around, checking that he was still alone. If he investigated it was likely he would arrive late at Brutus's residence for dinner, but given what they were going to be talking about he felt that he *ought* to investigate. Perhaps Caesar was visiting some mistress whose identity would cause a convenient scandal if revealed. So he followed.

At its end the alley opened out into a small square that Casca had never been in before. A few twisted trees emerged from holes in the pavement around it, and oddly they all seemed to be leaning away from the centre, as if trying to escape it, rather than all being bent the same way by the winds that sometimes swept through the city. In the centre of the square was a temple of grey, weathered marble, raised up on a wide platform of five steps. It was one of the many hundreds of temples scattered around Rome dedicated to one or another of the many gods in the Roman pantheon – a fair number of which had been appropriated from other religions and bought under Roman control.

The steps were cracked, and grass was growing out of the gaps between the slabs that formed them. Abandoned, perhaps – its worshippers a small cult or a foreign minority who had gradually died off?

The temple itself looked… wrong. The pillars all appeared straight when Casca looked at them, and the roof was set firmly and properly on top of them, but whichever part of it he concentrated on, his eyes tried to tell him that the other features were somehow twisted, or joined each other at odd angles. It was as if he was trying to make sense of the architecture while drunk, although he hadn't had any wine since the afternoon, and that had been weak. He might have ascribed the askew look of the place to the results of a long-ago earthquake, or some subsidence in the ground beneath it, but when he looked at it straight there was nothing wrong. It was just when he looked away, or past it, that it was disturbing. It made him feel queasy, and not just in his stomach. Queasy in his head.

Caesar glanced around, and Casca moved back into the shadow of the alley's walls. Seeing nobody, he climbed the steps and entered the temple.

Nerving himself, Casca crossed the open space and climbed those same steps.

He glanced upwards, to see if there was any carving running along the pediment on top of the temple that might tell him which god or gods it was dedicated to, but the way the columns appeared to curve together towards a roof that seemed to belly out towards him made him suddenly dizzy, and he looked away quickly. There *were* words there, however, and he braced himself to look again.

Iä Hastur cf'ayak'vulgtmm, vugtlagln vulgtmm, the words read.

It was a language he had never come across before. His lips moved, trying to form the sounds, but his mouth suddenly went dry and bile rose at the back of his throat, burning the sensitive skin there.

Tearing his gaze away from the letters, which seems to twist as he looked at them, he moved to the corner of the temple and looked upwards again at the newly revealed side.

Ph'nglui mglw'nafh Cthugha n'g Sothtoth n'gha-ghaa naf'lthagn.

The words still meant nothing. Was Cthugha the god worshipped here, or was it Hastur or Sothtoth? He'd never heard of any of them, and the way his stomach was churning he thought he probably never *wanted* to. Some of these foreign cults involved things like human sacrifice and worse.

There was a part of his mind – quite a sizable part – that was screaming at him to get out of there, but he took a deep breath, quelled his rebellious stomach and moved in past the pillars, through the portico and into the temple itself.

Inside was a large, rectangular open space. *Apparently* rectangular, because, like the outside, the corners and edges where the walls met didn't appear to be straight unless Casca looked directly at them, in which case they were fine and it was everything else around them that was wrong. At the far end of the temple a statue rose up to the ceiling, and Julius Caesar was standing directly in front of it.

If Casca had thought the strange, twisted architecture of the temple exterior and interior had caused him digestive problems then the statue in front of which Caesar was now prostrating himself very nearly caused him to vomit. It was a dirty grey in colour, with hints of green in the folds and creases, as if there was mould growing on it – or out of it. The stone itself seemed to be pocked with holes, like volcanic pumice, but it also looked *soapy*, with a strange glint where the light from the braziers set around the edge of the space reflected from it. Casca had seen many bizarre statues of gods in his time, but this one beat them all.

In form it appeared to be animalistic – like a recumbent lion, perhaps – but the angle of the limbs and joints meant either that it had several badly broken bones or that the sculptor had put the head where the tail should be and vice versa. Instead of paws it had claws, like those of a vulture but thicker and crueller, and its tail gave the distinct impression that it ended in a second head: blunt and featureless, but carved in such a way as to suggest it was somehow still *watching* the viewer with malign intent. It was the actual head that was the strangest thing, however. It seemed to be covered with globular excrescences that could only be eyes, except that there were hundreds of them of various sizes. It was watching all directions at once.

How could anyone in their right mind worship something like that?

But it seemed that Caesar was doing just that. He was now lying on the marble floor between the front claws of the statue with his arms extended towards it in supplication.

"I can't do it," he was moaning. "Please – don't make me. Let me go."

There was movement in the shadows of the statute, and a man walked into sight. Casca moved back into the shadows of the portico, enthralled. It was the man in the yellow toga, the man with ragged holes for eyes, and he stood over Caesar, looking down at him. The flickering light from the braziers made the shadows of the eye-sockets dance, and Casca thought he could even see the reflection of the red light off the bloody tissue within.

Casca pressed himself back against the cool marble. He thought he could detect something beneath the palms of his hands – a regular thudding, just like the noise he had heard earlier. Like someone hammering iron against iron, somewhere far below.

"There was an agreement," the man in yellow said, distracting Casca from the mysterious vibration. His voice was mellifluous, measured. Casca recognised well the sound of a man who was used to manipulating crowds or potential investors with his words, and with the tone of his voice. It was a tone of voice that Casca had successfully used himself – in politics and in business – and had heard Caesar use with equal success. This man, however, had mastered it perfectly.

"I didn't understand," Caesar moaned. Casca was shocked to hear the pain and anguish in his voice. He was used to Caesar being strong. Self-serving perhaps, even petty, but strong.

"That is the nature of agreements," the man in yellow pointed out. "The one party rarely understands what they have signed away to the other party until it is too late. You wanted absolute power – we gave you absolute power. *We* wanted influence – you will give us influence."

"I thought you meant favours, influential positions, *money!*"

The man in yellow laughed, but there was no humour in the sound. It was like something echoing in a dark room. "Those things are not influence. They are glittering baubles. Treasures for the foolish."

"I didn't understand," Caesar whispered. "I want out of the agreement."

"There is no 'out'. You are with us, or you are nothing."

Caesar rolled slightly, and his right hand reached clumsily behind his back. He was trying to reach something on the nape of his neck. "I reject you," he said, and it sounded to Casca as if there was something of the old Caesar in his tone. "You would destroy Rome, and I will not let you do that."

"*You* will destroy Rome, and we will watch." The man in yellow gazed down at Caesar's prone body. His face was devoid of emotion, but his voice had a note of slight surprise in it. Perhaps even the beginnings of respect. "But we confess that we had not anticipated the strength of your will. That was a surprise to us. We did not think you capable of rejecting the crown in the way that you did."

Caesar's fingers tightened on something that Casca couldn't see. He tugged at it, and his entire body convulsed. Whatever he was doing was agonising, but he continued to do it. "I reject you! I reject you and this abomination that you gave me!" With that he pulled hard, and *something* came away from his neck. For a moment Casca was confused – it looked like Caesar's hand was suddenly three hands, all connected together in some bizarre contortion – but then Caesar threw the thing that he was holding away. It bounced and slid to a halt, leaving red smears behind it on the marble tiles.

The thing that lay there on the cracked marble looked like two thin, white hands lying on their backs with long fingers that twitched and clutched at the air. The two hands weren't separate, however. They were joined at the wrist, forming a terrible whole with one set of fingers facing forward and one set facing backwards. A single creature made up of two impossible hands.

And that wasn't the worst. No, the worst was that the middle finger of one of the hands was covered in blood up to the second knuckle, and when Casca's horrified gaze slowly but inexorably moved back to Caesar's twitching body he saw that blood was trickling down the Dictator's neck from a ragged hole in the base of his skull.

The thing on the marble was shuddering now, the fingers fluttering as if it was dying. Its white skin seemed, to Casca's horrified gaze, to be shrivelling as he watched. Wrinkles were forming and running into each other as it shrivelled back to the bone beneath. If there was bone.

The man in the yellow toga bent down and picked up the conjoined hands. He held them, cupping them in his own hands, as if he was holding a sickly baby, and then with a single smooth motion he bought them up to his face.

The long, thin fingers tightened around his head and beneath his jaw while the thumbs slid into his empty eye sockets. When he bought his own hands down the *thing* was clamped to his face. *Over* his face, like a mask – a terrible, grotesque mask. The long middle finger that had been inside Caesar's *head* had left a smear of crimson on the man's cheek. Within moments the hands appeared to be filling out, the wrinkles vanishing as they absorbed precious life from their host.

"Something stronger is required," he said calmly, as if nothing untoward had even happened.

A skittering sound, like rats on a tiled rooftop, filled the temple, and as Casca's incredulous attention was drawn to the massive statue behind Caesar and his horrific master he saw that the statue's back was now covered with the double-handed creatures. They scampered, scuttled and ran across the stone in a sick wave, stopping around its haunches and its shoulders, eyelessly watching the events below.

The man in yellow didn't make any move, but as if at some signal, one of the creatures edged forward. It was bulkier than the rest, its long fingers thick and muscular rather than twig-like. Like a malformed albino spider it moved carefully forward over the statue's front limbs, then onto the podium on which the statue reclined. From there it walked with terrible intent upon its ten legs, five at the front and five at the rear, past the feet of the man in the yellow toga and up to Caesar's twitching body.

The Dictator had rolled ono his back by now. The blood from his skull wound was pooling on the marble behind him. He moaned, when he saw the thing, but apparently he didn't have the strength to pull away. It reached out with its front second and fourth fingers, using them like antennae, to touch his face. The tips of the fingers gently stroked his cheeks. Then, with a febrile motion, the creature sprang onto the side of Caesar's head and slithered around to the back. Caesar began to scream – a weak, pitiful sound – as the creature adjusted its position, readying itself so that one of the hands could slide down inside his toga and the fingers of the other could grip his neck. Once it was secure, it slid a thick middle finger up into the hole in the base of Caesar's skull with a sucking sound that made Casca's stomach twist.

"There," the man in yellow said. There was satisfaction in his voice. "Now you will go back and accept the crown for us. Do our bidding. Follow our will, as was agreed."

Caesar lay there, whimpering. There were tears squeezing out from behind his screwed-up eyes. Casca felt something he had never felt before for the man and never thought he would – pity.

Caesar pulled himself up to his feet, slowly and painfully. It seemed to Casca almost as if he was being manipulated by invisible hands, like some human-sized puppet. In fact, when Casca glanced at the back of Caesar's head he couldn't even see the hand-creature any more. Some of it was hidden inside Caesar's toga, of course, but surely something would have been visible? But no – it seemed to have blended with Caesar's body, disguising its presence.

Caesar turned to go – or *was turned* to go. Looking at his tear-streaked, agonised face, Casca felt sorry for him. Whatever was happening may have been his choice originally, but not anymore.

Casca pushed himself away from the stone of the portico and moved as quietly as he could to the temple doorway. He had to get away before Caesar left, and saw him. Perhaps there was still something in the man that he could appeal to, but Casca couldn't take the chance.

He stumbled blindly through the streets of Rome, his brain a confused morass of flickering thoughts that wouldn't cohere into anything sensible. Had those braziers been burning some incense which had caused him to hallucinate the whole thing? Had he fallen down, hit his head and dreamed everything? He wanted to run his hands across his head looking for injuries, but he was terrified that he might find blood at the base of his skull.

Eventually, more through luck than judgement, he found himself outside Brutus's residence. He knocked wildly on the door, and the slaves half-led and half-carried him through the vestibule, across the atrium and into the dining area.

Brutus and Cassius were already there, lying on couches around the central low table that was rich with plates of oysters, fish, poultry, olives and stuffed dormice. As the slaves laid Casca gently on the third couch, the two men made as if to rise. Casca waved them back down with a weak hand. A slave handed Casca a flask of wine, which he drained in one long series of gulps.

*"The long, thin fingers tightened around his head and beneath
his jaw while the thumbs slid into his empty eye sockets."*

Illustration by Malcolm Barter

"What have you seen, my friend?" Cassius asked gently.

"You would not believe me," Casca said, shaking his head. "There is no way that I could tell this story without it sounding like the ravings of a madman."

Cassius and Brutus shared a glance, and there was something in their expressions that persuaded Casca that they knew something he didn't. So, haltingly and punctuated by several more flasks of wine, he told them what had befallen him.

At the end of his story there was silence for a while. Casca realised that he was starving, and took the opportunity to grab food from the table. It was, as befitted Brutus's rank and reputation, all delicious, and all perfectly prepared. There was even a shallow dish of *garum sociorum* – the fish sauce made from mackerel that was, ounce for ounce, more expensive than the finest of perfumes.

"You don't believe me," he said eventually, through a mouthful of tuna. "I don't blame you. I hardly even believe myself."

"This temple…" Cassius said, waving a piece of bread, "did you by any chance feel a *vibration* through the stone, or hear a sound like Vulcan's hammer being struck repeatedly?"

Casca felt a surge of sudden joy. They *knew*. Or at least, they knew *something*. He wasn't mad!

Or perhaps they were all mad. No matter – they could be mad together.

Cassius could obviously see from his face that the answer was yes. "Nobody knows to which god the temple is dedicated, but it was built by foreigners from a country named Carcosa, whose location nobody seems to know. Caesar visited Carcosa on his way home from Egypt, although none of his soldiers or crew will speak of it, on pain of death. The sound has been heard by our agents, although none have traced it to a cause. Workshops beneath the temple perhaps – building weapons."

"Weapons?" Casca repeated, confused.

"We believe," Brutus added, "that Caesar has somehow fallen under the influence of some Carcosan cult. He worships their god now, not Jupiter and the gods of Olympus. Whatever he does, he does for them and not for Rome." He frowned. "Some kind of *take-over* is planned, an invasion from the inside, and it is up to us to do something about it."

"But what of those *creatures*?" Casca asked, shuddering at the memory. He couldn't quite reconcile what he had seen with what Brutus and Cassius were so calmly suggesting.

Cassius shrugged. "Some Egyptian cults use snakes or scorpions in their rituals, *that* much we know. The Minoans were known to venerate bulls, at least according to the ancients. Whatever these creatures are, they must come from Carcosa, and they mean *something* to the priests of the cult."

"I think," Brutus said slowly, "that we must all agree – Caesar cannot be allowed to take the crown. To have as Emperor a man in thrall to a foreign religion – he would either change Rome into whatever these priests want, or he would destroy it." He paused. "He must die."

"He didn't look well," Casca pointed out. "I'm not sure he'll make it past the ceremony of coronation."

"We cannot take the *chance*," Cassius said insistently.

"He will have guards around him," Casca went on. "He is protected at all times! And even when the soldiers aren't there, his general – Marcus Antonius – is always present."

Brutus raised a hand to halt the developing argument. "At the Capitol," he pointed out, "when Caesar approaches to enter, his guards disengage to form a ceremonial line. There are senators enough there, ready to greet him. If we attack then, in the crowd, we can cause enough confusion to cover ourselves while we withdraw." He looked over at Cassius. "We will need a base to withdraw to, out in the countryside, and we will need enough soldiers loyal to our cause to protect us and to engage the forces of his supporters afterwards."

"Gaius Octavius will form up against us," Cassius said thoughtfully, "as will Marcus Aemilius Lepidus…"

We're discussing killing Julius Caesar! Casca thought with a horrified thrill as the two men debated calmly, but then he remembered again the temple, and what he had seen, and he knew that what they were considering was right. History would judge their actions well, if of course history ever got to know about the cult of Carcosa.

"But who strikes the fatal blow?" he interrupted, hoping that neither Brutus nor Cassius were going to try to talk *him* into it.

He wanted to be on the outside of the crowd when it happened. Or, preferably, in the middle of some remote forest. This would be a real test of his negotiating skill.

"We will all strike the blow," Brutus said softly. "There are others with us, others who distrust Caesar and have heard about his attachment to this strange foreign religion. Decius Brutus supports our cause, as does Cinna, Metellus Cimber, Trebonius and Caius Ligarius."

"Cinna the poet?" Casca exclaimed, surprised. "What use will he be? Sharp words are *his* weapons."

"Someone will need to write about us, and what we do." Brutus smiled. "Best to have a poet on our side who can do that." He gazed from Casca to Cassius and back again. "If we are to do this then we all strike. We all kill Caesar together so that none of us individually does so. Is it agreed?"

It was agreed. Brutus and Cassius sent messengers out to their fellow conspirators to tell them to meet on the steps of the Senate the next morning. Caesar would arrive late, and with pomp and ceremony, as was his wont, and they would be ready. Casca accepted Brutus's offer of a bed for the night. He knew that Brutus was more concerned that he would run off and hide if he was left alone, but the truth was that Casca didn't *want* to be alone. He was worried about what might happen to him on the way home, or while he was tossing and turning in his bed.

He slept badly, his head filled with dreams of white crawling shapes, and when he was finally woken by one of Brutus's slaves, and was ceremonially washed and dressed, he felt like a man preparing for his own execution.

The sun was shining out of a perfect blue sky, and the ancient stones of Rome seemed to glow in its cleansing light. Casca could hardly believe what was about to happen, or indeed what had happened the night before, but as Brutus led him by the arm and helped him into a litter he slipped a knife inside the folds of Casca's tunic.

"For later," he said. "Wait for my signal."

The Senate was to meet in the Temple of Jupiter Optimus Maximus, located on the apex of the Capitoline Hill and positioned so that the entirety of Rome was spread out beneath it. The slaves carrying the litter were gasping and sweating by the time they had climbed the hill and pushed their way through the crowds that always assembled to see the business of Rome carried out. As Casca stepped from the litter he looked around at the various shrines, altars, statues and victory trophies that were displayed in the open area outside the temple. They marked the history of Rome – its triumphs and its failures, its conquests and its defeats, its people and its soul. And, if they didn't succeed in their business that morning, they could bear witness to Rome's ultimate failure.

"Stiffen the sinews," Brutus murmured, taking Casca's elbow. "What we do, we do for Rome."

He led Casca across to a group standing on the steps leading up to the temple's immense pillars. Cassius was there, as were the others who had been named the night before – Decius Brutus, Lucius Metellus Cimber, Gaius Trebonius, Caius Ligarius and the poet, Helvius Cinna. They each swapped dark glances that, Casca thought, should have been enough to give away their purpose to any soldier nearby. They virtually *stank* of conspiracy.

A stir in the crowd drew his attention. He glanced past Brutus and Cassius and saw a litter approaching. It was, of course, bigger and more resplendent than any other litter, and carried by more slaves than was necessary. Soldiers in gleaming metal and polished leather armour followed it. The litter drew to a halt amid cheers and applause from the crowd, and, after a dramatic pause, Julius Caesar climbed out.

He looked pale, Casca thought, and his eyes were shadowed as if he carried a great weight of worry. As he turned to acknowledge the adulation of the crowd with a languid hand, Casca tried to get a glimpse of the back of his neck, but he could see nothing untoward.

"I shall engage him in conversation as he approaches," Brutus said quietly. "When I shout 'Tyranny is dead!' then we all fall upon him. Is it agreed?"

"Yes," came the reply from everyone gathered around him.

As his guards moved to form a line along the lowest step in front of the temple, Caesar drew his toga around him and swept towards the conspirators. It seemed to Casca that he took a deep breath before he moved, as though bracing himself, or summoning what little strength he had left.

"Great Caesar," Brutus said smoothly, moving to intercept him, "might I petition you on behalf of Publius Cimber, brother of Metellus here, who you have banished from Rome for reasons that —"

"Bother me not here," Caesar snapped. "If you bend and pray and fawn for Publius Cimber then I spurn you like a cur. Know that Caesar does no wrong."

He tried to push his way past the knot of conspirators, but they drew closer about him. Caesar's face twisted in anger, but it seemed to Casca that there was something else there — gratitude, perhaps, or relief. He seemed to know what was coming.

Brutus opened his mouth to say something — probably the fateful words — but Caesar raised a hand to the back of his neck. His face convulsed, and he seemed to Casca, who was behind and slightly to his right now, that he was trying to tear something away. For a moment there was nothing in his clawed hand, but then Casca saw it — a white hand emerging from the folds of his toga, its skin moist and maggoty — that clutched at his neck with four of its fingers and would not let go. The middle finger, however, extended up into Caesar's hairline, where a thin line of watery blood trickled downwards.

Casca couldn't help himself. He grabbed for the knife inside the folds of his own toga and lunged at Caesar's back. He heard shouts from the crowd, and thought he could make out Brutus shouting, "Tyranny is— !", but his blood was roaring in his ears like a waterfall, blocking everything else out. He swept the knife up, and then down, skewering the fleshy white hand to Caesar's neck. Blood spurted, but so did a thin, yellowish fluid. The hand convulsed, fingers digging hard into Caesar's neck.

The other conspirators threw themselves on Caesar, hacking and stabbing, but Casca stepped backwards, hiding the knife within his toga. As the crowd screamed and surged, as the shocked soldiers advanced, he moved in the other direction. Eventually he turned and ran.

He didn't know where to go. Not home — if anyone was looking for him then that was where they would go. Not to Brutus's residence, for the same reason. If there was some gathering place for the conspiracy to retreat to in order to prepare for the inevitable attack by Octavius and Lepidus then he didn't know its location, but even if he did then he wouldn't have gone there. He just wanted to run to the middle of some forest somewhere and just sit there until all the hubbub and hullaballoo had died down.

Inevitably, however, his feet drew him to the Carcosan temple. As he stared up at its distorted lines, and felt rather than heard the regular pounding from somewhere inside it or beneath it, he knew that there was unfinished business there. Brutus and the others thought that assassinating Caesar would be enough. It wouldn't. Whatever was in the temple had to be destroyed as well, even if it cost Casca his own life.

There was an old, twisted tree growing out of the pavement to one side. He reached up and snapped off a branch.

Reluctantly he climbed the five steps and entered the temple.

It was hot inside. The bald man with no eyes was absent, and Casca stared up at the strange and disturbing statue that dominated the inside of the temple. Perhaps he had misremembered it, or perhaps the flickering of the braziers and the strange geometry of the walls and ceiling was confusing him, but it seemed to him that the statue's head had been canted to the left the last time he had seen it, but now it was pointing downwards, and slightly to the right. The myriad of blank marble hemispheres that were its eyes could, of course, have been looking in any and all directions.

He held the dry branch that he carried up to one of the braziers until it caught alight. If there was anything there that could be burned then he would burn it.

Casca could hear the sound of metallic tapping, or thudding, or clicking clearly now – more clearly than on the previous night. It seemed to be coming from around the back of the statue, and he followed the noise, circling the creature's stone flanks until he reached its rear, where he found a dark opening. He went through, holding the burning branch in one hand and the knife in the other.

Steps led downwards. He followed, until he found himself in a subterranean corridor, lined with damp brick from which green strands of fungus sprouted like the hair of a corpse. The metallic thudding was louder now, like the beating of Vulcan's own fiery forge. He followed the corridor to a corner. Bracing himself, because the thudding noise was shaking the very brickwork now, he turned the corner.

He found himself in a long catacomb with an arched roof, but the architecture took second place to the *thing* in the centre. It was… actually, he didn't know *what* it was.

There were wheels the size of waterwheels and cartwheels in there, whirling around madly, but they were made of flesh rather than wood or metal, flesh that was marbled with muscle and fat, and they were each encircled by jagged ivory teeth that meshed with the teeth of other wheels so that they all rotated in opposing directions but each driving the others. There were also great coils of muscle that seemed to be gradually unwinding, thick rods of glistening horn covered with thorn-like spines which rotated endlessly, and heavy knobs of bone that swung back and forth on lengths of tendon as thick as Casca's arms. In the middle, dimly visible through all the moving parts, Casca thought he could see leathery bellows inflating and deflating with a regular pulse. With a sick feeling in his stomach Casca realised that the wheels and rods and coils appeared, in some cases, to be impossibly passing *through* each other, as if they were occupying the same space.

Altogether it was a vision of complete madness: organised, regular and yet completely, entirely alive. The thudding sound it emitted echoed through his chest, making it hard to breath. That might have been a benefit, because the whole cellar was permeated with a cloying smell of faecal matter, sweat and bile.

What made his head swim was that, although the catacomb was on finite size, with walls and a ceiling, when he looked at the thing moving ceaselessly in the centre he knew he was looking at something vast, something without boundary or limit.

"Beautiful, is it not?"

He turned. The man with the yellow toga and no eyes was standing behind him, in the doorway. He still had the creature from last night clamped to his face, its thumbs plunged into his eye-sockets and its fingers clamping around the sides of his head. It covered his forehead and his ears, but left his mouth free.

Two other men wearing yellow togas were visible behind him, half-hidden in the shadows. They too had no eyes, but they seemed to be staring at him. The three of them could have been triplets, their features were so similar.

"Sothtoth, the cosmic timekeeper," he went on. "The regular beat at the centre of the universe, counting down infinity moment by moment until the Old Gods are free once more. Sibling to Azathoth, the amorphous blight of nethermost confusion which blasphemes and bubbles at the centre of all infinity. The order which defines chaos, without which chaos could not exist."

"Caesar is dead," Casca said. It was trivial, but it was the only thing he could think of. In amongst all the madness that surrounded him he was keeping a precarious hold on his mission, and on what the conspirators had achieved.

"Of course," the man in yellow said.

"You *knew*?"

"There are many possibilities, but then –" and he smiled, "there are many temples, many Old Gods. Whoever takes control of Rome will be one of us. Or *will* be one of us. The one you call Brutus worships at the shrine of Hastur the unspeakable and has done so since his time on the coast of Gaul. The one you call Cassius is a devotee of Azathoth, the amorphous blight of nethermost confusion which blasphemes and bubbles at the centre of all infinity. Every one has made a bargain which they do not yet understand. But they will. The Old Gods will be ascendant, one way or another."

"The conspirators who killed Caesar will fall themselves, eventually," Casca whispered, and he knew that it was true. "Octavius and Lepidus control far greater armies."

"And they have struck bargains with Ghatanothoa and Shub-Niggurath respectively," the man in yellow continued smoothly. "There is no escape. You make a bargain, or you die – but not quickly, and not well."

"There is a third choice," Casca said. It took every ounce of his skills as an orator to keep the trembling fear he felt from his voice. Before the man in yellow could move, he threw the burning branch into the centre of the moving wheels and rods and belts of flesh.

He heard it hit a wall and fall to the floor, but he couldn't see it. There was no effect on the thing in the catacomb, which apparently had just ignored the trivial attack. Or hadn't even noticed it.

"Sothtoth is not here," the man said, smiling. "Or, rather, Sothtoth is everywhere. You cannot stop the pulse of the cosmos."

"Then I can stop yours," Casca said, plunging his knife into the man's chest.

"My pulse is bound to that of Sothtoth," the man said pleasantly. On the conjoined hands that covered his face there was a sudden stirring. Skin drew back on both sides, above where the holes of the man's eye-sockets were, and Casca saw with little surprise two white hemispheres, like marbles the size of plumbs, staring at him with icy, malign intelligence.

He heard a rustling sound above him. Glancing up he noticed in resignation that the arched ceiling was covered with the conjoined hand-creatures. All of them were clinging to the brickwork with one set of fingers while the second set hung down towards him. Like leaves, he though numbly. Like white, marble leaves.

"Now," the man in yellow said, "let us discuss the terms of *your* agreement to serve, or the nature of your inevitable madness and death. Whichever you prefer."

The problem was – as Casca knew for a certainty – that it wasn't a choice. It wasn't *either* service *or* madness and death. It was one, and then eventually the other. That was the nature of the agreement. The only question was: how long could you extend the former before the inevitability of the latter?

He took a deep breath, and tried to recall every rhetorical and oratorical trick he had ever learned.

"Then let us talk, like businessmen." he said.

THE UNDISCOVERED COUNTRY

IAN EDGINTON

TRY AS I might, I cannot bring myself to murder my child.

These are not what are father's hands were made for. The hands that held her as a newborn, fresh to life, should not be the ones to smother that brief spark. I know a quick death would be preferable to the lingering fate that awaits us but I do not have the strength nor will in me for such an act. It is mercy at too high a price but I fear that may change as the days pass.

Were they around the throat of my usurping brother Antonio, though, I would have no such qualms. Yet even he would not sully his own hands with homicide, instead he cast us into this ailing craft and left us prey to the elements. He did not wield the dagger or draw the garrote but he has killed us just as surely as if he had. The wind and rain, hunger and thirst are his dread weapons.

She sleeps now, my angel Miranda. Swaddled in my cloak and sackcloth, in the base of this barque that has become the bounds of our world. She stirs and murmurs occasionally, calling for her dog. It was this that troubled her most, leaving her beloved pet behind. A boisterous, shaggy haired hound. I lie and tell her that he is safe with her uncle, that we will find another just like it when we make landfall. She knows the truth, she can see to the very core of me, as her mother once could but says nothing. Before curling up to sleep, she kissed me and touched my cheek.

"It will be alright, father. You'll see."

I felt my heart crack in my chest for my love of her and my soul howl at my impotence to save her. It was then, as the skies darkened and the seas began to churn and chafe, that I swore a dire oath. Should we live through this, I would never let my child be placed in harm's way ever again. I would brazen the heavens and shoulder the Earth from its axis if need be in order to keep her safe. But first we must endure.

*   *   *

THE SEA THRASHED and boiled. Lightening arced in jagged spears of white fire, briefly illuminating towering, foam-edged promontories that tore at the fragile shell of our craft. I lay next to Miranda, folding my arms about her. I felt her cry and quake with terror.

"I'm frightened," she said.

'So am I," I replied, "but whatever happens, wherever we go, we shall be together."

A surge slammed into the side of the boat, sending us spinning. Another hurled us back. We were nature's catspaws. I braced my arms and legs tight as I dared against the insides, pinning us into place. My limbs quickly burned with the exertion but to relinquish my grip for even a second would have sent us hurtling into the maelstrom. The sea and sky roared, pawing with claws of salt to find purchase in our tiny refuge. In petulant fury it hurled us high and far. The world and my mind span, darkness upon darkness. My hold loosened. Miranda screamed and then there was nothing.

I woke to a void, vast and absolute. I called out to Miranda but my speech found no traction. My words fell short from my lips, despite calling at the top of my lungs. The very air, if there was such, seemed closed about me, smothering my voice. Panic rose like bile and it took all the will I could summon to wrestle it back.

I walked forwards, though the ground gave no resistance to my footsteps. I could not be certain if even there was any surface. I felt dwarfed into insignificance by the seeming vastness of my surroundings. I had no perspective, no sense of dimension. I could have been a mighty colossus or an insubstantial mote, it mattered naught to this all-encompassing emptiness. Such an absence diminishes a man's soul, stripping it of all value, vanity and worth. He finds his true place in the scheme of things.

I stopped and stood as there seemed little purpose in continuing for there was nowhere to go. The silence was eternal. I had no reference point for distance or duration, only the rise and fall of my chest and the steady drum beat of my heart marked the passing of time.

It was then I felt the darkness shift.

I have no other words to describe it. I saw and felt no tangible movement but there was something. A fluctuation, a stirring, the rolling of a wave but on an incomprehensible scale. This new universe, this blank slate of creation, turned.

Before I could muse upon it, this strange world was riven by a line of white light. It was not illuminated in and of itself but was rendered luminous by its blatant opposition to the darkness. The line continued to widen its edges into the tenebrous expanse.

I retreated only to find myself moving up and back until I was looking down upon the scene. From my high vantage, I could see the line – now more a bilious pearlescent than pure white – did not continue unbroken but was punctuated by a dark delineator before continuing on. I felt myself retreating further and further, unable to manage my ascent until I was so far removed I could see the entire thing, whole and at once.

A taut, pallid ellipse whose transition was broken by another on a vertical plane. It was a putrescent green colour, flecked with yellow. I wracked my brain with thoughts to its purpose and then it turned to look at me.

It was an eye.

It was an eye and it was looking at me.

My fear found purchase and I screamed. I felt the fabric of my sanity start to fray when a clear bolt of hope was cast down to me.

"Father!"

Miranda's voice, as fresh and pure as the dawn, reached out to me and raised me up from the abyss – a lifeline by which I was able to haul myself safely to shore.

I AWOKE IN a nest of black rock, waist deep in seawater and my head aching. Miranda was pulling at my clothes endeavouring to keep me from sliding beneath the surface.

"Father! Wake up!"

My senses settled and I pulled her tightly to me as if to impress her into my very heart.

"Miranda!"

"I told you we would be alright," she said, as calm as you like.

"Yes, yes you did."

Reluctantly I let her go and groaning, pushed myself to my feet. Seawater sluiced from my clothes that hung heavy about me, yet regardless of the discomfort we were alive and together.

"Are you hurt?"

"No," she replied. "I thought you were when you wouldn't wake up."

"I must have hit my head but I am well enough now."

"Where are we?" she asked.

"I don't know," I replied. "The tempest could have flung us anywhere but some land is better than none. Are you up for a walk?"

Miranda nodded and took my hand.

The black rocks rose in a steady incline from the shore inland. Those at the periphery had been slathered with slime and seaweed but further in it was possible to define their form more clearly.

To call them rocks was a misnomer for they seemed to be a kind of obsidian. A dark, smooth glass, comprised of keen-edged planes. It was a landscape of lines and hard angles with no curves or ellipses anywhere to be seen. Unlike glass however, as mirrored as they might have been, they strangely did not hold a reflection. Nor upon, closer inspection was their surface in a pure ebon state but rather peppered with tiny whorls of nebulous light.

Staring deeply it was possible to see that each whorl was spinning upon a luminous axis and each spiraling limb in turn was spangled with further points of light and about those lights orbited other bodies and upon those bodies lay islands and oceans and upon those, vast cities whose architecture did not play host to the human form.

"Father!"

Once more Miranda's voice pulled me back. The tightness of her hand in mine anchoring me to this world.

"I was calling and calling but you didn't hear me. You just kept staring at the stones!"

The fear and concern was writ large in her eyes.

"I'm sorry, I didn't mean to frighten you. I think perhaps I hit my head harder than I thought. I shall have to be more careful."

We moved on through the piceous jumble. I took care not to rest my gaze upon any one for longer than I dared. I had no doubt now that we were in an unnatural place.

In my youth I had delved into the obscurities of wild magic. I sought to peer behind the warp and weft of creation, to discern the lattice upon which all life is laid. In honest humility, I confess I had developed a modest talent, but the passing of my father and the calling of my station as Duke of Milan meant that I was obliged to put aside such trivialities and set my mind to more practical matters.

I cannot but marvel now at my naivety. Where I took pride in my arcane dabblings I see now that I was merely wading in the shallows, while here, in this place, we were above the dark water.

"Look, a boat? Is it ours?"

Miranda was pointing back down behind us to a small cove further along the bay. There, buoyed amongst the rocks was indeed the tiny vessel that had saved our lives. Like us, it too had miraculously weathered the storm and appeared, at least to my eyes, to still be sea-worthy. I was half tempted to return to it and chance our fortunes to the water once more, but the small hand in mine gave me pause. Without provisions we would not last more than a few days. If there was salvation here, we had to find it.

With no small struggle, we crested the steep escarpment. I felt Miranda's hand instinctively tighten in mine again and with good cause. I was correct in my study, this uncommon geography was not made for the likes of men. It was clear now the beach upon which we had made landfall was but broken remnants of the interior that had migrated towards the periphery. The island proper comprised great spars of black crystal ten times taller than a man and wider around than a mill stone. Between them ran broad hexagonal plinths stacked and stepped in irregular tiers all leading towards the interior.

Nothing about this place spoke of the world we knew. There were no beasts, nor birds, nor foliage of any kind. It was as if all were fearful to set foot or take root here. I too shared their reluctance. This place was less of the natural world and more an intrusion of some alien other into our own.

Again, all of my instincts bade me turn back and depart headlong for the horizon in that fragile shell of a ship. It was to risk certain death to be sure but at least our immortal souls would remain whole and untainted, whereas to linger here I feared for more than our lives. Yet, despite this, I still placed one foot before the other, inexplicably drawn to the centre of this island by curiosity and a compulsion I cannot explain.

"You're doing it again."

I was the subject of Miranda's scrutiny once more.

"Does your head hurt? Do you want to stop?"

I could not help but smile at her concern.

"No, thank you. Although, I think I am finding this place strange and distracting. As if we should not be here but somehow it wants us to be. Don't you feel it?"

Her brow furrowed as she thought for a moment.

"Not really. I feel tired and thirsty, but that's all."

"Do you want to carry on?"

"Yes. Well, there's nowhere else to go really, is there?"

I could not refute her logic. She was considerably wiser than her six years. That she did not share my sense of dread or foreboding obliged me to question whether this indeed was all in my mind. Or perhaps her innocence and the purity of her soul shielded her somehow from the deleterious effects of this odd environment?

Slowly we pressed on. I lifted Miranda over certain of the plinths that she could not negotiate herself. We fell into a steady pattern of ascent until suddenly she gave a shrill, fearful cry.

The ache in my bones, and the weight of my water-logged clothes, counted for naught as I heaved myself over the brink. There, lay the body of a man. A Moor and a mariner, by his attire. A sword of deadly purpose and uncertain origin protruded from his chest. Miranda was staring at the corpse in strange fascination.

"It's alright," I said. "There's no need to be afraid."

"I'm not," she replied, matter-of-factly. "He made me jump when I first saw him, that's all. It's not the first dead body I've ever seen."

This was certainly true. There had been an outbreak of typhus in Milan the summer before. The bodies had been stacked high on handcarts en route to being burnt.She had lost several friends and a cousin before the infection was extinguished.

I have never shielded her from the fact that death is a part of life. A process and a passage, it is one of two certainties over which we have no control. We are born and we will die. How we choose to spend the time in-between is what defines us.

"What's wrong with him?" she asked. "Apart from being dead?"

I looked again and saw the reason for her curiosity. On closer inspection the corpse's skin was possessed of a faintly greenish hue. Not that of grave moss or putrescence but an iridescent shimmer more akin to that of fish scales. With my attention now attuned for similar irregularities, they seemed all the more evident.

The dead man's pupils were considerably wider and darker than was customary, and his teeth small, sharp and serrated. Spanning between his fingers was a translucent webbing while on his neck, below his ears, were several flaps of skin that I could only surmise were gills.

The body before me was a freakish impossibility and yet here it was. I grasped the sword and pulled it clear from his chest. The vile miasma that followed caused us both to gag.

"He smells like bad fish!" said Miranda, her hand over her nose and mouth.

"That he does," I replied. "But he also looks to be a sailor. Perhaps his ship is still here?"

"And perhaps so are the ones who killed him."

"It's a possibility."

"Are you going to kill them?"

"That too is a possibility, but let's hope it does not come to that. Are you ready to keep going?"

She nodded, her hand still clamped firmly over her mouth and nose.

I took the lead now, scouting ahead to make sure our route was safe before beckoning her to follow me. All the while I could feel a strange yearning in my chest, an aching fondness that you feel when you have travelled far and long and are within sight of home. Having never set foot here before, my reason counselled that such a sensation was not possible, yet my instincts felt the pull of this place, as if there were a line about my heart and I was being reeled in. I fought against it in quiet concentration, although part of me secretly wished to see it to the end.

The great black columns listed and tilted about us. Some were of an immense proportion, their surfaces graven with a scrimshaw of unspeakable hieroglyphics. The workmanship was of a skill without peer, images and phrases of an obscene beauty, many one and the same, hewn by hands on an inhuman scale. I do not know how, but I sensed that they were tales in testimony and tribute to races that are far removed from the world of men. They were ancient when the stars were but a nursery of nebulous gas and fume.

It was then I saw a face staring back at me, gibbous and manic. It was not my reflection, for the raven surface held none, but rather the image of a sea-hand like the other, yet still in possession of his human features. He screamed and pounded at his confine in wordless silence. I hammered back upon the obsidian surface but he could not see or hear me. Each facet of the pillar showed a different aspect of his person. From near and far, above and below. He turned and simultaneously ran away and toward me depending on the view within the crystal.

At times his face filled one entire section, distorted and tormented. At others, he was the faintest figure in an empty landscape. He was not bound into the pillar as if it were a prison cell but swallowed by some manner of malevolent architecture. He was imprisoned by angles, and he was not alone. Other columns showed scenes of similar madness. They were his shipmates, or some of them at least.

"Can we help them?"

Miranda was by my side. Her hand in mine.

"I don't think so. I think they're trapped in there."

"Will the same happen to us?"

"Not if we're careful. I don't know why exactly, but I have the feeling something wants us to be here."

"Father," she asked earnestly, "is this real?"

"What do you mean?"

"I'm tired. I am so tired. I don't know if I'm dreaming."

Scooping her up with my free arm, she wrapped both of hers around my neck and tucked her head tight into my shoulder.

"If you want it to be a dream, then a dream it is. Sleep, and I will wake you when we are done here."

With my child in one hand and my sword in the other, I continued onward towards the source of the unnerving compulsion. It did not take long to find it, or so I thought. Cresting the final hexagonal step I was faced with an object that obliged me to pause in fear and wonderment.

Before me, I beheld a monolith of such immense proportion its very existence seemed an impossibility. It possessed not just extreme size but unnatural weight also. It felt as if the very ground was straining to bear it up, and that matter was drawn to it by the magnetic nature of its presence.

Hewn from a fathomless black material, it was framed, on all sides, by borders inscribed with the same heathen scripture as before. The main front panel, on the other hand, appeared to be no more than a smooth black plane. I gasped in awe at the sight of its vastness.

"In his house at R'lyeh, dead Cthulhu waits dreaming," came a dry, fractured voice.

Sword clenched in my fist, I quickly sought its source and soon alighted upon a bundle of rags and sticks huddled in the lee of another base stone.

"Yet his death is but a brief punctuation and his dreams are all but done."

The ragged mound was a man, a Moor like the mariner but twisted and wizened like the roots of an ancient tree. His bare head was scarified with raised signs and sigils, as too was the rest of him. He looked at me with empty, hollow eyes, the sockets raw and caked with dried blood from where the eyeballs themselves had recently been plucked out.

"Do not look upon the tabernacle, lest he set hooks into your soul and make it his."

I pointed the blade at this wraith and clung tightly to Miranda but mercifully she did not stir.

"Speak, old man!" I growled. "Explain this madness to me!"

"You are already his to some measure, else you would not be here, but if you can talk and reason with me then there is still hope for you."

"Not just me but my daughter, also."

This spectre scrambled urgently to its feet with a robustness belying its age.

"There is a child here? Then you must leave while you can!"

"We have no sound ship to speak of. To chance the ocean would be certain death."

"To stay would be worse."

"Why? What is it that so afflicts this troubled place?"

The old man slumped back against the stones, his fleeting burst of strength now draining from him.

"This... this is a site of worship that beggars belief. It is both a temple and tomb for that which never truly lived and so can never die."

"There is magic here?"

"Deeper and darker than you can imagine. It belongs to the Great Old Ones, who came to our young world from the sky long before the ages of man."

He slumped and shrank back onto his haunches.

"They are dead and gone now, as much as such things can die. Entombed, inside the earth, under the sea, but they spoke in dreams to the first men who formed a cult that never died.

"In elder days, chosen men talked with them in dreams until the body of the Earth itself rebelled against them and the dread city of R'lyeh sank beneath the waves. The one primal mystery through which thought cannot pass... but the memory of them never died.

"But it is said that when the stars are right, the great priest Cthulhu will rise from his dark house to bring the world again beneath his sway."

My glance swept across the alien geography that surrounded us.

"And this is it?"

He nodded. His hands folded in his lap were rimed in a deep scarlet crust. His fingernails clogged with a ruddy ichor.

"As much as the Old Ones had their acolytes so too there were others set on keeping them bound beneath the ocean and the earth. When the storm came and the island rose, we thought we were prepared but we were not. I had my tools to bind it, my books and my staff but it was our flesh that was found wanting.

"It preyed upon the weakest of our number, turning them body and mind into its vassals. Those who were stronger fell prey to the abnormal geometry of this loathsome acropolis until only I endured. It sought to make a puppet of me. To read the words and give it egress. I resisted it the only way I could."

Miranda murmured and stirred in my arms. I hushed her and rocked her as I had done when she was a babe.

"You have to leave, for your child's sake!"

"If as you say such darkness is going to be unleashed upon the world, will there be any safe haven from that which lies here?"

"On some remote island, perhaps? Cthulhu is tied to this place and cannot free itself unaided. That is why it tried to use me to open the way. That is why I put out my eyes so it could not use me or my books."

"Then there's nothing to fear."

"There is all to fear, for you are here. You have been touched by magic and it can sense it. That is why it cast wide its web of the elements, to draw you in. And if it cannot use you, it will have your child. These things do not happen by chance."

I felt rage roiling within me like thunderheads.

"Where are your books now?"

"Scattered, by that cyclopean edifice when I spurned my sight. Do not go looking for them, it will take you too close to what lies within."

I already knew what I had to do. I debated whether to leave Miranda behind, but I could not. Whatever fate might befall us, we would face it together. She would not be alone; I would watch over her for the rest of my days. Sensing my departure the old man called out but I paid him no mind.

As we fell under the ominous shadow of that titanic presence all sound seemed to cease. I was reminded, unnervingly, of my recent time in that nether-space. Sweat beaded my face and body yet I shivered with the sudden cold.

There, up ahead I could see the sorcerer's books. An unassuming pair of thick, brown leather tomes fitted with brass clasps and locks as if to keep their contents from breaking free. I crouched down, laying the sword aside to tuck the books into a capacious buckskin satchel that lay close by. The floor was splattered with dark splashes of dried blood and gobbets of matter that I tried not to focus upon. I slipped the strap of the bag over my shoulder.

"Father?"

"Close your eyes, child. Go back to sleep."

It is the nature of children to be contrary, hence she sat up and stirred, surveying her surroundings.

"Where are we? I don't like it!"

There was an edge in her voice, a cracked note of genuine terror.

"What is that?"

She was pointing at the smooth featureless surface of the monolith. I was about to reassure her that there was nothing there when I stifled my words.

There was something – a tall beam of darkness, darker than the rest. A narrow ribbon of a void set between two intractable surfaces. My mind struggled to process what it was seeing when suddenly, instinctively, I took a step back as my body reacted to the revelation before my consciousness had fully absorbed the truth.

It was a door and it was open.

Only a crack, the merest sliver but it was enough. I knew what lay on the other side. I had seen it. I had been there in spirit at least.

"Father!"

I heard Miranda's voice, frantic and full of desperation yet it did not seem to be part of my world. It was as if she was in another room, remote and far removed from my presence. I was transfixed by that black window. It had a gravity all of its own, a singular presence that demanded my all. I had no other desire but to obey what lay beyond above all things.

Then the darkness shifted and I saw a familiar flash of sickly white. It was the eye.

"Fool!" came the cry and a searing blow landed across my back.

I staggered forwards, holding tightly to Miranda. I turned to face the old man, who was brandishing a staff almost as long as he was tall.

"Go! Now! While you still can!"

Stirred from my torpor I barely had time to respond when Miranda indicated several figures that were capering across the rocks with a reptilian gait. Even at this distance I could hear their shrill chittering and their nails scraping like knives upon the stone.

"They're coming! They're coming!" she wailed.

The old man grasped my arm with a fearsome strength and thrust the staff towards me.

"Take it and go!"

My mind was my own once more but I did not know for how long.

I gripped my daughter and the staff and ran back down the incline up which we had so recently struggled. I leapt from step to step praying my footing would hold. I tried not to think about the old man or the terrible, brief scream that cut through the air behind us.

Our woeful boat was still buoyed on the tide where we last saw it. I hastily put Miranda and the satchel inside before jumping aboard and using the staff to push off from the shore.

Several of the things that were once men reached the bay, shrieking and snarling at us as we departed. Some made to leap for the water but scampered back when I held out the staff, ready to defend us to the death. There was power in it and the books too, even if I did not know how to wield it yet, but I would learn.

The current caught us and swiftly yanked our frail refuge out into the wild water. Already the skies were darkening and the seas thrashing, echoing the impotent fury of the beast behind the door at our escaping its clutches.

LIGHTNING SHATTERS THE sky and the tides writhe in torment, but now I have no fear.

We will ride the maelstrom. We will find a safe haven that I will gird with magic to keep the flesh of my flesh safe from harm. I will brush this time from her memory so it takes on but the aspect of a bad dream and keep her innocence unspoilt.

I will steep myself in these books of magic, clothe myself in their words and bend the world about me to my will. I will become the tempest, wrathful and merciless and woe betide any who would seek to test me.

THE SUNS OF YORK

ADRIAN CHAMBERLIN

"Three glorious suns, each one a perfect sun;
Not separated with the racking clouds,
But sever'd in a pale clear-shining sky.
See, see! they join, embrace, and seem to kiss,
As if they vow'd some league inviolable:
Now are they but one lamp, one light, one sun.
In this the heaven figures some event."

Henry VI, Part Three: Act II, Scene I

"When the sun sets, who doth not look for night?"

Richard III, Act II, Scene III

MAY 5TH, 1502 – THE GARDEN TOWER, LONDON

SIR JAMES TYRELL looks a man at peace, at ease with the knowledge he will die on the morrow. But when I hold the lantern closer to allow his secret visitor to gaze upon the traitor's face, to dispel the shadows, darkness remains in the condemned man's features: his eyes are bloodshot and sunken, rimmed with black circles, the mark of one who has not slept for many a night.

He is in his fifty-sixth year, yet seems much older. He is weak from his sleepless nights and his inability to take sustenance – and his slumped, albeit broad shoulders and hunched posture on the edge of his cot show a man whose spirit is utterly broken by his guilt. My fellow jailers believe ghosts do haunt Tyrell when night rules the land, punishing and harrowing him for his role in the Boar's tyrannical rule, that he even bore responsibility for the disappearance of the two princes.

If he was responsible for the killing of the boy-king Edward V and his younger brother Richard, perhaps ghostly visitations are not beyond the bounds of reason, for Tyrell spends his last days in the same fortress the two princes spent theirs. My visitor sneered at me when I told him of the turnkeys' fantasies, ordered me to engage logic and reason over superstition.

That is easy for him to do. A student of law at Inns Court, Thomas More has access to learning I, a humble servant of the Constable of the Tower of London, will never see. He has trained his fine mind to analyse and critique every word spoken by man. His star is in the ascendant; despite his youth, he has been trusted with a very special mission, by royal command no less – albeit one that must needs remain uncertified. Secret.

More is seated at the rough-hewn table, his thin wrists and elbows jutting through the thick black robes like the bones of a bat through its wing membranes. He places his bundle – wrapped in red silk – upon the table and begins to sharpen his quill beside a stack of fresh vellum. His haughty posture and thin-lipped scowl show his disapproval of the surroundings; there is no comfort here. The tapestries and ornamentation of what were once the royal apartments, to lodge important prisoners of state in comfort and dignity, are not to be found in this small turret room. Slime-encrusted brick and cold flagstones are Tyrell's furnishings, a simple wooden cot with straw his sole comfort.

More has begun to write, his fastidious eyes taking in Tyrell's appearance and describing it in slow, careful movements of his quill. If he is surprised at the condition of my prisoner, he does not show it.

Tyrell's face is quizzical; a frown adds to the darkness lining his cragged features, and yet the pupils of his eyes do not constrict when I hold the lantern close to him; they widen, twin pools of blackness that seem to hunger for light rather than shun it.

The candle flame shrinks and the light dims. I blink, then Sir James lowers his eyes to the rough flags of the floor and the lantern shines more brightly.

"Visitor at this hour? Yet you do enter in secrecy – just as I did, all those years and bodies ago."

His voice is deep, the words elegantly delivered yet marred by that course northern accent. This was the voice that commanded armies at Barnet and Tewkesbury, that spoke into the Boar's ear to tell the usurper that his bloody wishes were fulfilled. It is a voice that still carries strength and command, belying the owner's enfeebled body and soul.

It is the voice of evil. I am aware of the dank smell of the chamber, the fresh sweat of the prisoner and the scent of fear, yet the fear is not of us. Sir James Tyrell has seen the bundle Thomas More has placed upon his writing desk. The red silk clings to it, betraying its cruciform structure. His breathing quickens.

I cast my eyes to the transom window. From this elevation Constable Brackenbury's garden is in full view, its early summer flowering a pleasing sight – yet darkness has encroached upon the shrubberies and rosebushes, the trees now silhouettes of distortion as the sun sinks. Only the white roses contain the remains of the summer sunlight, glinting like shards of skulls.

The white rose – the flower of York – now a symbol of death and destruction.

"The Flower of York in its last bloom."

I start at Tyrell's words, and turn from the window. He glowers at me.

"I know the Sun in Splendour, the Sunburst, to be the true symbol of your house," More speaks evenly, softly yet commanding. There is no fear in his tone. "Perhaps you know the king has ordered the symbol be struck from all heraldic devices."

Tyrell nods warily. "Another generation and it will be forgotten history. Perhaps it is for the best."

"That will be for the king to decide, Sir James."

Tyrell laughs. "Will it, sir? What exactly do you know of Richard? Of his reign, of Bosworth, of the two boy princes? Only what your masters tell you. And yet you come here to hear my story. Is Tudor's version of events so poor that even the young disbelieve it?"

Thomas More stands tall, to his full height, and sets his shoulders. "That is not why I am here. My royal master would know the true story of York's fall, from one who was there at the beginning and the end."

Tyrell shakes his head. "'Tis a story that should never be told, *boy*. Go now, believe in the comforting mythology your new lord and master Tudor is busily creating. Forget me."

He stands, and More takes an involuntary step back, surprised at how tall the condemned man is. The disturbed shadows rear around Tyrell, make him appear to rise to the very apex of the arched ceiling itself. There is an unsettling gleam in his dark eyes I have never seen before, as potent as the white glare of his teeth, and I cast an anxious glance over my shoulder to the locked door.

Thomas retakes his seat and attempts to hide his unease. He clears his throat and says, "You advanced highly and quickly through the ranks. By bloodshed. One who lived for slaughter. Quite a butcher's bill you racked up, Sir James. George, Duke of Clarence was your first assassination – yes, we know it was you — then Rivers, Buckingham, Stanley, Grey... All to secure your master's grip on the throne. A common soldier elevated to nobility, an iron fist in a silken glove... a blunt instrument painted with fair and deceptive colours."

Tyrell snorts. "You have a way with words, sir."

"A blunt instrument...but was it Richard who wielded you?" More extends a hand to the bundle and pulls the silk away. Despite the weak light from my lantern and More's candle, it is as though a sun has exploded in the cell.

The silver cross is two feet long. Its gilded foliate borders glitter like starlight; the solid gold circling the roundels of the arms, head and base shine like the midsummer sun.

Tyrell hisses with horror. His withered arm rises to hide the cross from his sight. His limb is hideous in the full glare reflected by the relic: yellow skin covers waxy, lumpy flesh, streaked along the skeletal shaft like melted candle wax. The stumps of his fingers are putrid, open sores, like obscene, cancerous polyps.

"A processional cross recently unearthed from Bosworth, Sir James. As the roundels display the Sun in Splendour – the York emblem – it was sent to the royal court for destruction. Fortunate that I, who am learned in matters of arcane geometry, inspected it first."

He taps the bronze alloy Corpus and the strange, ebony structure that has replaced Christ's head, while averting his eyes from the strange jewel. The light does not reach it; it appears a writhing pool of blackness. "This gem would appear to be of obsidian. It is no such thing. The material of which it is crafted is nowhere to be found on God's Earth, and the angular surfaces carved herein are beyond the wit of any human craftsman. To even look at it for longer than a moment will turn the mind to potage."

Tyrell is trembling. He refuses to look at the cross.

"It is known among the scholars of old as a Shining Trapezohedron, a polyhedron beyond man's capacity – and sanity – to craft." More stares hard at Tyrell. "The Pnakotic Manuscripts call it the Shining Splendour of Azathoth. The name Azathoth was last heard at Richard's court, one of the many curses uttered by Margaret of Anjou.

"Tell me of Margaret, Sir James. Tell me of the powers invoked after Tewkesbury. Of the sundering of the seal that separates this world from the next. Tell me what you know of the Shining Splendour of Azathoth."

Tyrell lowers his cancerous limb and fixes More with those hypnotic pools of blackness that have seen so much death and horror.

"It was birthed in the battlefield... in the burst of a sun..."

MAY 4TH, 1471 – THE RIVER AVON, ONE MILE SOUTHWEST OF TEWKESBURY ABBEY

WHEN THE LIGHT exploded, I forgot everything. I forgot the oppressive heat of the morning, the smell of spent gunpowder and smoke from both sides' artillery, the fallen arrows that turned the battlefield into a giant pin-pillow, the hot blood that stained my plate armour and filled my nostrils with the stench of death. I forgot the fearful whinnies of our dismounted horses, half a mile to our south.

I forgot the fear that had gripped our battle, the vanguard commanded by the king's youngest brother, Richard of Gloucester. And I forgot how the fear turned to joy with the success of our surprise force of over two hundred spearmen in the evil lanes of the wooded section of the Colnbrook that became a tributary of blood, feeding the Avon with the spilled life fluid of men from both Houses.

Until the sunburst we saw nothing but the billmen, rising from the hidden ditches within the ancient oak woods, their glittering curved blades surmounted by top and rear spikes atop ash poles that stretched to the sky, seemingly sprung from the depths of Hell to wipe out the Duke of Somerset's battle. And Hell is what we descended into, gladly and gleefully.

Their front formation fell to our pikes, three hundred men suddenly disembowelled, their innards entangling with the ancient roots that had pressed through the leaf litter and topsoil like the exhumed remains of ancient serpents, and our billmen dropped their halberds and finished them off with dagger and shortsword. Lightly armoured in sallets, mail standards and brigandines, the billmen had lost their advantage of surprise and distance and would be no match for the heavy plate armour, swords and maces of Somerset's advance had they not been joined by Richard's battle: innumerable soldiers in their own plate armour, wielding our own mace and sword.

We descended into the maelstrom of the *mêlée*, where each man lost sight of his comrades and commanders and fought for his own survival in a world of crashing blades, pierced plate and gored flesh, spurting hot blood that blinded, and barely human howls of agony that deafened.

The Lancastrian forces of the deposed king, Henry VI, and Queen Margaret, advancing from the north over the patchwork ground of foul lanes, hedges, and deep dykes, outnumbered us by over one thousand men. But not one hour ago King Edward IV, in a stirring address accompanied by an angelic chorus of trumpets, amidst a blaze of banners bearing the Flower of York, birthing within a glorious golden sun, had convinced us we would prevail.

Our eyrie is built in the highest cedar's top, dallies with the wind, and scorns the sun. For God is with the House of York.

The trees grew in height, reared above us and shut us into darkness; we fought without the blessing of sunlight, for now the sun scorned us.

A mace crashed into my side and I spun, almost falling to the churned ground. I arrested the second blow with my sword, pushed the pommel into the open visor of the armoured man and saw his mouth erupt in a shower of blood and broken teeth. I slashed, thrust back, and he crashed to the ground. To my left I saw our commander, Richard of Gloucester, his helm cast aside and terror in his youthful eyes, and I hesitated.

Richard was only eighteen, ten years my junior, but a natural leader whose prowess put more seasoned warriors to shame; he had distinguished himself on the fog-strewn battlefield at Barnet the previous month.

All that was now forgotten. He sank to the churned mud and carnage, on his knees, his sword abandoned. His hands clasped together, misshapen in steel gauntlets, and his head tilted forward.

Praying, in the midst of battle! A cold fury took me, to see our commander abandoning his natural ability and martial experience, to commend his soul to God rather than inspire his men to battle to the last breath. This is the moment when battles are lost: when men look to their lord and commander for strength and see only a mewling boy, resorting to grovelling on the ground like a tiny wren, hiding from mightier birds of prey.

"Richard!" I shouted, the protocol of using his title forgotten. My voice echoed through the slaughter field and I saw several combatants flinch. I strode toward him, stepping over opened corpses.

"Gloucester! To me, man!" I was within yards of him. He must have heard me, for I clearly heard his whispered words, his fevered exhortations – but I could not understand them. I froze.

His black hair was matted and drenched with sweat that ran down his lopsided cheeks. His words became guttural, his face distorted by a snarl, his thick lips twisted and drawn back from his uneven teeth so the prayer became even less intelligible – the snuffling, questing sounds of a boar. He shrank into himself, his drooping right shoulder exacerbating the crookback that his custom pauldrons usually disguised so well.

The darkness grew; shadows lengthened, hiding the carrion of battle carnage in their sinuous blackness. Plate armour and sharpened blades no longer reflected the summer sunlight – they became blurred, grey shapes from which the light shrank. I glanced up, and saw nothing above the treeline but thickening greyness, like the fog that had obscured the battlefield at Barnet.

But *darkening*. This was no repeat of Barnet; this was no natural mist. I looked down to the still muttering Richard, but the darkness was absolute. I put my hand out to where my ears told me he would be, laid gauntleted fingers on steel pauldron.

I felt fire, the overlapping steel and leather coverings no protection from the heat that scorched my fingers. An angry hiss interrupted the incantation, rolling into a roar that shook the grove. The ground trembled, the invisible fire continued to consume my hand, and then the light exploded.

I did not know its source – it came from all around me, from above me, below me... and *through* me, blinding me to my surroundings. It was not the golden light of a glorious summer sunrise, nor the cold glare of a harvest moon. It was not the harsh flickering fire of a candle trapped behind a magnifying glass, not the fierce rage of an inferno.

It was a light that is beyond my powers to describe, and yet there was something familiar about it. A feeling that I had seen its like before, many years ago. All I can say is that at the time, I felt I was being remade, forged in some unearthly furnace; *reborn*. And then I knew where and when I had seen this light before.

It was the light we all see just before we enter the world. When we leave the darkness of our mother's womb, just before we take our first breath to scream and cry with anguish at the pain of being alive. A light we forget immediately after, because man's mind is not able to ponder the awful power of the light of Creation.

I was a man, with a man's sensibilities and a man's knowledge of the world. I was not meant to see this light. To *feel* it, to *hear* it. To *taste* it, to *breathe* it.

To live it.

To be conscious of the things that exist within the light, and beyond it. Things that were aware of my presence, my intrusion, and turned what passed for eyes upon me.

I heard the roars of demons that were too horrific even for Hell, heard the fluting melodies of beings that were more beautiful than the most blessed seraphim in Heaven and I do not know which ones terrified me the most.

The light vanished before my mind turned in on itself. For the second time in my existence, I was deposited upon the physical reality of this world, amid the blood and carnage of my fellow sufferers, and I wept anew at my rebirthing.

Only when I became aware of physical sensations – of the water soaking my skin through my carapace of leather and steel plate; of the cramp in my legs from where I had lain unconscious; of the feel of cold, damp stone under my tear-streaked cheeks; of the metallic aroma of blood and spent life that assailed my nostrils; of the cries of disembowelled men thrashing and drowning in their own blood as the sons of York despatched them from this world; of the shivering of my body and the thirst that afflicts all men after battle – only then was I able to connect with this Earth once more, to be aware of my surroundings.

The ancient woodland had gone, changed for the cool sanctuary of the Norman splendour of Tewkesbury Abbey where Queen Margaret of Lancaster had sought sanctuary. Dying bodies twitched and writhed among the shattered pews of the nave, their spears splintered, the pikes bright with their owners' blood which fed the chill air with spectral wisps of steam as it cooled. In lifeless heaps of steel plate and mail, the broken bodies of armoured knights lay like destroyed siege engines. I examined one with trepidation, frowned at the blistered holes, glowing red hot, gouged into steel plate by what looked to be *hooves*...

I crossed myself hastily, an attempt to abjure the Dark One. For surely, only Satan and his children could make such footprints. The sun shone timidly through the glass windows, as if fearful of shining its light on the carnage and horror beneath it.

I got to my feet, my boots squelching with blood and river water where I had crossed the Avon in a trance. I looked for my sword, felt relief when I saw the familiar pommel – and horror and disbelief when I saw where the blade was embedded.

I would never be able to use the weapon again; the sword tip had punctured the knight's breastplate as though it were butter, the blade passed through and buried, impossibly, two feet into the stone flags of the sanctuary floor. Its edges glowed scarlet and blood sizzled and steamed where it met the escaping life fluid from the dead man's chest.

His visor was open, and his eyes stared at me with a look of horror that must surely have accompanied him to death. The gold circlet on his helm that marked him to be the young Lancastrian heir to the throne, Edward, Prince of Wales, was spattered with blood.

A loud keening reached my ears, an unmistakably female voice filled with grief and despair, cruelly amplified and distorted by the strange acoustics of the abbey church. I looked to its source, and a shadow shuffled across the altar. I regarded it, watched it unfold and rise, take shape with wings of scarlet and precious stones. And yet the grief on Margaret of Anjou's face was not for her dead son, lying pinned to the stones of the House of God. Her despair was directed to the vaulted roof, as though asking God Himself for forgiveness.

"I am Mother of Ruin." Her hands clutched to her heaving, shivering breast what I took to be the silver and gold processional cross taken into battle by the Prince of Wales. "A cockatrice hath I hatched to the world... Lord God, forgive me. Pour all your tears unto me, mankind, for I am your sorrow's nurse."

"*All will have cause to wail the dimming of your shining star, my lady.*"

I froze. The new words seeped into my ears, floating like mist, ethereal and unearthly, but there was no mistaking the voice.

Richard, Duke of Gloucester.

"*Tyrell. Turn and face me. Face your master... your king.*"

Edward IV, his brother, was alive, outside the abbey – I heard the triumphant rally of trumpets and heard the King's cries of thanksgiving to God, saw glimpses of banners bearing the Sun in Splendour through the parts of the altar window that had not been sheathed in blood.

Margaret took her eyes from the ceiling and her arms dropped when she beheld the thing that spoke behind me. The cross slipped from her fingers and I gasped at the carved figure within the radiant sunbursts. Christ's body writhed, the holy agony of His Passion, yet a blasphemy was embedded where His head should be. A black, gleaming gemstone, carved in crazed angles that reflected and refracted light that suddenly coalesced, focussed upon the man it knew observed it.

And now *I* was observed. A black portal opened to another realm where alien intelligences regarded me with hunger.

I took a deep, shuddering breath and turned, choosing instead to face a new horror.

No monster greeted me. Instead, Richard of Gloucester stood before the dispatched Prince of Wales. Fingers slowly unfolded from the hilt of the sword buried in the knight's chest, extended like serpents, and the hand rose, palm upwards.

I could see little of his face until the light that was his halo, as bright as a sunburst, faded. And the smile on his face was that of a saint.

"*Loyaulté me Lie.*"

May 5th, 1502 - The Garden Tower, London

"Loyalty binds me." Thomas More whispers the words, the translation of Richard III's personal motto. He has been as enraptured by Tyrell's account of Tewkesbury as I; his quill has not moved once.

"We were both bound to each other – but not by military brotherhood. Not by familial ties or duty. It was a loyalty that was forced upon us by... by the thing that came through the gate. Remember: I held his arm when the invocation finished. Our destinies were joined at that moment."

He grimaces and glances at his crooked arm.

"King Edward knighted me for my valour, soon after Henry VI met his end in the Tower at Richard's hand. Richard did sing splendidly of my actions to his royal brother, made me to be the hero of the engagement. 'The Soaring Eagle of Tewkesbury.' A mass murderer in the House of God, in the service of the House of York."

A grim smile twists his features. "I had no recollection of my journey from the ancient wood to the abbey, and only Richard bore witness to my killing of the Prince of Wales, and my slaughter of dozens of surviving Lancastrian knights."

I pause. The slaughter had been so great the abbey had to be closed for over a month until it was purified and reconsecrated. I tried to imagine the scene, the blood... I could not.

"King Henry *was* murdered, then." More is more focused on the lives – and deaths – of notable figures; the fates of the common soldiery is of little import to him. "Why did Edward allow his brother to do that? Did his conscience not trouble him?"

Tyrell laughs, without mirth. "Do you know what Richard said, to the newly restored King of England? "Conscience is but a word that cowards use. Our strong arms be our conscience, swords our law.' Edward did not resist; he shrank, allowed Richard to snuff out Henry's life. He even agreed to Richard's demand to have Margaret present to witness the killing."

Thomas has begun to write again. The writing is faster, the nib louder, scratching like rats in the walls.

"Bathed in that eldritch sunburst, the wren became an eagle." Tyrell grimaces. "But a darker bird of prey you would not find. His new direction was fuelled by what Margaret had unleashed."

"And you did aid him."

He glowers; the black pools of his eyes glitter. "Of course, I was his bondsman. 'Bound in chains of loyalty, forged by the light from the grove, my dear Tyrell. My servant and brother in darkness.' We were cursed, Master More, by our rebirth in that sunburst – we saw the realm of gods older than this world and the void that hungers to consume all.

"Human acts, politics, war, power plays – and the love and kinship we feel for each other – all these are nothing in the great scope of the universe. That is why I murdered with impunity, with no thought to my soul or the grieving of wives and children left behind.

"Richard could ask me to do what others could not. I worked in the shadows, as befits a creature of the night."

15TH AUGUST, 1483 - THE WHITE TOWER, LONDON

I LEFT THE shadows of the garden and felt those within the tower envelop me. I greeted Constable Brackenbury with a feeling of déjà vu. Five years previously I arrived here with murderous intent and royal sanction. Then, the snow and frost of that January night bit hard and deep but I did not need the heat of the cressets and torches within the bloody tower to warm me. I had engaged upon murder with alacrity and energy, joyful in my purpose. To secure the crown by despatching the dissembling Duke of Clarence, a man who had proven his unworthiness at Bosworth – even then, King Edward had kept him in his battle because he could not trust his eldest son. To drown him in the Malmsey butt was a novel experience for me; my despatch of the realm's foes had been in combat, with steel and wood, sword and armour. This was assassination, a cowardly way of ending a man's life, but the ends justified the means.

I had no such certainty this night. The golden twilight, the dimming of a glorious summer sun, gave way to a darkness blacker than that winter night. My heart was heavy, my conscience bare.

Children. A threat to the crown? Their bastardy was obvious now the dead King Edward IV's illegitimacy had been proven, but that was not enough for my master.

I would have abandoned my mission, defied the Lord Protector. No ends could justify the murder of children. The entreaty that these two were enemies of the kingdom was a feeble lie and only a monster would follow it through.

And yet, were these not monsters? Margaret's reckless invocation to Azathoth had gone far beyond eclipsing the three suns of York. Perhaps it would make no difference. Perhaps it would be a mere stay of execution for the realm, which was surely cursed when that sunburst fell upon earthly ground at Tewkesbury.

Brackenbury had aged greatly since I had seen him; the custodianship of the heirs to the throne had placed great worry upon him. He knew the threat to them would come from within the bloodline, not via a foreign enemy.

"Sir James," he said gruffly. He cast a cursory eye over the commission I handed him and grimaced. "Once more I am commanded to give you the keys for a night. This time, no names are mentioned. And this time, Dighton does not accompany you; you enter alone."

I did not reply. I would damn no other soul than my own, which was already commended to the Dark Ones that hid behind the shining veil. Brackenbury shook his greying head and handed me the keys.

"I trust your reward will be bountiful for what you are about to do."

I did not reply. I weighed the black iron keys in my good hand while he departed. They felt so heavy, like shackles to the direst torture chamber in Hell which surely awaited me.

I ascended the winding stairs slowly to the royal apartments, noting the fine tapestries and ornamentation that failed to disguise the true purpose of these chambers: a prison. A waiting room for death. Yet they were truly innocent, of their purpose in the tower and what awaited them; I heard their boyish laughter and wondered what games they played to occupy themselves.

The laughter ceased when they heard the key turn in the lock. I swung the door and attempted my most accommodating smile, but I had smiled little since entering Richard's service, and it must have showed. The golden-haired boys, sitting cross-legged on the hearth rug, took fright at my appearance and jumped to their feet, darting back to the four poster bed. Taking fright like tiny wrens when a mighty eagle sweeps upon them...

The Soaring Eagle of Tewkesbury. A murderer of wrens. I am certain my attempt at a smile turned even deeper into a rictus.

"Be at ease, Royal Highnesses." I walked into the chamber, my hands raised in supplication. "I come with gifts from your uncle."

They didn't reply. The younger prince, Richard, buried his head in his brother's chest. Edward V regarded me haughtily, confidence renewed by his role as protector of his brother.

"Uncle Richard has not visited us since we came. Are his duties so onerous that he cannot visit his nephews?"

I shook my head. "The Lord Protector is securing your inheritance from the enemies who wish you dead, Your Highness. His absence from you grieves him most painfully, but his duty to your throne must needs take preference."

Self-hatred at my lies speared me, and I averted my eyes. The fire burned deeply and welcome, its flames casting illumination on the richly-coloured illustrations of the book they had been studying. I recognised the book, and the inscriptions in the margins. Richard's handwriting, his own copy of *The History of Troy*. I knelt down and turned the book, smiling at the page's contents.

The passage described the advantages of fighting in the company of friends who share a common purpose despite overwhelming odds, and Richard's words "note well the fair words" underscored the picture of a mother wren defending its nestlings from a sweeping eagle.

I stared at the picture, then turned the page. The fate of the wrens was unwritten, but inevitable.

Unwritten. It must be so for these wrens of York also. Not just their despatch from this world, of which I knew history would judge me, but the means of doing so also.

MAY 5TH, 1502 - THE GARDEN TOWER, LONDON

MORE CANNOT HIDE his excitement. His eyes glint in the darkening, and sweat beads his forehead. His quill feather flutters; the scratching is clamorous. He is overjoyed to hear the confession at last, to resolve the mystery – and doubtless advance his ascendant star in Tudor's court.

He halts when Tyrell describes the means of despatch. He pales, his jaw drops, and his writing hand flies to his gaping mouth in terror.

I too am filled with horror at Tyrell's description, and his vivid recall of the horrifying details of the event. So much conjecture and supposition surrounds the fate of the princes, and now Tyrell has confirmed not only that they did indeed meet their end by suffocation but that mankind can resort to such blasphemous treatment of deceased bodies.

What is worse is that he relates the story with no guilt. A duty to be fulfilled, a job to be done.

"I was content when I opened their bodies, and saw what lay within. I knew then I was wrong to feel apprehension and pity. These were indeed monsters."

More throws his quill to the floor in disgust. "Monsters? You smothered, then *butchered*, the most replenished sweet work of nature – Man!"

Tyrell stares at him, with those emotionless, gaping black voids. He indicates the quill on the flagged floor. "Doubtless you will rewrite this, Master More, make it to be a tyrannous and bloody deed. You will emphasise their innocence, perhaps even exchange the book of war for a book of prayers? 'Twas no piteous massacre – 'twas extermination."

More eyes him balefully, not fearful of Tyrell's black eyes. "Did you say such when you brought these tidings to your bloody king? Was he as… indifferent to human suffering as you?"

"I was Knight of the Body. I slept on a pallet outside his bedchamber to guarantee his night's rest, but he slept little."

"Fearful is night to the guilty," More says, a little smug.

Tyrell shrugs. "Guilt did not trouble him. His mind had turned in on itself, became consumed with naked ambition. It is ironic that the human qualities he retained were evil ones; he rejoiced in slaughter. Yet it was all planned, all machinery in the engine of the curse."

"Sir James, you mentioned the 'eclipse of the sons of York. The Mother of Ruin.' Please elaborate."

"The eclipse... Think back to the battle at Mortimer's Cross, when our forces saw three suns rise on the morning of what would be our victory. Edward took it as a sign of God's favour – three suns rising, like the Holy Trinity, like the three brothers of York. Small wonder we thought God was with the House of York. And Margaret of Anjou was there; she witnessed this also. How long did she study, and what black tomes did she recite, for the right invocation to imitate this celestial phenomenon? To turn our sign of Holy Favour against us, to curse us with the dying of the sun – by each son of York?

"At Tewkesbury she realised, too late, that her invocation had worked against her. Two suns of York would fall to darkness, 'tis true. But the third one *became* darkness. When I spoke to her, I learned of the folly of those who would summon the power of the Old Ones. I learned that Azathoth is the ultimate source of power in the universe; He cares nothing for human affairs. But His servants do. They hunger for man's folly to open portals, to enter and feast royally on what we offer..."

DECEMBER 21ST, 1483 - THE RIVER AVON, ONE MILE SOUTHWEST OF TEWKESBURY ABBEY

LIKE ME, MARGARET was a creature of the shadows, and those of the court believed it was grief and despair that made her turn away from the sun. She looked older, more frail, with each day that had passed since her husband's and son's killings. Grief had consumed her and turned her in on herself, changed her from a noble and imperious queen to a twisted and harrowed crone who wandered the stone corridors of the royal palace, muttering curses and strange incantations.

There was no reason to keep her at court, but the Lord Protector – now King Richard III – would not allow her to return to Burgundy. It was deliberate cruelty to keep the royal widow at the Palace of Westminster, a trophy of war, to remind her of what her House had lost; to make her breathe, smell, taste, experience royal power without holding any. It would drive anyone insane, let alone one who had lost her husband and son to the man who gloried in kingly power.

That was before Richard's true madness. Before his body began to decay and the monstrous hump on his back grew to obscene proportions. Before the withering of his sword arm.

See how I am bewitched. Behold, mine arm is like a blasted sapling withered up. This is that Edward's wife, that monstrous witch, that by witchcraft thus has marked me.

"Well met, Sir James. How goes the court since my banishment?"

My steed hesitated, unwilling to go further, as if he too shared my memory of the sunburst enveloping me on this exact spot, twelve years ago. "Richard has appointed me Captain of Guisnes Castle; I am to leave for Calais this night. I am pleased to leave court – despite your departure, it remains full of womanly cursing. The Duchess of York, and now Lady Anne – mother, and reluctant wife – they all sound just like you. But now there are less ears to hear them. Rivers, Grey, Vaughan. Now Hastings – all despatched."

"By your hand, Sir James." There was no judgement in her voice, nor even question. A statement of fact.

I nodded. "Grey's last words were 'Now Margaret's curse is fallen upon our heads, for standing by when Richard stabbed her son'."

She laughed at that. "My curse? Ah, if only it *was* mine…"

I dismounted and unhitched the leather sack from the saddle's pommel, grimacing at the feel of the things sloshing within. I walked through the frozen leaf litter, my boots crunching. Margaret stood in the very spot where her son Edward had been despatched. The dying winter sun turned the snowbound tree branches to bloodstained limbs, and as it sank further it illumined her dress and furs. The threadbare, faded red brocade and silk now turned shades of bright scarlet and bloody crimson. No scarf or headdress shielded her head from the winter cold. Her breath did not mist in the evening air.

I noticed soil on her fingers, which were curled inwards like claws. I wondered what she had been digging. Or burying...

Margaret cocked her head at my arm, still hidden within my riding cloak. "And how does your arm fare, Sir James?"

The ride from London had been hard, every frozen byway and snowbound track an obstacle. My left arm was now unable to grip anything, and I shuddered at how much it resembled the king's.

Bound in chains of loyalty, forged by the light from the grove, my dear Tyrell. My servant and brother in darkness.

Queen Margaret smiled at precisely the same moment the thought crossed my mind. Here we stood, in the same grove where the light had shone in awful splendour to herald the end of the Lancaster line and the ascension of York. Where my hand had touched Richard's. A joint withering, an unmistakable sign that Richard and I were bound in bloody destiny. Damned.

"It has worsened since the princes' departure, my lady. Each day that passes, it withers more."

She nodded thoughtfully, no satisfaction or regret on her pursed features. "And none in the court suspect?"

"No, my lady. Only Richard and you know."

"Richard... And his crookback grows ever worse?"

"Aye, my lady. He is near bent to the ground when he rises; I do swear the hump has doubled in size since I saw him last. And..."

"It does move of its own volition, does it not?"

I shuddered, and knew it was not from the cold.

"Many times have I watched night turn to dawn with him in my arms, weeping with terror. I cannot comfort him... and I feel the life within his crookback. It does terrify me."

"Well it may, Sir James. Well it may." She turned and stared through the skeletal trees, where the sun touched the spires of Tewkesbury Abbey and turned them bronze and honeyed gold. There was a wistful look on her face. "I have not dared set foot on that holy ground since the death of my husband. I have... profaned it. Two suns of York have been eclipsed, yet the third remains. And through him the whole world will face eternal darkness, scorned forever by the real sun."

There was a similarity in this meeting to our first. In the royal chapel, following her crazed wanderings – not on the Lord Protector's orders, but out of my own curiosity – when she believed she was alone, and I heard her new incantation.

No mere curse this one. The words were of an unintelligible and hateful language – one that sounded as though inscribed by daemons in a corner of Hell even Satan dared not tread. Only the recollection of having heard them before made me pause.

Before they had been uttered by an eighteen-year-old duke. Watching her mouth twist and sweat pour down her cheeks, her spindle arms shaking as though fighting the invisible bars of some unearthly prison, the tone of *beseeching* and the wail of despair that whatever entity she prayed to would not listen, did not even care for her pain, made me realise what had happened in the grove and then at the abbey of Tewkesbury.

Richard, Duke of Gloucester, had not made this prayer willingly, or indeed knowingly. The unholy hymn had been spoken *through* him, by a female enemy who had called upon a darker, more ancient adversary to destroy the House of York.

I had never seen such despair on a woman's face before. This was the expression of one who, with the murder of her husband and son, surely had nothing to lose. And yet the grief on her face proved otherwise. Grief for what was to befall mankind, for the curse she had uttered with supernatural agency, defiling the House of God with invocations to an ancient evil to eclipse the three suns of York.

I had gone to her, allowed her to weep on my shoulder. Allowed her to tell me what she had done, what she had damned humanity to in her impetuous quest to destroy York by methods otherworldly and profane.

I prayed for the Sun of York to dim, for night to reign over its royal blood, Sir James. I embedded the Shining Splendour of Azathoth upon Our Lord's Passion and thus created that Sunburst at Tewkesbury. I broke the Seal, rendered the Veil, and opened the world to darkness. Earth gapes, Hell burns, fiends roar, and saints can no longer pray.

I would not have believed her, had she not shown me the light once more, birthed in that terrible dark jewel within the processional cross she had prayed upon at Tewkesbury, And then, when my arm began to wither, listened to what had to be done to prevent the curse spreading to all humanity.

Now I followed her gaze toward the shining abbey, resplendent in the dying winter sun, and the nagging, ever-present pain in my withered arm reminded me that I too am shunned by Grace. The glass windows in the nave turned scarlet; the river became a burnished lake of bronze. I remembered the slaughter of the Lancastrian men when they sought sanctuary there, and it seemed their blood had returned to ooze through the stones to remind me. Sacrilegious slaughter, and no holy sanctuary for me now.

The sun dipped below the horizon; the remnants of sunlight died, and the ancient wood consumed us with darkness. My horse whinnied in fear, and I heard scrabbling and scratching noises from behind. I turned, my heart pounding.

There was nothing to see in the dark, but I was aware of the presence. Something that stalked on hooves...

"You have the offering? Open it; place it by my feet."

I did as I was bid. I saw the freshly-churned soil, not more than a hand-span in length, and knew where she had placed the Sunburst. I imagined traces of that infernal light glowed through the soil.

And now, to reseal the portal...

The lungs and hearts were shrivelled, lifeless lumps of tissue that were even smaller since the night I had taken them from the young princes. The bowels were like dried bladderwrack, brown and leathery and bulbous. I had accidentally punctured one of the polyps during the drying ritual, and the sight of the embryonic monster within caused me to jump from the fire in terror.

The blood had been carefully drained from the bodies while on board ship to Flanders; not a single knife entry was made until the ground of England gave way to sea. Only then were the bodies opened, the blood drained into a Malmsey butt; the flesh parted from bone and placed within a second butt with the removed skins. The first butt consigned to the Black Deeps at the mouth of the Thames, under the gibbous moon and the recitation of the verse Margaret had ordered me to memorise.

The life-fluid was for the Lord Father of Deep Ones, that He may be content with the children's blood sanctified by Azathoth's Shining

Splendour and forebear from raising the levels of his watery realm to engulf England.

Everything else was to be taken to the site which birthed the Shining Splendour of Azathoth. The bodily remains of the two children lay like rags, and broken tree branches, and desiccated seaweed under the moonlight. I stood, retreated on trembling legs while Margaret advanced with her powder. She took a deep breath, closed her eyes and visibly willed herself to recite the words that so haunted me.

A second incantation, but harsher, more forceful, rather than the pleading of before. Not a summoning, but a banishing. I held my breath, steeled myself for the return of the light.

MAY 5TH, 1502 – THE GARDEN TOWER, LONDON

"AND THEN?" MORE is captivated by this episode. He leans over his ledger, as though his body is pulled into Tyrell's orbit by the dark, sucking pools of the condemned man's black eyes.

"Nothing. The light did not return. There was no sign of any response to her incantation, and we departed in utter despair. I to Calais, where I busied myself in my Guisnes duties, hoping to forget what England was to become. Margaret I never saw again – but I will never forget the sight of her standing over the spot where the Shining Splendour had birthed, where the remains of children were buried, and where the sun refused to shine. I have never seen such desolation. Richard once said, 'Let not the heavens hear these tell-tale women rail on the Lord's anointed.' And it appeared his dark prayer was answered; Margaret's was not.

"But distance from England made no difference. My arm continued to wither and my nights were filled with horrors. I shared Clarence's dream of drowning and Stanley's nightmare of a boar triumphant over England. I saw Clarence rise from the Malmsey butt like a serpentine sea beast from the deepest abyss, spilling blood that filled the tower and overflowed, drowning England. I saw a boar with Richard's face, and its crookback sundered to pour forth unspeakable abominations that burrowed into battlefield corpses and fed mightily, and animated the dead, giving them new life to ravage the kingdom with bloody strokes and mortal-shearing warfare forever.

"I dreamed of the princes, whose eyes were black, empty voids in which the light of stars birthed, lived, and died in an instant, and who gleefully told me: *The Seal has been broken by Anjou, the Mother of Ruin. Azathoth's dread servants are building a mighty eyrie to nest in, which will scorn your sun. And we will make prey.*

"I did not need the weekly dispatches to know the kingdom suffered under the usurper. I knew I was jointly responsible for the tyranny and despaired with the realisation there was nothing I could do, that it would only worsen. Until the following spring, when the sign that had so cruelly evaded Margaret shone in the heavens."

More looks momentarily confused. He flicks through his documents, frowning.

"16th of March, 1485," Tyrell says with a hint of reproach. "The death of Richard's queen. She passed on the same day as the sun was eclipsed by the moon."

More's hand trembles on the sheaf of papers.

"Even in Calais I saw it," Tyrell continues. "While some took it to be the final sign of England's damnation, that the Lancaster queen cruelly usurped by Richard had passed and God hid His sight from the world in despair, I saw what others could not."

His black eyes glisten. "I saw hope. I saw through the darkness, saw the light *beyond* this veil fade and vanish – and I knew the curse could be lifted.

"It was the same month Henry Tudor raised Wales and I knew: the Shining Splendour of Azathoth had birthed on the battlefield, so logic dictated it had to die on the battlefield. Two of York's suns had been extinguished, yet the third remained triumphant, his rays shedding darkness and damnation upon a benighted land. It was I who would eclipse him, and I knew how to do it. I had to return to England, fight Richard, and ensure his departure would seal the portal."

More's quill falls from his fingers. His jaw drops. "You fought at Bosworth. That is why King Henry did not punish you as he did the other Yorkists, why he accepted your service."

Tyrell nods. "I was at Bosworth. I note your king did not see fit to inform you of this. We are both being used, Thomas More. I a blunt instrument, you a more… elegant one. Yet used as tools by greater powers – who do not realise they themselves are toyed with by forces older and more terrible than Satan Himself – even older than the one who cast Satan from Heaven."

AUGUST 22ND, 1485 - BOSWORTH FIELD

SPEARS GUARANTEED YORK'S victory at Tewkesbury, and now spears would see the House fall at Bosworth. It would be a fitting end for the Boar.

I was welcomed to the armies of Richmond with open arms. I was not the first to turn coat against the usurper, and I would not be the last; Lord Stanley and his brother Sir William would commit their forces to the Tudor cause when the battle was at its height, and help Richmond win the day.

I had no men or arms with me, but I had intelligence of King Richard, how his mind worked, what tactics he would employ. That was enough, and I breathed a sigh of relief when I made my leave from Richmond's tent, thankful he had not asked me about my true reason for turning my coat. Yet I remember his hooded eyes resting on the chain around my neck, the bulge it made under my doublet. I remember the faint smile, and I wondered what he and Margaret of Anjou had discussed.

The Sunburst, the instrument of the eclipse of the suns of York, was no longer fearful to me. Digging it up from the failed sacrificial site at Tewkesbury had filled my heart with joy rather than fear. The hunger pulsing from that black and terrible jewel was still there, but I knew now I could turn this hunger to England's advantage.

"Sir James."

I halted at Richmond's softly-spoken, sinuous words.

"We thank you for your counsel. Yet, we would know more of the supernatural course that York is bent upon." He beckoned me, spoke in a whisper. "I know of the dreams that affect the Boar, for they did visit me."

"Dreams, my lord?"

Henry's knowing smile chilled me. "Rivers, Grey, Vaughan… Hastings, Buckingham… King Henry and the Prince of Wales. The princes in the tower. Their spirits did visit me, promising me victory, and cursing Richard. They spoke ill of you too, Sir James… *the instrument of their deaths*. Yet Lady Anne's ghost spoke well: 'Good angel will guard thee from the Boar's annoy; Tyrell be his name, and his spear will strike for joy.' What am I to make of this, Sir James?"

I thought quickly. "I would put little stock in dreams, my lord. Although… I was a billman once. My skill with staff and halberd will not have faded."

Richmond nodded. "That you were. At Mortimer's Cross, I believe."

I felt my cheeks grow hot. "You know my past well, my lord."

"I know *you* very well, Sir James. So be it: you shall be in the pike wall. I hope you will forgive me if I do not put you in a position of command; it will be better for you if the battle goes against me and the Boar prevails, that you be unseen and escape.

"I trust, however, that your withered arm does not make bearing a pike *too* arduous…"

These words ran through my mind as I watched the beginning of Richard's cavalry charge. Already the eighteen-foot stave with its steel head wavered in my hands, exacerbated by the near-uselessness of my withered left arm, but the sight of the Boar leading the charge with several hundred men – his whole battle – made even the experienced billmen around me, Frenchmen and Welshmen, tremble.

It was not the numbers of the Yorkist force that unnerved them, but the monster which led them. Even I was shocked.

Over his armour was a loose-fitting scarlet robe bearing the royal coat of arms and his personal badge, the white boar triumphant. And his face was the very personification of this rampaging beast.

Twisted, snarling, his lower teeth jutting like tusks, gleaming in the sun that shone behind us – and against him – and his body hunched over his huge mare like a gigantic spider clutching it and injecting venom, his crookback tight against his robe, bulging, pulsing like the spider's abdomen ready to give birth to monstrosities.

"Spur your proud horses hard, and ride in blood!"

Even his voice sounded different. Loud like thunder, echoing through even our massed ranks, and without a trace of desperation

"It was not the numbers of the Yorkist force that unnerved them, but the monster which led them."

Illustration by Tiernen Trevallion

or self-doubt. It promised death and destruction and made virtues of both, and his men loved him for it. Even I felt a stirring and a pang of loss, forever excluded from the company of York's warriors that had been my only family.

I shook myself. I saw the monster, and knew what he presaged; his followers did not, or had been blinded by the glory of York.

Richmond dismounted to present a less visible target. Pikemen pulled back from the vanguard, dropping back at a run, and closed round to protect him, forming a square that cavalry would be unable to penetrate: the Swiss Formation.

The front rank knelt with pikes sloping upward, the second behind them with their halberds angled, the third – of which I was a member – with pikes horizontal, at waist level.

Still the Boar and his mounted army came. The sun rose behind us, a disadvantage for an approaching army caught in its glare, yet the momentum of the horses carried them on, and Richard exulted. His eyes shone black in the reflected sunlight and his head tilted, a cry of joy roaring.

Just as I saw light, hope of salvation in the absence of sunlight after Lady Anne's death, he saw something that thrilled him in the blight glare of our most natural, wonderful, God-given sun – he could only have seen darkness, and gloried in it.

He bore no shield, and his sword remained sheathed in its scabbard, dangling from the saddle's pommel. His battleaxe was in his left hand, and looked unsteady; his right arm dangled uselessly by his side.

I gritted my teeth, sweat drenching my forehead underneath the leather liner of my sallet, pike wavering in my unsteady and unequal grasp, and my left arm felt numb, as lifeless as Richard's sword arm. Our shared sign of damnation, our martial weakness.

The York charge did not break until it struck the second rank. The horses careered into our Swiss Formation, impaled by steel, shattering pike shafts and unseating their riders. Sheared horseflesh and blood filled our vision, screams of man and steed echoed like thunder, and the thunder of approaching, fresher horses joined them – Stanley's army had joined our side.

The *mêlée* again, just like at Tewkesbury, world of spouting blood and torn flesh and crashing steel…

But this time there was a clear end: Richard of York was everywhere in my sight, his black eyes glistening in the sun, fixed hungrily upon Richmond's battle standard, hacking and pummelling and slashing his way ever closer.

Until the gap between us closed and I realised my comrades were nowhere to be found: dead, twitching their last under the hooves of the Boar's monstrous steed, or fled in terror.

"Tyrell!" The Boar snarled with hatred. "My brother in darkness, joined with the shallow Richmond, that milksop of Bretagne? For shame!"

His horse reared, its mighty hooves ready to crush my head into the blood-drenched soil of Bosworth. His battleaxe glittered in the sun, ready to finish what his night mare left. His golden circlet gleamed, as brightly as the blood that spattered the circlet of Edward, the Lancastrian Prince of Wales, and his eyes, as black as the void revealed by the light of Tewkesbury, glittered and hungered and exulted.

I dropped my pike; the effort required to hold it was too much for my withered arm. But I did not despair. The true spear to impale the bloody boar was around my neck.

"Let us to it, pell-mell, my brother in damnation. Not to Heaven, but hand in hand to Hell." I held Anjou's processional cross aloft, and the monstrous jewel made the Corpus within squirm and writhe and shriek abominations in my grip as it faced the final sun of York.

And Richard smiled. In that smile was relief, from one who knows his suffering is at an end, and that his true purpose is thwarted, and he can die a soldier on the battlefield. He could die a man, and not a mother to ruin and desolation. He dropped his battleaxe and extended his sword arm – his withered arm – to my own ravaged limb.

MAY 6TH, 1502 – THE GARDEN TOWER, LONDON

IT IS DAWN, and Sir James Tyrell's last sunrise on Earth shines through the window. The white roses gleam with summer freshness and purity. Tyrell looks through the window with gladness, cocks his head at the sound of birdsong and sniffs the scent of rose blossom.

"The sun is bright today," he says. "I know I can look upon it fully without despair."

I am as silent as More, who is still writing. I am still trying to envision Tyrell's description of Richard III's destruction and I fail miserably. How can Tudor's agent do it justice in mere words?

Who could? The veterans of Bosworth described an eldritch light around Richmond's standard and can remember little else until the moment Richard's crown was hacked from his head. Only the most demented – the ones who live and breathe in the taverns, obliterating their minds with drink – recall a scene from Hell wherein Richard III died, hacked to pieces, and his crookback exploded in a welter of flesh and blood and light, and birthed monsters that defied human imagination.

They say a holy fire did burn upon the site of Richard's fall, and a solitary pikeman held aloft a cross that emitted the fire of three suns to cleanse the land of the Boar's corruption. Some saw the shade of a woman in red rise from the holocaust, a regal figure who looked the image of a Lancastrian queen, and her smile was that of a saint.

Others say they heard the last king of York cry out for a horse, offer his kingdom for it, and that a pale horse appeared, upon which sat a pale rider.

I suspect More's frantic scribbling is an attempt to rewrite history, that what he has heard is too shocking, too terrifying – too *real* – to be recorded.

He does not accompany Sir James Tyrell to his execution, and I remain at the window. He has left white-faced, trembling, clutching his parchments and books and documents to his chest.

He has left the processional cross with the dark jewel. I wonder if that was deliberate.

Only when I hear the priest's last words to the condemned man, and know this chapter of England's past is at an end, am I able to move from my frozen position.

I see the headsman's axe rise, but the roses hide its descent. The dawn sun shines upon them gloriously, at one point turning the white blooms to red. They flare, flash, like a sun in splendour.

And the light shines gloriously and deeply within the cell, the last resting place of the third sun of York's enabler and destroyer, before darkness falls across my eyes and natural light denies me – the sun has scorned me.

In the darkness I hear childish laughter, young voices with ancient tongues, telling me of an eyrie, which will scorn the sun and from where they will make prey upon this world.

And then a light bathes me. Words spill from my lips, yet I do not recognise the voice.

"*Loyaulté me Lie.*"

"We will unite the white rose and the red. Smile, Heaven, upon this fair conjunction..."

Richard III, Act V, Scene VII

A Reckoning

Guy Haley

"When a man's verses cannot be understood, nor a man's good wit seconded with the forward child, understanding, it strikes a man more dead than a great reckoning in a little room."

As You Like It, Act III, Scene III

ELEANOR BULL OWNED the house.

Small places full of vice and sin, with such houses Marlowe was well acquainted. Mistress Bull's was low-beamed and dark with smoke, a place where light did not penetrate easily on the brightest day, and on the darkest not at all.

Within three others awaited him, his death upon their right shoulders surely as ravens perch upon the gibbets of unrepentant men. Fellows so sick with a malignancy of the soul, from whom the caladrius would turn its snowy face without demur. All three his comrades once, some soon to be his enemies.

Still he must meet them, and so he responded favourably to the invitation to a feast. Red blood flowed in Marlowe's veins, not whey. Under a lintel borne down by sorrow's weight and desperation's call, Marlowe stooped, his hand upon his sword's pommel, a smile upon his lips.

The widow Bull expected him, and took him from the common spaces of the victualling house into a little room, wood warped from true, only big enough to contain the table, benches and a couch behind. Marlowe went into it as a fish swims into a trap.

Ingram Frizer, Nicholas Skeres and Robert Poley were present. Their guarded talk ceased at Marlowe's entrance. All were garbed as generosi, but in habit they were far from gentle. Marlowe, fairer dressed than they and fairer in countenance, took his place among them. Make no error, all were wealthier than the run of men. Grim work pays a goodly wage. Fine clothes clad them, pearls adorned them. But the clothes of the three — Frizer, Skeres and Poley — seemed the dirtier, though they were not in objectivity smirched.

Marlowe, Marley, Kit or Christopher. He was as much a liar and cheat as the three, but the lies he told were beautiful, his gift to cheat a man of cold reality for an hour or two, and replace it with something higher. The three had none of that, though their wits were sharp. This one, Skeres, had a charming mask where weasel's eyes lurked cruelly. His words were lures to the unwary, and their purses oft became his. Frizer, his accomplice of old in such deception, was a darker man in both hair and in temperament. His smile was wide but hid a terrible bite.

Poley's truths were everything but he was an issuer of lies more tangled than a knot of eels. Marlowe trusted none of them.

They rose and greeted Marlowe in a flurry of false amity. Hard eyes hid murder.

"Kit! Kit!" called Poley in cheer as hollow as a serpent's tooth, and just as full of venom. "Now the company is complete!" He slammed his mug against the wood. "Food and ale, or matters first?"

"Marley," said Skeres. Frizer nodded, eyes hooding all but his contempt. Mistrust opened a gulf between he and Marlowe long before. They vied for the affection of their late master, Walsingham, too hard, to the detriment of good relations. No resolution to their contest could likely be attained, now Sir Francis lay coldly in his grave.

"Bring me wine, and meat," said Marlowe to Mistress Bull.

"I shall fetch it," she said. The low chatter and loud laughter of the common room was cut as she closed the door, and the little room grew smaller still.

Marlowe took a seat besides Poley on the side of the table by the couch, in opposition to Frizer and Skeres. Forever thick as thieves, the pair were wont to sit close by.

"Why call us here?" said Marlowe. "Too public! Safety is not your paramount desire, Ingram."

"I merely wish to entertain you, to gladden an old friend."

"Your pamphlets have you in poor regard across the city," said Poley, his mirth — false or not — slithering away. "You curse us by association. Railing against the French and Dutch protestants will have you hanged."

"So that is why I have been called," said Skeres. "I thought this meeting no product of charity."

"Stop now, Nick! This is a grave affair. Marley scolds allies of this nation," said Frizer.

"Why stop there? Spit at the queen while you are at your sport, the result would be the same. Better bait a bear!" said Poley, grinning into his mug of ale.

"The act was that of others," said Marlowe softly.

"Kyd," said Skeres knowingly.

Marlowe shook his head.

"Not Kyd?" said Frizer. "He languishes now in the tower, no less, and has suffered the torturer's attention. I hear he sang quite the tune. Your name spilled sweetly from his lips, along with a measure of his blood."

"It was not Thomas Kyd, I insist," said Marlowe. "In his torment my dear friend implicated me. How could he not? Every bird sings when its feathers singe."

"Implication! Ha! Implication? Implication enough to be caught like a coney and dragged before the Privy Council," said Poley.

"And there accused of blasphemy, of possessing a book of saying that Christ himself is not supreme, but the made vessel of God," said Marlowe.

"Not a sodomite as you have averred?" said Poley, mocking surprise.

"Did I say such a thing?"

"You have said such things," said Frizer. Poley laughed his lunatic laugh.

"So some say," said Marlowe. "So now why bring me to their presence if these sayings be commonplace knowledge? No record of the meeting was kept, no demand for my arraignment made. Only that I attend upon the Privy Council weekly, until licensed otherwise. I have stepped too far. They seek to snare me."

"They wish to keep your leash short, Kit," said Poley.

"That is no reassurance."

"If such import can be attached to this meeting with the high men, how do you still walk the streets?" countered Frizer.

"Because like you, Frizer, I am useful to our Lord Burghley. He angles me, I am hooked, he plays me on the line, but I am not gaffed yet. He waits to see my intention. Pray if you find yourself impugned as I, he judges your service so valuable that he does not strike you dead forthwith."

Frizer scowled. A serving boy knocked upon the door and entered without waiting. The company fell silent again as he handed Marlowe a bottle, bread, a plate of meat and a fine glass at odds with the low character of Bull's house. Marlowe poured a large measure and drank it down in one, then he poured a second. Poley followed the movements of his hands, and noted well they shook a touch.

"Something has you frighted."

"Perchance my time is done," said Marlowe. "The noose tightens."

"Us? You mean us? Dear Marley! Then why come here?" said Skeres.

"We have ever been colleagues in diverse ventures, if rarely friends," said Marlowe. "I must make my testimony, and sympathetic ears must hear it. Hear what I have to say, and you will understand better why I am here, and you are with me, and why the Privy Council set me free only to set a rope around my neck so they may lead me whither they will."

"I like this not one jot, one piece!" said Skeres. "If this be your fate, why not ours? We should leave. Frizer, this was a poor idea."

"Hear him out," said Poley. "Are we all not men who ken behind the curtains? We know what men of substance hide. I wish to hear his tale. He has knowledge; all knowing is useful, sharp to the knower or not."

"Sharp blades cut. We put ourselves in danger..." said Skeres, though doubtfully.

"Stop your mouth with beer, Nick," said Frizer. Poley laughed again, too loudly.

"I shall not," and Skeres placed his pot upon the table. "Marlowe must speak. Did we not snare Babington on lesser notice and by our action topple a queen for Walsingham?" said he.

"We did," said Poley proudly.

"Then who's to say Kit has intelligences worth the less in this instance? Not I, not afore I have heard them," said Poley.

"Then speak, though I urge you most reluctantly," said Frizer. "And expect no favour for the telling from I. I will not accuse myself for you, nor bring myself to any harm on your account."

"So be it," said Marlowe. "This tale must be told, I like it not in any way, and wish it were not true, but it is."

Pallid-skinned in the inn's gloom, Marlowe began his tale.

"It was Baines, that low pointer of fingers who has turned his coat and turned it again until even he knows not which colour it displayed. When caught in Flushing by the governor's men, he said I was guilty of petty treason, an utterer of false coin to the Catholic cause, when he himself is a papist first, selfish second, and loyal subject never. Burghley makes use of him, be that on his own conscience. I shared a room and proper duty with Baines, passing false coin to the papists to condemn them at Burghley's leisure. Never did I meet a man so twisted in his words. Why, not even Hob here speaks a lie so easily. Lord Burghley dismissed the claims against me this last year."

"We know," said Frizer and let his malice show.

"You did not know that I was set again to find this man early in the spring."

"You were in Lord Strange's employ, working at your plays," said Poley.

"I see you have me watched."

Poley saluted with his drink. "Not watched, but it pays to keep an eye about."

"Your eye did not see me leave. Two weeks I was gone to Holland. Burghley suspects Baines plays all sides for fools. He hid the dies when we were caught. Bad coinage remained his to give. Burghley wished to know to whom. If not disbursed in England's interest, then in whose? I said I wished no more to play spy, my lord retorted I had no choice."

"Burghley's words," said Skeres. "He has us all by the codlings."

Muttered affirmations followed. More ale was drunk, more wine poured. "Listen and I will tell you more..." said Marlowe.

BAINES I COULD not find anywhere in all of Flushing where we last met. I was of a mind to present myself to the governor to ask for aid, though it would tax me sorely for he thought little of me, and was half in mind that I was guilty of the accusation that Burghley freed me from. Then serendipity showed her fair face, and I saw one whose acquaintance was known to me in the market square. He knew nought of my and Baines' ill feelings, and this man greeted me as a friend. His name I shall not reveal, for he was a goodly man and goodly men should remain free of strife.

"Baines, Mister Baines?" he said. "Why, he is gone to Friesland, for what reason I cannot say. I put him upon an oyster boat myself not a week since."

"Ah," said I, affecting sorrow. "Such a pity that is, I wished to reacquaint myself with he, to show consideration for our time together here. It was most profitable, and I thought he may desire an interest in my latest venture."

"Which is?" he asked.

I dropped my voice. "A new trade is open. I speak of the East India Company, lately formed. A second fleet looks for capital."

The man's eyes lit with greed. "Perhaps, dear sir, you might advise me. I was ever your humble servant here in Flushing."

That was so, and I told him what he wished to hear, all truth. A petty revelation, but one that may serve him so that he might serve me again. He thanked me roundly. His memory excited by the prospect of profit, he remembered more. "The boat that carried Mr Baines, it was the *De Diepe Fischer*. If luck be with you sir, you shall find it at the docks. I do not rightly know where Mr Baines was headed, but they shall."

Fortune was upon me again; there at the dock was *De Diepe Fischer*, a small black oyster boat of no great consequence. The captain was a surly man, squint-eyed and harsh-tongued as the Low Dutch are. The flash of silver amended his manner. He could tell me nothing of Baines' purpose, but agreed to take me north to the same destination once he had sold his cargo. I whiled the day away in a rough tavern overlooking the port, whence I could maintain a steady eye upon the boat. He returned before nightfall, as the tide rose up its highest. I went to join him. He accepted me aboard without comment, and we set sail.

I will not labour to describe the journey, for it is the least of what occurred. I determined that this boat not only trawled, but bought the trawlings of smaller craft, for it was in some ways bigger than the other smacks we saw. The sea is crowded with them around that coast, so rich in abundance of fish and shell-fish. North we went, over the shallow waters of the German Ocean that wash the Low Countries. In places dark and muddy where strong currents perturb the waters, others clear and bright, the reefs of oysters shining blackly beneath our keel. The captain, Meerdammer, said little; his crew of two less. One was so averse to speech he was nearly mute, the other spoke the rough speech of the Fries. He conversed well enough in Dutch with his companions, but my ear could find no purchase on his accent. His voice was a rasping, bereft of meaning to me.

One night brought upon us a tempest such as I never witnessed. I feared we would founder in the seas, but it passed, and we sped on, and I thanked providence, though I bethink myself now that other Powers had a hand in the journey, and not those inclined to charity. Cursed luck! It is no friend to man. Destiny moves us uncaringly. We are as autonomous as chessmen.

Past the mouth of the Isel Sea, into the Wadden Sea, where brooding islands lurk low to the water, in shape like the leviathan that might, at any moment, strike out with its tail and crush so small a ship as ours.

Meerdammer brought me into Zoutkamp, a small village by a Spanish fort which, though now in the hands of the Hollanders, still subdues the spirit by its presence. He brought no cargo, the silver I gave him more than recompense, but before he left I saw his boat so laden with herring barrels it sat low in the water. A profitable journey for Meerdammer, but not for me.

I took care to hide my face, lest I come across Baines by chance. Furthermore, Zoutkamp entertains a large garrison, though it is of no large size itself. The fates do conspire to place two Englishmen in small villages side by side, and that in so remote a place would draw the attention of those I would rather avoid, to whit, the State's soldiery.

But of the man Baines, there was no trace. I asked in the sole inn, with difficulty extracting the intelligences I required. Frustration caused me to raise my voice, and at last a man who spoke a tongue I might understand was found.

"The other stranger," he said, and described Baines to my satisfaction, although he thought him German and had another name for him, "he is outside."

So poor was his command of the common Low Dutch, I thought he meant that Baines was in the street. Further questioning made sure that I was incorrect, and that Baines had taken ownership of a hovel outside of the village. I resolved then to pay him a visit before night fell.

No Englishman has known such desolation as the seaward marches of the Seventeen Provinces. Hard winds rattle without cease through the stalks of miserable reeds. Every fifty paces is a black ditch. The heath sinks into the sea meekly, and the waves arrogantly proclaim their mastery with frequent invasion onto land. The dykes and banks the Dutch build are everywhere to be seen, but put men of higher nations such as ours in mind of ruined palaces, where greensward has taken the place of wall and floor, marking out lost glories. It is chill there, but rarely fresh. The churning of the waves disturbs the mud from its bed, and the waters thereabouts are brown. No less hospitable country have I ever set foot in. And yet there Baines was, and there perforce I must be also.

His domicile was of driftwood and sod, in the dunes within sound of the sea. I could not truly conceive that a man of any station would bear to dwell within, but someone assuredly was. The smoke of a turve fire crawled thickly from the chimney. The door was ajar.

I approached side on, and bent low. Baines saw me, and let fire with his pistol. The ball passed far away from me, and I ran then, vaulting the low bank between track and house. Baines face was white, eyes goggled. Yet he charged the weapon quickly, as one of long practice. He fit the spanner, but could not wind it before I was upon him.

I drew my dagger, but not my sword, for I wished to menace and not kill him. He proved unwilling, tossing up the gun and catching the barrel, aiming such a blow at my skull with the butt that would have shattered it, had I not thrown my cloak around his arm and fouled his hand, and so did drag him toward me, whereupon I put him to the floor, and pricked at his throat.

"Mercy, mercy!" cried he. "I beg mercy."

"Speak freely to me, without hindrance of loyalty to your true masters, and perhaps I may yet give it you," I said. I pulled aside his pistol and tossed it from his grasp. "A pretty wheellock for one such as you, Baines. How came you by the money for it?"

"Mercy!" he said. He writhed under me in such a way as might excite a man in more lustful moments, but I would not let him free from that worse prick at his neck. He set up a wailing such as would shame a babe. I stood from him in disgust, drew my sword, and kept it close to his breast.

"Lord Burghley requires his property," I said.

"Lord Burghley!" he snotted. "I am here at his command!"

I prodded him, a sixteenth inch. Enough to bring forth a bloom upon his jerkin. He squealed and went deathly still.

"The dies," I said.

He blinked. "But I require them. I am here to do the work of England, for Burghley!" he said.

"Lies!" I said. I turned the tip of my dagger in his wound, and his teeth snapped together.

"The truth! The truth, this I swear!"

"What work of England?"

"Atheists," he said. He sat himself upright, and placed a hand to his hurt, his eyes ever on mine accusingly. "Men of your kind, after a fashion."

"I make no secret I care not if man chooses to worship God," I said. "Be it on their conscience."

"They are enemies of the state."

"They are not in the state of England."

"Therein lies your mistake," said Baines. "This anti-church has some connexion with men whose gaze we should not draw – high lords!"

"Raleigh's Night School?"

"Worse!"

This I did not believe. We were at the ragged edge of Europe, where mud and fish are the only currencies. The wretch looked to the floor, seeking his dignity there. "Upon the island of Schiermonnikoog, that is where the anti-church meets. A group of loathsome sorcerers to which I have made incursion." With an inclination of his head he indicated the island lurking on the near horizon. "This night I am to attend their ceremony, where I am to deliver the dies. The play is the same as in Flushing, good Kit!"

"Ah, so you will betray me anew?"

"I had my own skin to preserve," he said sullenly.

"Who asked this of you?"

"You know who would ask me to perform this task," he said. "Do not make me utter his name again, it is bad enough to utter the coin."

"Burghley.'Twas Burghley sent me to find you."

"'It was he set me on this task, I swear." With great and trembling care, Baines rose to his feet. "The dies are spoilt, made to his design. Small letters on the face are turned about so. The coin struck by them can be followed from hand to hand."

"You ever were a deceitful man," I said. "I cannot believe you."

"I dissemble only ever in England's service," he retorted. "I am true in my heart. There is a great deal of gold come lately to England. Our mutual benefactor wishes to know the well from which such a flood is drawn. It is not Spanish gold, it is strange, with a most peculiar lustre. It is here, I say. Here!"

I looked about the grey desolation of the Frisian wastes. "There is no gold here."

"So I thought. I was mistaken. It comes thence. Many months have I spent to uncover the source." He pointed to the grim island.

"Then to the island we must attend," said I. "Collect your dies, Master Baines. I shall accompany you as your guard. If challenged, you shall present me as such."

"And not my keeper?"

"That also."

Baines retrieved a pack from the rude hut; he condescended to show me the dies, and their spoiling, before shoving them quickly away as if spies hung on the wind. We went back to the village, he in front and I behind where I might do him injury should he flee. I kept his gun, powder and balls, and my own hand I kept wrapped upon the hilt of my sword.

You may wonder why Burghley set the two of us at odds. He weaves a tricky web, he is not the weaver Sir Francis was, but he has his talents. Baines' story may have been true, but I could place no reliance on his words. After all we experienced that night, he would yet turn on me if he saw advantage. He is a greater rival to me even than you, Frizer.

I purchased a jug of ale and links of sausage and good Dutch cheese to sustain us. Fresh bread was not to be had, owing to the lateness of the hour. Finding a boat to the isle, though near it was, was harder than the vittles. The channel is so narrow I warrant it might be swum by a hearty man, were the water warmer. I fancy though such an attempt would end in cold disaster, certainly in the month of February, and a boat we sorely needed. The fishers in the harbour looked upon us with blank idiocy, most not understanding Dutch or English, nor the French or High German I essayed, and both tongues I speak fairly. Two that did comprehend made the mark of the eye in the air and turned away at mention of the isle. One man took pity on us.

"What business have you there?" he asked in rotten French, thickened by his Frisian tongue.

"Our own," said I.

He understood my reticence. "We do not go there very much," he replied.

"There are villages there," I said. "Is there no trade?"

A peculiar mien settled upon him, and he shook his head at me slowly, biting upon his lip. "We do not go there, but they trade here, from time to time. One of them is here now."

How odd, that he should say so with such tremulous voice, I thought. "You will not take us?"

"I will not."

"Then two silver pennies if you take us to the one who hails from there." To this he agreed and led us to a small rowing boat where an ill-favoured, stooped fellow with a peculiar look about the eyes slopped out fish scales from an emptied barrel. Our Samaritan acting as translator, the stooped fellow refused us passage. But then Baines stepped forward and showed to him a curious medal of greenish gold, whereupon he agreed to carry us over water to Scheermonnikoog for fivepence, for he said he dwelled there and must return for the night. An outrageous fee, but it was not to be helped. Passage purchased, we left Zoutkamp. It was a miserable village, and I was not sorry to see it behind me. The place was burned by pirates at the beginning of the Spanish war, and only recent taken back from Catholics. The fort is much rundown, but full to misery with soldiery. Merchants might make merry at a like garrison's presence, but not the villagers, who looked upon the State's Soldiery askance, ever worried for their daughters. Baines and I were obliged to hide ourselves from their notice. Soon enough, news of two Englishmen in port would reach unwelcome ears, and I designed to be away before it was. There was no time to be had for wrangling with authority.

Out, out over the heaving sea, past mudflats haunted by the shrieks of lonely birds, too akin to ghosts. Once salt was made in old Zoutkamp, but the little ponds, all walled about with dykes, were clogged by mud and no more used, their gates broken. An air of dejection hung over all, so different to the bustle of the Dutch cities, whose vitality makes the heart of a man run quick. These drear places are great in number, and reflect the soul of that strange nation more than Amsterdam or Haarlem. Mark that well, should you ever come to that land.

The hunched man rowed us over, bent double and staring at the strakes. As he pulled hard upon his oars, I could not help but observe him. His eyes were bulbous, unto that of a frog or cod, and his breath came all wet and rasping. Long sleeves covered the twain of his hands, but once chance permitted a short viewing, and I saw that partway up his finger's length were webs. I have seen this before on blighted men, but this was different. No aberration of the human form, it was rather natural in its unnaturalness, if you apprehend my meaning, as if such webbing was fit to him as my feet are fit to me or the webbing of a goose's foot is fit to the goose.

As we proceeded over the waves, the steady knock of water upon the wood sounding an unfriendly beat, an unsettling sense came upon me. The more I stared at this man, the more I became convinced he was not a man at all, but something other. Mayhap you think that the cold must have affected my wits, for cold it was. Wind of such frigidity blew upon us from the north, biting at our exposed flesh with teeth of ice. I yearned for a heavier cloak. My face was soon blasted raw, and in the tips of their gloves my fingers lost all feeling. But it was not the cold, and nor were my wits addled. The man was not right.

He rowed us straight to the shore. The boat rasped hard upon the sand and he leapt nimbly into the water. Though crook-backed, he was strong and hauled the boat from the ocean, I and Baines within, untroubled by difficulty. I paid him his fee. He said nothing, but watched us with those hideous protuberances as we departed the beach.

If the lands around Zoutkamp were desert and poorly suited to human life, that of Scheermonikoog was by far the less desirable.

A rolling place of shifting sand, treacherous in footing, more beholden to Neptune's law than any rule of man. Five of the clock came and went by as we reached the centre of the shaggy heath that made the isle's heart. On all sides the pounding of the waves, relentless in their monotony, beat out a march. No effort of any magician could have brought on such a melancholy of the soul as the sound of that thumping on the sand.

We gained the highest point of the island; a poor peak no more than a dozen feet tall. Three villages around the edges gave themselves away as lanterns blinked yellow eyes at the drawing of the night. Baines pointed to the north, where the isle narrowed and took on a curled shape, like that of a tadpole. The tattered dunes that way were black, no light I beheld, but that was where he indicated nonetheless.

"Whither are we to go?" I said.

"The monastery," he said. "A ruin. That is where the meeting is to be held."

"At what hour?" I asked.

With level stare he did respond, "Midnight, Mr Marley, when else?"

Darkness dropped, heavy as velvet curtains. The dunes increased their efforts to drag at our feet. The moon was a way from rising, and the world was reduced to the hiss of sand, the boom of surf, black land and black water, the uncertain, ever-changing border sketched in dim white.

"We are here," said he. "Quietly now."

He led me to the brink of a dune and before us was a monastery church's tower, standing tall from fields on which the sands had already greatly encroached. This half of the church was well rooted in the turf, but the hind parts, the nave and the most part of the apse, had been washed clean away. The black shadow of walls broke in the water, cut clean. Extant blocks broke the paleness of the beach, and tumbled masonry made a little reef in the roil of the surf. The footings there were buried in the sand. Half the remaining building was in the ocean, half upon the shore. Doors of greyly-weathered oak barred the way into the tower from the landward side.

"Monks were here since King Stephen's time," Baines explained. "Until Papacy was overthrown in these lands. When the storming of the churches was done, this one and its brothers hereabouts survived the breaking, only for a storm to rise ten years to the day since the first statue was wrested off its perch in Antwerp, and all the monastery save this ruin and its tower carried off to the deeps by the wrath of God.'"

"On whose side does God's wrath fall?" I asked. I had no truck with such superstition, not least from Baines, who I held to be a monstrous Catholic, no matter how often he states himself being the contrary, an opinion I was soon to revise. "On the side of the Papists, or that of the Calvinists?" Baines scowled at me.

We had many hours to pass, so we ate and pissed and took our rest. We lit a small fire, which the wind beat at with gusting fists until it was small and cowed and incapable of shedding warmth. When the wind died a moment, it roared up high, and forced us back, and so no comfort could be got.

The moon emerged from racing clouds. I grew tired of Baines and the cold. I bade him stand and follow me into the church.

"We must wait!" he said, most agitated.

"We may as well stand as sit," said I. The production of my sword sealed the argument in my favour.

The gates were locked and so we came in from the seaward side. The water crept up the beach, and would soon hold congregation within the ruin, but we entered without difficulty. The church retained some fitments of wood, much rotted, but present. The destruction appeared therefore recent though it was over twenty years wrecked, and so total in its exercise that the storm took full half the building down into the sea.

"Watch your feet," I said to him, for there was much debris and sea-wrack about.

"We should not be in here!" said he, and a panic seized him, so that he became rooted as a tree, and I must poke him again unkindly to force his movement.

By the light of moon I examined carvings upon the antique pilasters. All were gargoyles of the most hideous sort, but of a type I have never seen in a church. Strange chimerae having features of man and fish, twining one around another lasciviously, hunting the beasts of the ocean with long spears; dolphin-fish, the whale, and the seal. In one window shone fragments of glass. The light was so dim I could not clearly see, but there was an image held in the corner of the remainder, as is the habit of the Catholics, and I strained my eyes to perceive. A fat-bodied angel, I thought at first, for there was a spread of wings behind the figure. Then I espied the writhings of worms at its mouth, and drew back.

"What manner of church is this," I said, much at unease, "that has devils in its windows?"

"One we should not set foot in," he warned.

"There is a door there," I said. I stepped over rotten boards and stinking seaweed to gain the drier end of the church and the safety of the tower. I stepped up to where uneven flagstones yet covered the earth, and I was gladdened by the feel of them under my feet. Forty feet further, and I was firmly upon solid earth, the tower overhead and the great doors before me. I could hardly credit that such a church might be so, one foot in the soil, the other in the sea, without collapsing to utter devastation long since. In the base of the tower were set a run of stairs. Those leading upward were open, but a rusting grate barred the portal down, a heavy lock upon it. Spiral steps led beneath to a crypt.

"What is down there?" I asked.

"We must leave!" he said, and plucked at my sleeve. He pointed out to sea. There was a ship of substantial beam, three-masted and rigged after the Dutch style, drawing close to shore and all lit up by lanterns. Borne by wind, I heard shouts and by moonlight beheld the movements of sailors in the ropes.

"We cannot be found inside!"

The ship halted, and the rattle of an anchor chain preceded the lowering of a jolly boat.

"We have to depart now!" said Baines, his voice all a-hiss.

"No," said I. "You must go. I will secrete myself in the tower." Baines blinked at me. "I have seen your medal," I said. "I have none. What suppose you shall happen if I fail in the production of the same?"

"It is for the best," he nodded rapidly, all too readily.

"Do not think of running, Baines, you must see this through or I shall know your story to be a base lie. If it proves so, I will chase you down, and deliver you to Burghley myself, and if you betray me to this anti-church, I shall make sure to kill you before I am undone."

He exited the ruin backward, nodding and blinking all the while as his feet splashed in the nearing sea. I looked upward, and braved the stairs.

The stone steps were firm, but the wood of the tower floors much rotted, and I dared not try them. To the roof I went, where lead remained and kept the timbers sound. I lay myself behind the low parapet, and waited. I had a good view. The moon was at its highest, and I was enabled to see directly to the ship offshore and the boat filling now with figures.

A line of lights drew my eyes to the west, a procession of torches closing in on the ruined church. Baines may or may not have been telling me the entirety of the truth, but there was to be a gathering that night, that was apparent. The boat came first, making shore twenty yards up the beach from the church.

Seven figures came out, cowled and covered all over with robes, and the boat returned to the ship to repeat the journey, and repeat again, until twenty such stood on the shore. They took to themselves lanterns from their boat, and lit them in a huddle against the wind, then came laughing and jesting to their church from the landward quarter, unlocking and entering through the battered oak doors and passing under me and my hiding place.

For a moment I feared they might come up, so loudly did their voices boom in the hollow ruination of that fane, but they passed on, and out to the juncture of the floor twixt land and beach within the church, and arrayed themselves there. Their voices fell to silence one by one, and all became so quiet I could hear their robes fluttering as pennants in the breeze.

From afar, I heard a mournful chanting, and the rattle of irons. The torches drew closer so that I did perceive the faces of their bearers, all swart and ugly as the man who rowed us to that place. Three score, perhaps, or more. Amid them were seven who were not of the island, for they possessed not that piscean look, and they were bound in shackles, and greatly terrified. The islanders arranged themselves not within the church with the men, who appeared so juxtaposed against the islesmen to be much fairer and cleaner of limb than the Frisian wretches, but upon the shore, where they stood two ells between each of them, either side of the church.

They faced the water, so close to the sea that it ran up over their feet and they flinched not from the cold, but continued with their singing. All but seven, who led the youths inside from the broken end of the church. The tide now made its way from the lost altar to the tower, so that the youths' feet were wetted by the ocean as much as their faces were by tears. They were Dutch and German youths, they cried out in those tongues, and some were girls and some were boys. Each was appointed a keeper, who led them upon a chained leash, and so they were arrayed before the men from the ship, who were twenty in number.

A twenty-first joined them, garbed likewise in the robes. Baines, for certainly it was he. I wondered to myself if he had other robes for me, or if he intended to betray me to these men after all, and if he would yet reveal my presence. They were no atheists, I determined. He said sorcerers, I recalled. I put small stock in the divine, but for these creatures it was not so; they were steeped in superstition. I looked upon a witch's sabbath. With great care for the bluster of the wind on the pan, I primed Baines's pistol, and put the spanner to the lock so to tighten it, muffling the sound of the device with my robes and hand.

The men upon the dry floor of the church spoke among themselves, several approached the man I was sure was Baines, and I heard English voices among High German, Low German and Dutch. A bundle was exchanged for a purse; the dies for coin. Then silence. The youths as made noise were beaten hard, and so we had more quiet, where the wind joined chorus with the islander's dirge. The sea stole closer. Its many tongues lapped hungrily at the stones of the floor where the twenty-one men stood. I longed to drowse, but dared not, and kept my eye upon the church, and the islanders, and the sea. This last drew all my thought, for out beyond the ship appeared a glowing, as of candles behind glass, but in this instance under the water.

At some signal unseen by me, twenty of the twenty-one stepped back. The first, the nearmost to the sea, stepped instead to the fore, and placing one foot upon the sand of the beach within the church, and the other remaining upon the stone, raised his hands and cried out in an ungodly tongue whose sounds were unfamiliar and noisome to the ear. The islanders responded, then the rest of the twenty-one in their turn. He shouted again, something different but in equal measure vile, and again the phrase was repeated in two jarring rounds. I distinctly heard Baines' voice among it. Baines was a devout man. I could not believe that he might mum these words and remain in good conscience. He had come to these creatures not as spy, but as fellow. Was there anything he might not do? The more I lay there, the more likely it seemed that he was of this coven of diabolists and I might meet my end.

On this exchange went. From the sea came a response, a lowing song that ended in dire screeches. The lights in the water shone the brighter, and drew nearer to the shore. By now, I was making sense of the awful speech of the chief witch, and, allowing for my poor understanding, I might repeat it here.

Ph'nglui mglw'nafh Cthulhu R'lyeh wgah'nagl fhtagn. Well might you shrink from it, or bare your teeth, Frizer, for it is a, dread speech. And I, who say no man should be beholden to the fear of hobgoblins, have tasted that fear.

Beyond the breaking of the waves, dark shapes moved, rolling in the sea. Dolphins, or the orcus, I thought, but no, these things had heads, and they rose as black orbs on the silver water, and then I thought seals, but no again, for they had arms and legs as men and they came forth out of the sea, walked upon land as men walk. They approached, passing through the cordon of islanders. They clicked and whistled as they passed, and the villagers called glad greetings. Then these mermen passed within, and gathered in the church – twenty-one of them to the twenty-one robed landsmen.

Their leader came forward. I cannot drive the sight of it from my mind. If our boatman was a man with the look of a fish, then this creature was the reverse, a fish with the look of a man. He was scaled, with huge eyes that gleamed; bald, without nose or lips, and frills at his neck like a living ruff that rose and fell with his inhalations. It stood before the foremost man, and put one foot forward, so that it too had one foot on the land, the other in the foaming water of the high tide.

It spoke. Not human words, but speech of a sort, its voice more croaking than the most loathsome Dutch nightingale.

"Gold," explained one of the islesmen beneath me, clearly, and in English. "Dominion."

"Flesh!" said the chief warlock, and gestured extravagantly. "Flesh for the lords of Atlantis!"

The creature made much croaking and bowed, and the youths were pushed forward into the press of pisceans by the islesmen.

They stood unmoving around the youths, then all of a sudden fell upon them, rending their clothes unto their wearer's nakedness, and then with thrusting members and gaping orifice they ravished them all, male and female alike, in the seething of the sea.

Such a savage mating, mercifully brief. The creatures cawed and made clicking in their throats, and whistled, and hooted out as they disported themselves and sated their lusts. So brightly did their teeth flash I thought they meant to consume the youths after their rapine, but they withdrew when they were finished, and the men and women were pulled weeping from the surf by the Frisians, and had blankets thrown about them. So they were led away. I heard the lock upon the gate, and clang shut moments later. I readied myself for the death of any man that might attempt the stair, but none came.

Four of the beings then went into the sea, so that they were submerged, and came out again bearing an iron chest. They placed it in the receding surf, and threw it open. A resplendence of gold was revealed to all.

Their leader rumbled and burped its speech.

"Gold!" said their translator.

"Dominion," said another of the twenty-one, a Dutchman. "Speed our ships across the world, let us claw back land from the sea."

At this, the lead of Neptune's throng croaked and whistled at length.

"English ships, Hollander ships, all pass safe, all over worldsea," said the Frisian. "This shallow sea your land, if you take it. But there must be a reckoning paid. My lord demands more flesh. Flesh of the English, German and Dutch. Flesh for his sport, flesh for our children to grow within."

"More flesh shall be procured," said another Englishman. And then I knew that voice, oh but I did not.

The chief piscean bowed, a mockery of courtliness, and the creatures returned to the water. As they went, several of the islanders shuddered horridly, and departed after them into the surf, shedding clothes and human form it seemed as they went into the waves, apprenticed to new and awful masters. Was this the trade? A tithe of flesh like Athens' pay to Crete for Minos' dread son? Vessels for the creature's seed to grow and live, before taking to the water? Spies of Neptune upon the shores of the Low Countries, and perchance too soon, of England?

The company dispersed, the men to their ship and the islanders down the coast. Baines said nothing of me; doubtless he was afraid of my pistol, for he knew I had the will to use it. When I dared come down, he was gone with all the rest. Why Baines did not reveal me immediately he was beyond the range of my shot, I know not. He means me ill, I am sure of it. I am drawn into his intrigue.

At the bottom of the stairs waited an islander so hideous I thought one of the mer-men had remained. I dispatched him from behind with a thrust to the neck. I rolled him over with my foot and beheld his face. Truly, this was the offspring of a devil, a creature born of woman but sired by one of the monsters from the sea. A hag-seed.

Up the stairs from the crypt, candlelight shone. I heard the weeping of the youths, but the gate was locked fast, and I could do nothing to aid them. Regret clawing at my innards, I ran.

As I made haste to the far side of the island and drew nigh to the further shore, a cry went up, and shortly torches dotted all the dunes. Baines, perhaps, or the body of the mixed man had been discovered. A further possibility was the boatman, who sharing some talk with his fellows had divined the truth. Howsoever it came to be, I was pursued. I ran like a hart with hounds behind, coming once more to the place where the boatman had brought us. A guard had been set about the little boats on the shore, six of the islanders, many ugly and afflicted with the squamous features of the dwellers in the deeps, waited my arrival. I came out of the dark into their torchlight, and had the advantage, for they were night-blind and they were plain for me to see. Two I ran through before a shout might pass their misshapen lips. The rest, though four, were no match for an armed man, and I finished them all without need of the pistol. Precious time I spent in the slaying. Already more came out of the isle's interior, flaring torches in their hands. I slashed the boat's painter and pushed out into the water, now after the falling of the tide some yards away. As I reached the sea, so the islanders reached the beach, shambling after me. It was to my fortune they kept no dogs.

I scrambled aboard, putting all my strength to the oars. They came at me, splashing into the water, the most fishlike hurling themselves headlong into my wake, but though they swam well, they could not catch a man rowing so hard as I. They ceased their chase and instead they stood in long line and let out a shrieking, savage call.

The events of the night were not done, not yet. I rowed hard, the shore of the mainland so desperately far. Things surged through the waves, and came at the boat. They knocked me hard, lifting the side of the craft and slopping water at me, and I feared I would sink. I could row, but these were the masters of the ocean, Neptune's deadly warriors. I put up the oars, though it seems foolhardy now, and watched them, and brought out my gun. There I waited in stillness. A lamp flash of eyes rising drew my gaze. I took aim, waited so that the water would not stop the shot, and when the head broke streaming through the surface, I discharged the pistol, slaying the piscean with a ball to the brain. At this the islanders let out horrible wails, though we were far away, and set up a great commotion, and the other shapes receded. More fool them, for I had time once again to recharge the pistol.

The next time I fired I did so too early, and the water broke the impetus of my shot, but I inflicted some hurt, for the second thrashed the water into spume, and sped off. That was enough. I had shown my teeth, and the dwellers in the sea retreated. I took up my oars again. The current speeded my efforts toward the land, and I was nearly free.

I did not step out of that boat until wood kissed sand and I could leap onto the beach without a drop of saltwater touching my boots. Then I was away as quick as I might toward the lights of Zoutkamp and its garrison of State's Men. Let the deep ones try to take me there, I thought.

I returned to Flushing via land.

MARLOWE FINISHED HIS story along with his wine. Skeres and Poley looked aghast.

"Have you lost your mind?" said Skeres. "Frizer lures us here with promise of revelation, and you tell us this bogey-tale?"

"I cannot credit such a story," said Poley, all mirth gone. "Not at all."

"You might not, and Skeres won't," said Marlowe, "but there is one here who knows full well of my report's sincerity, is there not, Ingram?"

"Be careful whom you accuse, lest you be accused yourself."

"Well then, we are done," said Marlowe, locking eyes with Frizer. "I think I shall keep the identity of the man whose voice I knew so well to myself, it may yet prove useful to me."

"Not all things are as they seem," said Frizer.

"Yet some most assuredly are," said Marlowe. "I shall depart now to await my Lord Burghley's next command. You shall hear from me anon."

Frizer gripped at Marlowe's arm, displaying a hand adorned by a large ring of strange design, made of greenish gold.

"Wait! We must pay the reckoning first," said Frizer.

"Aye. Such gold as that must be accounted for in blood," said Marlowe, and grabbed for Frizer's knife.

On 30th May, 1593, the spy and playwright Christopher Marlowe was killed in mysterious circumstances involving Poley, Frizer and Skeres — three known government agents — shortly after being arrested by the Privy Council and interviewed at a meeting of which no record was kept.

Though his death allegedly came about after an argument over the bill for the feast, it is possible that Marlowe was assassinated on the orders of the government. Numerous theories abound as to why, but one is that he was about to expose members of the Privy Council as atheists.

Richard Baines was hanged in 1594.

Ingram Frizer, who struck Marlowe dead, was cleared of murder by reason of self-defence. He became a church warden, and lived a life of respectability. He died in 1627.

The Green-Ey'd Monster

Danie Ware

A coil of pain and eyes that seethe with green

As loyal foe brings clever words to flaunt

And horror rises where there was no grief foreseen,

A heart now mock'd by jealous jab and taunt.

Beneath the surface curls a roil of hate

And darkness flares, a fury without name;

It rages beyond reason, fact or fate,

Is blinded to the truth, sees only blame.

And Desdemona cries with her denial,

But cries ignored, her protests lost unheard,

Love's innocence rejected and reviled

And breath all stops, death caught on final word.

The tale ends in truth stark in cold air.

The gods have drunk their fill, and do not care.

Act Three

"As flies to wanton
boys are we to the
gods.
They kill us for their
sport."

King Lear, Act IV, Scene I.

Exit, pursued by...?

James Lovegrove

I will tell you this, scribe: it is not as I have always said it was.

For nigh on twenty years now, whenever anyone asks me how I came by my injury, I have lied. I have rigorously maintained that the stiffness in my shoulder, the jagged scars which extend from it halfway up my neck, the chunks of missing meat, are all the gruesome handiwork of a bear. The culprit was no more uncommon a creature than that. A roaming black bear pursued me, caught me up in its claws, and tore a pound of flesh from my body with its ravening teeth.

No one queries this reply. Bears are a familiar enough sight in these parts. Bohemia's forests are riddled with them. Few who dwell in the country's rural areas can say they have not encountered one at some point in their lives. Most have lived to tell the tale, although some have not been so lucky.

At any rate, with this explanation I have been able to deflect such slings and arrows of curiosity as are loosed at me. Upon hearing it people will offer sympathy, perhaps, or wince as they contemplate the agonies I suffered. I will in turn dismiss their coos and blandishments. "Let us not make a fuss about it," I will say, sounding brave. "It is much ado about nothing."

Now, at last, as I lie upon what must surely be my deathbed, I wish to confess the truth. For the first and final time in my life since the terrible events of that night on the storm-tossed southern shore of this land, I, Lord Antigonus, formerly a noble of Sicilia and once close associate of and trusted advisor to her monarch King Leontes, hereby state for the record that I was not attacked by any bear.

No, it was no bear.

It was something stranger and much worse.

This will sound like a tale for a winter's eve, the sort of ghoulish, phantasmagorical story that should be recounted by a bard beside a roaring hearth to an audience whose faces are illuminated by the flickering firelight and also carry the inner glow that derives from a tankard or two of good sack. It may, contrarily, seem like some feverish dream of the kind that visits us on a hot, sweltering midsummer night.

It is, I assure you, scribe, neither. Everything I am about to say to you is gospel. Do not judge as you write it down. Do not attempt to assess its reliability as your quill traverses the paper. Merely copy verbatim what I say, and save your incredulity, if such is the sentiment I am to engender in you, for after. I bid you enshrine these words measure for measure, as though they are my last testament, my Will. Thus shall you earn the purse of coins I have promised you.

IT BEGAN WITH a storm.

I do not mean a meteorological tempest, although there was one of those too, later on.

I mean a mental storm, and it afflicted King Leontes, who got the notion into his head that his queen, his beloved, fragrant Hermione, had been unfaithful. Worse, she was dallying behind his back with King Polixenes of Bohemia, who was not simply Leontes's lifelong friend but like unto a brother to him. Worse still, said dalliance had resulted in the conception of an as yet unborn child, a sibling to young Prince Mamillius.

What provoked Leontes into this mania of misconstruction, I cannot say. It may have been the eating of some improperly cooked food, or a temporary inflammation of the brain. Note that I am trying to attribute it to a physiological cause, but I fear that it was actually a madness with an emotional basis, arising from some deep-rooted insecurity – a defect in his personality which had long lain buried but rested unquiet in its grave until, needing only the right prompting, it came squirming to the surface.

Hermione could not have been more innocent of the charges Leontes levied at her, and likewise Polixenes of the calumnies Leontes uttered against him. Great affection indeed was there between the queen and Polixenes, as was only meet and proper. She regarded him as any wife ought her husband's bosom friend, with the purest love and respect. Only in Leontes's mind was there aught other to the relationship than that. He alone supposed that the seed swelling in Hermione's womb was any man else's but his.

I know this beyond a shadow of a doubt because I had become well-acquainted with Queen Hermione through my years of service at the royal court and knew her character; but also, a surer test, because my then wife, my lovely Paulina, was her confidante and intimate companion. Paulina, if anyone, would have been aware had Hermione betrayed her marriage vows. She insisted to me that she had not. Therefore, as doting, trusting spouse to that most intelligent and insightful of females, I could be in no doubt that this was so.

How dreadful it was to see Leontes belittle and spurn his queen and make that merry wife of his so wretched. How saddening to watch the king leer and sneer at a woman for whom he had previously had only looks of adoration. I sought to guide him away from his unwarranted jealousy and spite, as did my fellow lords-in-waiting, yet our voices of reason fell on deaf ears. Hermione, though great with child and near term, was consigned to prison. Polixenes fled Sicilia, fearing with justification an attempt on his life by Leontes. Mamillius – sensitive, lisping little Mamillius – perished of a seizure, which was doubtless brought on by anxiety over his mother's plight. Then, to compound the misery, came the report that Hermione herself had died, having succumbed to the bloody throes of labour, for all the ministrations of the midwife Lady Margery. Such an outcome is, alas, all too often the case for a woman during childbirth, but the privations of imprisonment cannot have helped, nor the intolerable strain Hermione was under owing to her husband's cruelties.

Where once life in the royal palace had afforded all the laughter and gaiety of a comedy, now it was riven with tragedy. But that is not the real problem with this history of mine.

For I, loyal Antigonus, was charged with a task such as no man should be entrusted to perform. I, at my king's express edict, was to take the babe whom Hermione had lately brought into the world, at the cost of her own life, and bear it to a "remote and desert place". There I was to abandon it in the wild and let Mother Nature, as unforgiving as she is giving, determine its fate. I was threatened with death were I to refuse to obey this abhorrent order, and I would fain have faced the executioner's axe than do as the king demanded. However, the penalty extended to my Paulina as well, and I could not in all conscience imperil her life. I was forced to choose between my wife and the newborn, which Leontes reckoned a bastard, and I chose the latter. I defy any man to say he would have done differently.

SUCH A BEAUTIFUL little girl she was, scribe, that babe. Every inch the image of her mother, but also showing the dignity of bearing that typified her father, at least until his antic fit overtook him and turned him spiteful and cold. As I voyaged from Sicilia by sea with the infant, I nursed and cared for her and grew entranced by her eyes, which seemed wise beyond their years, and by her sweet little smile. I dandled her and fed her and let her grasp my finger with her tiny hand, and I grew as fond of her during those days of travel as I was of any of my own three daughters.

Our ship rounded the heel of Italy and sailed northward up the country's eastern flank, and by the time we moored at Venice to buy supplies from merchants there, I could almost not bear the prospect of being parted from the girl. It was agony to think that I must leave her in some uninhabited spot and hope against hope that she would somehow survive. As we set forth from Venice and headed east along the curve of coastline adjoining Italy to Greece, I spied many a desolate stretch of land where I might fulfil King Leontes's command. Yet I kept postponing the evil hour. The captain would ask me when he should give the order to put in and weigh anchor, and I would say repeatedly, "Tomorrow. Tomorrow and tomorrow and tomorrow."

In the end I could not delay any longer. We had arrived at Bohemia – and to those who claim the country has no coastline, I say that geography is malleable and borders shift. Believe me, it had a coast back then; perhaps it does not now. There seemed a kind of symmetry in depositing the child there, at any rate, for though she had not been sired by Bohemia's ruler King Polixenes, nonetheless she had been accused of it and been born into the turmoil created by Leontes's calamitous suspicions about his erstwhile friend.

Further informing my decision was the fact that I had a dream – although it was more like a nightmare – about the babe's dear departed mother. The shade of Queen Hermione visited me in my cabin and instructed me to discharge my onerous duty at the next suitable location. Moreover she told me to name the child Perdita, meaning "She Who is Lost", and foretold that never again would I see my Paulina, a punishment by the Fates for the wicked deed that I was being forced to commit.

Dreams like that, so vivid that they seem more akin to reality, are not to be ignored. They have the same power of augury as divine oracles, such as the one that was delivered to Leontes immediately prior to Mamillius's death, a message from the shrine of Apollo himself at Delphos, which the king stubbornly rejected even though it exonerated Hermione.

At first light the ship hove to at the mouth of a rocky natural harbour and launched its boat, with a mariner aboard, myself, and little swaddled Perdita.

Now we come to the point where my account stops being a comedy of errors and darkens into a litany of terrors.

Kindly pour me some water, would you, scribe? I am desirous of taking a sip and moistening my throat. Ah! The hurting is upon me again. I must wait. It will pass. It will pass. There.

A canker festers within me, you see. I am no stranger to pain. My shoulder alone is testimony to that. The wound may have healed but its ache has been my constant companion since its infliction. That pain, though, is naught compared with the pain of my disease, which waxes and wanes but never fully fades. The gnawing in my innards has worsened steadily in the months gone by, like a hunger that can never be quenched. At the very first I reckoned it no more than the colic. Within a fortnight, as no relief came and no physic seemed to ease the discomfort, I realised that I was experiencing the onset of mortality. There would be no surcease. Something was growing in my belly that would, as Perdita did Hermione, end my days. I was, in a sense, giving birth to death.

But to my narrative I must return. I am postponing the moment. I must screw my courage to the sticking-place and continue on.

I now delve into the most sinister memory which is mine, one I have striven not to recollect yet still attends me in unguarded hours and hounds me during the long, dark watches of the night, ever unbidden.

SLATE-GREY CLOUDS WERE amassing on the southern horizon as the little rowing boat plied its course across the water, entering the lonely bay. The mariner worked the oars, sullen and uncommunicative. Perdita was perched in my lap, restless and fretful. She seemed to sense that was all was not well and would not end well. I shushed and soothed her as best I could, but she would not be mollified.

Although a storm was looming, the air was still and the bay eerily quiet. The plash of the oar blades echoed sibilantly. No thunder yet sounded. No gull or mew uttered a cry. The atmosphere was, not inappropriately, funereal. I fancied that this might be how it was to cross the River Styx to Hades, the sombre sailor my Charon.

"This is an accursed place," said he, casting an anxious eye about our surroundings. "I like it not. I would prefer an isle full of noises, sounds and sweet airs to this hushed, barren emptiness. It weighs upon my soul like a dead hand."

He rowed on, but grew yet unhappier as we passed through the lilting shallows towards a strip of steep pebbled beach. By the time the boat's keel dug into shingle he was muttering to himself, offering half-formed prayers to the gods. Is there anyone more superstitious than a seaman? And yet I could myself not help but feel a twinge of unease. All around us rose granite cliffs, Cyclopean and forbidding. Our ship, visible between the tips of the bay's promontories, seemed impossibly far-off, as though it were retreating from perception, vanishing to some other realm. The distance could not have been more than a quarter-mile but the vessel might as well have been on the other side of the world for all that we could have reached it. That was how it felt, as though we were enacting our business on an altogether different globe.

"Make it quick," the mariner said as I debarked onto dry land. "This storm will not wait. Nor may I."

"I go, I go," I replied impatiently, "look how I go, swifter than arrow from the Tartar's bow."

Besides Perdita I carried a scroll stating her name and a fardel I had prepared for her, a bundle of gold and other trinkets of value. I still harboured the hope that she might be discovered by some passing stranger and taken in, and I wished to offer that person an incentive for performing this benevolent deed.

As I forged up the slope of the beach looking for an overhang or a sheltered cleft wherein to set Perdita and her attendant offerings, the coming storm gave its first warning growl. A flash of lightning played, casting weird dancing shadows, and the thunder rumbled after. A wind was gathering. We had but minutes, thought I, before the storm commenced in earnest and surmounted us.

To my surprise and delight, I spied a pathway that wound into the cliffs. There were crude stairs, hewn from the rock. The bay, then, was not unfrequented. There was every chance that someone might happen by and discover Perdita.

One might argue that this was absurdly optimistic of me. I cannot convey how lonely and ill-omened that place was. It seemed as far from civilisation as the surface of the moon. Yet, having divined a flimsy straw of consolation, I clutched at it and clasped it tight to my bosom, even as, with much hesitation, I lay Perdita down at the foot of the stone steps.

She cried out as I relinquished her. It was a sound to shatter the stoutest of hearts. Her gasping sobs grew in volume and frequency as I turned away from her. This was the most difficult thing I had ever had to do. Tears blurred my vision. I had accomplished my labour and it felt as though I had lost a love. I stumbled down the beach, away from her whose short life I had almost certainly doomed, and it was only as I reached the waterline that I perceived that the boat was gone.

THE MARINER HAD not tarried but one moment. No sooner was my back turned than he brought his little barque around and began rowing

225

strenuously out to sea. He was already four hundred yards hence and moving apace. I called to him, demanding that he come back, but peals of thunder overmatched my voice. I waved and gesticulated. He, with his back to the stern and his face to the bows, could clearly see me but affected not to. He just lowered his head and heaved all the more strenuously at the oars.

It can only have been dread that compelled him to flee, without reck for his passenger. Fear got the better of his nature and he abandoned me with less circumspection than I had abandoned poor Perdita. He could bear to spend not one second longer in that bay, and never mind that that meant marooning me.

I gave up remonstrating with him from afar. It availed me naught. The storm was now on top of us, pelting us with rain. The wind howled, lashing the waves to a seethe. I hurried back to where I had deposited Perdita, so as to be in the lee of the cleft and out of the tempest's teeth. My last glimpse of the mariner showed me him toiling through an increasing swell, the boat bobbing and rocking with such violence that with every oar stroke in three he pulled at thin air. I cannot say whether or not he made it back to the ship. A vindictive part of me wishes he did not, but if he did, what fabrication did he tell his captain? How did he account for his returning alone? Some spurious concoction no doubt sufficed. Mayhap he related that I had drowned, or had become disorientated and failed to find my way back to the boat, or had tripped and dashed my brains out on a rock. Or it could be that he claimed I had refused to leave Perdita untended and elected to stay on the beach with her, despite his protestations. It is a matter for speculation only. You may prefer whichever scenario you see fit, scribe. As you like it. What you will.

We huddled, Perdita and I, in the defile wherein had been carved that staircase. I shielded her body with mine as the wind blew hard enough to crack its cheeks and the rain came down in torrents such as could have drowned the roofs of temples. Thunderbolts leapt and struck, as ear-splittlingly loud as an oak being cleaved in twain by some Titan's axe. Presently I was soaked to the skin, and Perdita was shivering helplessly in my arms. I knew that if we did not find a better haven, we would neither of us survive. Gathering her up, along with the scroll and fardel, I began to ascend the steps.

It was treacherous going. The stairs were slippery underfoot. The wind made me totter with every vaunting gust. I fell and barked my shins more than once, but never did I allow injury to be visited upon Perdita. I protected her person at the expense of my own.

Then, deep within the cliff face, the stairs abruptly ended. I had climbed some fifty feet above sea level, by my estimation, yet had not gained the summit of that crag. It appeared that I had come to a dead end. Why, then, had the stairs been constructed at all? What purpose did they serve, if they went nowhere?

My puzzled dismay cleared as my rain-stung eyes espied a narrow fissure to my left. It was just large enough to admit a man. Within lay darkness. A cave of some sort.

I wormed myself into this cave, out of the elements. Half-walking, half-crawling, I penetrated it to a distance of some dozen paces, whereupon both Perdita and I were safely sequestered from the storm's blasts. I sat back against the dark, damp wall, and with Perdita nuzzling against my breast, the both of us sodden and exhausted, I slept, and so did she.

How long did we slumber there? For as long as it took for the storm to blow itself out and some warmth to return to our bodies. By that time it was well past noon and we were both hungry. Perdita mewled, and I comforted her by letting her suckle on the tip of my smallest finger. It was a temporary measure, I knew. I had to find sustenance for her somewhere, and for myself too. That was my imperative.

I made the decision to return to the beach, but once we got there I was struck by its utter sterility, which I had not really remarked hitherto. No whelks or cockles clung to the rocks, nor any limpet. No sea kale sprouted from the shingles and no kelp floated amidst the shallows. I could not even descry any fish in the water. The bay, it seemed, supported neither fauna nor flora. It was host to no life. Nowhere can have been deader.

I cast a glance beyond the promontories in the vain expectation of the ship still being there. Of course it was not. Nor could I see any sign of a sail on the horizon.

I trudged back up the steps to the cave. "There must be some reason these were carved here," I mused aloud as I walked. Perdita looked up at me with her big, trusting eyes, listening intently even though she could not comprehend a word I said. "They afford access to the cave. What if the cave is a mere vestibule, a portal between the bay and some other location?"

Upon re-entering the cave my hypothesis was confirmed, for I could feel a breeze flowing across me, a zephyr I had been innocent of before, while the storm was unleashing its shocks and buffets. An air current was passing through the cave. That indicated that we were not in some blind hollow but rather a tunnel of sorts, one which might lead from shore to land proper.

Apprehensive yet hopeful, I ventured further in, with Perdita as ever in my arms.

I HAD NO torch nor means of lighting one. I had only my probing hand and what scant illumination came in via the cave mouth. The latter soon dwindled and was gone, leaving me to rely solely on the former. Blind as winged Cupid, I fumbled along, becoming aware from the multiplying echo of my footfalls that the passage was widening and its ceiling getting higher overhead. This encouraged me to think that I was right and the cave would eventually disgorge us elsewhere, for why would it be enlarging if it were not a branch of some great subterranean system with one or more entrances inland? The fact that the floor was on a downward incline, the cave therefore drawing us deeper into the earth, was something I refused to allow to trouble me. Although I would rather we had been going upward, I consoled myself that there would at some point be a correction to this course. No descent can continue indefinitely, unless it were to take us to Hades' realm, and even that might be welcome, for this would at least be a destination, a terminus.

Light then glimmered before me. It was clay-coloured, dim and evanescent, yet could not have been more welcome. My eyes began to apprehend the rough contours of the cave wall. I could place my feet more confidently on the ground, without having to shuffle and quest with my toes.

Shortly I found myself in a gully. The cave had opened out onto more of those uneven steps, and I clambered down them, blessing the overcast sky and the diffused glow of Helios.

I was in a town.

It took me some moments to appreciate that that was what this was: a small, secluded agglomeration of dwellings. They were not houses as you or I know them, scribe. They were stone hovels meanly burrowed out from the gully's all but sheer sides, with misshapen doorway apertures and paltry glass-lacking windows. The most primitive residences imaginable, they rested atop one another much as a child might pile his wooden building blocks, with scant regard for order or design. Aside from these the town boasted just one other feature of note, a teetering structure at the landward end of the gully which rose perhaps two hundred cubits high. This pillar was mottled and grooved, and adorned with what appeared to be a myriad of detailed carvings, somewhat like Trajan's Column in Rome, although at such a distance as stood between me and it I could not distinguish what they represented.

At first I assumed the town untenanted. There was only silence and stillness within the gully, as profound as at any necropolis. I had come upon some ancient fishing community, methought, whose inhabitants had long since died out or moved to pastures new. Here and there lay a discarded remnant of domesticity – a clay pot, a frayed twine net, a hatchet with a flint head. It was hard to fathom how long ago the town might once have thrived, when had been its green and salad youth. Could somewhere as unprepossessing and ill-favoured as this ever have had a heyday?

I was resolved to investigate that strange pillar, to see if I might learn something from it about the nature and origin of the town. Then, through the window of a nearby house, I caught the glint of a pair of eyes staring at me.

As my skin crawled with horror, Perdita began to cry. Whether she sensed my sudden perturbation and was instinctively responding to it, or simply could not abide her hunger pangs any more, I cannot say. Whatever the cause, she bawled as loudly and lustily as was in her power to, and her caterwaul rang across the gully, filling it to the brim with sound.

Thereupon the person who had been covertly observing us rushed out through the doorway of the house and flew towards us.

She was a woman, although the description is not wholly apt, for she was more like a tatterdemalion, or one of the Harpies of legend. She had lank, grey hair and was clad in filthy rags. Her eyes were wide and her arms flailed as she ran at us, her mouth hissing words in I know not what language. She made to seize Perdita, and I snatched the babe out of her clawing grasp and delivered her a smack with my free hand. Undaunted, the hag tried afresh to lay her paws on the child. I bellowed at her and kicked out. A dire stench emanated from her body, a stink like rotting fish, and it fair sickened me, yet I close-grappled with her and fended her off. She would not have Perdita, not while there was breath in my body.

More of the townspeople emerged from hiding, drawn by Perdita's yelps and my shouts. They joined in the fray with an urgency I took for avarice. Though I could not discern quite why they wanted Perdita so badly, I could only assume the worst. They were all of them emaciated, starveling things, mere walking anatomies who appeared not to have eaten a decent meal in their entire lives. Appalling though the idea was, it occurred to me that they were eager to enjoy a feast of succulent infant flesh.

With their sheer numbers they overwhelmed me. Perdita was torn screaming from my clutches. I fought to regain her, battling through the throng of reeking, skeletal bodies that now surrounded her.

To my great consternation, the hag who had originally accosted us now possessed her and was spiriting her off into the house as though she had won some living trophy. I beat aside the crowd and followed. Had the townspeople been less enfeebled than they were, and I less desperate, I might not have managed this feat.

No sooner did I enter the dwelling than I was confronted with an astonishing sight. The hag had not, as I feared, set about carving Perdita up or sinking teeth into her. Far from it. The babe lay ensconced in the embrace of a younger female. This girl — for she could have been no more than sixteen or seventeen years of age — had produced a pendulous swollen dug from the folds of her threadbare tunic, and Perdita, having latched onto the teat, was taking deep and greedy suck.

The assembled townsfolk gathered in the doorway to peer in. The hag chivvied them away with blows and imprecations, screeching at them in that unknown guttural tongue of theirs which sounded to me like no language anyone had ever spoken nor should speak. They, as if reminded that they had other business to attend to, disappeared back to their homes. In no time the gully outside was empty. The town seemed again deserted.

I, for my part, was seeing the hag in a new light. This shrewish creature had been, as it were, tamed, and while I found both her and Perdita's newfound wet-nurse repugnant, especially in such close propinquity, I also had cause to be grateful to them. This I expressed with all the courtly courtesy that was mine to employ, making low bows and other obsequies. Julius Caesar, accepting tribute from the conquered barbarians of the north, could not have been more gracious.

In return, the hag tried her utmost to explain something to me, using signals and dumb shows. She pointed to the sky, mimed stormy weather, then implied the fall of darkness, which was imminent, for dusk was already smoking the air and night was on its way. Then she pointed seaward and drew the triangular shape of the cave-mouth fissure in the air with her hands, followed by an indication of somebody walking through. I thought she was referring to me, but she repeated the action – two fingers striding like legs, over and over – until I gathered that she meant several individuals.

People were coming. That much I was able to glean. After dark, in the wake of a storm, the town received visitors.

Who those visitors might be, and their purpose, I had no conception. But I was shortly to learn.

PERDITA, STOMACH REPLETE with milk, duly sank into sleep. I, meanwhile, partook of a thin fish broth the hag cooked over a pitiful flame.

Afterward, my hunger somewhat sated, I pointed back and forth significantly at Perdita's wet-nurse and then the hag. By this means I was able to ascertain from the latter that the two of them were, as I had suspected, daughter and mother.

I then attempted to establish whether the daughter had herself lately become a mother, for why else would she be capable of giving milk? The hag affected incomprehension, but a certain furtiveness in her mien told me that she understood all too clearly what I was asking. I could only deduce that her daughter had had a baby but had lost it, perhaps to disease or infirmity. That or the child had arrived stillborn. It was, evidently, a taboo subject. The hag did not wish to discuss it, and I was consequently loath to press the point. I owed these women a debt. They were my and Perdita's hostesses, sharing with us what meagre provision they had, and to offend them would be not only impolite but impolitic.

My assumption was that Perdita and I would be spending the night in this humble abode. Then, come morning, we would leave the town and proceed elsewhere. It struck me that my and the little princess's fates were now inextricably bound together. The ship was gone. Captain and crew must presume us dead. On this foreign shore Perdita and I needs must accept whatever came our way. A divinity had shaped our ends, rough-hew them how we would, into something as bewildering as it was unforeseeable.

As darkness entirely engulfed the town, I expected that we would all settle down to rest. However, there was a marked tension in the air. Might it have some connection with the imminent arrival of visitors?

I expressed this enquiry to the hag as best I could. Her answer was a single word, uttered with a kind of dark, deep-rooted dread, more shuddered than said.

"Y'ha-nyarthlun."

Perplexity must have been writ large upon my face, for she repeated the word again, and then again, making it insistent by repetition.

"Is that a name?" I said. "The name of a location, or perhaps a person?"

After I had offered much gesticulation to illustrate my query, the hag nodded. I was right. Y'ha-nyarthlun was indeed a location, but also the name of the race who inhabited it.

What the hag told me next, however, made little sense. For Y'ha-nyarthlun, by her account, lay due south, somewhere out in the ocean, not too many leagues thence. But it was not an island. It was a city. Moreover, unless I sorely mistook her, Y'ha-nyarthlun did not stand proud above the waves but rather beneath them.

My scepticism was great. A submarine city? But what sort of beings could dwell in such a place? What form of life could a seabed city house?

It was ridiculous. The hag was in the grip of some superstitious fantasy. People from the depths, coming to this town. The very idea of it! I did not believe then, as I do most assuredly now, that there was more to heaven and earth than was dreamt of in my philosophy. I used to be a rational man until experience taught me to be otherwise.

The hag sensed my doubt and dismissed it with a kind of grim fatalism, as if she knew I would soon be disabused of it. She damped down the cooking fire, and then, in hazy darkness, we sat and waited. Perdita remained cuddled in the daughter's arms. This impromptu wet-nurse seemed pleased to have a babe to care for, even if it was not her own. Her gaze was fixed on Perdita and seemed both melancholy and resolute, that of a grieving mother finding temporary solace in a substitute child.

I was wrong about that, as I had been about so many other things.

The night wore on. The atmosphere in the hovel grew yet more febrile, yet more freighted with dire anticipation. I myself had a hankering to see these people from Y'ha-nyarthlun, whom allegedly the storm had prompted to leave home, swim up from the deeps and grace this town with their presence. They seemed to me the stuff of travellers' tales, like the wild reports from far-off lands of anthropophagi and men whose heads grow beneath their shoulders. I surmised that they might in truth be merely some seafaring tribe who donned outlandish guise to make themselves appear monstrous and otherworldly, as though they genuinely resided in lodgings at full fathom five. The aim of this practice was to strike fear into the hearts of those whom they called upon when they made landfall. Thus might they intimidate locals into according them veneration and paying them tribute.

I was beginning to drowse off when a whisper of distant voices caught my ear. At once the hag and her daughter both stiffened. It sounded like chanting, and the language used was identical to that spoken by the townspeople, full of stops and starts and thick syllables and unnatural growls. But it was not a chant such as one might hear a priest employ at the altar when offering libation or sacrifice to the gods. It was, rather, in the nature of an invitation. Hypnotically it echoed through the town's meandering streets, like a summons. The visitors from Y'ha-nyarthlun — for that could only be from whom the voices originated — were calling in lulling, beguiling unison. "Come forth" was unmistakably the tenor of their words. "Come forth and show yourselves."

Within the hovel I could see only the glint of wide, terrified eyes. The hag's daughter was paying attention to Perdita no more. I could feel both women trembling, the very air vibrating with their fear. The same sentiment conveyed itself to my limbs too.

Now, alongside the chanting, was audible the shuffle of footfalls. These were wet and sloshing, such as of creatures who found it a challenge to walk upright on land. As the sound grew louder, so did my apprehension of its unnaturalness. Nothing human, surely, could walk with such a moist and slovenly traipse.

I dreaded to see what sort of being was the source of it. Yet I yearned to as well. Does that make sense to you, scribe? I was seized by an awful curiosity. Against the hag's hissed imploration not to, I raised my head to the window aperture. I peered out.

Would that I had not.

THEY WERE FURRED, those things from Y'ha-nyarthlun. They had coats sleek like otters'. They had bodies much like men's, but for hands and feet they had the clawed flippers of seals. They slouched as they moved, shoulders bent, legs slow and straining, as though their own weight was a burden to them. There were gills in their necks, gaping as they sucked in air, and their mouths had a plump-lipped, froglike cast. As for their eyes...

Oh, their eyes were the blackest orbs imaginable. Bereft of emotion or life or anything that one looks for in a human's eyes. Spheres of pure void.

I was able to distinguish their features so clearly thanks to strange lights which several of them carried — stringy seaweed sacks filled with soft egg-shaped baubles which exuded a wan greenish glow. These illuminated the things from Y'ha-nyarthlun with an eldritch lambency as they shambled past the hovel. The hue and pallor of the light made the creatures even more ghastly-looking than they already were.

As I beheld that sinister parade of inhuman sea-bred beasts, I found myself praying to the gods, in whom I had but the slimmest of belief. I entreated them to protect Perdita and me from the creatures. I begged Zeus and his kin to preserve us with all their divine might and see to it than no harm befell us. Faith comes to all men in times of extremity, scribe, does it not?

The gods listened, or so I thought. The sea beasts, a dozen of them all told, passed the hovel by. Still they intoned their chant, but none in the town heeded it. Nobody left his hovel to face the Y'ha-nyarthlunians and receive whatever grim depravity was theirs to bestow.

I sank back from the window, feeling bloodless and wrung-out. My gaze met the hag's, who simply nodded with solemn wisdom, as one might to another person who has just been initiated into an unwelcome mystery.

It was then that I noticed that her daughter was absent.

So was Perdita.

NEITHER THE HAG nor I had marked the daughter leaving. She must have slipped out of the hovel as the things from Y'ha-nyarthlun were approaching, Perdita still snug and fast asleep in her arms.

The hag was appalled by this turn of events, albeit nowhere near as greatly as I. She gnashed her teeth in anger and distress. Her daughter had betrayed her trust, it would seem. She would never have given her Perdita to look after had she known the daughter might then abscond.

She hurried from the house, I at her heels.

The procession of Y'ha-nyarthlunians had reached that carved pillar at the landward end of the gully. There they had gathered in a small knot, and as the hag and I hastened towards them I perceived that the hag's daughter was the nucleus of their assembly. To my disgust and utter dismay I saw her hold up Perdita before them. She was like a dignitary offering a bribe to a group of ambassadors, currying their favour. I must assume – although I do not know it for sure – that the Y'ha-nyarthlunians had taken her own child on their last visit to the town. The way she was surrendering Perdita to them now, she seemed forlornly to be hoping that they would take this child in the other's stead and return her offspring to her. This was all some urgent ploy to recoup that which she had previously conferred, willingly or not, on the creatures.

I gave vent to a roar of purest rage and anguish. I quickened my pace to a run and launched into the Y'ha-nyarthlunians like a ball into ninepins. The element of surprise lent me the advantage. I knocked brine-damp bodies aside and wrested Perdita from the daughter's hands.

The jostling awoke Perdita and she began to keen, but that was the least of my concerns. For we were right in the thick of the creatures, and their baleful black eyes were staring with fixity at the babe. At last I could glimpse the minds behind those glassy orbs, and they were greedy and implacable and abominable. Disturbed from their aquatic routine by the churning of the storm, the Y'ha-nyarthlunians had roused themselves to intrude on the isolated, beleaguered little town and take what they felt was theirs by right: a human life. Whatever tribulation the storm caused them in Y'ha-nyarthlun, this was the horrid reward they habitually granted themselves in exchange, time after time.

They were all around me. The hag remained outside their circle, too fearful of them to come to my aid. The daughter was shrieking in maenad-like hysteria. I could see no way out of this predicament. The Y'ha-nyarthlunians closed in. Perdita was doomed, and so was I.

Unless…

I was old even then, grey-haired and spindly-limbed, with but a modicum of the strength I had known in my youth. Yet a forcefulness – a liveliness – entered me, one born of the desire to protect Perdita at all costs.

I thrust her securely into the front of my raiment, so as to free up both my hands. Then I turned and climbed.

The pillar bore so many carvings in its surface that it afforded numerous handholds and footholds. It was sheer but scalable. It was thin for its height, too, scarcely six feet in circumference. I had no notion of what I would do once I gained its summit. All I could think about was getting away from the Y'ha-nyarthlunians. They, with their flippered extremities, surely could not follow where I was going.

As I ascended I was vaguely conscious of the nature of the carvings which were giving me assistance. They were images of entities that even now I shudder to recall. Among them there were figures that were humanlike but with too many limbs, too many mouths, too many eyes. There were creatures that had no analogy to any on this earth, while certain others seemed a gallimaufry of animals of differing species, part amphibian, part reptile, part mammal. The rest were mere shapes, geometrical patterns such as even wise Euclid could not have imagined, yet they evidently represented beings who possessed sentience, for the sculptor – whoever that mad genius had been – had rendered them with the same vibrant verisimilitude as the other, more obviously life-imbued likenesses. Betwixt and between all these were arrayed the forms of men, far smaller in stature, who either cringed in obeisance to the monsters or permitted themselves to be eviscerated and consumed by them.

Sooner than I might have thought possible, I was atop the pillar. I thought myself safe, at least for the time being, but when I looked down I realised that I had underestimated the Y'ha-nyarthlunians. Several of them had elected to give chase after all. They clambered clumsily, but they were coming up nonetheless.

I looked around me, frantic. The end of the gully was not far. Perched on that narrow pinnacle I was almost level with the land surrounding the town. I could have sprung from the pillar and grasped the lip of the gully wall and hauled myself over, were it not for the fact that the gap was some twenty paces, much too far to cover in a leap from a standing start.

Perdita was grizzling at my breast, terrified. I contemplated hurling myself from the pillar's apex to the ground, ending it all for both of us. Even death seemed preferable to winding up in the Y'ha-nyarthlunians' clutches.

Ever higher the creatures inched towards us, and I became aware that the pillar was shaking. Though wrought of solid stone, it was fragile in its slenderness. It had never been intended to support additional weight. With myself, Perdita and now several of those sleek-pelted monstrosities at its summit, the pillar was top-heavy and becoming unbalanced.

I sensed, with gut-wrenching inevitability, what was about to happen.

Sure enough, it did.

THE PILLAR BEGAN to topple. The Y'ha-nyarthlunian nearest me was within reach of my foot, and I saw its eyes register a kind of dull, panicked surprise as the column of stone tilted creakily over.

Huge cracking noises emanating from its base, the pillar fell with a sweeping acceleration towards the gully wall.

More through instinct than calculation, I jumped, using the pillar's plummet to lend me momentum.

Somehow I managed to catch onto the gully's wall without crushing Perdita between me and it. I hung on for dear life as beneath us the pillar collided with the wall and broke into a score of shear-edged chunks. Y'ha-nyarthlunians tumbled from it, flailing, shrieking. One of them alone had aped my example and abandoned its purchase on the pillar before it struck. The creature now clung to the gully's wall too, on a tiny ledge some ten feet below. The rest were dashed to the ground amid the rubble of the pillar.

I scrambled up over the lip of the wall and threw myself prostrate on the horizontal terrain beyond, hunched over Perdita. I was panting and gasping and whimpering all at once, a wretch who was pathetically grateful to have survived when death had seemed a near certainty.

When at last I raised my head, I saw the silhouette of a forest in the far distance, a touch of verdure in an otherwise unpromisingly bleak and bare landscape of blasted heath. It seemed to offer sanctuary, and I made for it, limping, weeping, with poor Perdita wailing every step of the way.

Amid the trees I became disorientated and lost. I kept walking simply so as to put distance between us and that accursed gully and the nightmare we had endured there. In time, I spied the glitter of torchlight moving between the trunks. I halted and hallooed. The torch came to a standstill. I had been heard. Help was surely at hand.

"Among them there were figures that were humanlike but with too many limbs, too many mouths, too many eyes."

Illustration by Kev Crossley

In relief I set down Perdita and also the scroll and fardel, which had contrived to stay on my person throughout the alarums and excursions of the night. I straightened up – and at that moment something pounced on me from behind.

It was the Y'ha-nyarthlunian who had also leapt from the pillar. The creature had hoisted itself up from the gully and been stalking me ever since, I all unknowing, too sunk in confusion and disarray to sense it shadowing me.

It had teeth.

Its great thick-lipped maw resembled a frog's in every respect save that it contained rows of fangs as sharp as needles. These it sank into my shoulder, eliciting exquisite agony. I could not help but scream. I wrenched myself away and felt a tearing and rending of flesh – my flesh. I collapsed to all fours, and my hand happened upon a fallen branch, thick as my own wrist. With next to no thought I snatched it up as a weapon and swung it round. It caught the Y'ha-nyarthlunian a smart blow across the face. A hit, a very palpable hit. I struck again. The creature wheezed in distress and emitted a string of words which I took to be invective. A third blow to its crown stunned it so that it sank to its knees. A fourth, delivered with the last of my ebbing strength, smashed open its skull and robbed those eyes of their dim, dark intelligence. The Y'ha-nyarthlunian keeled over, dead.

I, too, keeled over. Blood poured down my back. My senses dimmed.

I could hear Perdita crying and reckoned that it would be the last sound ever to reach my ears.

MAYHAP YOU KNOW, scribe, of Perdita. You know how a girl of that name, beautiful and beloved by all, used to live in a village not far from here, raised by a shepherd and his son. You know how that shepherd enjoyed a richer estate than is habitually due one of his humble station. You may well have seen him at fairs, decked out in modest finery, pompous but well-meaning.

You know too, I imagine, that Perdita is now betrothed to Bohemia's Prince Florizel and resides in the country of her birth, Sicilia. There, she is reconciled with her father and has been reunited with her mother, the good queen Hermione, whose death proved to have been a mere subterfuge concocted with her favourite lady-in-waiting Paulina so as to keep her safe from King Leontes until such time as the balance of his mind was restored to him. Sixteen years it took, but for them all there has been a happy ending.

Likewise for me, after a fashion. I was found and presumed dead by the shepherd and his clownish son. Those rude mechanicals left me where I was but took Perdita, along with the scroll and fardel, and returned the several miles to their home. The body of the Y'hanyarthlunian they did not discover. It lay where it had fallen, concealed in undergrowth nearby. They should count themselves lucky that it was veiled from their view thus. Their simple minds might not have survived the shock.

When I came round some while later, near dead from blood loss, I managed to stagger to a nearby hamlet, where I was taken in by a kindly widow who staunched my wound and brought me back from the brink of death. Eleven whole days it was before I recovered. Only on the twelfth night did I regain my senses, and even after that I was for some goodly while a gibbering, incoherent mess.

I stayed with the widow for months thereafter, for the simple reason that I was too frail to be moved anywhere else. I ought to have tried to return to Sicilia and my dear Paulina when I was well enough, but the memory of my dream of Hermione, in all its prophetic gravity, prevented me. When I learned from a passing vagabond named Autolycus that a shepherd and his son had adopted Perdita as their own and were bringing her up together, that settled it. My duty was to ensure that she came to no harm. How could I go back to Sicilia and admit to mad Leontes that I had disobeyed his command and his daughter yet lived? Paulina and I would both be beheaded.

The widow's home became mine. She and I developed an understanding. She has no idea to this day who I used to be. She knows me not as a nobleman in self-imposed exile but just the poor, near-dead shipwrecked Sicilian whom she rescued and nursed back to health. I am content to leave it that way.

And now my narrative – my confession – is done. I have told this tale to shrive myself of guilt and shame, as I face my final journey, the trip to Dis's realm which all men must sooner or later make. I trust that Hades shall not punish me too harshly for the wrongs I have committed. The torments of Tartarus, anyway, hold no fear for me. When one has encountered the horror that is the Y'ha-nyarthlunian race, all else pales into insignificance beside.

I told the widow, with whom I now live as a man does with a wife, that it must have been a bear that attacked and mauled me in the forest. This version of events has become the universally accepted truth round these parts. Why would anyone assume it was otherwise? A bear. Of course a bear, and not anything else.

Your eyes bespeak your own mistrust, scribe. You think me deranged, an old man babbling nonsense in the last hours of his life.

I cannot reproach you for that. It is possible that that thing which was not a bear did not take just flesh from me, but a portion of my sanity as well. Who can say? Perhaps I am verily mad. Were some playwright to pen my story, which would he choose? Would he have me pursued by a bear, or by some misshapen, misbegotten monster? Which would be received better by those for whom he intended his work to be performed?

A story is only as credible as its teller, and only as acceptable as its audience deems. Mayhap I am a mere deluded fool, and this is a tale told by an idiot, full of sound and fury, signifying nothing.

As I make my exit from the stage of life, I leave it to you to choose. Truth or folly? Which is it to be, or not to be? That is the question.

THE KING IN YELLOW STOCKINGS

ED FORTUNE

WHEN THE DUKE Orsino announced, "If music be the food of love, play on, give me excess of it; that surfeiting, the appetite may sicken, and so die," I have to admit, I laughed. Such a pompous, self-important man who loved himself above all others and could no more love another than he could love a mirror. I had been laughing at the Duke for some time, of course. The man had made rather a nuisance of himself to my lady's court. I miss him terribly.

Little did I understand at the time that this was no grand statement of desire, nor the pretentious squawking of some bored noble who was venting his frustration at his inability to woo my mistress Olivia. None of us knew at the time that it was a summoning, a dire call into the wild cosmos, where things beyond our ken lurked and plotted events that would lead to the demise of us all.

The courts of Illyria were once a grand and special place. The dancing, the song, the plays; I hated it all but, by the Lord Almighty, do I miss it now. Maybe it has been my own fine sense of taste and disgust at unnecessary revelry that has saved my soul thus far, or maybe I am more deserving of torture than most. Now nothing changes, nor will it ever do so. Nothing will grow here, not love nor wheat.

And so I scratch parchment with quill in an attempt to relate to you how Illyria fell into this dark and unyielding temperament, to be lost forever more beneath the waves of ill-passion.

IT BEGAN, AS these disasters always do, with a stranger. The herald Cesario was new to Illyria. I pride myself on my spies and my sources, though if I were to be modest (as I often am, though I consider it more a vice than a virtue) I would admit that my spies are drawn from simple folk who are wont to tell elaborate tales for simple coin. Thus

I took the far spun stories of Cesario's origin to be simple hyperbole. The fair-skinned eunuch didn't look like he had come from anywhere more exotic than the land of Messaline, although having kin in that blasted and vile land would be enough for any man to hide their origin. Had I only asked what he was a herald of then perhaps we would have all been spared. In hindsight, I should have been more cautious and listened to those in my employ more. Fool that I am, I had already begun my own obsessions, and the pounding of my heart had deafened the wisdom pouring into my ears. I had begun to dare to hope that my Lady Olivia had looked upon me with a more favourable eye than I had ever imagined. Little did I know at the time that I was being deceived.

I HAD FREQUENTLY dismissed Sir Toby Belch, my lady's uncle and a true cove and knave, yet long considered him an ally. He had seen off suitors to his niece in the past as a matter of course. Many of the fine men of Illyria had attempted to woo the Lady Olivia only to fall foul of Sir Toby's kind and welcoming smile and an open bottle of wine.

At the time, I had concluded that the man was a drunk first and a fool second, but for a time he was a confederate of mine. Suitors would come and we would conspire to ruin the chances of any and all of them who came to pass. If a simple wrong-footing from me failed, then Toby was there with his repulsive habits of wine and song to lure the unwise into a ditch, where they lay ashamed and typically short of purse.

I could have put a stop to the practice, but I was so enchanted by my lady that I simply turned a blind eye. Well as much as I could; my distaste for the man was immense and he would often abuse the hospitality of anyone who showed him kindness.

He possessed none of the beauty of his niece, his face red and his hands yellowed. His body was a monument to neglect, as if he was slowly forgetting that he had anything but a belly, and a mouth and hands with which to fill it.

I SHOULD HAVE seen the signs. I should have realised that when his friend Sir Andrew Aguecheek arrived that the man was merely a servant of a greater darkness. But how could I have known? I was never one for plays or merriment. And as I say, I was distracted.

A letter from my lady took my mind. I was led to believe that the Lady Olivia had affection for me. Love is a dagger often pointed at the heart, and I was cruelly wounded by this plot. I know now that it was no cruel jest. The letter bid me to wear yellow in a way that pleased Sir Toby's dark master, rather than the Lady Olivia. Its instruction, and his cunning, led me to act the fool, and yet worse, lead me to forget who I was.

I am the famous steward of the Lady Olivia, the one named Malvolio; it was I who was responsible for her safety. Even if the letter was true (and it was not), I should have done my duty and protected her from all the suitors who sought to use the widow's grief against her and plunder her wealth.

It is my belief that Sir Toby's machinations were ritual in design. For not only did I wear the banner colours of his secret lord, I was bid to behave in a way that was not in my nature. I sacrificed the things I that made me who I was, not only for the folly of love but for this dark force that lurked all too close to us all. Such behaviour would see me locked away, which is only right for those who have lost their minds. Only fortune's fair smile let me escape such a mire, and only the scratching of a quill helps me stay clinging to what little sanity remains. I have my freedom, but only because my jailer was a fool.

It was I who let the herald into our court. My lady has often entertained the Duke Orsino; his position is such that our usual tricks have never been attempted on the likes of him. Fortunately, the man is such a narcissist that there was never any hope that she would fall for him. Cesario, his page, was another matter entirely.

Orsino's herald was blessed with an illusionary blush of youth and seemed to have the ear of anyone he cared to talk to. He arrived in the strangest garb I ever did see; long robes and a pallid mask, his long arms covered in pale white silks. All of this was used to great effect; the mask a disguise to reveal the equally pale but alluring youth beneath. Little did I understand what the herald truly was.

My sources of course had too many wild stories to tell about this herald. That he was in fact a she. That she had survived a recent shipwreck and had lost her brother in the same tragic wreck. An unlikely story, nothing human survives the shores of Illyria.

These were the least of the outlandish claims. Others said that he did in fact have a brother, a monstrous one who had indeed come from the sea but that the sea was also his home. Some said that the herald's true name was Viola. Others claimed it was a more foreign name, that the herald hailed from the long lost land called Carcosa and was in truth its renegade prince, Hastur. Never dismiss anything as fanciful nonsense. It may well end you.

I PIECED TOGETHER the full deception. (Remember that I had drunk deep of the food and wine of love and was in my cups with misplaced passion.) Cesario (or whatever his name may have been) was playing a different game from that of love with both the Lady Olivia and the Duke Orsino.

To my lady, he was her pallid king. Though I was not privy to their private conversations, I feel that the results were plain to see. Illyria's finest beauty lay ruined by the promise of the exotic and the unknown, her wit and regard eaten away by promises and lies meant to confound earthly wit.

To the Duke, I understand the idiot simply fell for the fey herald's mystery. His coy innocence and strangeness broke the bounds of brotherly love into something other.

He was once such a kind man, though a fool. As his humour changed, so too the city under his charge. The banners that bedecked its walls were replaced with a yellow sign; one that made your eyes leak to even look upon it.

It was then that the ague began. Men, strong as an ox, losing all sense of who they were and suddenly behaving as if they were someone else entirely. Elders who had spent their lives on this land suddenly forgetting the place they were standing and calling each street and river by strange and foreign names.

The Duke had changed, poisoned by the food of love.

IT WAS THE Duke who announced the play. A strange and foreign play, one that I had thought was banned (and yet I was too filled with the idea of grand romance to speak up). He was always one for song and dance but this was the strangest of plays. Illyria is not short of playwrights and actors; they infest this land like they do anywhere that allows a man to stand idle. Yet the performers came in their hordes, each to try out a role.

The bars along the docks swiftly filled as actors came to the Duke's newly opened theatre to try out for this fantastic play. Never will I see a more ragged bunch; those who came to audition never seemed the same again, their eyes sunken, their faces slack. Rumours of disease spread like wildfire, of course, and then the docks were full again, this time with fine citizens looking to flee whatever ailment was coming from that awful playhouse.

The exodus began on the calmest of days. Illyria has never seen such a ragged fleet. Each and every ship filled with people, all leaving. The Duke, refusing to issue even a simple quarantine, had announced his new play ready and that the opening night would be that very evening.

I suspect that those with enough sense were urged to flee faster. Maybe had they not been in such a hurry, then fewer would have drowned. But few survive the shores of Illyria.

The waves were the size of mountains. Those of us who still had our wits, and had stayed behind, watched agog as the elements themselves struck out at those who had the courage to leave. I have never seen water move like that, lashing tendrils of spite and malice, ripping the ships apart and devouring them whole. The storm had a shape; something that looked to be not a bat, nor bear, nor squid, nor shark, but something all the more monstrous, lurking, titan-like in the darkness as a tempest.

I watched solemnly as the few who remained filed, one by one, to the playhouse, surrendering to the inevitable. I have not seen them since. I'd even welcome the presence of Sir Toby, but he was first in line to see the final play; this was his goal all along, to embrace the ultimate excess and be drawn into this dark madness of music and pomp which eats the very soul.

I RETURNED TO my lady's court, to find it empty save for her. In her hand she held a pallid mask, and she wept openly into it, her wit stolen from her by this poisonous love. Cesario had fled to be with the Duke. The cad had suggested that she throw herself at the mercy of his brother. A strange foreigner with a stranger sounding name.

Still, I have always been my lady's most humble servant. So, as my ink runs out and the scratching sound of the quill ceases, I will take the Lady Olivia to meet this brother, this stranger. This man, if that he be, named Cthulhu.

THE TERRORS OF THE EARTH

PAT KELLEHER

I

GAZING OUT THROUGH rheumy eyes at his three daughters, gathered courtiers, nobles and servants, Great Leyh'r, son of Bladud, son of Lud, King of the ancient Isle of Albion, sat throned in Troynovant's Great Hall.

Outwardly, he bore the stately manner of a King of Albion. Inside he howled like a man condemned, beating at the confines of his cell, unable to escape his fate; a fate thrust upon him by Divine Right of Succession and the Blood of Albion that ran in his veins. He had seen some fourscore years, threescore of those upon the throne of Albion, the previous score in the company of his father, King Bladud, and his dark obsession, of which the rule of the kingdom was but the least of it.

Leyh'r felt the ineffable yoke of his office press down upon him like the years on his back that weakened his sinews, agued his bones and misted his sight. If he could bear it a little longer he might yet do some good, even though he must still carry the heavier portion of that burden alone toward death.

For lack of a son and heir he was forced to cleave his kingdom between his daughters, lest his eldest daughters' husbands, Albany and Cornwall, fall to war over it.

Leyh'r stirred on his throne, his voice echoing from the high vaulted ceiling.

"Know we have divided in three our kingdom and desire to publish our daughters' several dowers and divest ourselves of rule, interests of territory, and powers of state. Which of you, should we say does love us most? Goneril, our eldest born, speak first."

Expecting her and her husband to inherit all, Goneril quickly tamped the flash of anger in her eyes but her gaze continued to smoulder with resentment as she spoke; each honeyed word weighed and valued for the revenue it would return.

"Sire, I love you more than any child loved a father, more than eyesight, air and freedom. I love you as much as life itself."

Leyh'r knew the ill disposition in which she bore him and did not blame her. He rose and turned to the large tapestry map of Albion that hung on the wall.

"Of these bounds," – he pointed at the map – "even from this line to this, we do make thee lady."

The brief glint of avarice in Goneril's eyes, before she and Albany bowed their heads, did not go unseen by Leyh'r as he turned to his next eldest, so much like himself they often had their differences.

"What says our second daughter, our dearest Regan, wife of Cornwall? Speak."

Regan bowed, the hint of a sly smile on her face imparted toward her self-satisfied sister. With time to think, her answer was well-crafted and fashioned to appeal to the old man's vanity.

"Sire, I am made from that same spirit as my sister and consider myself her equal in all but this; she falls too short of the love I bear your Highness and that only in your love do I find happiness."

Leyh'r nodded, satisfied. "To thee and thine I give this ample third of our fair kingdom, no less in space, validity and pleasure than that conferred upon Goneril."

But guilt roiled in Leyh'r's belly like a venomous distillation, for he knew that in claiming their thrones thus they had damned themselves and their descendants, as surely as the Blood of Albion ran in their veins, too. Yet he had another daughter.

He turned to his youngest, his beloved Cordelia, Coeur de Leyh'r, the very object of his heart, and his determination almost faltered for she was too much like her mother. Her nature was so far from doing harm that she suspected none. For her, though, there would be nothing. Cordelia would never sit upon the throne of Albion. He had sworn it, even though to do so meant that it would cost him her love and that he would never see her again.

The thought raked afresh the memories of his wife's death. That he should lose a wife, a queen, and they a mother, that he should now so lose a daughter. But he knew Cordelia's faults, though they were slight, and had crafted this very stratagem to catch her and her alone. Nevertheless, the words almost turned to ashes in his mouth as he spoke.

"And now, our joy, though our last and least, what can you say to draw a third more opulent than your sisters? Speak."

Cordelia, fretted, her hands worrying at her girdle, her voice the cautious song of a sparrow after a storm: "Nothing, my lord."

"Nothing?"

She met his gaze, her eyes imploring him not to do this to her. He had seen that same look in her mother's eyes once and, broiling in shame, he looked away.

Cordelia stepped forward, appealing to him. "My lord, I cannot heave my heart into my mouth. You have begot me, bred me, loved me, and I return those duties back as are right fit. I love your majesty according to our bond, no more, no less."

He felt bound upon a rack of fire and that if he let his tears fall they would scald like molten lead. Yet he could play his part as well as his other daughters had played theirs.

"So young," said Leyh'r, aghast, "and so untender? Better thou had not been born than not to have pleased me better! By the sacred radiance of the Sun, and all the mysteries of the orbs from whom we do exist, I hereby disclaim all my paternal care, kinship, and propinquity of blood. Your third I part between your sisters and hereby banish you my sometime daughter. Four days I give thee to provision yourself against the world and on the fifth I grant thee safe passage to Gallia, never to return!"

Bewildered glances flashed between Regan and Goneril as if they would speak up. "Come not between the dragon and his wrath!" warned Leyh'r in a low growl. Cowed, they stood in silence and said nothing.

Cordelia looked at him in shock, her face caught between hurt, confusion and betrayal as he stripped away her very world, all she knew and all she thought she knew. It was the ghost of a look that had haunted him all these years.

He wanted to gather her into his arms, tell her he was sorry, that he loved her, that he was at the mercy of greater forces and all that he did, he did to spare her. Instead, he turned his face to hide the welling tears and flung out his arm.

"Go. This shall not be revoked!"

Cordelia fled the court, her sobs echoing round the hall. Perillus, one of Leyh'r's councilmen, may the gods bless and favour him, followed after.

Leyh'r's priest, Skalliger, stepped forward from his station behind the throne. "Royal Leyh'r has spoken. The session is over."

Leyh'r sat unmoving as the courtiers, guards and servants withdrew. When the great wooden doors closed on them with a sepulchral finality, he slumped against the throne, the dammed tears breaching his manhood, eroding the remains of his resolve. Tectonic heaves wracked his shoulders and his regal facade collapsed to reveal a frail old man who barely filled the great seat upon which he sat, or the robes he wore.

Skalliger strode around the dais, his robes flapping like an agitated rook.

"Cordelia banished?" he demanded.

Leyh'r looked up, eyes red, white beard wet with tears and mucus. He drew himself up, his limpid gaze frosting to a glare.

"Reason not the need, Skalliger! You may be party to this but I am Priest King of Albion as was my father before me. Prescribe not my sacral duty. I would have something saved. Something pure. Give me that at least. There is blood enough in the succession of Goneril and Regan for your purposes.

"No, do not speak. By Nodens, I have spoken. I am firm. Albion will endure. And so will my Cordelia. Beyond you, beyond this accursed isle, safe in Gallia and bounded by Nodens' protection.

"I have but one concern now and it is but the main; these late eclipses of the sun and moon. The stars are right and the Old One, Goemagot stirs from his slumber beneath Albion." He paused, laying his hand on Skalliger's shoulder, his voice wistful. "I had hoped this cup might pass from me that I might yet see out my dotage in quiet reflection and peace. But fear not. My duty is clear. Though I wish it were otherwise, I have been preparing my entire reign. And, as Daughters of Albion, so too will Goneril and Regan once they are crowned and initiated, and learn the secret I have tried so long to keep from them."

"Goemagot will yet sleep, thanks to you."

"Aye," sighed Leyh'r, as if that were of little consolation. "Come Skalliger. We must prepare for the ritual. Send forth and summon hence the Pnakotic Order, lest to Goemagot I be no warder."

II

IN ONE OF Troynovant's many cloisters a shadow resolved itself into a man. Edmund, the dutiful whoreson, had returned to Troynovant having spent years away out of sight, out of mind. But now the time was right. Now he returned to confront the old lecher, Gloucester, who begot him and his legitimate half-brother Edgar; heir to the lands, revenue and title of the Earl of Gloucester, a title he once coveted but now a mantle so meaningless and fleeting in the face of what was to come that Edmund sneered. Stepping forth from the darkness, he held a book beneath his coat, at pains to hide the thing from sight in such a place.

"Brother Edgar, you came."

"How could I not, brother?"

Edgar stared at his half-brother. He had not seen him for over a year and he had changed. His skin was pallid and his watery eyes bulged.

"Edmund, you're ill. Shall I fetch the apothecary?"

Edmund waved away his concerns with an unnervingly wide smile. "This is no illness, plague, or pestilence, brother. This is who I am, the unnatural fruit of your dear father's loins."

"You mean our father. He has ever held us both alike in his affections."

"No. He is your father, not mine. He but sired me. My true father does yet sleep till I wake him."

"I do not follow. What game is this?"

"Your father," said Edmund, patiently, as if teaching a recalcitrant child its alphabet, "consorted with unnatural things in blasphemous acts and brought me into the world. See for yourself. I have the proof of it here in this book. Look well where I have marked it."

He thrust the book into Edgar's hand.

Edgar's brow furrowed at the strange and indecipherable script.

"I cannot read it."

But then a kind of comprehension dawned as the heretical script spoke not to the eye but directly to the mind, wherein Edgar began to conceive the meaning of the marks.

"Oh gods, gods! Blasphemy!"

He fell to his knees and his bright eyes dulled as reason fled. Contaminated by its necromantic touch, he thrust the book away from him, as he might a poisoned dagger or envenomed cup. Seeking to put distance between himself and the foul tome he fell, scrabbling back to the corner of the cloister.

Edmund calmly closed the book, smiling. "Why brand you us with 'blasphemy', 'blasphemer', 'blasphemous?'"

But Edgar was no longer listening. His eyes were wide with a vertiginous terror that threatened to pull his mind into the abyss. Overcome by an overwhelming desire to flee, Edgar dragged himself up by means of a column and ran.

Edmund watched his maddened brother stagger off. It mattered not. The burning ember of corruption had already taken hold of Edgar's mind and would consume what wits he had left, like a spark to tinder.

He put a hand into the leather pouch at his waist and felt the small graven image there and smiled his unnaturally wide smile.

"Of late a rumour I dripped into unsuspecting ears, that it should spread like a canker and blacken the name of Gloucester. I have word that my invention thrives. Now, Goemagot, stand up for bastards."

Edgar stumbled through the claustrophobic passages and stairwells of Troynovant until he found a gate that opened from the suffocating stones into the open air, his place in this cosmic creation only too clear to him now as he fell to his knees beneath the vast cold firmament that neither knew nor cared of his existence. Looking up at the night sky, his mind was swamped by a cold immensity until he felt diminished. Insignificant. Lost.

"Edgar, I nothing am!" he screamed.

III

The untimely rage of the King unsettled the Court and, in the following weeks, whispers, like water running downhill, trickled quickly through the corridors and cloisters of Troynovant.

"Is our Royal father mad?" asked Regan. "He has ever been cold and distant as the stars with us, while he shone like the sun on Cordelia. But now he has removed our youngest sister from his affections as surely as our mother's o'er hasty death removed him from ours."

Goneril shrugged. "We know the guilt he bears for our mother's early death; we were old enough to grasp some measure of the gulf that grew between them and to know the blame was his, even if we know not the reason. Yet was Cordelia too young to know anything."

"Aye, he has long doted on her in atonement for our mother's passing; how is it that she bears the full brunt of his fury? 'Tis madness. And now he girds his personage with strange and riotous knights of gods know what provenance. No doubt his tortured mind sees foes where there are friends, and fears phantasmic reprisal."

"If he is mad, it is well he did what he has before he lost all his reason," replied Goneril.

"Aye, we have waited long enough for this. Now the kingdom is parted betwixt us we have no need of caring. Thus may we truly regard him with that scant worth he is due and turn him out like a mad dog that has bit its master, for in truth I know not when he will turn his wrath on us."

"You speak my very thoughts, sister. Once we return to our seats for our coronations and become true Daughters of Albion, he shall have no succour from me or mine. We shall turn our faces and bar our doors against him and whatever knights now attend him, for fear of our persons."

IV

The Earl of Gloucester was troubled. The vigorous knight who once championed the king had long since run to an amiable bulk. An old man, ruddy of complexion and silver hair a-wisp, he stared into the blazing hearth, lost in thought. He had no doubt that those who envied his friendship with the old king would move against him. In times such as these with a crown divided, allegiances shifted, loyalties were bought and sold, accusations of conspiracy and treason spread as rivals sought to curry favour with the newly ennobled. Recent rumours concerning his own character had given him more cause to worry.

Gloucester glanced up from the fire. The youth loitering in the shadows beyond the heat of hearth did little to ease his concern. Edmund had been away at Bladud's Great University, and away he would again. But the whoreson must be acknowledged.

"You look ill," said Gloucester, returning his gaze to the flames. "Have you seen Edgar? I have not had word from him these three nights past."

Edmund sat down across from him and leaned forward, resting his forearms on his knees and gazed intently at the old man.

"You say I am ill. Very well," he said. "Glean what afflicts me."

The old man studied his son's face. It appeared familiar yet different. His wiry brows wrestled with the enigma until finally they reared up in alarm.

"You... you have the Deeping look!"

"There we have it!" said Edmund bestowing his wide smile upon the old man.

Gloucester was on his feet, shaking his head vehemently. "No. No! Your mother was ever fair and you were as well-proportioned as any honest issue."

Fire-cast shadows writhed across Edmund's face. "You consorted with a lineage more ancient than your own, in black and blasphemous acts. And such was the rumour I dropped like a poison into the ears of the court."

"Oh, villain! Blasphemous villain. It is not true!"

"Oh, it is." Edmund's voice was inhumanly calm, no longer slave to the choleric humours to which Man was heir. "At the university I discovered heretical texts collected by the old necromancer Bladud himself. In them I learned the secret of the Blood of Albion, whereupon I began to have such strange dreams.

"Compelled by my visions, I wandered into the Deepings hard by the university. There I found my mother in the village where you left her and she revealed to me my true nature. When you lay with her, you consorted with a Deeping One, a follower of the Old Ones. That which I inherit proceeds from the maternal."

"Fie on you! I brought you up a son of Gloucester. You owe me thanks, boy. Obeisance."

"You cannot appeal to my filial duty. But you do have that for which I must be thankful: your still soliciting eye and your bawdy lusts. And if not for your foppish conscience I would have fared little better than the rest of my outcast clan. If it is the legitimate you seek, then the Deeping Ones have more claim over this land than any hereabouts."

"Oh, treason!"

"Don't mock me with false outrage. I owe you no fealty. That I owe to a greater power. The Old Ones are my gods now and to their law my services are bound. My 'true' father, Goemagot, does but sleep 'til I wake him. Then I shall see him do such things! What they are yet I know not, but they will be the terrors of the earth!"

"You're mad!"

"Oh no, not I." He reached for the leather pouch at his waist. "Here. See the truth of it for yourself. She gave me this in commemoration of him."

He thrust into Gloucester's face a small graven image, worn with age, its features all but rubbed away through reverent handling.

"Look! See what a dread and terrible purpose is seated on this brow?"

Gloucester saw the truth of it, and far more. He shook his head, and rubbed the calloused heels of his hands against his eyes to abrade what he had seen, the horror of what he had done in begetting Edmund. And in his mind he saw the writhing bulk of the graven creature, as large as a hill fort, rise up from beneath the earth and turn its eyes upon him.

In a paroxysm of terror, he wormed his fingers into his eye-sockets and with a bestial howl tore out the profane organs, as much as for what they had seen as what they failed to see.

He collapsed to the ground, pain briefly numbing the horror he felt as, tender and newly blind, he flinched from repeated kicks as Edmund drove him toward the door as one might a beggar, casting his father out into the night.

Edmund regarded the bloody orbs on the floor, naught now but offal. He ground the jellies into the flagstones, feeling them burst beneath his heel.

"Now to attend the Daughters of Albion and to draw from them that which my Gloucester-father loses, no less than all. The Old One rises when the young doth fall."

V

NAMELESS EMISSARIES, HERALDS from distant kingdoms where learnèd men kept watch on the stars, and eldritch scholars from Bladud's University, came daily to Troynovant. Their haunted visages and truculent manners did nothing to assuage the Court's opinion that the old king was mad. And some courtiers repeated the oft heard refrain that he was never the same since the death of the queen. Strange knights whose shields bore heraldic devices of unknown origin arrived at Troynovant by ship in the dead of night, the sounds of chanting could be heard from the royal chambers and the smell of strange incense drifted about the cloisters.

The arcane practices continued until one morning, just before dawn, when a column of a hundred Knights of the Pnakotic Order rode forth from Troynovant, accompanying Leyh'r, Priest King of Albion, his high priest Skalliger, and a small group of acolytes and scholars, north along the King's road.

The land gradually rose, leaving the rich forests and wide-skirted meads behind. The road gave way to drovers' trails and cart ruts that wound up sparsely-populated valleys, through banks of brown withered bracken where scabrous sheep watched them pass without interest.

Soon even the tracks and trails petered out, and cairns and waymarkers vanished, along with any sign of human habitation.

They reached the top of the moors to be met by a howling damp wind laden with the threat of rain. There, open before them, lay the foul Fell; a vast undulating, almost featureless plateau, where low-lying mists clung to the sodden earth like a cawl, the horizon permanently lost in a haze of mist, haunted by the spectres of hillocks and solitary menhirs marking the Fell's boundary. Here and there splintered crags thrust up through the pustulent surface of the moor like the shattered bones of a decomposing corpse.

In this place, Man seemed nothing more than a skim of civilisation, a daub on the wattle of an ancient, unknowable world. The might and intelligence that built Troynovant, Caerbran and Caerleir held no sway here.

Leyh'r felt a wave of despair and shivered. It fell to him now, as High Priest King of Albion to discharge the last of his divine duties, one he did not relish, but he had lived a long life. He was ready, Cordelia was safe and he had spent the last weeks purifying and preparing himself, learning the ritual incantations.

Nonetheless, he wished he had been a bloodier and more belligerent King, then he might have died in glory in battle at the height of his manhood and been long dead ere the stars crept toward their blasphemous alignment. Yet he had overseen a reign of peace and his life had been a long and healthy one, unperturbed by war. But even those kingdoms with which they had treaties regarded Albion with dark suspicion and thanked their gods for the intervening sea.

Among the expanses of bogs and rounded hillocks scoured by ancient ice, an occasional carved, weather-stained cyclopean block of unsettling dimensions emerged through the swirling mists, as if some titanic hand had tossed them there. On a barren plateau that admitted no other imposition of intelligence, their presence was disturbing.

An intermittent keening wind, if wind it was, howled through the crags and hidden hollows with an awful inhuman lament, bringing with it a surge of unnameable fear. The Order of Pnakos unfurled their banners, embroidered with the Elder Sigil, and muttered wards of protection under their breaths.

The horses became skittish and recalcitrant as they wound in single file between black viscous pools, and their riders struggled to control them. One knight's horse panicked and lost its footing, sending both rider and mount into a quagmire. Despite desperate attempts to save them, both were lost to the foul sucking mud.

After that they abandoned the horses, leaving some men behind to tend them. Leyh'r strapped the ceremonial sword to his waist, drew the satchel carrying the forbidden scrolls containing the ritual formula over his shoulder, and proceeded on foot.

Loud cracks and rumblings from the ground stirred up pestilent vapours from the clinging bogs, and by midday heavy storm clouds had filled the firmament from horizon to horizon, to be met there by the spectral mists that clung tenaciously to the Fell.

As they wound across the bleak unforgiving landscape, a nagging anxiety continued to sweep through the accompanying knights. They had not the training and eldritch knowledge to fortify their minds as Leyh'r and his acolytes had, and throughout the day the maddening drip of apprehension and fear continued to diminish the train's numbers. Men lost themselves in the low mist and slunk off, a rising dread smothering their shame.

With night approaching, those of the Order that remained made camp on a rocky outcrop that stood proud of a fetid mire where strange pale plants grew, their thin tendrils whipping sluggishly at the air.

"What, half my men gone?" protested Leyh'r when he heard.

"What need have we of a hundred?" reasoned Skalliger. "Fifty will do."

"What need we of fifty, my lord?" asked another. "Ten will suffice to see you delivered to the Stones, and each will gain a greater part of the glory when Albion is safe again."

Leyh'r smiled indulgently. There could be no glory in this place, of that he was sure, but there was no reason to disabuse a man clinging to what hope he could.

Unable to sleep for fear of the dreams he knew would come, Leyh'r watched the slow sweep of the stars that brought the awakening of Goemagot ever nearer, along with his own indentured end. The temperature dropped. Frost crusted the peat and a brittle ice spread over the boggy pools as if, in their passage, the cold stars had touched the Earth itself.

Leyh'r shuddered, and not from the night's chill.

VI

THE NEXT DAY brought a relentless freezing rain that soaked into clothing and sapped morale. More knights had slipped away in the night. Those few that remained looked tired and haggard, their sleep tormented by the same strange dreams.

The cyclopean ruins grew more numerous and water sluiced off the weathered blocks as if nature itself sought to wear them away through stubborn erosion. The rain filled stagnant pools to overflowing so that the ground became a sodden treacherous bog of sucking peat, the water cutting rivulets through the Fell into the becks before rushing headlong over rocks, through crevices, cascading over ledges and lips in great spates of foaming rust-coloured water that roared down off the malignant moor.

It seemed to Leyh'r as if the entire landscape had been so suddenly thrust up from the sea that the water sought its way back to the ocean in torrents.

The heavy clouds lent a greenish preternatural cast to the light and violent gusts of wind drove the rain almost horizontally across the Fell, reducing visibility until Leyh'r and Skalliger lost sight of the remains of the Order entirely. Still, they had one concern and it drove them on. They had but to head in the direction from which the emanations of dread issued, pulsing out in great waves that threatened to swamp their resolve.

Crashes of thunder added their tumultuous reports to the chaos, answering the rumbles from beneath the ground as if two vast and primordial titans clashed. Leyh'r had no doubt that it was Nodens wrestling with the waking Old One.

"Goemagot stirs!" bellowed Skalliger over the storm.

"We have to be at the Stones when the stars are right or else all is lost!" Leyh'r called back, as the storm lashed around them.

Assailed by another wave of unutterable dread, Leyh'r recited Belshim's formula, a ward of protection from the Pnakotic manuscripts, attempting to furl the sails of his mind against the psychic tempest lest they be torn to ribbons, and all that was Leyh'r wrecked and sunk without trace.

However, his mind, more frail than it had been in his youth, gave way to the supernatural assault. His wits broke free of their moorings and Leyh'r vanished beneath another swell of malevolent terror, forgetting all purpose and design, clinging only to the guilt that weighed him down, drowning him in anguish and remorse.

He stood upon a rock, his tattered mantle clinging to his slight frame, his threadbare white hair and beard plastered to his head. His hands grasped at unseen things; fleeting memories illuminated by the lightning before they were lost and scattered to the winds like leaves in a hurricane.

Merwin, his wife; beautiful, serene, smiling fondly at their two young daughters laughing in the sunlight of Troynovant's gardens, the babe Cordelia at her breast.

Merwin, her face red, contorted in anger and abhorrence as she raged at him, beating him with such small fists.

Merwin lost, silent, eyes vacant.

Merwin...

"Merwin!" Leyh'r beat at his head and let out a tormented howl of grief. "Oh, why should a dog, a horse, a rat, have life and you no life at all?"

VII

SKALLIGER DESPAIRED AS his King, on whom everything still depended, snatched at phantoms in the storm. He seized Leyh'r by his arm, but the old king shrugged him off, his attention caught by something else. Leyh'r cocked his head, listening intently.

Skalliger drew his sword, stomach clenched tight in anticipation of he knew not what. "Who's there? Make yourself known!"

Skalliger could not bring himself to call what crawled out of the tempest a man. Naked but for a cloth around his loins, his skin was a confusion of bruises, cuts and abrasions, his hair knotted and bedraggled and his body smeared with the filth of the Fell.

He loped cautiously toward Skalliger, all the while flinching from some invisible assault. "Beware the Foul Fiend!"

"What's that it says?" asked Leyh'r, peering curiously at the stranger.

"The Foul Fiend has led me here through whirlpool, bog and quagmire!"

"What are you called?"

"Called? I had a name once. Edgar." At his mention of the name, the man's limbs spasmed in a fit that quickly passed. "The Foul Fiend took it, fouled it and left me with nothing and so will he do to everything else when he awakes, walks Albion's hills once more, and builds again his old demesne. Poor Tom's a-cold."

Leyh'r crouched down on his haunches to inspect the creature hunkered on the ground, his back to the rain. "I saw you and I thought a man a worm." He nodded sagely. "So are we all in face of the Old Ones."

Skalliger noticed that mention of the Foul Fiend seemed to draw Leyh'r from his phantasms to something like his purpose and dared to hope that this benighted creature may do Leyh'r some good.

In the distance he spied a titanic ruin.

"My liege!" Skalliger yelled through the storm, half-blinded by the rain. "Over yonder lies some refuge. Come. Let us wait out this present squall there."

He led Leyh'r, who continued to talk in earnest with his new companion, out of the stinging rain and biting wind and into the relative calm of the ruins.

Although the partial shelter of the ancient ruin gave them some respite from the storm, Skalliger did not wish to dwell upon what foul purpose it might have been put to when it was first raised here.

The roof had long since collapsed and the rubble worn and weathered was softened by lichens. Most of the building stood open to the elements, but one intact section provided a windbreak from the worst excesses of the storm.

Skalliger ushered Leyh'r into a cove, along with the unkempt madman calling himself Tom – for the name Edgar seemed to provoke in him such dread that his body rebelled against it.

A voice from further in the shadows called out a warning.

"Come no closer, I beseech you. If you are of sound mind and limb and uncorrupted by the spawn of Goemagot, come no closer. I am a broken man. Vile and unnatural copulation has been my sin!"

The man stepped from the shelter of the shadows, his hand groping clumsily along the wall, his fingers and nails bloody and ragged from such wear.

"It is not the Foul Fiend," said Tom, after consideration "for of eyes he has a hundred. This poor man has none. See there, the unhappy hollows of his face?"

Skalliger peered at the man. "I know you," he said. "Are you not Earl of Gloucester? How came you here?"

"Sir, having no eyes, I smelt this place out, its preternatural stench leading me here that I might yet see some mischief on my ill-begotten bastard's scheme. There is harm set against Albion by one who would liberate dread Goemagot from his dreaming, whose sigils and signs are seared into my very mind. They craze my wits and I have no eyes left to shut against them. My whoreson Edmund, who I did beget with a Deeping One in abhorrent union, has vowed to see the Old One rise and his unnatural fortunes with it."

Leyh'r reached out, touched the old man's face and nodded in sympathy. "I know well the guilt a father bears."

Gloucester cocked his head and winced. "I know that voice. Is't not the King?"

Leyh'r sighed in reverie. "Aye every inch a king, yet not so, for I lack a queen. I had one once, but she discovered my duty; to wit that my life has been forfeit since my coronation as was my father's before him and his before him.

"For those of royal blood are, by Divine succession, the Priest-Kings of Albion. Our duty is sacral and sacrificial, that at the end of our days, or when the need arises, we give in ritual our life and blood so that Goemagot the Great Old One remains a-bed.

"Conceiving three royal daughters of Albion, my sweet Merwin then by unhappy chance conceived the arcane knowledge that their sacred lives, too, were forfeit. That the children she bore me, and those they might bear in turn, could one day face the same fate as I by virtue of the blood they shared. My queen, her maternal instincts o'erwhelming her Royal duty, grieving my perceived betrayal at our daughters' fate, fell into a rage and from there into a melancholy, and thence into a madness from which not even her children could rouse her. So, confining her to keep her from harm or harming, one day in the grip of a lunatic fit she escaped and leapt from a high tower rather than bear a son and heir to inherit such a dread mantle."

Leyh'r hung his head. "I have mourned her ever since and sought a way to right the wrong I did her."

Gloucester gasped. "Disowning and banishing Cordelia."

Leyh'r nodded. "It is not all, but I hope that saving one daughter from the curse of Albion's Blood is enough. Now I go to make my peace and perform my sacrificial duty 'ere the stars are right, that Goemagot may not yet wake."

"Then we must go, my liege," Skalliger declared. "We must brave the storm again to reach the Stones, but the way is treacherous and we may not make it."

"Then it is madness to go out there," said Gloucester. "Here is a way that delves into the earth, and under it. I have taken refuge in it before and it leads to a passage."

"This is Goemagot's domain," countered Skalliger, "and I have no doubt the Fell is but the barrow that entombs him. If he sleeps yet, then we may reach the Stones in time."

VIII

GLOUCESTER FELT HIS way along the gigantic blocks, his fingers inching over glyphs that Skalliger could scarce see, but those illuminated by bursts of lightning told a story he had only previously known from forbidden texts. Here, in carvings made by some primeval hand, he saw glimpses of great cities populated by amphibious men serving monstrous creatures, the sight of which was mercifully all too brief, underscoring the fact that the places through which they now walked were once sovereign to greater powers than Man. Giants once walked here. This land, of which Albion was nothing but the surviving promontory after the greater share of it sank beneath the waves, was theirs and would be again if Leyh'r failed.

The party continued to edge their way down to the gloom. Here Nature stood on the very verge of her confine and other laws held sway. Water that seeped down ran in unnatural directions. The walls and angles seemed wrong and confused the eyes, inducing a nausea. It was all they could do not to flee.

Only blind Gloucester seemed sure of his footing. "Take my hand, let me guide you. I have not eyes to deceive," he said.

Leyh'r placed his hand on Gloucester's shoulder and Skalliger on his, while Poor Tom, with no mind left to lose, made his own way, canary-like, watching for signs of the Foul Fiend.

Even with their eyes closed, they were not immune to the strange geometries of the place. "I think we go the wrong way. We labour down precipitous slopes into the depths and I fear we may fall," protested Skalliger.

"Nay the ground is even," declared Gloucester.

But it was not enough to take it on faith. Skalliger opened his eyes. The space was lit my some faint luminescence from deep below only serving to confirm what his other senses told him. "Nay, 'tis horrible steep, the walls rise and others drop away and the angles of the stone... Methinks we look down from a dread summit into a bottomless pit."

"Close your eyes lest your brain turn and your deficient sight send you tumbling into the unnatural abyss to which these perverse geometries are but the brink. I tell you, the ground is even!" declared Gloucester.

Leyh'r heard Tom sniff the air in long draughts, and caught a hint himself of a foul odour that almost made him retch as it drifted up on some warm updraft from unspeakable depths.

"The Foul Fiend. I smell him. He comes, he comes!" Tom cried.

Leyh'r reached out blindly, laying a palsied hand on the crouching madman's shoulder, seeking to quiet him, remembering that it did as much in thunderstorms for Tray, Blanche and Sweetheart, Merwin's favourite dogs.

As the unnatural stench assailed his nostrils, Skalliger let go of his liege's shoulder and drew his sword. Hearing a gelatinous heaving and slapping, he opened his eyes again.

"My lord! Flee! Oh, gods –"

Skalliger managed to scream before something wet and heavy abruptly silenced him and dragged him into the depths.

The rest hurried as fast as Gloucester's hands could find the way and they soon felt the cold wet breeze on their faces, and the rocks became wet and slippery under their hands as they emerged onto the surface of the Fell again.

Rain, driven by a chill wind, began to saturate Leyh'r's robes anew. He listened briefly for sound of pursuit, and heard nothing but the wind shrieking over the blasted heath. They had come out under the summit of a large hillock atop which stood a circle of seven large stones, each twice as tall as a man.

Leyh'r's shoulders slumped. The weight of his duty was almost tangible now and his fragile mind buckled under another wave of malign emanations from the Old One below, the psychic assault beginning to crumble what fragmentary resolve remained.

"Enough. Let it be now. The stars do not pause in their journey and neither must I. The hour draws near."

He looked to the blind Gloucester and to the madman, Tom, who had got him this far. He would ask no more of them. But his body was frail and he was exhausted mentally and physically, and he loathed himself for it.

"Fellows, take me but to the crest of that sacral hill. I have one last act as King that I must yet perform; my final abnegation."

He could have wept in gratitude when they each took to his side and step-by-step the three of them laboured against the buffeting wind until they reached the summit. There, the great stones rose about him and in the centre stood the stone altar, stained dark with the Blood of Albion, where his predecessors had sacrificed their lives.

He clapped his companions on the shoulders. "Go now, there is work to be done that is not for the likes of thee. Bid me farewell and let me hear thee going."

Edgar took Gloucester's hand and began to tug at it, urging the blind man away.

"Come, sirrah, come. The Foul Fiend approaches!"

They had reached the edge of the circle, when from the shadows of the nearest standing stone stepped one whose skin was like to the stones themselves, wet and glistening with a batrachian sheen. Edmund, sword in hand, his wide eyes nictating, herded them back.

"No, stay. The great Goemagot awakens and I would have you witness my rise before you fall."

A surge of indescribable terror rippled through the circle, paralysing the trio with fear and loosening bowels. Their minds roiled in its wake and the men sank to their knees crying out in anguish.

Only Edmund seemed immune. He strode over to where aged Leyh'r clung to the altar, his hands pressed in a rigor against the stained and weathered stone, his thin skin clinging to his bones like damp cloth. He took the ceremonial blade from Leyh'r's scabbard, weighing it in his hand.

Leyh'r looked up almost without comprehension, his body still gripped by a peristalsis of fear.

Edmund leaned down. "Oh, I do not mean to kill you. Not yet. I need only delay your death until Goemagot awakes."

Tears welled up in Leyh'r's eyes and he slumped against the altar stone. The passing convulsions of fear leaving him drained and defeated. His entire life had brought him to this point. Everything he had sacrificed, all he had lost, and he had failed.

Edmund circled the stones, holding the blade aloft in triumph and calling out in an ancient tongue that had not been heard on those hills for eons.

Lightning spat angrily around the stones. The ground rumbled its defiance in return.

"Beneath Albion, Goemagot has dreamed!" cried Edmund with apocalyptic zeal. "Now he awakens!"

One of the great stones toppled as the bulk of the hill heaved upwards. Goemagot stirred. Thick black pseudopods burst from the earth, writhing mockeries of the stone sentinels that had stood there immobile since time immemorial.

Seeing the great tentacles, Leyh'r despaired until a terrible thought took hold. The ritual required only blood and death. The ceremonial sword was an affectation, quick and painless, but it was no longer in his possession. And yet there were other methods of self-sacrifice, if one were desperate enough.

"Oh Leyh'r, Leyh'r, Leyh'r! Beat at this gate that let thy dear folly in and thy dear judgement out!"

He smashed his head against the altar stone. Again and again he dashed his skull against the rock, speaking the words of the ritual, punctuating them with pain and blood. But it was too slow. He would lose consciousness before he died. Despondent, he collapsed.

IX

CURLED UP AND whimpering, a moment of lucidity forked though Tom's mind like lightning, a moment in which he fully knew himself again but briefly; a candle guttering against a draught. He must act before the flame went out.

Naked and bleeding and with an incomprehensible bellow of rage, he launched himself at his half-brother, driving him to the ground, the ceremonial sword spinning from his grasp.

Edgar, feeling the tide of madness rise to swamp him once again, seized the sword and thrust it into his half-brother's body.

Edmund's eyes met those of his strange sibling in pained surprise. He watched as Edgar's keen intelligence struggled vainly against the madness that threatened to consume him again, even as death clouded his own vision.

Edmund pulled Edgar toward him and hissed venomously, "My death comes too late, brother. I have murdered the Daughters of Albion, Goneril by poison, Regan by dagger. The bloodline is finished. Nothing now can stop Goemagot. Nothing..." And with that, the Deeping One's unnatural spawn died.

Edgar recalled that he could not read the words in the book Edmund had shown him, yet even written down they contained such power as would strip a man of his mind. He wondered, did the words need to be spoken aloud at all?

He crouched by the bloodied, semi-conscious Leyh'r, opened the satchel and took out the parchment containing the words of the ritual.

He pulled the sword from Edmund's lifeless body and thrust the parchment onto the point of the blade, intending to drive both into the body of the waking giant, trusting that intent alone would suffice to complete the dread ritual, or at least do some harm. Pushing the parchment down to the hilt he turned, ready to impale the unspeakable creature.

A flash of lightning illuminated the sheer immensity of the creature as it now reared high above the stones and in that one brief fantastic glance, the afterimage of the creature seared itself on his mind's eye with such terrible force that what was left of his sanity, and Edgar, burnt away. He dropped the sword, envenomed with words so ancient the human tongue could barely speak them, and howled in anguish.

Gloucester crawled towards the sound, sightless, groping at the wet earth until he came upon him and stroked the face that he would never see again.

Tom groaned. "The sword..."

"No words, no words. Hush."

The old man felt around until he found the abandoned blade. Unperturbed by the sight that so unhinged his son, Gloucester stood up. Though blind, his mind reeled from the emanations pulsating out from the creature. All he had to do was to charge toward their source.

Leyh'r sat, numb with shock.

His daughters dead? Goneril and Regan? Oh gods! His burden, the Blood of Albion, had brought them to their premature deaths, as it had his wife Merwin.

He watched, resigned, as the great terrible mass writhed above him, shaking off its slumber as a deep resonant rumble filled the earth.

Blinking away the rain, Leyh'r saw Gloucester pick up the ceremonial blade, with the ritual parchment still skewered to it, and charge at Goemagot as fearlessly as the Earl once charged the foes of Albion.

But no champion could stand for Leyh'r now. The last of the Blood of Albion resided but in him. Only Leyh'r could succeed. He struggled to his feet and staggered between the blind old knight and his foe, reciting the ritual incantation even as Gloucester made his thrust.

The blade pierced Leyh'r's heart as Gloucester drove on into Goemagot and the creature cried out. The seismic reverberation of the hideous sound burst Gloucester's heart, killing him instantly.

Impaled upon Goemagot's corrupt flesh by the blade and its skewered parchment, Leyh'r continued with a wanton determination to pronounce those syllables that would yet banish Goemagot as the

Blood of Albion pulsed ever more weakly from his body. Even as his heart beat its last he knew that his true heart, Coeur de Leyh'r, lived free from the curse of that self-same blood and if this was the price then he would willingly pay it to keep her safe.

As the last syllable of the ritual passed Leyh'r's lips, lightning lashed down from the sky, striking the pommel protruding from his chest. In one furious moment of reaction, sword, text, blood, incantation and lightning combined in an alchemical superflux, as if Nature itself struck out in abhorrence of the thing.

Leyh'r's lifeless body ignited, sticking like burning phosphor to the Old One's degenerate bulk, tearing a terrible scream from whatever obscene orifice the thing used for a mouth. Attempting to recoil from the pain, it contracted like a slug from salt, until the last of the primordial giant slithered back into its barrow beneath the Earth, although its screams haunted Albion's dreams for days after.

X

POOR TOM AWOKE in the remains of the stone circle. He didn't know whether the abomination was dead, sleeping or merely licking its wounds, but overcome with revulsion for the place, he picked his way across the Fell. Several days later, bruised, bleeding and grimed in filth, he staggered down off the moor.

Living among Troynovant's back alleys and middens he scratched a meagre existence, lost in the endless liturgical babble with which he sought to ward himself. Whomsoever he met, he warned against the Foul Fiend and no discouragement by rod or stocks dissuaded him from his ministry.

One day, drawn out by the sounds of celebration, he pushed though the crowds to see jugglers, acrobats and dumb shows. Heartened for the first time in a long while, he approached a gentlewoman.

"What festival is this?"

The woman scowled at him irritably. "Surely every fool knows that?"

Tom smiled blankly at her.

"Tis the coronation of Queen Cordelia, of course. Her as was exiled to Gallia by the old King, but with him gone, and her sisters dead she's the rightful heir, so she is returned to be crowned Queen this very day. Her mother, Queen Merwin, would be so proud, gods rest her spirit."

Tom's smile vanished as a stark realisation chilled him to the soul.

Cordelia didn't know. Upon her coronation, the priests would induct her into the true purpose of her sovereignty, condemning herself and any future children to the very fate from which Leyh'r sought so desperately to spare her.

He pushed urgently to the front of the crowd lining the procession route as Cordelia passed by, waving happily to the crowds.

He cried out in warning, "Beware the Foul Fiend! Beware the Foul Fiend!"

But his voice was drowned out by the chorus of joyous cheers and she was gone.

Later, when the bells rang out in honour of the newly crowned Queen, a shadow of despondency fell over him. Consumed by a rising anxiety he rocked back and forth with increasing agitation.

"Tom's a-cold," he whimpered. "Poor Tom's a-cold."

"In one furious moment of reaction, sword, text, blood, incantation and lightning combined in an alchemical superflux..."

Illustration by Tony Hough

Exeunt

John Reppion

Act One: Two Noble Kinsmen

BANKSIDE, LONDON. MARCH, 1616.

"MY DEAR FRIEND, I do not see why it is you torture yourself so. *Cardenio* is a fine work, though I say it myself. I am proud of what we have done together. The King's Men will make an outstanding job of it under your guidance."

William Shakespeare bent to clap a reassuring hand on the shoulder of the figure hunched at the desk.

"More than that, it is precisely what the people want. Comedy, tragedy, these are the things you have a gift for."

Fletcher, the fingers of one hand entwined in his dishevelled locks, glanced up sullenly at his companion.

"So say you, a man who has never been content merely to give the audience what they want."

William stood, raising his hands in a gesture of defeat, then traversed the small, ill-lit room.

"You cannot force an idea. There is time yet to let the notion form. To develop, to germinate, over years if necessary. You are but thirty-five."

John Fletcher threw himself back into an upright sitting position with exasperation, his chair creaking in protest at the maltreatment.

"Thank you, o ancient magus for your words of wisdom. What fortune is mine in having such an owlish mentor? Help yourself to another cup of sack, won't you."

William was already pouring out two measures of the sickly sweet sherry wine, a smirk upon his lips. He handed one cup to his friend then drank deeply from his own. John stared down at the liquid, black and viscous in the flickering candlelight.

"*The Tempest* is your master-work, William. I believe it absolutely, and you have said as much yourself. Is it the ache in your bones and the white in your beard that made it so? Must I wait until I am so old and bent and ugly as you to achieve such?"

Spluttering laughter broke forth from the pair and, his sulking thus interrupted, Fletcher knocked back his syrupy wine in one draught.

"All the world's a stage, and all the men and women merely players." John, staggering slightly, retrieved the sack and sloshingly re-filled his cup. "Yet Prospero is more than that. He is the author of his own tale. His art is artifice; his witchcraft is stagecraft. You are he, and he is you."

"In some sense," Shakespeare conceded with a contemplative swig of his drink. His mind drifted back to a half-forgotten fever-dream of his early career when the plague had struck down players and audience alike at The Rose Theatre. He had been ill himself and his memories of the time were a strange confusion of real and unreal horrors. His disquieting reminiscences were cut short by his friend.

"Yet, even as our dramatis personae suffer, we know why it is we make it so. We pluck at the heartstrings because we – the playwrights, the sorcerers, the Gods of the stage-world – know how to elicit a response. We know the bitter-sweetness of longing, the sting of loss, the gnawing of revenge, the ecstasy of love. Raw emotion becomes music upon the page and in the mouths and on the faces of the players. What though, if we were as indifferent, as uncaring, as the author of the world outside that window?"

Fletcher's index finger stabbed towards an un-curtained, diamond-paned portal. Outside the sky was a starless void, a mere piece of black cloth – a backdrop – suspended there in likeness of night.

"Everything we do is simplification. Our skill is in bringing order out of chaos. People want to see their lives and experiences rendered thus, made sense of, but it is a lie! If we could only turn our hand to the truth, just imagine the impact it would have."

Feeling unsteady on his feet, Shakespeare sat. The chair seemed to groan beneath him as if it had not anticipated such a burden, an unwelcome reminder that he was not the man he once was. The ache in his bones, so comedically alluded to by his companion, was genuine. He felt it more acutely now, the veneer of youthfulness the drink provided unexpectedly stripped away.

"Our conversation runs in circles, my friend. Have a care lest in a moment you are returned to your desk, head in your hands, telling me you cannot explain yourself any better than you already have. I say to you once again that I am very proud of the work we have done together, but cannot conceive of this idea you hint at. This grand tragedy. This idea, the substance of which eludes even you, its originator."

John Fletcher opened his mouth to interrupt but William held up a hand, forestalling him.

"There are truths in tales, truths in songs, truths in plays truer than any in the mundane world. Love was never so perfect, death never so tragic. We are liars? Is the weaver lying when she tells us the wool from a sheep's arse is now a hat? Is the brewer a liar, passing off mere water as ale? You and I sir, are alchemists turning the lead of human drudgery into pure gold. You say what if we gave them reality? They have reality! They live in reality, out there, ankle deep in the shit and the piss where the people swarm like rats and the rats swarm like insects and disease.... disease..."

Shakespeare faltered. He passed a hand over his eyes, squeezed them shut wiping away a pair of tears.

Fletcher knelt suddenly before his senior and eagerly took him by the hand.

"Yes. You see. You see. I speak not of the unvarnished truth. Not mere reality. I speak of experience heightened and honed by our craft, by our words. Never was a true love so perfect, nor a real death so tragic as in one of our little entertainments? What of the love of a father? What of the death of a son? What of your own boy Hamnet, William?"

William, shocked, tried to pull his hand free but the younger man held it fast. Further tears came unbidden.

"You wrote of it, didn't you? How the plague took your only boy from you in his eleventh year. You have said you did not but how could you, the great William Shakespeare, not? And how could you not, with your skill, sharpen it?"

"Enough!" Shakespeare rose to his feet abruptly, pulling free as he did so, thick sack wine splattering on the wooden floor like a gout of blood. "Why do you seek to torture me so?"

Hurriedly, he began snatching up his things from about the room. His cloak, his stick, his hat.

"William, please. I did not mean to wound you. This is what I have been trying to make you understand. Imagine a play wherein the truth of which you spoke, truth which has dealt you such pain, was revealed. Not fleetingly, how humanity usually views such, but methodically, unflinchingly. Utterly."

Shakespeare, his hand now on the door's handle, turned and raised his stick in a threat to the other should he attempt to follow.

"The ultimate tragedy!" John continued, entreatingly. "Gods, if Gods there be, do not care for or about us. The Olympians do not play with us for sport. There is no reason, no order, there is only chaos. All the world's a stage, and there is no script. No second act but death!"

William wrenched the door open and began a hasty descent of the creaking stairs. Fletcher did not follow but called after him.

"We are alchemists whose words turn leaden drudgery into gold! What could we make of that which every man knows but dare not face? William? William, wait! Please!"

THE NIGHT OUTSIDE was cold and wet. The sky just as blank and lifeless as it had seemed through Fletcher's grimy window. William hurriedly fastened his cloak and set off at a pace along the narrow, busy street. He felt old. In his very marrow, his heart, his mind. Old and weary.

Why had he even returned to London this time? What hold did this filthy city have upon him that he could not be content to leave it behind once and for all? He should be in Stratford with Anne. She was alone in the house now, Judith married and gone only one month ago, and yet here he was.

Mud and shit sucked at the wrinkled leather of his boots as he stamped along. He did not need to think about where he was going, his feet knew the way. He walked on, lost in thought, oblivious to those he passed, many of whom recognised him and some of whom he should have recognised himself.

At the mention of Hamnet it had been as if a great sorrow sunk deep within had risen and burst to the surface of William's being. Sorrow and guilt too, for he had not been with the boy at the end. Had not seen nearly enough of him in his short life.

Tears were on his cheeks once more but they were almost indistinguishable from the sooty, spattering drizzle which fell over all.

No, that was not right. Though it had been John who had spoken Hamnet's name, the boy's spectre had already been summoned by William's own thoughts and words.

How had John known though? Could the answer be that he was indeed a true friend? A man who knew William's sadness and understood how he had suffered. He said he had not meant to wound him, and yet –

William squelched to a halt at a gateway off Borough High Street. He shoved the gate inward with a painful creak which felt like it emanated as much from himself as the straining hinges. Arranged around three sides of the yard beyond were the *higgledy–piggledy* buildings of The Tabard Inn – a hostelry which had been in business for more than three centuries. Despite the rain there were some whose merry-making had spilled out into the court, several taking advantage of the yards darker corners to satiate those urges and appetites drink so often provokes.

Upon entering The Tabard, William was immediately accosted by a party of theatre-folk. He knew a few by sight, only one or two by name, yet felt no inclination to decline their insistent invitation. Indeed, he had more or less counted on as much. His cup was kept full, food ordered and eaten. Either they would pay for the pleasure of his company, or else he would be left with a hefty bill to settle. He did not much care which. Their inane, self-important jabbering was a welcome distraction from his earlier vexation and the renewed rawness of his sorrows. He laughed when they laughed, slapped their backs as they did his, until at last, in his cups, he stood upon the table and bellowed a toast.

"Oh, that men should put an enemy in their mouths to steal away their brains! That we should, with joy, pleasance revel and applause, transform ourselves into beasts!"

A roar of approval. The meaning and origin of the speech lost on almost all present. William, wobbling on the table-top, laughed then coughed until his eyes watered.

"And now," he cried "I must piss!"

A roar even louder and more exultant.

Out in the yard Shakespeare planted his feet firmly and sent forth a golden arc, frothing a puddle until upon its surface was a head worthy of an ale. Triumphant, he looked to the sky. The rain had ceased, the clouds dispersed, and the heavens were now filled with stars.

"Will." The voice came from across the yard, little more than a whisper.

Adjusting his breeches, William peered into the shadows. A figure slowly melted into existence out of the darkness near the gateway. The man looked familiar, Shakespeare realised. He had passed him in the street on his way to The Tabard. He had been there among the drinkers in the tavern too. A young man with flowing locks, his cheeks bare, upper lip and chin adorned with but a teenager's growth of hair. The face was one he knew of old.

"Marlowe?" William staggered forward, splashing through the still steaming puddle.

"You see me now then, old friend. I began to worry I was forgotten," Kit Marlowe chuckled softly "Twenty-five summers have passed, after all."

With the awed over-familiarity of drunkenness Shakespeare placed his hands upon Marlowe's face and squeezed the flesh, felt the jaw and skull beneath. The young man only smiled and chuckled again.

"Yes, dear Will, I am real."

"How can this be?" the drunkard held tightly onto the squished yet amused face of the other, examining it through eyes too blurred to be believed. "You are dead."

Kit took his friend's hands in his own. "Indeed," he grinned. "Come with me, and all shall be revealed."

Act Two: When Shall We Three Meet Again?

EXHAM, LONDON. APRIL 1616.

THE PLACE WAS like no tavern either Michael Drayton or Benjamin Jonson had ever set foot in before.

Their journey had begun in Blackfriars and it had taken more than an hour of snaking through a labyrinth of filthy riverside back-streets to find their destination. Already each was beginning to wish they had not made the effort.

Shakespeare's hand-drawn map, though it appeared crude at first glance, had proved incredibly complex. On it were marked thoroughfares which were not at all apparent to the everyday traveller. There had been more than a dozen occasions on their journey where Dreyton and Jonson felt sure they must have taken a wrong turn, yet once the supposed dead-end was approached some hitherto hidden way was revealed. Some of these passageways were barred by people, seemingly mere loiterers, who enquired casually where the pair thought they might be headed. When "Exham" was given in answer — the name of the mysterious district which neither man had ever heard of before but noted on Shakespeare's map — the path, such as it may be, would be immediately cleared.

Neither Drayton nor Jonson were thin men and the way was on several occasions so narrow that they were forced to turn sideways, sliding their backs and their bellies along walls whose greasy surfaces bore evidence of others having done likewise. It was due to these manifold stresses, strains, and complexities of their journey that, despite the length of time they had already spent together, no opportunity to properly discuss the circumstances which had brought them there arose before they were finally seated in The Swine.

The tavern's odour lived up to its name in every way; an acrid, gamey mixture of pig-pen and the slaughterhouse. Ale was ordered, the men taking their places in a dingy corner at the insistence of the large and imposing barkeep who recognised them instantly as "Shakespeare friends". He was missing an eye, or at least could not open one — a great knot of mottled scar-tissue covering it and most of the right side of his face, its tautness pulling his upper lip into a brown-toothed leer.

Thirsty from their journey, Drayton and Jonson each took a long draught of his ale, which turned out to taste not nearly so foul as either had expected.

"It is as well Fletcher did not come, I think," said Jonson "I doubt his nerves would have stood the journey," he glanced about himself before adding, "nor the setting."

"You said you spoke with him; what reason did he give for declining Will's invitation?"

"John is beside himself. In a fair terror of Will, or anything connected with him. He said that he wished never to hear from him again."

"A falling out over a play, is it?"

Michael Drayton shifted in his seat uneasily, leaning in and trying to turn his face away from the rest of the room as he spoke. He was increasingly aware of being watched by The Swine's other clientele, some of whom he almost thought he recognised from the labyrinthine journey.

"It is exactly that," replied Jonson, his own eyes flicking suspiciously in the direction of some of the curious drinkers, "but not in the manner you mean it, I fancy. Will sent him something he had written, or at least begun to write, some twenty years ago. It was about the death of his boy, Hamnet, and John said it was enough to break his heart. Yet, the letter which accompanied it said it was John's to do with as he wished. That he may re-work and claim authorship of it, should it suit his purposes."

"His purposes?"

"John and Will had been discussing the notion of a grand tragedy – the ultimate tragedy – something more affecting than all that has gone before. John said that he could see that Will was thinking of Hamnet and, though he regretted doing so, tried to use that pain, that loss, as an example to help him evoke such. Will was greatly offended."

"I see." Thirst and unease had caused Drayton to drain his cup quickly and he set it down upon the table with a rattle that seemed jarringly long and loud, threatening to draw yet more unwelcome attention "Why then, did he send the manuscript?"

"Because, according to Will, it was of no consequence. Insignificant. He wrote that since John and he had spoken he had come to understand something of what a grand tragedy may be and that it undoubtedly rendered his own loss, indeed all such personal losses, petty in the extreme."

The scar-faced barkeep thumped another two ales down on the splintery table-top between the pair, causing each man to start.

"Thirsty." It was not a question. He bared those of his teeth not already exposed in what might have been an attempt at a smile. Picking up the empties in one oversized paw of a hand, he left them once more.

"We are to expect Will in a black mood indeed, then," Drayton reflected, taking a nervous gulp of beer. "Strange. He seemed bright enough in his invitation. Excited even."

"Indeed. I have a notion why. I believe you and I may be about to read a new Shakespeare play. John said that Will began sending him ideas – notes and suggestions at first but eventually whole acts in rough. As the play developed so John's terror grew. So affecting were these passages, so acute had his fear become, that he confided in me he had burned the most recent letters without so much as opening them."

"What on Earth is the play about?"

"Oh, there was some lost, far-off land, some monarch or other. A masked king I believe John said, but he said little more. He could barely bring himself to speak of it. I fear the whole thing has had an ill-effect upon him. He pleaded with me not to come today, warned against reading anything Will has written in the last month."

"Wine!" a voice bellowed.

The duo, who had been leaning in closely as they spoke, looked round in surprise. William Shakespeare was striding towards them, a broad grin upon his face.

"And meat!" he added.

At this a strange ripple of excitement passed through The Swine's patrons, and the barkeep moved hastily to meet the playwright's orders.

Drayton and Jonson stood and clasped their host's hand in turn as he joined them at their table.

"I'm so glad you could come," grinned Shakespeare, removing his cloak with flourish, "but where is John?"

Drayton and Jonson exchanged an awkward glance before the latter cleared his throat.

"He is unwell. He sends his apologies."

A great onion-shaped bottle twice the size of a man's head was plonked on the table before the trio, its glass opaque, its surface thick with dust and cobwebs. Three pewter goblets clattered as the barkeep set them down and began to pour the wine. It was a deep red with a heavy, spicy odour and Drayton suddenly became aware of some of the other drinkers trying to catch its scent.

Emboldened by Shakespeare's arrival, and his apparent comfort in such strange surroundings, Drayton looked fully upon the faces of some of his fellow customers for the first time. Several were indeed men and women whom he and Jonson had encountered upon their strange journey, only now they had unfastened their shabby, stained cloaks, and uncovered their pallid, greasy heads.

It seemed, to his horror and disgust, that all bore the taint of some illness or other. Some seemed too thin and wan while others appeared bloated and sebaceous like great swollen toads. Pronounced dark rings were around the protuberant eyes of some, while still others had flesh mottled and marked with crazed networks of blackened veins. He thought in horror of the plague.

There was no doubt now that they had caught the heavy scent of the wine, some actually closing their eyes and taking great chest-swelling breaths, drawing the odour in. Appalled, Drayton turned back to his companions to see if they had seen as he had. Shakespeare's face was much closer to his own than he had expected, the wide grin still upon his lips. He clapped a hand on Drayton's shoulder.

"And you. Are you well, Michael?" he enquired.

Drayton glanced uncomfortably towards Jonson but he was fully occupied in drinking deeply, apparently much enamoured of the aromatic wine.

"I... I am fine, Will." he managed weakly.

"Good. Good!" came the emphatic reply. The smile and gaze remained fixed and intense until at last, after what seemed like an age, Jonson spoke.

"Ah, fine stuff. I've never tasted its like."

The goblet was barely on the table before the barkeep was filling it again.

"Thank you," grinned Shakespeare, "and now to the kitchen, if you please."

The huge man growled an acquiescent chuckle and staggered off. Drayton saw the man lick his lopsided lips as he departed and, to his growing discomfort, thought he caught sight of some of the other drinkers doing likewise.

"John told me you have been working on a play, Will. How goes it?"

Shakespeare stared at Jonson for a moment, his smile unwavering but his eyebrows knotting into a frown as if he had to search deep to make sense of what was being asked.

"Oh that," he laughed, slapping the table. "I should not have troubled poor John with all that nonsense. I couldn't see it then. I hadn't got it, you see." His laugher continued and Dreyton thought he heard stifled sniggers from across the room.

"Hadn't got what?" Jonson asked, taking another gulp of wine.

"Why the joke, of course. The Joke!" Shakespeare wiped tears from the corners of his eyes as he fought to master himself. "There is no Grand Tragedy, you see. It's a comedy. It's all a big joke. One great big –" Words failed him as he broke into a paroxysm of laughter once more, the mirth in the room at large growing in response. Dreyton caught the baffled Jonson by the wrist.

"I think we had better leave, Ben," he said, as emphatically as he dared.

"No, no, no," managed Shakespeare, rubbing his hands across his face vigorously in an effort to control his mirth "No. I-I apologise. I am getting carried away. Please, you are my guests and I have something very special I wish to share with you."

Seizing his goblet, he raised it in a toast.

"I drink to the joy of the whole table!"

In a moment Jonson, seemingly already a little groggy from the heavy wine, raised his own drink. The pair looked to Dreyton who reluctantly lifted his goblet to meet theirs.

"And to that of the whole room!" Shakespeare added loudly. A cheer went up among the other drinkers. Some of the voices sounding eerily inhuman.

Drayton nervously touched his cup to his lips, taking a sip of the wine. Its fragrance was almost overpowering; the taste peppery and dusty beneath the excessively rich perfume. His tongue tingled at the touch of the liquid, the back of his throat burned as he swallowed. He choked and set the vessel down hastily. Neither of his companions seemed to find it disagreeable, however, each drinking heartily of his tankard.

"So then," Jonson rubbed at his tingling lips with the back of his hand, "the play is a comedy."

"There is no play, Ben," Shakespeare laughed. "I could not hope to capture even a morsel of it in my writing, in language at all. That is why I must show you. Why I must share the experience."

"I see," said Jonson more sceptically. "Tell me, Will, is this a religious experience you speak of?"

Shakespeare clapped a hand over his mouth and shuddered for several moments with suppressed mirth. He raised the index finger of his free hand and wagged it to and fro, as if admonishing Jonson for making an unfair joke.

A collective gasp alerted the trio to the return of the barkeep. He appeared stooping out of a low curtained door behind the bar, carrying a huge platter in both hands. As he approached the table The Swine's other patrons followed to surround the trio of men.

Upon the platter was what Drayton took to be a roasted pig or boar. All four of the creature's limbs were absent but the torso, still studded here and there with tufts of coarse black hair, was as broad and long as that of a full-grown man. The head was intact and by far the most unpleasant part of the thing: its snout and jaw shallower than those of any true pig, its ears small and set at the sides of its skull rather than the top.

There was something disgustingly simian about the face of the beast, something obscene about its blackened empty eye sockets, set close in the front of its skull, and even the bruised apple in its small, almost child-like, mouth.

Shakespeare eagerly shifted the great onion-shaped wine bottle and the goblets onto an adjacent table where the inn's sallow clientele began thirstily helping themselves to their contents.

The platter was so large it overhung the table at either end, legs creaking under the burden. A cloud of greasy steam hung around the body of the beast, settling like meaty sweat upon the faces of the trio. Three sharp carving knives and three tri-pronged forks were retrieved from the sticky puddle of fatty juice that pooled around the creature and distributed among Jonson, Drayton, and Shakespeare.

"Today we feast as Romans feasted in Londinium, and as our own ancestors feasted long centuries before," Shakespeare grinned. "That is how Marlowe put it to me, and it seems fitting enough."

He stabbed his fork into the shoulder of the animal and began hacking off a great slab of juicy, pink flesh with his knife.

"Marlowe?" asked Jonson, somewhat reluctantly carving himself a modest piece of pig-meat "Christopher Marlowe? You mean to say you came here with him in the old days?"

"Not in the old days," Shakespeare replied through a mouthful of flesh, spraying saliva and swine-juices across the table, "only last month. You see," – he swallowed with a great gulp then grinned, showing dangling tendrils of fat caught between his teeth – "I met him in The Tabard that night after I saw John and he brought me here."

"But that is impossible," interrupted Drayton desperately. "Marlowe has been dead for decades!"

He looked towards Jonson imploringly. Surely this had gone too far for him too, by now? To his disgust Drayton saw his companion chewing a mouthful of the flesh with an expression bespeaking his utter pleasure at its taste. Jonson, noticing him at last, made a motion as if to suggest he could not talk with his mouth filled, yet immediately began carving himself another, much thicker, slice of the body.

Feeling a nudge at his back Drayton turned and saw that a fight over the great wine bottle had broken out amongst some of those who now crowded around them. Others simply leered from the table's edge at the great steaming corpse of the hog-thing, salivating.

Shakespeare raised his voice over the growing clamour: "Michael, you know as well as I the rumours that always persisted about dear Kit. He was a spy they said, and indeed he was. He was Lord Strange's man. And aptly so, for he told me that he learned many strange things, saw many strange sights in his employ. Some, in Holland, or rather in the sea off its coast, proved to be his end... in a manner of speaking. The end of his career – both careers – at the very least."

"You mean to tell us that Marlowe did not die at all," – Jonson's jaw worked on the succulent meat as he spoke – "that he has been in –?" His question was cut short as he began to choke.

His mouth opened wide as he struggled to cough up the chunk of flesh which seemed to swell to fill his throat. Drayton tried to pull back his chair to stand and help his friend but their audience was so tightly packed around him that there was not room to do so.

"In God's name, someone help him!" he shouted urgently.

Jonson's eyes bulged, his face reddened. Shakespeare, apparently oblivious, carved himself another slice even as the fighting and jeering in the rest of the inn seemed to intensify.

Drayton in panic and fury shoved hard at the edge of the platter, driving the curiously tailless rump of the pig corpse into Jonson's chest. His friend folded over the steaming hog-arse, an under-chewed hunk of the beast's flesh flying from his gaping jaws.

Jonson gasped for air, then coughed painfully. In moments he was bringing up his meat, wine and ale in steamy convulsions upon the platter before him. Drayton had to cover his mouth to stifle his own reflexive gagging at the sight and the stench. Shakespeare however, merely chuckled and popped a final slice of meat into his mouth before declaring, "Well, it seems we have had our fill."

As Shakespeare made to move back his chair, the scar-faced barkeep shoved those closest to the playwright back a few steps to give him room.

All around the table people jostled to get closer. Some began making furtive grabs at the beast on the platter, digging their dirty fingernails in to scratch out chunks of greasy flesh. There was the smashing of glass followed by a high, gurgling scream from somewhere among the crowd.

Jonson, still clutching at his throat, staggered to his feet with the assistance of the barman. Rounding the table, the giant pushed away some of those closest to Drayton so that he too was able to stand. The table barely deserted, the odious customers began to fall bodily upon the hog-thing's carcass, tearing at it and each other like a pack of ravenous wild dogs.

The barkeep shoved and elbowed his way through the fevered crowd toward the squat doorway behind the bar, the threesome following closely in his wake. Jonson, catching his breath at last, managed to croak out, "Where are we going?"

Shakespeare clapped him heartily on the back.

"Down," he grinned.

BEYOND THE STAINED and tattered curtain, a series of well-worn wooden stairs led steeply down into blackness. The playwright took the lead and began to descend the creaking stairs, whistling a happy tune as he did do. Jonson and Drayton, much afraid and for the moment stunned into silence, were encouraged to follow with grunts and nudges from the now unseen giant.

A heavy door of wood and iron was closed and barred by the Cyclops guide, blocking out all light for a moment. Horrific sounds as of an orgiastic and bloody riot could be heard from The Swine above. The stairwell took on a soft red glow as Shakespeare opened another door at its bottom, immediately disappearing inside.

The room was a kitchen, clearly centuries older than the hostelry above. A large fireplace occupied most of the wall facing the doorway. Embers glowed amid a great pile of ashes, the metal turn-spit on which the hog-thing had been roasted shimmered greasily above.

It was here the beast had evidently been butchered too; blood and offal oozed from a collection of battered buckets. The legs of the pig-thing were suspended from hooks driven into the beams of the low ceiling to cure, their surface encrusted with salts and herbs. Though they terminated in what appeared to be malformed trotters, the limbs were far too long and too thin to have come from any normal pig. Drayton tried to imagine how such a creature might move when alive and intact and shuddered at the thought.

Nicked and tarnished knives and cleavers, battered pots and pans, and other cooking implements hung from hooks or lay in piles on the blood- and shit-stained floorboards. There was, Drayton and Jonson realised in the same instant, no means of exit other than the door through which they had come. As one they turned, only to see the barkeep closing and barring the kitchen door.

"What in God's name is going on, Will?" Jonson managed croakily.

Shakespeare, bent and searching amid the buckets of death-reeking swine-guts, did not seem to hear the question.

"What just happened up there?" Jonson asked with more vehemence, his voice hoarse and raspy as he tried to raise it. "What are we doing down here?"

Shakespeare turned to face his associates with a manic grin, a long-handled axe gripped in both hands. Wordlessly he crossed to the fireplace and began raking out the smouldering ashes onto the floor with its head. A spot thus cleared, the axe was dropped with a clatter. The Bard stepped into the fireplace and in a moment seemed to disappear up the chimney with a cackle which echoed eerily.

The barkeep now held a lighted oil-lantern which he offered to Drayton with a grunt.

"Follow," he prompted, pointing towards the fireplace.

Above their heads something thudded heavily upon the floor of The Swine. The disembodied limbs hanging from the rafters shook with the force of it.

"Come" – the voice from beyond the fireplace sounded distant and ethereal – "and bring a light, won't you?"

At the rear of the fireplace, three or four feet up the chimney, the lamplight revealed an age- and soot-blackened metal door set into the wall. Clambering through the aperture with some difficulty – especially Jonson who was the larger of the two men – the baffled pair found themselves in a damp and draughty passageway hewn out of stone. It was evident that this was a tunnel carved into the very bedrock of London itself. Shakespeare waited there, positively dancing with exhilaration and agitation.

"Now look here!" he snatched the lamp from Drayton's grasp and jogged off down the passageway.

"Where are you going?" Drayton called before reluctantly trotting after, Jonson wheezing along behind him. "What is this place?"

Shakespeare had stopped and was examining a portion of the wall closely, holding the lamp up to it and throwing long-tentacled shadows from his fingers as he ran them over the surface. He was tracing some ancient, angular characters graven into the rock. They were crudely done and worn away by centuries of dripping damp yet, looking over Shakespeare's shoulder, Jonson thought he read CORNIGER MATER FILIORUM M.

"Roman," Shakespeare declared, beaming. "I told you ours was a feast straight out of Londinium. But the Romans did not make these tunnels, they merely improved upon them. Did you recognise the name on the map I gave you? Exham? There was a scandal around the Baron of Exham – Walter de la Poer – a decade or so ago. Beneath his family estate there are Roman remains just such as these, and beneath those... well, Kit told me that all such places – and many remain hidden here in England – have since acquired the nickname of Exham."

Drayton, moving to the edge of the field of light cast by the lamp, bumped hard against something in the blackness. There was a scraping of metal.

Shakespeare wheeled round and shone the light in his direction. Drayton had collided with what appeared to be an ancient well-head set into the floor, a rusted, metal lattice fastened across its top. His leg stung and when he put his hand to it, it came away bloody. A single drop fell from his finger-tip, shining crimson in the lamp-light as it dripped off and down through the grated well-covering. For the first time Shakespeare looked uneasy and raised a finger to his lips signalling for his companions to be quiet. Curiously tense but silent seconds passed before he spoke again.

"We must be on our way," he said quietly and was off down the passageway at a run. "And take care where you tread from now on!" he warned, glancing back over his shoulder.

At first Drayton thought it was the wind whistling in the depths of the covered well, but even as he and Jonson resumed their chase, the sound blossomed into a terrible screeching howl. The shuddering light of the lamp showed half a dozen similarly covered shafts as Shakespeare dodged past each one, fleeing along the tunnel. Jonson and Drayton, barely able to keep up, had to try to remember where they had seen the obstacles lest they crash into another. The same terrible sound was coming from all of them – like the baying of some desperate half-starved beast of the forest with its leg caught in a huntsman's trap, only now it was accompanied by awful long-nailed skitterings and scrabblings.

Ahead of them Shakespeare rounded a corner and disappeared from view, the light fading with him. Making the turning in haste the duo were confronted by a gigantic figure, its head crowned with an array of vicious looking horns or spikes, its caprine eyes blank and white. The statue reclined upon a vast marble plinth. Though it had evidently occupied the centre of the small vaulted temple they now found themselves standing in, the statue had slid a few feet to one side by means of some cunning and ancient mechanism, revealing a hidden stairway beneath. Down this stone spiral Shakespeare was already descending hurriedly.

"We can't go down there!" said Jonson desperately, grabbing hold of Drayton.

"Will!" Drayton called down the stairs as loud as he dared. "Will! For God's sake, man!"

Shakespeare stopped and looked up, his eyes glittering in the lamp-light.

"The ghouls will not venture down here. Their graveyard tunnels merely intersect with these and they take their sustenance, and their trophies, from the dead alone. Besides, they know better than to intrude upon the domain of the All Mother." He flashed a grin which might have been reassuring had not his words been so strange, then continued downward.

Reluctantly Drayton moved to follow him but Jonson, still holding him, stood fast. Behind them the howling was joined now by a scraping, screeching, clattering – the sound of the rusted covers of those wells, or pits, being rattled by whatever had skittered up from their depths.

"This is madness," he croaked "we don't know what's down there!"

The light was fading as Shakespeare continued his descent. Jonson and Drayton stood staring into each other's eyes, paralysed with indecision. Then, from the passage behind, there came the sound of crumbling bricks and the clang of metal upon the stone floor. One of the howling things had broken free.

Jonson let go of his companion and leapt for the staircase, almost stumbling down the steps in his haste. Drayton followed but having descended a few steps turned to catch hold of the end of the marble plinth. He pulled with all his strength and felt the huge statue shift slightly. It was not enough.

"Ben!" he screamed "Help me, Ben!"

He was in almost complete blackness now. To his terror Drayton felt the heat of panting breath upon him and smelt the stench of fetid meat. Jonson's hands joined his, grasping at the barely visible slab, and together the pair pulled with all their might. It moved slowly at first then, aided by whatever unseen mechanism enabled its motion, closed so suddenly and with such force that it slipped from their grasp. The sound of the statue thundering into place overhead was mingled with a pained, bestial scream giving the men hope that whatever had sought to peruse them had been crushed, or at least injured, by it.

The spiral staircase was tight, its steps and walls treacherously slimy and uneven. For a time, the pair moved in silence, their quick breaths and pounding hearts the only soundtrack to their blind descent. Then there came the sound of Shakespeare's whistling – the same cheerful tune as earlier – echoing up out of the darkness. He sounded as if he were fathoms below and neither man had it in him to call out to their insane guide.

After what seemed like an age they saw light coming up from below. They soon discovered it came not from Shakespeare's lamp but from flaming torches set into soot blackened niches along the walls. These burned with curious flames of blue and green. At the same time the duo became aware of the sound of water somewhere below, and as they continued downward a hiss became a roar.

Shakespeare stood on the near shore of the rushing black river. He still held the lantern in his hand, a mere fraction of the cavernous space being lighted by the strange flames of blue and green. He greeted Drayton and Jonson with a smile and a cheery wave, beckoning them.

Not knowing what else to do, the weary pair trudged across the ebon sand toward him. With a shudder Drayton noticed that the subterranean beach was littered with bones. Jonson stopped to examine an incomplete skull whose pseudo-humanoid aspect looked unsettlingly like that of that swine-thing slain the cellar-room somewhere far above their heads. He retched and kicked the thing away in disgust.

"Where are we?" Drayton had to shout almost into Shakespeare's ear to make himself heard above the roar of the river.

"At the threshold," grinned Shakespeare "at the very edge of the world we think of as our own. What a piece of work is man! How feeble in reason! How infinite in delusion! Our domain is nothing more than a layer of scum upon the surface of the true world. As the tiny beasts which suck blood while we sleep might suppose the bed and its occupant to belong to them, so we imagine that the Earth is ours, made for us."

"You are ill." Jonson was standing at Shakespeare's other side now. "We must get out of this place. All of us. Together. You must return to Stratford. Return to Anne!"

Shakespeare laughed. "Indeed. So I shall. So shall we all. But I must show you first. Show you what Kit showed to me."

There was an almighty thud, followed by another, and another; like the beating of some unbelievably vast heart. The pounding rhythm, beat out on some unseen gigantic drum, filled the air and rattled the bones of the trio. On the far shore an eerie crimson light began to glow into life, illuminating a previously unseen cave. Within the mouth of the cavern a host of silhouetted figures seethed and cavorted. Though the river was wide and the light but dim, it was clear that many of the shapes did not belong to anything human.

A many-legged, shadowed thing on the far shore waded into the rushing water, dragging a coracle-like boat behind it. For the first time Drayton became aware of a mossy, aged rope suspended high above the water, linking the two banks. Reaching half a dozen of its spindly limbs up to take hold of the rope, the thing scrambled crab-wise into its vessel and began pulling itself across the river towards them.

Jonson set off at a terrified sprint along the black beach into the absolute darkness of the cave. Drayton tried to call after him but, to his horror, discovered that he could not even hear his own cries above the roaring water and the echoing thunder of the drum. Shakespeare stood beneath the vibrating rope dancing from foot to foot, eagerly awaiting the arrival of the inhuman ferryman. Desperately, Drayton considered his options.

He did his best not to look directly at the thing as it scuttled up on to the shore, dragging the boat with it. Its body was roughly the size of a man's and he glimpsed a quasi-human head set necklessly into the swollen torso. An impression of too many eyes set into a face that was covered with thick black hair threatened to overpower his strained composure but he forced himself to look away.

Hanging his lantern from a hook which projected from the prow of the little boat, Shakespeare eagerly clambered aboard and gestured for Drayton to do the same. There was not enough room in the craft for the spider-thing as well as the men, and at first Drayton thought the creature had merely shoved them off into the river. The boat was spun sideways by the current but then caught and held fast.

Despite his best intentions Drayton, now seated at the rear, glanced up at the rope only to see the abomination dangling between it and the boat. Three of the thing's hands – almost child-like in their delicacy, yet repulsively skeletal – held on to the lip of the craft. It began to pull itself hand over hand over hand along the rope.

Drayton, struck with the full force of terror and revulsion, rained down a succession of two fisted blows upon the creature's digits which he felt crack hollowly. The boat whirled away only to be caught by the tips of another set of the thing's fingers.

Shakespeare was grabbing at Drayton now, shouting unheard angry words into his face. Drayton kicked hard at the bony fingers which burst pulpily beneath his heel. To his horror he saw Shakespeare launch himself sidelong into the raging river. Again the boat spun, this time uncontrollably, the lantern swinging wildly upon its hook as he fought to steady himself. As he was borne by the current, Drayton saw Shakespeare dragged out of the water by the spider-thing, the rope bending under the increased strain of his weight.

DRAYTON REMEMBERED LITTLE of the journey through those nighted crypts, those titan arcades, barely glimpsed by the light of a single flickering oil-lantern as he clung feverishly to the ever spinning water-craft. He recalled but dimly the chance grounding of the boat upon a sandbank close to which a herd of pallid grunting things grazed upon stinking heaps of refuse, and how Jonson, half mad with terror but also relief, had leapt into the craft, shoving it off into the current once more. London has more than its fair share of lost and forgotten subterranean rivers and eventually their boat made its way out into the Thames. There they lay upon their backs and drifted freely beneath the night sky thanking God until the sun rose above them.

WILLIAM SHAKESPEARE DIED on the 23rd of April 1616, at the age of fifty-two. He departed this world within a month of signing his will, a document which he begins by describing himself as being in "perfect health". No extant contemporary source explains how or why he died, yet fifty years later John Ward, the vicar of Stratford, wrote the following in his notebook:

"Shakespeare, Drayton and Ben Jonson had a merry meeting and, it seems, drank too hard, for all grew ill and Shakespeare died of the fever there contracted."

Shakespeare was buried in Holy Trinity Church upon the banks of the River Avon in Warwickshire. In accordance with the custom of the time there was no coffin, only a winding sheet to cover his body. The stone marking his final resting place was inscribed with the following verse:

Good friend, for Jesus' sake forebeare
To digg the dust enclosed heare;
Bleste be the man that spares thes stones,
And curst be he that moves my bones

Many believe that the Bard himself penned the curse, arguments once made for Ben Jonson's authorship now largely overlooked and forgotten.

The warning was thought to have proved effective for four centuries, the grave showing no signs of ever having been disturbed. Yet, in 2016 a strange discovery was made. A team using ground-penetrating radar in an archaeological probe of the tomb found that something was missing. Shakespeare's head – his skull – was gone.

Beneath the spot where his head had lain, the archaeologists detected a curious disturbance in the soil; it was as if the skull had not so much been exhumed as dragged downward. Radar evidence which seemed to show a collapsed network of tunnels beneath the church and its graveyard has been dismissed as mere supposition and "bad data". Nevertheless it is now widely believed that the head of William Shakespeare was taken as a trophy, and a ghoulish one at that.

Epilogue

> "Life's but a walking shadow... it is a tale, Told by an idiot, full of sound and fury, Signifying nothing."

Macbeth, Act V, Scene V.

SOMETHING WICKED THIS WAY COMES

GRAHAM MCNEILL

Act I: Tempt Not A Desperate Man

I.

DON'T LISTEN TO this.

Seriously, don't.

I'm not joking, put down the damn phone or whatever the hell it is you're listening to me on, and do yourself a favour by smashing it with the first heavy object you can find. Or if you're somehow reading this, burn it. Find some matches and light it up. Please.

I know, I know, why bother recording this if I'm just going to tell you to smash it up, right? Well, if you know who I am, then you'll know I'm an actor; a narcissistic, egomaniacal prick of an actor. If you don't know me, then for God's sake go and see a play sometime.

Still here? Have it your way then. Let me introduce myself. My name is Mackenzie Baladan, and if you're going to stick around to listen to my last words, then I damn well want you to pay attention to what I'm going to say. So what if I ended the world? What actor could ask for a greater curtain call than that?

Right, let's get on. I probably don't have much time left. I can hear branches scratching at the door to the roof, roots gnawing the earth and leaves thrashing at the glass. The woods have come to Dunsinane, just like it said they would in the Bard's play.

But I'm getting ahead of myself. I need to tell you what coaxed me out of London and brought me to this isolated rooftop in Scotland.

It was the Whenschal Sisters, that's what.

I should have bloody known.

*　　*　　*

II.

I DON'T REMEMBER when I first heard rumours of the part. Last year sometime. Spring maybe? No, not spring. I remember it being dark. The arse end of winter maybe, sometime black. Anyway, word was going around the usual Soho bars and clubs patronised by the luvvie community that something special was in the wind (though calling that pack of raptors and four-faced liars a community is a joke). No-one could say for sure where it started, but there were whispers that a juicy script had turned up that was going to be a star-making turn for whichever lucky bastard was able to land the lead role. Of course it was a role for a man; big parts like that don't come up for women these days, no matter how progressive we like to think we are. No, this was going to be a doozie, a role that would open the doors to Hollywood royalty, a chance to be King of the World!

Naturally I had Imogen do some digging. If anyone could get to the truth of the matter it would be her.

Imogen Boite (never once was it expected she would take my name when we married) is my wife and manager, someone who, even if you only have a passing acquaintance with this business we call show, you'll have heard some wicked stories about, most of which are probably true. Her nickname in agency circles is Chainsaw, which, publically, she brushes off with a spotless hand, but behind closed doors... Oh how she revels in it. She's fought tooth and nail to get me parts in productions up and down the country and even secured a couple of lowbrow movies across the pond. Nothing major yet, nothing that's going to land me one of those cute golden statuettes in February, but there's a steady stream of scripts been sent our way over the years. Tosh, mainly, but it never hurts to keep one's options open.

By means both fair and foul, she's found ways to get me roles earmarked for actors who, if I'm honest, were much better choices. But Imogen can be *very* persuasive. She's not averse to spreading the odd bit of salacious gossip to trip up some younger wannabe sniffing around a role she has her eye on for me. Remember that dashing young star from *Casualty* everyone was touting as the next big thing last year? The one who was in the running for a role I was after? Yeah, the one who overdosed after he was caught cheating on his wife.

Guess who passed the address of his Camden love nest to the gutter press?

Anyway, Imogen's got contacts everywhere in London, from the Palace of Westminster to the smack dens even the music industry guys don't know about. But even she was stymied. All she could uncover were half-heard fragments, whispered gossip and stories of closed casting calls. Now rumours like this surface every day and mostly they're complete nonsense. But this one had a whiff of truth to it; just enough details to make it plausible, just enough vagueness to keep people interested and sniffing around.

Most of what Imogen learned was smoke and mirrors, but one nugget gave a veneer of truth to the mutterings; an original manuscript of some major work had apparently turned up and was being put into production by the Whenschal Sisters. Eventually that rumour became fact when the Whenschal Sisters themselves finally revealed their new acquisition. Somehow, they'd come into possession of the original hand-written manuscript of William Shakespeare's *The Tragedy of Macbeth*.

The foremost Bardic scholars from Oxford, Cambridge and Miskatonic had verified its authenticity with the breathless, manic excitement of lunatics. One even went so far as to claim that it differed so wildly from the versions we'd previously seen on stage and screen that it would change the world as we knew it. Another managed to get onto the BBC and scream that no-one should ever read it, that it was an abomination of perversions and monstrous secrets. He lasted all of six seconds before the producers cut to the weather girl.

The excitement buzzing around London was palpable, and every actor was crawling out of the woodwork in hopes of securing an audition. Macbeth was a juicy role; show-stopping moments in the spotlight with plenty of lurid murder and sex. I'd played the role twice before, and Imogen assured me I was a natural fit for the part.

Then the casting call went out and I knew the gods hated me.

The sisters didn't want to meet with me. It was that chisel-faced cunt Duncan Pryor they wanted for the lead. The tabloids and the *my-ghost-hubby-got-me-pregnant-and-now-he-wants-custody-of-our-baby* magazines were full of Duncan telling everyone how his Macbeth was going to blow everyone away. With a total lack of irony, he wittered on about how this production was going to light a fire under ailing British theatres, like he was their personal saviour. I couldn't pick up a trade paper without seeing his clean cut face and ripped physique staring out at me like some horny peacock. I tore out every page I came across, and even wiped my arse a few times with his smugly handsome face.

As you might have guessed, Duncan Pryor and I have a history.

We'd started out as friends, fellow RADA survivors who'd come up the hard way, scraping walk-ons in *The Bill* and *Holby City* before earning recurring roles in *Eastenders*. We both got our breaks at pretty much the same time; him in a Shaftesbury Avenue production of *All My Sons*, me in a remake of *The Singing Detective*. Over the years he'd beaten me out to a lead role in half a dozen shows, parts that earned him acclaim and prizes galore. Not that I didn't do well myself, you understand, Imogen won me some plum parts, but nothing to compare with the accolades Duncan was getting.

So when I heard that Duncan Pryor had won the role of Macbeth, I gritted my teeth and publicly wished him well, all the while praying for some hideous degenerative cancer of the anus to spread to his face. One by one, every role was filled until the entire play was cast, but there wasn't a dickie bird left for me. The closest I'd get to the proscenium would be if I could get a seat in the front row. Maybe I could put Duncan off and get him to corpse on opening night.

III.

THEN THE MUSES smiled upon me.

Imogen returned to our flat in Mayfair at 4am on a Sunday, waking me from a disturbingly erotic dream of an oil-slick forest where the branches swayed like drifting smoke and the bark split like leering mouths with tongues that drooled a milky sap. I remember waking with my balls throbbing and an almighty erection, which would normally be an occasion to grab Imogen and make the most of it, but she wasn't beside me. I looked up and saw her leaning against the doorframe of our bedroom, silhouetted in the light from the hallway.

There was something wrong with her outline, as though black smoke drifted towards edges that were only just reassembling her form.

I blinked away the afterimages of the dream and sat upright, fumbling for the lamp. Light filled the room and Imogen was just Imogen again, partially clad in a cocktail dress that left little to the imagination and a good deal more of the goods on show.

"How much do you love me?" she asked.

I whipped back the sheets to expose my engorged member.

"This much."

She cocked an eyebrow and said, "Impressive."

"Thanks. Hop on. Take it for a spin."

"In a minute," she said, waggling a finger. "I've got something to show you that's going to make you happy."

"Happier than this? What is it? Cate Blanchett's sex tape?"

"Better," she said and sat on the edge of the bed.

She handed me an iPhone I didn't recognise.

"What's the code?" I asked when I saw it was locked.

"4820. Go to the Photos App."

I unlocked the phone and did as she instructed.

At first I wasn't sure what I was looking at. Then I thought it couldn't possibly be real. It had to be a fake, didn't it? I looked up and Imogen arched an eyebrow in a, *yeah, I know* fashion. I looked at the pictures again.

"Jesus Christ! How did you get these?"

"One of the Twins," she said, meaning either Nathan or Sebastian Chamberlain, the identical twins Duncan employed as his PAs. "The one with the goatee."

"That's Nathan."

"Nathan, yeah. Must have been Sebastian's night off. Anyway, I ran into him at a wine bar in Kensington and he was acting all weird, like he had a secret, but didn't dare tell it. So I slipped a little something into his champagne to loosen his tongue. A quick snog in the gents and he told me Duncan was at a Hush Party in the penthouse upstairs. Invite only, of course, but it didn't take much more than a quick fumble down his Calvin Klein's to get the flat number and the entry password out of him before he passed out."

Imogen's breaches of the bounds of our marriage never bothered me. It would have been massively hypocritical, given my well-hidden addiction to prostitutes.

"You went upstairs, of course?"

She nodded and now that I'd adjusted to the light, I saw the gleam in her eyes from too much coke and booze.

"It was amazing," she said with a cat's grin, breathless at the memory. "There were things going on I didn't even know were possible. People intertwined in knots of flesh. Impossible to tell where one person ended and another began. There was some strong weed being passed around and a weird piping music that seemed like it was coming all the way from the sky, but was being played by a drunken Peruvian llama herder."

"Sounds... wonderful."

"It was," she said, flopping back on the bed, arms over her head.

"Where was Duncan?" I asked.

"In one of the bedrooms."

"Did he see you?"

"No, I think it's fair to say he was a bit preoccupied."

"I'll say," I said, swiping through the pictures once again.

A dozen images of Duncan Pryor getting spit-roasted by a pair of greased-up, musclebound gym-rats in zippered gimp masks. Men and women in outlandish costumes that made them look like freak show abominations surrounded him. Grotesqueries filled the background, but the unmistakable face of Duncan Pryor filled every shot. Actually, the pictures were quite arty; nicely framed (appropriate, I know) and vividly coloured. Had the subject not been a famous actor, I could imagine them on the wall of some swanky Knightsbridge gallery.

"What do we do with these?"

"What do you think we do with them?" she said, sliding her hand onto my groin. "You e-mail them from that little shit's phone to every newspaper on Earth."

"I love you," I said.

"Yes, you do," she answered.

OF COURSE, THE tabloids murdered Duncan.

He sacrificed the Chamberlain twins on the altar of public opinion, and for a few days at least, it looked like he thought he might get away with it. After all, everyone in the biz indulges in a bit of slap and tickle on the side. He did the obligatory doorstep confession and apology to his fans and wife, looking gloomily contrite with his uncomprehending children propped up beside him. I could read his thoughts like subtitles:

Eventually I'll be forgiven and this will all be forgotten. I'm a movie star, for God's sake. The rules don't apply to people like me.

Except this time, they did.

They crucified him, made him the laughing stock of the nation. A hundred memes were spawned every day, a great many created by Imogen, who had a real knack for twisting the knife in someone's back. Then it came out that Nathan Chamberlain had taken a razor to his wrists, unable to cope with the guilt of having apparently betrayed his beloved employer in a drunken haze. His brother had a very public kiss-and-tell at Duncan's expense, swiftly followed by a complete psychotic breakdown. The grief of being fired and then losing his brother was too much, and he was locked up in one of the cheaper Priory facilities and no-one could get access to him for love nor money. Then the papers got hold of Sebastian's financial records, which detailed Duncan's escort habit in meticulous detail and made my addiction to working girls look like harmless flirting.

Duncan denied everything, but it was already too late. Nothing could save him. He was a dead man and everyone knew it.

Just as I knew there was only one actor who could replace him.

The show, as they say, must go on.

I.

I SUPPOSE I should explain a bit about the play then, yes?

But first let me tell you what I know about the Whenschal Sisters.

Bugger all.

Actually, that's not quite true. Everyone knows *of* the Whenschal Sisters, they're a production company in London. But that's about it. No-one knows where their offices are or when they started up. Or even who they have on their books. Their Wikipedia page is useless and they've kind of, well, *always* been part of the fabric of London as far as I can tell. Some folk say they have an office somewhere near Hampstead Heath, others that they weave their magic from some anonymous tower in Canary Wharf. I've never met anyone who's been to their offices — wherever they are — because they only ever come to see you. And when they set a time to meet, it's *always* with something juicy, something star-making. The kind of once-in-a-lifetime script that'll set an actor on the road to stardom. If they want to meet and offer you a part, you don't refuse, no matter what. You're getting married that day? Cancel it. It's the birth of your first child? Get your wife to close her legs and keep the brat inside a few more hours.

And no matter how much the scandal rags offer, so far no-one who's ever sat around a table with them has said so much as a single word about what happened. So this'll be an exclusive for you, right here, the first recounting of a meeting with the Whenschal Sisters.

II.

IMOGEN TOOK THE call on a Friday morning, and from her expression, I knew our fortunes had changed. I went into the kitchen and called Carl Banks, my pet writer. I keep him on speed-dial for when I need a script punched up with extra zingers or to make sure all the juiciest lines go to me. He's a hack, but he's *my* hack.

"Banky! How the devil are you, you old scrote?" I said when he eventually answered.

"What do you want, Mackenzie?"

"Lovely to speak to you too, Carl."

"Whatever it is, I'm too busy."

"What? Got another bunch of ad-libs to script for *Wags to Bitches*, have we?"

"No, I'll have you know it's a —"

"I don't care," I said. "I need you."

"I'm not interested."

"It's the new *Macbeth* film from the Whenschal Sisters."

The line went quiet and I knew he was hooked. Of course he was. He'd be mad to pass this up and we both knew it.

"Where and when?" he said with the usual wheedling need and self-loathing I'd come to expect from the miserable old fart.

"Get your scrawny arse to Dunsinane House Hotel."

"Is that north or south of the river?"

"It's in fucking Scotland, you thick twat," I told him and hung up.

III.

WE FLEW TO Aberdeen just after lunch the next day, landing in the Highlands in glorious sunshine, which made a pleasant change from London rain. A car was waiting for us, a swish, gloss-black Jag with a slender driver who moved with feline grace and whose eyes were entirely hidden behind impenetrably dark sunglasses. We made no attempt at conversation and he returned the favour, which was just as well, as I was tired and cranky from being delayed in the fourth circle of Hell that is Terminal Five of Heathrow Airport.

We climbed into the back seat and the driver pulled out with all the elan of a professional who knows exactly how to use his vehicle. Once the airport was lost to sight, the scenery was magnificent and far less urban than I'd been expecting; all soaring mountains, rolling forests and swathes of rugged moorland. I hardly spotted any signs of habitation at all, just a few whitewashed cottages halfway up the hills and some quaint looking farms. It was like we'd travelled back in time. I grew drowsy as the rolling motion of the car lulled me towards sleep. Imogen was peering out the window at the scenery, her brow tensed in a little furrow just over the bridge of her nose.

"Everything alright?" I asked.

She nodded, but didn't answer, which was usually a sign of trouble ahead. Imogen almost never passed up the chance to make some observation about hating being away from London. Instead she stared at some ruins on a wooded hilltop as if she half-expected a blue-faced Mel Gibson to charge out in his kilt, waving a sword.

I slept until the driver finally pulled into the gravelled driveway of Dunsinane House Hotel. The name was misleading, as it was more of a castle than a stately home. Its walls were grey granite, moss-covered and thick, the windows tall and slim and paned with leaded glass. A piper was waiting for us by the door, which the owners probably thought was a nice, welcoming touch, but which only made me want to put my fingers in my ears. I'm no expert on what bagpipes are supposed to sound like, but this monotonous piping was like fingernails down a blackboard.

Inside were more trappings of a forgotten yesteryear. Suits of armour, swords on the wall and huge, cowhide rugs spread over marble flagstones veined with a queerish green. A bottle of what looked like *very* pricy whisky sat invitingly on a small table next to the roaring fire burning in an enormous hearth. The cat-like driver brought our bags in and departed without a word. I wondered if he *ever* spoke.

"It's a scene straight off a shortbread tin," said Imogen.

I wanted to echo her caustic assessment, as I have a famously low tolerance for all things rustic, twee and *regional*, but I felt strangely at home here. Oddly, it felt as though I'd seen this place before.

"It looks expensive," I said, taking a few steps around the room.

Paintings of strange landscapes were framed on the stone walls, like windows to other worlds. They made me faintly queasy to look at them, and I couldn't decide if it was because they were bad prints or just bad paintings. They were stupidly hard to see properly, the colours twisting and blending in chaotic patterns like they'd been smudged in the printing process. Or maybe it was just shit modern art.

I don't know, but with the strange sensation that the places in the paintings were somehow... *Waiting*. I turned my attention to the bottle by the fire. I'm more of a vodka man, but I've never been known to refuse booze when it's expensive and free. I poured a couple of generous drams, handing one to Imogen and clinking glasses with her.

"Help yourself, Son of Coinneach," said a rasping voice behind me.

I jumped and almost dropped the bottle. Three women dressed head to foot in black had entered the room without a sound. All three were clearly related, but differed wildly in age. One was a fall in a nursing home away from the grave, another looked barely old enough to be out of her school uniform. The third was a matronly woman, with the most enormous breasts I'd ever seen. She had a motherly bearing that made me feel more at ease than I'd been in weeks.

They couldn't possibly be sisters, could they? There had to be at least seventy years between the eldest and youngest. Maybe the *Sisters* part of their agency's name was just an affectation and they were actually grandmother, mother and daughter. I took a sip of the whisky to gather my thoughts. I grimaced at the taste. Whatever this was, it wasn't whisky, but as its amber warmth spread through me, I felt my reservations about coming here ease.

"My father was Robert," I said. "I don't know anyone called Coinneach."

The oldest of the women laughed, a croaky, rasping sound that spoke of a lifetime of filterless Capstans. Her teeth were black like the homeless hags you see cackling under Waterloo Bridge. She shook her head and indicated I should pour her a drink. I did and held it out to her. She took it from me with icy fingers and I almost gagged on the mulchy smell emanating from her, like wet earth after the rain. She winked and downed the not-whisky in one swig.

"The man who sired you, aye," she said, wiping a hand with skin like corrugated card over her lips. "But he's not your true *faither*."

"Forgive my sister," said the youngest of the three, and I felt the absurd need to keep her safe from harm, like she was an innocent wildflower in danger of being plucked. "She has the *an da shealladh* and sometimes says things she shouldn't."

I didn't know what that meant, but said, "I know the feeling."

Imogen and I took a seat on worn, but comfortable couch before the fire. The middle sister sat across from us and it was all I could do to keep myself from staring at her pendulous breasts. I just wanted to bury my head between them. The youngest sister knelt on the floor beside me and rested her head on my knee like a loving daughter. The eldest poured herself another drink and paced the carpet behind me.

They all began speaking at once, their words hard to separate at the time and harder now to recall which one said what. They had a hypnotic rhythm to their speech, as if they'd practised this routine many times before. I found myself almost drifting off, but I remember being faintly unsettled by their words at the time. God, if I'd known what they meant, I'd have run screaming into the night and not stopped until I reached London.

"He's no Duncan," said one.

"No," agreed another. "But greater in parts."

"Lesser in most."

"Will he suffice? Will his seed be fruitful in Magna Mater's belly?"

"We'll know when the Black Goat comes to Dunsinane."

"When will that be, sister dear?"

"When the stars align and the words are spoken."

"By the light of dead stars," said the ancient crone behind me. "Corpses of those who lived when the universe was young watch over you, yet you see it not. Their hand is at your throat, yet you feel it not. He's a bigger monster than any I've seen."

"Not him, her!"

Imogen and I listened to their ravings with a growing sense of confusion. We'd guessed, given their reputation, that there'd be some strangeness to the meeting, but this was getting truly odd. These women didn't seem like they had anything to do with the production of movies or plays, more like escapees from a nearby psychiatric facility. I glanced over at Imogen and saw a tightness to her jaw that usually signified someone losing their career. I took another drink, savouring its numbing heat and sat back, ready to watch the fireworks.

There were fireworks alright, but they didn't come from Imogen.

IV.

I DON'T REMEMBER much about the rest of that night. Or the following few days for that matter. I seem to remember taking lots of walks in the grounds of the hotel by myself, where I found an overgrown maze filled with statues that time and wind had weathered oddly, with textured curves and angles that ought to have been impossible to render in three dimensions. I went to touch one, but some instinct made me pull my hand back just before I made contact with the stone. I remember drinking more of the strange whisky from the bottle by the fire, a bottle that never seemed to diminish, no matter how blind drunk I got.

Despite the copious amounts of booze I drank, I never had so much as a sniff of a hangover. I woke from smoky dreams soaked in sweat, but curiously rested. I don't think I'd ever felt as energised.

Imogen, on the other hand, was having a foul time. She spent most of her time feeling unwell or raging at her phone provider's shitty service and cursing the lack of hotel wifi. What made it worse was that we hadn't seen so much as a single member of staff to complain to since we'd arrived. Our room was always cleaned by the time we got back to it and our meals were always ready just when we felt hungry. Food was served in a wood-panelled dining room with a high-backed throne at the head of an enormous banqueting table. It looked so authentic, I wondered if it could be pressed into service as part of the set. Maybe it already was and we were simply poor players strutting upon a stage.

The rest of the cast and crew began drifting in over the next few days, and since I was playing the lead role, it would be me that set the tone for the production. On some sets it's the director who does that, but once you meet Michael Duff you know straightaway he couldn't lead a thirsty horse to water, let alone make it drink. He's a journeyman director and he knows it. He's quite happy to leave the motivational stuff to the kind of person who loves the spotlight. Which in this case, was me, and I was more than ready to lead this dance.

Like the hotel's staff, the Whenschal Sisters hadn't shown their faces since our first encounter by the hearth, but a handwritten note I found next to the strange whisky one evening promised we'd meet again before filming started. I still hadn't seen a script, which was starting to worry Imogen some. The longer things went on, the harder it would be to get out of this deal if things went tits up.

I arranged a big get together for everyone on the Friday night, a chance to spend some of the production budget and get everyone better acquainted. The acting circles are a lot tighter than you'd imagine, and it's always good to see what dynamics form early on. I sat at the head of the table, at the centre of everything so I could get a good view of the rest of the cast. I have an eye for spotting who's going to be fucking who over the course of the production. Always ready with an appalling pun, Banky calls it my sexth sense. It might not seem like much of a talent, but it can save a great deal of heartache down the line when you know how things are playing out in the trailers after shooting has wrapped for the day.

The food arrived and it was as sumptuous a banquet as any king might have commanded. Like everything about Dunsinane House, the food felt like we'd jumped back centuries, and even the vegans didn't complain when the hog-roast was brought out and carved by two extras with ruddy great claymores they lifted from the walls. The champagne and wine was flowing freely — a little too freely in some cases — and the atmosphere was decidedly convivial. I offered smiles and nods of the head as needed, a beneficent monarch dispensing favours with a glance. I was in my element.

Then Banky turned up and ruined it all.

V.

I HADN'T SPOKEN to Banky since I'd called to tell him to get his arse to Scotland. It's a cliché, but the man never had a deadline he didn't miss or an appointment he wasn't late for. He'd sit around in bloody Starbucks all day answering e-mails and "researching" without doing any damn writing at all. Then, whenever a deadline loomed, he'd panic like his head was on fire for the next few weeks, becoming functionally nocturnal and churning out just enough words to justify begging for another few weeks. Typical writer. He thinks that just because he can string a sentence together we all ought to fawn at his feet like he's some kind of heroic, tortured artist. Well, let me tell you that on every set I've worked on, the writer's place in the food chain is somewhere between the security guard at the gate and the man who takes my shoes off to be polished.

But this was late, even for him.

The night was in full swing. Everyone's public appetites were sated and I'd pretty much guessed which couples were going to pair off. I'd just turned to whisper something to Imogen when the doors to the dining room burst open and I saw Banky. For a moment I thought his hair was actually on fire, then realised it was the hearth in the other room I was seeing. He held what looked like the script in his hand, waving it around like some desperate autograph hunter.

"You can't do this, Mackenzie!" he yelled, rather killing the mood.

He shuffled into the banqueting hall, and I squirmed in my seat as I saw the state of him. He looked bad; bleary eyed and unshaven, which I'm led to believe is kind of the dress code for most writers. Nobody would make eye contact with him, which reminded me of how in Japan when some business type is disgraced, everyone physically moves away from them, like that person's dishonour might pass to them. Everyone in the banqueting hall recognised a moment of career suicide when they saw it and turned away. The smiles grew a little more fixed, the jokes and bawdy anecdotes got a little louder. Everyone knew he was making a beeline for me, so conspicuously kept their gazes averted. Banky might as well have been invisible for all the attention anyone paid him.

"Shitting fuck," I muttered. "The old man's finally gone mad."

"Let me handle this," said Imogen.

I put a hand over hers.

"I'm sure I can handle Banky. He's just drunk."

She shrugged and raised her eyebrow before sipping her wine and settling back into her chair.

I got up as Banky almost threw himself at me, wild-eyed and frantic. Pages of the script fell around him as he gripped my arms. For a scrawny sort, he was stronger than he looked. I gently guided him towards the back of the hall where an impromptu bar had been set up with enough booze to get the entire House of Lords drunk thrice over. I wanted to get him as much out of earshot as possible.

"Listen, old fellow," I began. "What the hell's the matter with you?"

"Have you read this?" he said, holding out a crumpled handful of yellowed pages. "No, of course you haven't, you never do."

I shook my head. "No, I haven't read it. It's bloody *Macbeth*. I've played the role before, how different can it really be?"

"It's not *Macbeth*," hissed Banky, "Not like you know it. Not like *anyone* knows it. That's why he rewrote it for the masses."

"Who rewrote it?"

"The Bard, for fuck's sake! Shakespeare!" screamed Banky. "He didn't want anyone else to know what *he* knew. Clever bastard, but I know the rules, the structure. I know what he couldn't help but slip into all his manuscripts — the magic, the monsters and the sorcerers. The poor sod probably didn't even know he was doing it, but the words... The word... Once they're in your brain they have to come out somehow. They have to come out or you'll go mad! I've been going over them all since I read this one. Every play, every sonnet! I haven't slept a wink."

"What are you talking about?"

"This isn't a script as you've ever seen it," he said, again waving the crumpled pages under my nose. "It's more like a... A... A way to rip aside the veil. A storm of the oldest words, a hurricane to strip away the blinkers we wear to keep us from going utterly mad at the sheer monstrous, uncaring void of the cosmos."

I wondered if that hadn't already happened to poor Banky, and only refrained from saying that by a herculean effort of will. I still didn't really understand what he was talking about.

"I think you're just exhausted, Banky," I said, turning to pour him a stiff whisky. "Come on, let's get you another drink, yes? Here, have a little nightcap, eh? That'll settle you down."

Banky nodded and took the drink, which reassured me that this situation wasn't totally beyond saving.

"Now, come on, old fellow, what's *really* got you all riled up?" I asked. "Is it the script? It can't be *that* bad. If it's a stinker, well, it's not the end of the world, is it? Imogen can get me out of it. Remember how she got me out of that godawful Uwe Boll movie?"

Banky shook his head. "This isn't a bad script. It's a work of insane genius. It's a work of absolute truth."

That took me back.

"Then why can't I do it?"

"Because some truths we're not *meant* to know," sobbed Banky, sliding to his knees and throwing his arms around my waist as he wept into my crotch. "Some truths are just too awful to face."

"What kinds of truths?" I said, trying to pry him loose.

"The secret truths!" yelled Banky, but no-one paid any attention. "Weren't you listening? The things behind the masks, the monsters upon whose flesh we crawl, believing it to be a world of solid rock! We don't see it because we don't want to, because we'd go mad if we admitted what we know in the darkest part of our souls. That this world was theirs and will be again!"

I.

BANKY WAS FINALLY ejected by some of the extras who'd be serving as assorted castle guards, but what he'd said — though it was utter gibberish and made not an iota of sense — had unsettled me enough that I didn't feel able to return to the feasting. I apologised to everyone around the table and climbed the steps to my room as Imogen gathered up Banky's pages and exhorted everyone to have another drink.

I climbed into bed without undressing and was asleep as soon as my head hit the pillow. Almost the instant my eyes closed I fell into the best, most vivid, most erotic dream I'd ever had. A real sheet-soiler if you know what I mean. Imogen and I hadn't had sex since we'd arrived at the hotel. No sooner had we unpacked than the Red Oktober sailed into her nethers and she felt so sick that the very thought of fucking made her want to puke.

I tried not to let that bruise my ego.

I dreamed of the forest again. In my dream I was on my knees before a dense swathe of a thousand black-trunked trees with waving branches. Not the sexiest thing to dream about, I know, but each of those trees was like a beckoning invitation to something unimaginably forbidden. Have you ever done something just because it was so taboo that you just *had* to do it? Something so carnal that you didn't even care if you were caught? Well, this was like that, times a thousand. And at the centre of this dense forest of desire was something vast and insatiable, an outline of something I wanted to *fill*, something that ached for me to spill my seed in its endlessly fertile womb. I was powerless to resist. I stood and wasn't surprised to find I was naked. I took a step towards the forest, feeling wet caresses of glistening branches as they bent to brush my bare skin.

The trees parted before me, drawing me deeper into the woods. The ground was moist underfoot, soft and pliant like raw meat. Blood welled around my toes, and I felt bones crunch underfoot. Dreary pipe music drifted through the trees, filling the air with a song that drew the forest onwards.

Knowledge filled me with every step, whispered in the spaces between the mad piper's notes. I was walking on the corpses of a vanished time, an epoch of life on this Earth that ended unknown billions of years ago, long before our species of upstart ape stole the world's throne. How many civilisations had died before ours arose? How many species had claimed this insignificant blue globe as theirs before the inexorable forest had devoured them, only to shit them out again as something new in a stinking froth of rebirth? None could say, for whatever mark they once made on this world had been utterly erased.

An ache spread from my groin, a pressing need that I willed to keep inside me. My dick was like a divining rod, pointing the way onwards as I pushed deeper and deeper into this dark, dripping forest of extinction. The elephantine trunks of gargantuan-limbed trees loomed all around me, vast and organic, veined and undulating with deep, peristaltic motion. It looked like nests of worms threaded their trunks, wriggling and burrowing in an endless cycle of birth, death and renewal. The thought of worms infesting my flesh only made me more determined to reach the centre of the woods.

I climbed higher through the slow-moving leviathans, feeling the ache swell to encompass my entire body. Every aspect of this dream was revolting and hideous, but I saw beauty in it, a beauty I never expected to feel while walking on the corpses of failed civilisations. That ours would be next seemed certain, but at that point I didn't care.

The sky grew radiant with a sickly yellow glow, and I emerged into the centre of the forest. Again I went to my knees. It wasn't the sky that was alight, it was the being *filling* the sky. My eyes went wide and I felt the all too fragile pathways of my mind fray and shred at the sight of it. Cosmic and nebulous, a life-giving sun of mouths and eyes, a being of radiant splendour. Yet it was also a destroyer, a thing that cared not that its spawn extinguished that which had nourished its very creation.

Smoky tendrils reached down from the sun, coiling towards me like snakes as a soft chanting built from the forest. I'd seen no-one there to give voice to any sound. Were the trees singing to their goddess?

Iä! Shub-Niggurath! Iä! Shub-Niggurath! Iä! Shub-Niggurath!

The words were unintelligible, but their meaning was clear. Understanding burned into my brain like a scream. This wondrous being was the All-Mother. The Magna Mater and wife of the Not-to-Be-Named-One. From her infinite, bloated womb a new age would begin, wiping away the world we naively believed belonged to us. But the truth of it is that we were squatters only, vermin lodged in the cracks of their flesh like a parasitic infection. All the millennia we claimed dominion over the Earth was an eye blink to the world's true masters.

The tendrils lifted me up gently. The frond-like limbs of the forest caressed me as I was borne towards the gaping maw of the hungry sun. I would die here, but I would be born anew, becoming the spark to bring life in the face of species doom. As endings go, this wasn't a bad one, and I laughed like a maniac as the sun swallowed me.

I woke with a sudden wrench at the sound of breaking glass. I blinked away the dreamsight of the woods and the memory of the undulant wetness of the sun's interior. The sense of loss and frustration was almost unbearable. I felt the reality of the room and everything in it to be hideously frail and absurdly temporary. The solidity of everything I'd thought permanent and unchanging was now rendered horribly precarious, a house of cards that could be brought down by the trembling of a single atom. Air heaved in my lungs, harsh and toxic after the woods where every intake of breath was an act of destruction, every exhalation a joyous rebirth.

Grunting at the heaviness of my flesh, I rolled over to see Imogen kneeling by the hearth with her back to me. She was naked and her long hair hung low over her half-turned face. The fire had burned down to cherry red embers, and I could only see her silhouette in the dim glow. Torn shreds of paper surrounded her, the pages Banky had left behind before being ejected from the banqueting hall. The remains of the smashed whisky bottle glittered on the hearthstones around her. The peaty aroma of the fire filled the room; primal, damp earth and sulphurous fumes like the many long-vanished worlds upon which I'd walked. Something in the soft tremors of her movements unsettled me. Then I realised what it was; Imogen was crying. Droplets fell to the floor, a puddle made red by the firelight.

In all the years I've known my wife, I've never once seen her shed a tear. Not for orphaned kids, not for kicked puppies and not even the ending of *Cinema Paradiso*. So to see her weeping scared the shit out of me.

"Imogen? What's the matter?" I asked when I finally found my voice.

She shook her head. The line of her jaw was so perfect, so delicate. I couldn't see her eyes, but her cheeks were wet.

"What's done cannot be undone," she said, lifting the wadded up paper from the floor. She threw it in the fire, which crackled hungrily as it devoured the ancient pages. "The things we've done... Our hands are steeped in blood, Mackenzie, and all the perfumes of Paris will not sweeten their foulness."

"Are you drunk? What are you doing?"

"What Banky should have done. Ridding the world of this."

"Is that the manuscript? Jesus, that's the original!"

Even as I said the words, I felt their hollowness. What did it matter if the ancient words of a madman from Stratford were fed to the flames? The world was on the brink of ending, and I was worried about a bloody *play*? But old habits die hard, and the thought of something precious being burned to ashes struck a long dormant chord within me.

I tried to get out of bed, but my limbs wouldn't obey me. I couldn't move a muscle. I could only watch helplessly as my wife, page by page, burned the honest to God, original fucking manuscript of *The Tragedy of Macbeth*.

"Christ, Imogen! Stop!"

"The things I read," said Imogen, finally turning towards me. "The things I saw. The things *they* showed me... I couldn't..."

My wife wasn't crying. The puddle wasn't red because of the firelight.

She'd gouged out her eyes with the broken neck of the whisky bottle.

Horror swept over me like a surge tide. My heart thundered in my chest, but my skin was cold. Crimson tears streaked Imogen's face and her eye sockets were ruined craters of blood and glutinous matter. Strings of nerves hung down her cheeks like tattered weeds.

"Holy Fucking Christ!" I cried as a knot of sickness made a fist of revulsion in my gut.

"The White God can't help either of you," said a sweet, innocent flower of a voice. "The All-Mother devoured him long ago."

I turned my head and saw all three of the Whenschal Sisters at the door to our bedchamber, hooded in black and wreathed in a haze of yellow fog. The smell of damp, rotten earth and wood emanating from them made me gag. The cackling crone shuffled over to Imogen and bent to lift something from the floor. She placed it my wife's hand and I saw with mounting terror that it was a dagger-like shard of glass from the broken bottle.

"Imogen, no!" I cried, desperate to stop her doing any more harm to herself. "Please, don't. Whatever drugs they've given you, listen to me! It's Mackenzie, your husband! Your husband! Stop this, just put the glass down, please!"

Nothing I was saying was having any effect.

Typical. The one time I needed the truth to *really* matter in my delivery of a line and it fell flat. I wondered if Duncan Pryor would have managed to sell that line. Probably, but it was too late for regrets now.

"This needs to end," she said.

"No, Imogen, no! Don't do it, stop, please, no!"

But I could only watch, impotent, as Imogen lifted the shard to her skin. I screamed as she drove it in. She twisted the glass, digging deeper into the meat and gristle of her neck. Finally she hit an artery and blood squirted from the wound in arcing jets. It sprayed the wall like a fucking sprinkler that just kept going. Jesus, who knew she had so much blood in her?

I called her name over and over as she fell forwards onto the floor, unable to look away until every last drop of blood had spilled out. The Whenschal Sisters circled her like bullies ready to taunt a kid with buck teeth, their bare feet slapping the bloody flagstones.

"Get away from her, damn you!" I shouted.

They turned to me, and I saw that, beneath their hoods, their faces were no longer recognisable as anything human. Instead, each skull was a writhing mass of worms and scuttling insects. Millipede mouths and cockroach eyes; carrion feasters ready to devour the corpse scabs of the old world in readiness for the arrival of its new masters.

Disgust overcame terror and my limbs were mine to command once again. I scrambled backwards, thankful I was still fully clothed as the three hideous things I'd once thought were women moved towards me. I screamed in gut-wrenching terror, a scream I didn't know my throat was capable of making.

I ran into the corridor, not knowing where the hell I was going, but just needing to be away from those heralds of the apocalypse. Fog filled the passageway entirely, and I could barely make out anything to give me a sense of direction. Just ghostly outlines of suits of armour, paintings that seemed to be slithering free of their frames, and heavy shields on the walls. I wrenched a sword from one of the armoured figures, not that I knew how to use one nor expected to face anything I might actually be able to harm with it. But it felt better having *something* in my hand. I staggered down the corridor, feeling a warm wetness spilling down my thighs in a pulsing stream. It soaked my trousers, and I felt my strength ebbing with every lurching step, but I didn't dare look to see what it was.

I knew I couldn't escape, but that didn't matter. I didn't know if whatever the Magna Mater needed from me had already been taken, but I sure as hell wasn't hanging around to find out. More by luck than any knack for spatial awareness, I found the door to the stairs. Fully expecting it to be locked, I laughed hysterically when the handle turned in my hand.

The same obscuring fog filled the spiral stairs, clawing up from below in filthy yellow streams. More of the idiot piping skirled up from below, and the floor heaved with the motion of millions of worms and burrowing things. No way down, so I ran up the stairs, bouncing from the walls and scraping my flesh raw until I emerged onto the roof. The cool night air was a balm on my skin and my soul.

I turned and slammed the door behind me, pushing the dead-bolt home and backing away. I heard slithering *things* moving behind it, testing the wood, perhaps gnawing on it. I was under no illusions that something as prosaic as a door would halt things that could end worlds, but I'm only human and such small things comfort us mortals in our times of need.

Moving to the centre of the roof, I threw back my head and howled at the stars. Many years ago, I'd loved to look up at them, filling my notebook with their names and drawing each constellation with painstaking care. These were not those stars. These were not the twinkling lights that once brought comfort to a frightened child, these were baleful eyes leering down with ancient hunger. My stomach heaved and I vomited, feeling all moorings with this world and my sanity slipping away.

Laughter bubbled up inside me. Ridiculous, I know, but you tell me what the sane response is to the end of the world.

I stumbled like a drunk to the edge of the roof, resting my hands on the cold stone of the parapet. The air was thick with the reek of corruption, but from that corruption another world awaited its birth. I looked out over the landscape, and wasn't surprised to see a thousand of the black trees moving through the darkness towards Dunsinane House like an advancing army. Looking beyond them, I saw the lights of mankind go out, one by one.

It was never a play, was it, Shakespeare, you mad bastard?

No, it was prophecy. I felt the last vestiges of sanity crumble and knew I didn't have long before my every faculty was gone. I reached into my shirt pocket and took out my phone. I giggled stupidly, thinking I might call my mother, but then quickly quashed that idea. After all, what would I tell her?

Hi mum, it's me, sorry the world's ending. Just thought I'd tell you I'm sorry for all the shitty things I did. Bye!

No, in my last moments, I decided that I would record a eulogy for the world. A clue for anyone who might live to see the new one rise from the mulch of the dead. Something that might let them know who ushered in the return of Earth's first masters.

So there you have it. We've come full circle.

I hope my tale has brought you some measure of illumination, whoever you are. Or *what*ever you are. I'm stepping onto the parapet now, and the ground is so very far below me. I feel hot winds billow as the timbers of the roof door begin to crack. They're coming for me. They want to feed me to the Magna Mater.

I look down into the host of writhing tentacles and suppurating maws of the shambling black forest. Behind me, the door shatters into splinters, and words to greet the end of the world rise within me.

Life's but a walking shadow, a poor player
That struts and frets his hour upon the stage
And then is heard no more. It is a tale
Told by an idiot, full of sound and fury.
Signifying nothing.

I'll speak them as I fall.

Curtain

"The play's the thing."

Hamlet, Act II, Scene II.

#TEMPEST

@Siegel_Jan

@StageDirections

Massive storm, ship wrecked in rocky cove.
Clouds withdraw to reveal Greek-style desert island.
Enter @BeardieWeirdie and @GeekGirl.

@BeardieWeirdie

I did elucidate
how that my evil brother drove us forth
and is in his own vessel now bewrecked
by my enchanted skills. Markst thou not?

@GeekGirl

Father, I mark't. I merely wisht to scan
my twitterfeed to see if aught could holp
and if my gentle tweets could soothe their screams

@BeardieWeirdie

Doubtest thou me? Thinkst thou I would kill
these minor characters thus randomly?
Have I not pow'rs beyond that crude device?
Am I not>

@BeardieWeirdie

> a veritable Gandalf in my strength
and yet a hobbit in my kindly heart?
All shall survive. E'en my accursèd kin
my brother and his son >

@BeardieWeirdie

> a likely lad
who may yet heal this deadly fam'ly rift
when his keen gaze doth pierce thy untouched heart.

@GeekGirl

He little knows I have no heart for boys
but I have met online one Sycorax,
a single-parent Goth girl, supercool,
whose witchy orbs >

@GeekGirl

> did sear my soul
and in whose arms I would fulfilment find.
Alack, upon this lonely desert isle
I can but masturbate and dream.

@BeardieWeirdie

Go forth, my child. 'Tis time to meet thy fate.
Instant romance must end our tale of hate.

@GeekGirl

Ah, wtf. He thinks I'll love this twat.
To 'scape this doom, I'd eat his wizard's hat.

@StageDirections

Exit @GeekGirl.

@BeardieWeirdie

When fair Miranda sees this noble youth
rising thus Bond-like from the churning waves,
his six-pack beaded with the curdled foam, >

@BeardieWeirdie

>his dripping breeches like to clingfilm mould
all the fine details of his manly form —
Ah then her maiden innocence will melt>

@BeardieWeirdie

>and in the union of their new desires
past treacheries will all dissolvèd be.

@BeardieWeirdie

And now, with wizard's sight, let me observe
how Ariel, my spirit-slave, performs
the several tasks that I have tasked him with.

@BeardieWeirdie

He is a being made of air and light
a soap-bubble that drifts upon the wind,
yet thru such minions greater pow'rs are mine >

@BeardieWeirdie

>than other mortals wield. Howe'er, he is
oft easily diverted from my straight commands.
He hath a tendency to suck with bees >

@BeardieWeirdie

>and sim'lar habits of the herbal kind.
Ariel, come thou hence!

@StageDirections

Enter @AeryFaery, an androgynous youth in tight jeans and a
rainbow satin jacket.

@AeryFaery

Come unto these yellow sands
dance all night to dodgy bands
feet it footly there and here
wear a cowslip in your ear.

@BeardieWeirdie

What ditties warblest thou? Are these
th' enchanted tunes of those thy faery kind,
the latest Club Ibiza and its ilk?

@AeryFaery

Hast hit the spot, my master. Summer next
Full fathom five will be the biggest hit.

@BeardieWeirdie

Enough! Seest thou young Ferdinand
he of the sixpack and the beachboy looks?

@AeryFaery

I mark him well, o master. And methinks
the clinging of his sodden breeks doth steal
the very rhythm from my beating heart.

@BeardieWeirdie

Thus shall his manly limbs inspire
the untried passions of my daughter's soul.
Bring them together! On this sea-girt isle >

@BeardieWeirdie

> as yellow-beached and palm-tree-fringed as e'er
Ibiza boasted, she can ne'er resist
the triple lures of sun and sea and sex.

@BeardieWeirdie

My long-lost bro will then welcome me back
to la famiglia of Naples fame
and all will be forgiv'n. Or else
an endless feud may then ensue –

@AeryFaery

Alas, the tempest that we called
was wilder e'en than forecast could predict. Your brother
sleeps with the fishes.

@BeardieWeirdie

Bugger me. We have a problem here.
A sentimental bond might well have sealed
all fam'ly discord, but now my other kin >

@BeardieWeirdie

> my uncles, cousins, and an aging aunt –
this desert isle retreat being now revealed –
may yet go to the mattresses. Where do they couch?

@AeryFaery

In yet another cove — this isle
being well provided with a dozen such—
they were benighted. Now do they wring
their clothing and their hands

@BeardieWeirdie

And do no doubt bemoan
the evil fortune that has brought them here. What of Caliban?
My brother's henchman, and a killer famed >

@BeardieWeirdie

> for murders beyond count. Three garrotted,
one drownèd in his bath, two more
poison'd by their own carbonara sauce,
some sleeping kill'd –

@AeryFaery

My master, say no more! I fear
this Caliban, a beast in human form,
doth yet survive, and in the secret cove
attends upon thy aunt.

@BeardieWeirdie

A pox upon them both! My brother's death
hath ruined my cunning plan, and sweet romance
will ne'er bring final end to this our feud.

@AeryFaery

I heard in Verona they tried that plan
between the fam'lies Montague and Capulet –
no happy denouement was there,
a suicide pact –

@BeardieWeirdie

Nay, 'twas a mere divorce.
But piss no more upon my doomed parade!
My pow'rs are all exhausted. The tempest of last night >

@BeardieWeirdie

>has drained me quite. Get thee to Starbuck's, slave!
Put thy girdle round about the earth
in forty seconds. Bring me a triple shot>

@BeardieWeirdie

>of mocha latte topped with extra cream
and we may yet devise what can be done
to extricate me from these deadly straits.

@StageDirections

Exit @AeryFaery, reentering moments later with mocha latte.

@AeryFaery

Master, while standing in the stilly queue
that, barely shifting, as tho petrified
waited implacably their coffee turn>

@AeryFaery

>over the shoulder of one geekish youth
as tho foredoomed, I read a summons dread
to call a creature from the ancient world>

@AeryFaery

>one deadlier than any since devised.
Know'st thou the name, of nunciation grim
and all uncertain?>

@AeryFaery

>Hast thou heard
the rumour of that place where he was spawned
in some dark kingdom fathoms undersea?
These are no pearls that were his eyes

@BeardieWeirdie

Say no more! I know of what you speak
(or whom, the grammar is not clear).
A monster vasty as the ocean deeps
from which he comes, a thing>

@BeardieWeirdie

>of botched-together horrors, dragon-clawed,
lepidote body sprouting flightless wings,
the face a groping mass of tentacles,
the whole>

@BeardieWeirdie

>a nightmare made in playdough by a child
swollen to overgrow Gargantua. Cthulhu!
To conjure him would be idly to ope
Hell's darkest portal.

@AeryFaery

Even so. He sleeps
in unpronounceable R'lyeh's halls
dead but dreaming, doomed to wake
at the last trump that hails our end...

@BeardieWeirdie

No that's the Kraken. Never mind.
To rouse him for my petty trials would be akin
to taking a chainsaw to a sardine tin.

@AeryFaery

Yet Master I have some small skill
in music that can soothe the savage breast –
and breasts come not more savage than this beast.

@BeardieWeirdie

Thinkst thou in truth thy faery airs
could lull him, once roused, back to deathless dream?

@AeryFaery

I know a song
could quench the fire in a dragon's maw
or still the thunder of the great god Thor>

@AeryFaery

>transform a witch's brew to harmless whey
and turn the wildest night to limpid day.

@BeardieWeirdie

That bad? But stay!
Bring me Miranda and young Ferdinand.
We must be fenced within a circle sure>

@BeardieWeirdie

> of strong protection 'gainst the monster's rise.
My spells will ring us in a field of force
like to the mystic singularity.
Dost thou see?

@AeryFaery

Indeed.
When the wind is nor' nor' easterly
I can tell a Hawking from a handsaw.

@BeardieWeirdie

Go then! Bring me Miranda and her hapless youth.

@StageDirections

Exit @AeryFaery, reentering with @GeekGirl and @Beachboy.

@Beachboy

Of your kindness, tell
who is this beauteous being whose sweet voice
drives from me all the horror of the storm?

@BeardieWeirdie

My daughter Miranda.

@AeryFaery

My name is Ariel.

@Geekgirl

I have a DM from sweet Sycorax!
Tomorrow morn she hopes to sail this way. The ship we'll know
by its black sails emblazoned with a skull.

@Beachboy

You seem a geeksome maid. I wish you well
with your fair Goth.

@Geekgirl

I thank you sir. And Ariel, a sprite I long have known
is surely well deserving of your love.

@BeardieWeirdie

By all the gods, I swear I'm much inclined
to cast them forth into Cthulhu's clutch
for wimpish ways and limping soppy words!>

@BeardieWeirdie

>But as it haps, their wayward affections
effect no change of plan. Come close, all three!
I must a small event horizon weave>

@BeardieWeirdie

>to shield us from the new apocalypse.
My daughter, thou shouldst hide thine eyes from sights
too fearful for a maid to look upon.

@Geekgirl

Nay father, thou dost
underestimate me quite. I would not miss this day
for all the teabags made in far Cathay.

@BeardieWeirdie

So be it. Ariel, prepare!
And I will summon Cthulhu from his lair!

@StageDirections

'Tis now my turn to take the centre stage
with bold directions conjure Cthulhu's rage.
Divers alarms are heard, and mystic chants>

@StageDirections

>And soundless now Prospero rants.
The waves upswell to rearing height
the sunless sky is black as night
and then at last the scabrous hide>

@StageDirections

>shows thru the backdraft of the sucking tide
and monstrous tentacles come writhing out
entangled with a swaying waterspout.

@StageDirections

We glimpse the giant beak, the ragged teeth
and livid goo bubbles from underneath.
Prospero's foes are plucked from rock and shore>

@StageDirections

>and meet their end with SFX galore.
Against the background of their dying screams
wide-eyed Miranda tweets and beams>

@StageDirections

Ferdinand in fainting mode is seen
while Ariel looks a little green.

@BeardieWeirdie

Silence! I've had enough of rhyme
'Tis back to blank verse just in time.
(Bugger.) Ariel, use your music fey
to make the damn thing go away.

@StageDirections

The storm fades, and a haunting tune
stills the dark waters spread beneath the moon;
Cthulhu, sunk once more beneath the wave>

@StageDirections

> in vanished R'lyeh finds his dreaming grave
while on the shore the few survivors stand:
wizard, sprite, girl, and hapless Ferdinand.

@BeardieWeirdie

After this act, I must my pow'rs forswear
'tis customary to sink into despair
expiring haunted by the horrors past>

@BeardieWeirdie

> but frankly, guys, I really had a blast.
Minions of Cthulhu all, I wish you well!
And know we'll party one day soon in Hell!

Dramatis Personae

"All the world's a stage, And all the men and women merely players."

As You Like It, Act II, Scene VII.

ABOUT THE AUTHORS

MISTRESS NIMUE BROWN

NIMUE BROWN IS the author of graphic novel series *Hopeless Maine*, in which there are a lot of tentacles and strange creatures. She started reading Shakespeare when she was about 12, and a great deal can, verily, be blamed on this. In order to calm the madness rampaging in her head, she writes both fiction and non-fiction books, and blogs at **www.druidlife.wordpress.com**

MR MICHAEL CARROLL

MICHAEL CARROLL IS the author of twenty-five(ish) novels, including the acclaimed *New Heroes/Super Human* series of superhero novels for the Young Adult market. He currently writes Judge Dredd and DeMarco, P.I. for *2000AD* and *Judge Dredd Megazine*. Other works include Jennifer Blood for Dynamite Entertainment, contributions to the Titan Books edition of John Higgins' *Razorjack* graphic novel and the e-novellas *Judge Dredd Year One: The Cold Light of Day* and *Rico Dredd: The Third Law* for Abaddon Books. A former Herald of Galactus, Mike lives in Dublin, Ireland with his wife Leonia and their twin imaginary children Tesseract and Pineapple. He is over half-a-hundred years old and some days it really shows. Visit his website at **www.michaelowencarroll.com**

MR ADRIAN CHAMBERLIN

ADRIAN CHAMBERLIN LIVES in the small south Oxfordshire town of Wallingford that serves as a backdrop to the UK television series *Midsomer Murders*, not far from where Agatha Christie lies buried, dreaming in darkness. He is the author of the critically acclaimed supernatural thriller *The Caretakers* as well as numerous short stories in a variety of anthologies, mostly historical or futuristic based supernatural horror. He co-edited *Read the End First*, an apocalyptic anthology with Suzanne Robb (author of the acclaimed thriller *Z-Boat*) and edited the supernatural warfare novella collection *Darker Battlefields*, coming from the Exaggerated Press in summer 2016.

He is aware of the concept of "spare time" but swears it's just a myth.

Further information can be found on his website,
www.archivesofpain.com

MR IAN EDGINTON

IAN EDGINTON IS a *New York Times* bestselling author and Eisner Award nominee.

He is currently writing *Batman '66 meets The Avengers* (Steed and Mrs Peel, not the other ones!) for DC Comics as well as Judge Dredd, Stickleback, Helium, Kingmaker and Brass Sun for *2000AD*.

Other titles include such iconic characters as Wolverine, Batman and the X-Men. He has also worked on a number of film and television properties including *Star Wars*, *Star Trek*, *Aliens*, *Predator*, *Terminator*, and *Planet of the Apes*. He has written for the videogames *Hellgate: London*, *Dead Space*, *Kane and Lynch*, *The Evil Within* and *Assassin's Creed*. In addition, he has written the audio adventures *Doctor Who: Shield of the Jotunn* and *Torchwood: Army of One*.

He has adapted into graphic novels works by bestselling Young Adult novelists Robert Muchamore, Malorie Blackman and Anthony Horowitz as well as literary classics, *Pride and Prejudice*, *The Picture of Dorian Gray*, *A Princess of Mars* and the complete canon of Sir Arthur Conan Doyle's Sherlock Holmes novels. He has also written several volumes of Holmes apocrypha, *The Victorian Undead*, has adapted H.G. Wells' *The War of the Worlds* and written several sequels, *Scarlet Traces*, *Scarlet Traces: The Great Game* and *Scarlet Traces: Cold War*.

He lives and works in Birmingham, England.

MR ED FORTUNE

ED FORTUNE HAS been telling stories since he was very small and he is now too old to stop. He writes about books, table-top games and comics for *Starburst Magazine* and hosts a very popular podcast about genre. He also happens to be an award-winning games designer, which is nice. He has written for magazines as diverse as *Time Out* and *The Fortean Times*. He lives in Greater Manchester in a cave surrounded by bears and is powered by tea and chocolate hobnobs.

Mr Guy Haley

A writer of science fiction and fantasy, Guy Haley is the author of *Crash*, *Champion of Mars*, the *Richards and Klein* series and others. He is also a prolific contributor to Games Workshop's Black Library imprint.

Previously a science fiction journalist and editor, Guy finds making up his own strange worlds even more fun than writing about those created by other people.

You can find hundreds of reviews, interviews, opinion pieces, free pieces of fiction and more on Guy's blog at
www.guyhaley.wordpress.com

Mr Pat Kelleher

Pat Kelleher is a freelance writer. He served his time writing a wide variety of TV licensed characters, across a bewildering array of media, has several non-fiction books to his credit and a collection of children's stories published by Bloomsbury. His *No Man's World* series of pulp sci-fi novels is published by Abaddon Books, along with his *Gods and Monsters* e-novella, *Drag Hunt*. He also worked on *Sniper Elite 3*, the latest in the video game series from Rebellion and has short stories published by Tickety Boo Press and the award-winning Fox Spirit Books.

Mr Andrew Lane

Andrew Lane is the author of eight books in the *Young Sherlock Holmes* series as well as several *Doctor Who* related dramas for Big Finish Audio, and is currently working on a new set of adventure books with the overall title *Crusoe*. He has recently written Cthulhoid fiction based in the South-West of England for the anthologies *Secret Invasion* and *Dead Letters*. He studied *Julius Caesar* for his "O" Level English, which renders him suitably qualified to be included in this anthology.

MR JAMES LOVEGROVE

JAMES LOVEGROVE IS the author of more than 50 books, including *The Hope, Days, Untied Kingdom, Provender Gleed*, the *New York Times* bestselling Pantheon series, the *Redlaw* novels and the *Dev Harmer Missions*. He has produced three Sherlock Holmes novels and is working on a Holmes/Cthulhu mashup trilogy, *Cthulhu Casebooks*, with the first volume, *The Shadwell Shadows*, out in late 2016 with the follow-ups, *The Miskatonic Monstrosities* and *The Sussex Sea-devils*, due at yearly intervals after that. He has also sold well over 40 short stories and published two collections, *Imagined Slights* and *Diversifications*. He has produced a dozen short books for readers with reading difficulties, and a four-volume fantasy saga for teenagers, *The Clouded World*, under the pseudonym Jay Amory.

James has been shortlisted for numerous awards, including the Arthur C. Clarke Award, the John W. Campbell Memorial Award, the Bram Stoker Award, the British Fantasy Society Award and the Manchester Book Award. His short story *Carry The Moon In My Pocket* won the 2011 Seiun Award in Japan for Best Translated Short Story. His work has been translated into over a dozen languages, and his journalism has appeared in periodicals as diverse as *Literary Review, Interzone* and *BBC MindGames*. He reviews fiction regularly for the *Financial Times*. He lives with his wife, two sons, cat and tiny dog in Eastbourne, not far from the site of the "small farm upon the South Downs" to which Sherlock Holmes retired.

MR GRAHAM MCNEILL

HAILING FROM SCOTLAND, Graham McNeill worked for over six years as a Games Developer in Games Workshop's Design Studio before taking the plunge to become a full-time writer. Graham's written thirty SF and Fantasy novels and comics, as well as a number of side projects that keep him busy and (mostly) out of trouble. His Horus Heresy novel, *A Thousand Sons*, was a *New York Times* bestseller and his Time of Legends novel, *Empire*, won the 2010 David Gemmell Legend Award. Graham lives and works in Los Angeles for Riot Games, and you can keep up to date with where he'll be and what he's working on by visiting his website, **www.grahammcneill.com**

Mr Jonathan Oliver

Jonathan Oliver is the author of two sword and sorcery novels, a plethora of short fiction and the twice British Fantasy Award-winning editor of *The End of the Line*, *Magic*, *House of Fear*, *End of the Road*, *Dangerous Games* and the forthcoming, *Five Stories High*. He has also twice been nominated for the World Fantasy Award and was a nominee for the Shirley Jackson Award. *Star-Crossed* is his first foray into explicitly Lovecraftian fiction, though a thread of the weird runs through all his fiction. He lives in Abingdon, Oxfordshire with his wife, two daughters and a cat called Fudge.

Mr John Reppion

John Reppion was born in Liverpool, England in 1978. His writing career began in 2003 when he collaborated with his wife Leah Moore on a proposal for a six issue mini-series entitled *Wild Girl*. The proposal was accepted and the series was published by Wildstorm in 2004/05.

Since then the duo have written many classic characters including Doctor Who (in *The Whispering Gallery* with artist Ben Templesmith), Sherlock Holmes (in two original mysteries for Dynamite Entertainment), and Dracula (their adaptation of which is now on several university reading lists).

John's interests in Fortean phenomena, esoterica, folklore, philosophy, theology and horror have led to his writing articles and reviews for numerous magazines and periodicals including *The Fortean Times*, *Strange Attractor*, *The Daily Grail* and *SteamPunk Magazine*. 2008 saw the release of his first full length book *800 Years of*

Haunted Liverpool, published by The History Press. His Lovecraftian Liverpool tale *On The Banks of the River Jordan* was published in 2014 in Ghostwoods Books' *Cthulhu Lives!* anthology.

MR JOSH REYNOLDS

JOSH REYNOLDS IS a freelance professional writer and the author of over twenty novels. Despite what you may have heard, he is not an 18th Century painter, a footballer or a comedian. He is fairly non-Euclidian, however. His works include stories in anthologies such as *Atomic Age Cthulhu*, *World War Cthulhu*, *Steampunk Cthulhu* and *Historical Lovecraft*, as well as publications such as *The Lovecraft eZine*. For a full list of his published work, visit **www.joshuamreynolds.wordpress.com**

MISTRESS JAN SIEGEL

JAN SIEGEL WAS twenty-four when pulled out of the slush pile at Faber for the prestigious *Introduction* series. Faber wanted her to be a "literary" writer but she was keen to write popular fiction and has published in several genres, under several different names, with several major publishers (including Hamish Hamilton, Viking Penguin, Little Brown, Century Arrow, and Harper Collins). She prefers SF and fantasy realism and has won/been nominated for awards and received wide critical acclaim in all genres. Her fantasy is often bracketed with Philip Pullman and J. K. Rowling and her SF has been compared to Stanislaw Lem. As Jemma Harvey, her excursions into romcom (more com than rom) led her to be picked by *Heat* magazine for their Top Ten Summer Reads. She also writes poetry, usually incorporated into her novels, and is currently involved in a major project to promote great poets.

MR ADRIAN TCHAIKOVSKY

ADRIAN TCHAIKOVSKY WAS born in Woodhall Spa, Lincolnshire before heading off to Reading to study psychology and zoology. For reasons unclear even to himself he subsequently ended up in law and has worked as a legal executive in both Reading and Leeds, where he now lives. Married, he is a keen live role-player and occasional amateur actor, has trained in stage-fighting, and keeps no exotic or dangerous pets of any kind, possibly excepting his son. He is the author of the critically acclaimed *Shadows of the Apt* series as well as standalone works *Guns of the Dawn* and *Children of Time*, and numerous short stories.

MISTRESS DANIE WARE

DANIE WARE RUNS the social media profile of cult retailer Forbidden Planet, and has organised their signings and events calendar for more than a decade. When not at work, she remains geek and gamer, warrior Mum, outward-bound cyclist and fitness freak.

She went to an all-boys' school (yes really), studied English Literature at UEA in Norwich, then joined a Viking re-enactment group and spent her twenties fighting, writing, and rolling certain multi-sided dice. At thirty, she made an attempt to grow up and didn't like it much; at forty, she spends her time with her son, in the gym, or making up for missing the battlefield by writing epic stories about it.

Author of the *Ecko* series, published by Titan Books, follow Danie on Twitter @**Danacea** or at **www.danieware.com**

MR C L WERNER

EXILED TO THE blazing wastes of Arizona for communing with ghastly Lovecraftian abominations, C L Werner strives to infect others with the grotesque images that infest his mind. He is the author of almost thirty novels and novellas in settings ranging from Warhammer and Warhammer 40,000 to the Iron Kingdoms and Wild West Exodus.

His short fiction has appeared in several anthologies, among them *Rage of the Behemoth*, *SHARKPUNK*, *Kaiju Rising*, *A Grimoire of Eldritch Investigations*, *Edge of Sundown* and *Marching Time*.

ABOUT THE ARTISTS

MR MALCOLM BARTER

SPAWNED IN 1957, Malcolm Barter studied Illustration & Design at Ipswich School of Art. He has freelanced in Publishing, Editorial & Advertising, notably illustrated Ian Livingstone's classic Fighting Fantasy gamebook *The Forest of Doom*. He is also a fully qualified Horticulturalist. Now back illustrating, his recent work has included more Fighting Fantasy, having been tracked down and dragged back by French publishers in 2013. He currently resides in Suffolk with his daughter Poppy and a modest bonsai collection.

MR KEV CROSSLEY

AFTER 15 YEARS designing video games, Kev Crossley turned his hand to illustration, contributing to numerous D20 gaming books alongside work for comics including *2000AD*, *Mam Tor* and *Kiss4k*. His art and writing have appeared in over twenty art books published by Quarto and Ilex among others, and he is the author and illustrator of three books of his own; *Fantasy Clip Art* (2006), *101 Top Tops From Professional Fantasy Painters* (2011) and *Character Design From The Ground Up* (2014).

Kev writes and illustrates regularly for *Imagine FX* magazine and affiliated publications, and in 2012 he illustrated Ian Livingstone's 30th Anniversary Fighting Fantasy title, *Blood Of The Zombies*. In 2015 he produced illustrations for Total Warhammer and Jonathan Green's *Alice's Nightmare In Wonderland* gamebook.

MR TONY HOUGH

TONY HOUGH HAS been a fantasy and SF illustrator since 1987 and a Lovecraft fan for even longer. He studied *Macbeth* and *A Midsummer Night's Dream* for English Lit and thought they were "quite good".

His eclectic work has featured in many magazines, books and games as well as on a snowboard, which rocks!

MR RUSS NICHOLSON

RUSS NICHOLSON IS an illustrator of Fantasy, best known for his contribution to Fantasy Gamebooks, such as the Fighting Fantasy series, including the first such book, *The Warlock of Firetop Mountain*, TSR's *Fiend Folio*, Games Workshop publications, including *White Dwarf* Magazine and for the seven books in the Fabled Lands series. Recently he has produced work for Le Grimoire, Dungeon World, Goodman Games, RuneQuest, Kobold Press, Scriptarium, Calific, Tin Man Games and the American folk punk band Blackbird Raum, as well as others.

MR NEIL ROBERTS

NEIL ROBERTS IS a freelance illustrator, sculptor, 3D modeller, writer, lecturer and comic book artist residing in deepest, darkest Lincolnshire, UK. He is responsible for the covers on the *New York Times* bestselling series, *The Horus Heresy*, which has sold over one million books. His art also covers *2000AD*, *Doctor Who*, *Battletech* and much, much more. A classically trained painter, Neil spent many years in the video games industry working on a wide range of games and believes in applying a traditional approach, using modern technology, to create memorable imagery.

MR TIERNEN TREVALLION

TIERNEN TREVALLION HAS worked as an Illustrator and artist since being convinced to leave school in the early '80s. Most recently his work has included comic strips for *2000AD* and Renegade, illustration for the Black Library and cover and promotional art for Pink Floyd's *Wish You Were Here – Symphonic*. Tiernen is also working on several collaborations and projects of his own, which may or may not involve angry puffins.

ABOUT THE EDITOR

MR JONATHAN GREEN

JONATHAN GREEN IS a writer of speculative fiction, with more than sixty books to his name. Well known for his contributions to the Fighting Fantasy range of adventure gamebooks, he has also written fiction for such diverse properties as *Doctor Who*, *Star Wars: The Clone Wars*, *Warhammer*, *Warhammer 40,000*, *Sonic the Hedgehog*, *Teenage Mutant Ninja Turtles*, *Moshi Monsters*, *LEGO*, *Judge Dredd* and *Robin of Sherwood*.

He is the creator of the *Pax Britannia* series for Abaddon Books and has written eight novels, and numerous short stories, set within this steampunk universe, featuring the debonair dandy adventurer Ulysses Quicksilver. He is also the author of an increasing number of non-fiction titles, including the award-winning *YOU ARE THE HERO – A History of Fighting Fantasy Gamebooks*.

He also edits and compiles short story anthologies, including the critically-acclaimed *GAME OVER* and *SHARKPUNK*, both published by Snowbooks.

To find out more about his current projects visit **www.JonathanGreenAuthor.com** and follow him on Twitter **@jonathangreen**

ACKNOWLEDGEMENTS

AN ANTHOLOGY SUCH as *Shakespeare Vs Cthulhu* is, like the performance of a play, the artistic accomplishment of many individuals, both those who appear on stage and those who work hard behind the scenes to help make it a success.

Obviously I must start by thanking the authors and artists who contributed their work to this book, to mark the 400th anniversary of the Bard's death. However, I also owe a debt of thanks to Emma Barnes of Snowbooks, first for being so open to new models of publishing and supporting *Shakespeare Vs Cthulhu* from the start, and then for doing such an excellent layout job on the book as well as publishing it.

And then, of course, we come to the Kickstarter that crowdfunded the book in the first place. I must give special mention to Tim Bayley, whose short story *Lovecraft's Labours Lost* was one of the perks offered to backers, and Nicole Wykes, who produced the postcards that were another Kickstarter reward.

Which brings me to those people who put their faith in the concept of Shakespearean Cthulhu, or Lovecraftian Shakespeare, in the first place and backed said Kickstarter. Without them, *Shakespeare Vs Cthulhu* could not have happened at all. So here's to you, all of you. Or as William Shakespeare himself might put it:

**"I can no other answer make but thanks,
And thanks, and ever thanks."**

Twelfth Night, Act III, Scene III.

KICKSTARTER BACKERS

BOTTOM

"I have had a most rare vision. I have had a dream; past the wit of man to say what dream it was."
- *Bottom*, A Midsummer Night's Dream.

Roger Huntman • Andy Elijah Walker (Look, Mom, my name is in a book!) • Antonio Campos Jr from McAllen, Texas • Kenneth J. Wiant Jr.

MALVOLIO

"My masters, are you mad?"
- *Malvolio*, Twelfth Night.

James A Hirons • Jasper Bark

RICHARD III

"Now is the winter of our discontent, Made glorious summer by this sun of York; And all the clouds that lour'd upon our house, In the deep bosom of the ocean buried."
- *Richard III*, Richard III.

Robert Biskin • Adam Matthews • Mark R. Froom • Hycgan • Jeremy LaMastus • Karli Watson • Heesung Yang • Duncan Young • Elisabeth McWhorter • Michael Carr • Sune Bøegh • William A Hay • Larry McConnell • Christopher Reed • Steff Green • Emily Cox • William Ching • Ayalon Levy • Vincent Rospond • Mike Speedling • Zack Kline • Mark Gerrits • Leshia-Aimée Doucet • Nick Tyler • Xeromancer • Robert Stevens • Henry D Weisenborn • Paul Freelend • Emma and Rosie's daddy • Bobsacks • Justin McFarland • GMark Cole • Alicia Cameron • Loki Carbis • Bill Strangely • Chris Gannon • John D. Hobkinson (I voted to stay in Europe) • James Smith • Janet Oblinger • Vivienne Dunstan • Jason Hunt • Michelle Matel • Scott

Campbell • Kevin T. Likes • Matt Sanders • Mathew Hargrove Farabee • James "Jeimuzu" Payne • Elizabeth Crane • Alexander Redshaw • Jon Auty • Justin Bolger • Flavien "Fl4v1en" Luquin • Yosef Maayan • Mat • John Merklinghaus • Lordspielmeister • Hayley Johnson • Andrew Craker • E. M. • Kathryn Luznicky • Nichole Doucette • Ashley Miller • Thue Eriksen • Rameses McQueen Taylor III • Tyler McCauley • Lester Smith • Melanie Spitzer • Jeff Lowe • Malcolm SW Wilson

YORICK

"Alas, poor Yorick! I knew him, Horatio: a fellow of infinite jest, of most excellent fancy"
- Hamlet, Hamlet.

Danie Ware • Jonathon Green & Laurell Hamilton • Delusional Lies

MACBETH

"It is a tale, Told by an idiot, full of sound and fury, Signifying nothing."
- Macbeth, Macbeth.

Matthew Churchill • Matt Zitron • Ashley Knight • Steven Vest • Jason Seddon • Zacharias Chun-Pong LEUNG 梁振邦 • Steve "LeBeau" Dempsey • Erik T Johnson • Brian Brunswick • Andrew D. Wild-Woods • Mike Scott Thomson • Colin Oaten • Martin Gooch • Master Theodore Drew • Niki Lybæk • Emma Holohan • Martin Andersson • 林立人 Lin Liren "Seeker of Truth" • Morgan Baikie • Heather L Telfer • Allan Schnoor • Jeanne Milostan • Jordan Semeniuk • Hiram G Wells • Jessica Enfante • PJ Montgomery • Thomas Walker • Corina Hinz • Stefan "Stephano Andronicus" Anundi • Pete Sutton • Joe Kontor • [Yes] • Anthony McClung • David Tavakoli • Jessica Wilbert • Willhameena Power • Jon Pam • Tiffany Michelle Brown • Mama Jane • Adam Kennedy • Pamela Adams • Paul Leone • Kerry T Peterson • Will Templeton • Snortlet • Rupu Gupta & Trudi Miller • Matt Bowkett • Cat Treadwell • David J. Graham • Vincent V Cava •

Shannon Sofian • Adam T Alexander • Adrian J Wright • Jane Hanmer • Jørn Johansen • Robert K. J. Killheffer • Tina Mammoser • James Aukett • Kyle Verkuil • Doktor Martin Theiß • Richard Wysor • Andy Tregunna • Daniel J. Wild • Stephen Thomas Bayley • Marjorie-Ann • Eversong • Neil Sayer • Emily Beamon • Peter L. Larson • Scarlett Letter • J. Isaac MacFarlane • Antoine "Bardin" Dijoux • The Abhorrent • Luke Morton • M3rauer • Therese Öberg • James Rose • Rachel Ferris • Yes

FALSTAFF

"The better part of valor is discretion, in the which better part I have sav'd my life."
   - *Falstaff,* Henry The Fourth, Part I.

Mark Patrick Oughton

ROMEO & JULIET

"My bounty is as boundless as the sea, My love as deep. The more I give to thee, The more I have, for both are infinite."
   -*Juliet,* Romeo and Juliet.

   Ant O'Reilly • Megan Orr • DonDon • Steve Gill • Lennhoff Family • Zachary Brown

HAMLET

"To die, to sleep; To sleep: perchance to dream: ay, there's the rub; For in that sleep of death what dreams may come..."
   - *Hamlet,* Hamlet.

   JonJesus • Stuart A Harris • Adam Selby-Martin • Jordan Carey • Marc Thorpe • Phillip Bailey • Iain Smedley • Scott Maynard • Mark Myers • Mike Meltzer • Chris Douglass • Paul F. Murphy • R.M.Williams II • Eugene "Tinman" Doherty • Winston Kou • Russell Smeaton • Joe Abbruscato • Frank Lopez • Chris Angelini • Furrida • Stephanie Irwin-Booms • Émeline Dalmaz • Mark Lazare Owen

• Traci Belanger • Science Fiction and Fantasy Writers of America (SFWA) • Keary • Susylee Hendy • Andrea Lo • Neddy Games • Michael Brookes • Robert P Stephens II • Keegan Christopher Duda • Paolo "Mathu" Pasquali • Ben Wenger • Philip Barnes

HENRY V

"Once more unto the breach, dear friends, once more; Or close the wall up with our English dead!"
- King Henry, Henry V.

Eric Priehs • M.L.Goforth • Derek Mayne • Steven Parry • Kieran Scully • David Hemsworth • Andrew Alvis

JULIUS CAESAR

"The evil that men do lives after them; The good is oft interred with their bones."
- Antony, Julius Caesar.

Katy Costello

PROSPERO

"This thing of darkness I acknowledge mine."
- Prospero, The Tempest.

Peter "Malkira" Lennox • Matthew Carpenter • Jeremy Heitjan • Tim Lonegan • Jon Hudson

KING LEAR

"That way madness lies."
- King Lear, King Lear.

Kieren Wilson